BENDIGO SHAFTER

BENDIGO SHAFTER

LOUIS L'AMOUR

BANTAM BOOKS
TORONTO • NEW YORK • LONDON • SYDNEY • AUCKLAND

BENDIGO SHAFTER

A Bantam Book

PRINTING HISTORY

Elsevier-Dutton Publishing Company edition / January 1979
Bantam paperback edition / September 1979
Louis L'Amour Hardcover Collection / February 1985

Book design by Renée Gelman

If you would be interested in receiving bookends for The Louis
L'Amour Collection, please write to this address for information:

The Louis L'Amour Collection
Bantam Books
P.O. Box 956
Hicksville, New York 11801

ISBN 0-553-06270-0

Published simultaneously in the United States and Canada

Bantam Books are published by Bantam Books, a division of Bantam Doubleday Dell Publishing Group, Inc. Its trademark, consisting of the words "Bantam Books" and the portrayal of a rooster, is Registered in U.S. Patent and Trademark Office and in other countries. Marca Registrada. Bantam Books, 666 Fifth Avenue, New York, New York 10103.

PRINTED IN THE UNITED STATES OF AMERICA

10   9   8   7   6   5   4   3   2

AUTHOR'S NOTE

The town in my story is fictional, the locale is not. In the area there were three settlements, now ghost towns, or practically so. These were Miner's Delight, South Pass City, and Atlantic City, the latter so-called because of its location on the Atlantic side of the Continental Divide. The site of the town in the story is actually close to that of Miner's Delight, but not identical. The inhabitants of the town are fictional, although similar characters made the westward trek.

The first woman ever elected to public office in the United States was Esther Hobart Morris, in 1870. She was elected Justice of the Peace, but bears no relationship to the Ruth Macken of my story. The Honorable William H. Bright pushed through the legislature the bill that gave women the franchise in Wyoming. This was in 1869.

The Medicine Wheel lies at the northern edge of the Big Horn Mountains of Wyoming at an elevation of 10,000 feet. Who its builders were, we do not know; its purposes were obviously astronomical, and a somewhat similar Wheel in Canada has been dated at 2500 B.C. Similar structures were built in many parts of the world at about that time.

When I first visited the area some 35 years ago the central cairn was much larger than at present. Vandals have carried away stones for some stupid reason of their own. Indians to whom I talked at the time knew nothing of its origin, merely saying it had been built by "the people who went before."

On the relatively flat top of Medicine Mountain there are numerous holes, and stones dropped into these holes may be heard to fall for a considerable distance. There are numerous caves in the area and it has been suggested the entire mountain may be hollow.

One thing seems apparent: The Medicine Wheel, although considered a sacred place by many tribes, was actually built before any of the historical tribes arrived in the area.

v

THE MEDECINE WHE

UNORGANIZE

CASCADE MTS

Yakima R.

Yakima
Basin

Klickitat

Goldendale
Rock Cr.
Pine Cr.
Alder Cr.

Columbia R.

Umatilla Landing
Umatilla R.

The Dalles

Emigrant Spr.

Brown Town

Grande
Ronde

Union

Baker

Snake River

Wallowa Mts

OREGON   TERRITORY

BLUE MOUNTAINS

CONTINENTAL DIV

Boise R.

Indian C.

Camas Prairie

Wood R.

Lost River

Lost River Sinks

LAVA BEDS

Eagle Rock

Fort Hall

Fort Hall Trail

Oregon Trail

Snake River

SIERRA NEVADA

CALIFORNIA

THE GREAT BASIN

Humboldt River

Ruby Mountains

Diamond Mts

Great
Salt Lake

Fort Bri

Salt Lake City

Mormon T

Ruby Valley Sta.

+Granite Mt.

Diamond Springs

UTAH   TERRITOR

NORTHWEST U.S., 1850

Scale of Miles

0   50   100   150

Eureka

WYOMING TERRITORY

BIG HORN BASIN

BIGHORN MOUNTAINS

Lodge Grass Cr.
Little Big Horn R.
Wagon Box Cr.
Medicine Wheel
Bald Mt.
Granite Pass
Soldier Cr.
Hidden Tepee Creek
Horse Cr.
Spanish Point
Black Butte
Meeteetse Creek
Big Horn River
Tensleep Canyon
ABSORKA MTS.
Spring Gulchy
Wagonhound Cr.
North Fork Owl Cr.
South Fork Owl Cr.
Powder River
OWL CREEK MTS.
Sanee Cr.
BRIDGER MTS.
Red Cr.
Crowheart Butte
Bull Lake
Wind
WIND RIVER BASIN
Sage Creek
River
Bear Peak
North Fork
Little Wind R.
Mt. Baldy
Fork
Agie R.
South Fork
Moccasin L.
Rock Springs
Black Mt.
North Fork
Popo
Twin Creek
WIND RIVER RANGE
Middle Fork
Beaver Creek
Deep Creek
BEAVER RIM
The Town
Boc
Strawberry Cr.
Willow
Sweetwater River
Tabernacle Butte
ene Cr.
Oregon Trail
South Pass
Oregon Buttes
CONTINENTAL DIVIDE
GREAT DIVIDE BASIN

CENTRAL WYOMING TERRITORY, 1868

Scale of Miles

0   20   40

Map by William and Alan McKnight

PART I

ONE

Where the wagons stopped we built our homes, making the cabins tight against the winter's coming. Here in this place we would build our town, here we would create something new.

We would space our buildings, lay out our streets and dig wells to provide water for our people. The idea of it filled me with a heartwarming excitement such as I had not known before.

Was it this feeling of creating something new that held my brother Cain to his forge throughout the long hours? He knew the steel he turned in his hands, knew the weight of the hammer and where to strike, knew by the glow of the iron what its temperature would be; even the leap of the sparks had a message for his experience.

He knew when to heat and when to strike and when to dip the iron into the water; yet when is the point at which a group of strangers becomes a community? What it is that forges the will of a people?

This I did not know, nor had I books to advise me, nor any experience to judge a matter of this kind. We who now were alien, strangers drawn together by wagons moving westward, must learn to work together, to fuse our interests, and to become as one. This we must do if we were to survive and become a town.

3

No settlement lay nearer than Fort Bridger, more than a hundred miles to the southwest . . . or so we had heard.

All about us was Indian country and we were few.

There were seven men to do the building, two boys to guard our stock, and thirteen women and children to gather wood and buffalo chips for the fires of the nights to come, and kindling against a time of snow.

Only now did we realize that we were strangers, and each looked upon the other with distant eyes, judging and being judged, uneasy and causing uneasiness, for here we had elected to make our stand, and we knew not the temper of those with whom we stood.

It was Ruth Macken, but lately become a widow, who led the move to stop while supplies remained to us, and we who stood beside her were those who favored her decision and joined with her in stopping.

My father had been a Bible-reading man and named his sons from the Book. Four of our brothers had gone the way of flesh, and of the boys only we two remained. Cain, a wedded man with two children, and I, Bendigo Shafter, eighteen and a man with hands to work.

Our sister was with us. Lorna was a pretty sixteen, named for a cousin in Wales.

"You will build for the Widow Macken," Cain said to me. "Her Bud is a man for his twelve years, but young for the lifting of logs and the notching."

So I went up the hill through the frost of the morning, pausing when I reached the bench where their cabin would stand. A fair place it was, with a cold spring spilling its water down to the meadow where our oxen and horses grazed upon the brown grass of autumn. Tall pines, sentinel straight, made a park of the bench, and upon the steep slope behind there was a good stand of timber.

The view from the bench was a fine one, and I stood to look upon it, filling myself with the quiet morning and the beauty of the long valley below the Beaver Rim.

"You have an eye for beauty, Mr. Shafter," Ruth Macken said to me, and I kept my eyes from her, feeling the flush and the heat climbing my neck as it forever did when a pretty woman spoke to me. "It is a good thing in a man."

"It works a magic," I said, "to look upon distance."

"Some people can't abide it. Bigness makes them feel small

instead of offering a challenge, but I am glad my Bud will grow to manhood here. A big country can breed big men."

"Yes, ma'am." I glanced about the bench. "I have come to build you a cabin, then."

"Build it so when spring comes I can add a long room on the south, for when the wagons roll again I shall open a trading post."

She turned to Bud, who had come up the slope from the meadow. "You will help Mr. Shafter and learn from him. It is not every man who can build a house."

Ruth Macken had a way of making a man feel large in his tracks, so what could I do but better than my best?

The morning chill spoke of winter coming, yet I notched each log with care and trimmed them with smooth, even blows.

There is a knowledge in the muscles of a workman that goes beyond the mind, a skill that lies in the flesh and the fiber, and my hands and heart held a love for the wood, the good wood whose fresh chips fell cleanly to the left and the right.

Yet as I worked my thoughts worried over the problem of our town. We were ill-prepared for winter, although our sudden decision to stop left us better off than had we pushed on to the westward.

Going on would have been simple, for travel is an escape, and as long as our wagons moved our decisions could be postponed. When one moves, one is locked in the treadmill of travel, and all decisions must await a destination. By choosing to stop we had brought our refuge tumbling about us, and our problems could no longer be avoided.

The promised land is always a distant land, aglow with golden fire. It is a land one never attains, for once attained one faces fulfillment and the knowledge that whatever a land may promise, it may also demand a payment of courage and strength.

To destroy is easy, to build is hard. To scoff is also easy, but to go on in the face of scoffing and to do what is right is the way of a man.

Neely Stuart already regretted the stopping and spoke of continuing on to California in the spring, and Tom Croft, who listened to Neely, was a man who never knew whether the course he had taken was the right one. So he was always open to persuasion. Nor was his Mary of a different mind.

Evan Webb talked of going on when spring should again bring grass to the hills, yet he had been the first to break off from the wagon train and follow Ruth Macken in her decision. He was a discontented, irritable man, always impatient for change, yet he was also strong and resolute and would stand up in an emergency. He had a son, an arrogant, disagreeable boy named Foss . . . short for Foster.

John Sampson, my brother Cain, and I were for staying on, which left only Ethan Sackett, a single man who had been guide for the wagon train but had chosen to leave it when we did.

"What has he to do with us?" Webb demanded, when I wondered aloud if Sackett would stay on. "He's a drifter, not one of us."

"He chose to stay with us, and that makes him one of us."

"He chose to stay because of Mrs. Macken. Would he have come with us had it not been for her? I say he does not belong here."

It was our first night around the fire, the first after leaving the wagon train, and we huddled close to the flames for there was an autumn chill in the night. The truth was we were all a little frightened at what we had done, and our nerves were on edge because of it.

"He won't be with us long," Neely Stuart said. "His kind have no stability. He is more like an Indian than a white man."

"Who among us," John Sampson asked mildly, "has wintered in this country? I think before the winter is gone we shall be glad he is among us."

"We could have been miles from here," Stuart complained. "We were fools to stop."

"Mrs. Macken," I told them, "will open a store, come spring."

"To sell what?" Stuart scoffed. "And to whom?"

"She will sell boots and clothing she and her husband packed against that purpose and vegetables we ourselves will raise. Whenever possible she will accept goods in payment, goods to be sold again."

"A silly woman's dream!"

"There might be good trade with the wagon trains," Webb admitted, "but no matter. When it is warm again I shall move on."

"I shall stay."

It was the calm voice of my brother, to whom all men listened. Until then he had remained silent, watching the leap of the flames and thinking his thoughts.

Cain's face was square, massive, and might have been hewn from oak. His body was also square, but large and powerful. He moved easily, as one who is in complete command of himself and his every muscle. He was not a man given to talking, speaking only when his mind was made up, not as many men do who shape their thoughts as they speak.

"I shall open my smithy and a shop for the mending of guns. I believe the Widow Macken knows what she is about."

"Stay on if you wish," Stuart said defensively. "I shall not." Yet his tone had weakened before the weight of my brother's decision.

"I shall leave with the first grass," Tom Croft said. "The wilderness and the thought of Indians distresses my wife."

The sickness of disappointment lay upon me, for if they left our strength would be pared to nothing, and we must also go. We were too few as it was, and if attacked by Indians our chances would be slight.

This valley we had chosen lay upon a highroad for the Shoshone, but it was traveled by the Sioux as well and occasionally by the Ute or Blackfeet. Our presence invited trouble.

On the morning I went up the slope to build for the Widow Macken. There was a fringe of ice along the stream's edge, and the meadow was white with frost. My breath showed in a cloud, and the bodies of the cattle steamed as they worked, hauling down the logs after I felled the trees.

The morning air sang with the hum of axes, a fresh and lovely sound on a chill morning. Looking down from the bench to where the town would lie, I could see my brother pacing off the limits of his cabin site.

The blade of the double-bitted axe sank deep, and chips as large as a man's palm fell into the needles under foot. From time to time I paused to listen to the squirrels, scolding from the pines nearby, yet the pauses were few for the time was short. There is a pleasure in working with the hands and muscles, a pleasure in the use of good tools, and I gloried in the grip of my hands upon the axe and the smell of honest sweat and fresh pine wood.

When I went up the slope with Bud beside me, I chose the trees with care, choosing not only for size and straightness, but to leave the forest as it was, to give the trees room to grow taller and thicker.

"Trees are a crop, Bud Macken," I said, "to be taken only with care and a thought for the forest."

"But there are lots of trees," he protested.

"A forest is a living thing like a human body," I told him, "each part dependent on all the other parts. A forest needs its birds, its beaver . . . all its animals and plants. The forest gives shelter to the birds, but they repay the debt with the insects they eat, the droppings they leave, the seeds they carry off to plant elsewhere.

The beaver builds dams for himself, but the dams keep water on the land, and although the beaver cut trees to use and to eat, their ponds provide water for trees during the hot, dry months."

For a moment I held still. "Listen," I whispered, "and you can hear the forest breathe."

This was a lesson my father had taught me, that we only borrowed from the land, and borrowed with discretion and a thought for the years to come.

He taught us that to live *in* the wilderness one must live *with* it. Live from it, but allow it to live also. Such was my intention now, and so I explained to Bud Macken my reasons for choosing trees as I did.

What I had received from my father and Cain, this I would pass on to Bud and perhaps someday to sons of my own, for a bee that gathers honey must pass the honey on to those who can best use it. Yet it was little enough that I had to teach and much I had to learn.

When I had felled my third tree, I put Bud to trimming the limbs, watching him first to be sure he knew the use of an axe, for this was no country in which to be left without a foot. I was beginning the fourth tree when Ethan Sackett rode up the hill to draw rein beside me.

He leaned on the pommel of his saddle and watched for a moment before he spoke. "Bendigo, at this time of year there will be few Indians about, but do you take a walk up the ridge now and again to look over the country. If they are about we must know it, so keep your eyes wide for a sign."

"You believe they are holed up for the winter?"

"Soon . . . but a body can't be too caring. Bendigo, I count on you. I cut little ice with those men down yonder, but neither do I pay it much mind. But if there's trouble comes I figure you'll stand. You and that brother of yours."

"Webb will fight. I have a feeling you can count on him, too. He's a mean, cantankerous man, but come fightin' time, he'll be around."

"You are right, I am thinking. You keep shy of that man, Bendigo. He's dangerous."

He rode away then, and as I worked I gave thought to what he had said and began to gather the sense of it. There was a temper in Webb that flared sudden and often. At first I had thought him only a sullen, disagreeable man, but as the days passed on the westward way I saw him change. He took no pushing, and when somebody moved toward him he pushed back . . . hard.

The westward way had a different effect on folks, and many of them grew in size and gathered in spirit. John Sampson was such a man. Back home in the States he had been the village handyman, and nobody paid much mind to what he thought about anything. He did his work and he took his pay, and that was the sum of it. Folks turned to teachers, ministers, storekeepers, and bankers for opinions.

But once you got out away from home on a wagon train, a minister or a banker wasn't much help; a handyman could keep your wagon rolling. Time and again, on the trip west, Sampson helped folks out of trouble, and finally they began to ask his advice on things. When they got it, it was good advice.

When we crossed the Mississippi and rolled out over the grass lands some folks were scared of the size of it all. Miles of grass stretched on all sides, the vast bowl of the sky was overhead, and there were a few who turned around and ran for home, their tails between their legs. There were others, like John Sampson, who began to grow and to take big steps in the land.

Webb grew, too, but in another way. There had always been a streak of violence in him, but fear of public opinion and fear of the law had toned it down. Now a body could see the restraint falling away. Nobody had a reason to cross him, so all had gone smoothly so far, but Ethan Sackett had read him aright.

The work was hard, but none of us had led easy lives, and we buckled down to it. John Sampson and Cain were the first to start their cabins after I began on Mrs. Macken's place. Neely, he sat on his wagon tongue talking to Tom Croft about what fools they had been to stop. Webb sat listening for a spell, and then he went to whetting his axe.

Come noontime he was close to catching up with Sampson.

My eyes kept going to the hills, and my ears reached out for sound; we lived with fear.

This was a savage land, a lonely land, yet here the foundations of our homes would be laid, and here we would sink the roots of our lives. Here, for some of us, our children would be born.

We accepted the danger but took no unnecessary risk. It is a fool who invites trouble, a child who is reckless, for life holds risks enough without reaching out for more.

There would be cold, there would be hunger, there would be snow, and no doubt before spring brought life to the plains again we would suffer hardship. We had not enough food to last a long winter, and when our cabins were built the hunting and the cutting of wood must begin.

A day passed and then another. Three or four times each day I went up the slope, then scaled the sheer white cliff above it, finding several ways a man could climb easily and swiftly, almost as though steps were built for him. Each time I scanned the country for Indians, and also to know the country. In my mind I measured the steps to the next creek, to the tall, lightning-scarred pine, to the swell of ground.

In a blinding snowstorm or the dark of night such knowledge might mean the difference between life and death, and later when I could walk the ground I would know it better.

John Sampson and Cain were placing their cabins so the ends could be joined by a palisade. Stuart and Croft were building opposite them and Webb a bit further along, yet all could be joined by a wall or the wagons to make a fortress of sorts.

Stuart came up the hill to watch me work. "She's crazy," he said, "to build so far from us."

There was something in what he said, for her house would be all of a hundred yards from the others, and such isolation could be dangerous. Yet I knew she built for tomorrow, and she accepted the risks. But I, who must do the building, planned the house strong and true.

The logs I chose were thick and heavy, and I fitted them snugly together. There would be no chinking in this cabin, for I worked each log smooth with a broadaxe and adze, and laid them face to face. Eighteen inches thick at bottom was each wall, tapering to twelve under the eaves, and the fireplace was built of stones artfully chosen.

On the fourth day Ethan Sackett came down from the hill and took up an axe and worked beside me. He was a strong, lithe man, easy with his strength, and he handled an axe well. He worked with me an hour or more, then went down the hill and worked with John Sampson, who was the oldest among us.

Twice during the week he brought in game. The first time it was two antelopes. "Not the best of eating," he said, "but it is fresh meat."

The second time it was a deer that dressed out at nearly two hundred pounds. He cut it well and passed it around, leaving some meat at each fire.

Tom Croft, who was a good worker when he put his back into it, stayed on the job better than Neely Stuart, who was forever finding something else that needed doing to keep him from work. He'd be going to the bucket for a drink, or talking to his wife.

And then it began to snow.

TWO

When the first flakes fell I was up on the ridge cutting poles for
the roof, which was half-finished. I'd paused a moment to
catch my wind, and when the first flake touched my cheek I felt a
chill of fear.

By now the passes to the west were closed, and the way to the
east was long. We were trapped in this lonely place, building our
town. The winter would be cold, hard, and long, and we were
ill-prepared to face it.

Flakes sifted down by twos and threes, then faster and still
faster. Bunching my poles I threw a half-hitch on one end and a
timber hitch on the other and started the team back along the
slope.

From the ridge where I'd been cutting I could see the shape of
our town. Cain and John Sampson had left off working each on his
own and were roofing Cain's house, with Ethan passing poles up
to Sampson. Mrs. Sampson was hustling bedding from her wagon
into the cabin.

Ruth Macken's cabin was a worrisome distance from the others
but had the finest site.

Smoke was lifting from Cain's house, the first inside fire in
town. I could see the women-folks and youngsters coming in from
gathering sticks. Sampson was only a shadow through the snow,
still working on the roof.

11

When I got the poles to the cabin I climbed up on the roof, and Bud handed the poles up to me. One by one I laid the poles in place, forming the temporary roof that would keep the Mackens warm until spring came when we could add a solid plank roof. When the last pole was in place I came down, and we started pitching dirt on the roof to seal it tight.

Ruth Macken went inside and started a fire, and when she returned to the door Ethan was there to help her move her bedding inside. She had brought her husband's favorite chair, knocked down and packed flat, and a chest of drawers she said came from the old country.

When I saw the books she carried I looked at them wishfully. I had never owned a book, nor had the chance to read but four or five, although I'd read those carefully and often.

Of a sudden there was a pounding of hoofs, and Ethan turned sharply around, his gun half-drawn under his buckskin shirt.

It was Neely Stuart. He leaned from his horse, trying to peer into the door. "Is Mae here? She went out with the little Shafter girl and Lenny Sampson."

"They were over in the creek bottom when I was cuttin' poles atop the ridge. They should be back by now."

A gust whipped snow into our faces and there was a moan in the wind. For a moment the wind caught our breath and we could not speak.

"Come on!" Neely said. "We'll roust out ever'body and hunt for them."

"You go out there with a lot of tenderfeet," Ethan said, "and you'll lose some of them."

"Who asked you?" Neely shouted. "That's my sister out there!"

Ethan was in no way put out by Neely's anger. "How much experience have you had in blizzards, Stuart? A man can lose himself in fifty yards, and judging by the sound of the wind, this one will be pretty bad."

"Ethan's right," I admitted. "You can't even see the other houses now."

"You coming or not?"

"We're coming," Ethan said. He turned to Ruth Macken. "You'll be all right, ma'am?"

"Bud's here, and we've some unpacking to do and a meal to get. When you come back, come to supper. I'll have some hot soup waiting."

We rode down to town, unable to talk for the wind blowing our words down our throats, yet we thought of what was to come; not one of us was fixed for winter.

It was amazing the way the snow piled up. In the few minutes it had been falling there were two to three inches on the level, and it was starting to drift against the north side of the cabins.

Neely had reached Cain's house ahead of us, and when we came through the door accompanied by a gust of blown snow he was talking. ". . . if that Sackett opens his mouth in here, I'll . . . !"

"Whatever it is you'll do," Ethan said mildly, "you'd better save it until later. We've got to find those youngsters before they freeze to death."

"You stay out of this!" Stuart shouted. He turned on the others. "Scatter out and hunt for them!"

Ethan squatted on his heels against the wall. "You'd be wanderin' blind in the snow. You start seven men out in a storm like this and some of them aren't comin' back. You've got women-folks will need you before spring comes."

Neely started to shout, but Cain stopped him with a gesture. "What did you have in mind?"

"Bendigo here, he saw those young uns down along the creek, and if they were doin' what I figure, they never saw that storm comin'."

He turned his eyes to Cain Shafter. "I should do the hunting because I know this country better than anybody here, and there ain't anybody going to mind if I don't come back. I'd like Bendigo, if he'd care to come along."

"What about me?" Webb demanded. "I grew up in snow country. I seen a sight of it."

"You're welcome. I spoke of Bendigo because he's single and he's steady. Doesn't fly off the handle. A blizzard in this country is nothing to play around with."

"While you sit here talking those youngsters are freezing!" Neely's voice shook with anger. "Don't you try to tell me what to do! I'm going out!"

"All right. Where do you figure to look?"

"Out there!" Neely flung a wide arm.

"Big country." Ethan got to his feet. "Better take it slow. You get warmed up and you start to sweat. The first time you slow down or stop to rest the sweat will freeze, and you'll be wearing a thin coat of ice next your skin."

"You think they stayed with the creek?" Cain asked.

"Sure. There's hawthorn along the creek, and my guess is they found some late berries hanging. Sometimes they stay on until

January, and the first day here I rode down there and saw the bushes heavy with them. Those young uns are hungry for sweet, and it's there, so they probably just went on from bush to bush. When they realized it was snowing heavy they probably stayed right there, knowing we'd come for them."

Ordinarily that would be good thinking, but knowing how flighty Mae Stuart was, I couldn't see her using that much judgment. Mae was sixteen and pretty, but mighty notional. She'd put up her hair about a year back, and she was flouncy, feeling her oats, like. She'd been making eyes at men-folks since she was shy of thirteen and was getting to where she wanted to do something about it.

Ann Shafter, Cain's oldest, was only ten. Lenny Sampson, although a bright youngster, was six.

"Bendigo, Webb, an' me will go over to where the brush thins out and work north from there.

"Neely, if you're bound and determined to go, you and Cain can cross to the upper creek and work back. We'd best search every clump of brush. They'll not hear yelling in this wind."

He looked around. "The rest of you stay put, and don't leave the house for any reason at all." He was listening to the wind. "In this weather a man shouldn't get fifty feet from shelter."

Ethan had shortened his distance from fifty yards to fifty feet, and when we stepped outside I could understand why. At the door he paused to say one more thing.

"If we don't find those youngsters by the time we meet up, then we'd best all come in. Then Bendigo and me will go out again.

"It's a long time until spring, and if anybody can be spared it's us. There's more to be considered than those youngsters out there."

We went afoot and it was cold. No use for horses in that kind of weather, not where we had to look, down in the brush where it was a tangle of deadfalls.

A time or two I'd seen blizzards, but nothing like this. The wind came down off the mountain like there was nothing between us and the North Pole. The snow no longer fell in flakes but in frozen particles that stung the skin like blown needles.

Even walking across the wind it was hard to catch a breath, but we tucked our chins behind our collars and breathed through the merest slit of a mouth.

When we reached the stream at the foot of the cliff it was a relief. The trees were mountain alder, clumps of quaking aspen, willow, hawthorn, and an occasional spruce.

Everything was buried deep in drifted snow, the smaller bushes looking like snow-covered hummocks of earth or rock. If we found those youngsters it would be a miracle.

The cold was intense. Here or there the snow had heaped itself over a fallen tree or some rocks to form a hollow where an animal or child might have curled up, so we dared pass none of them. Once, slipping on an icy log hidden beneath the snow, I had a bad fall.

When I got up I saw Ethan squatted on his heels, studying something.

It was a rabbit snare, rigged at the opening of a run. The snow around the snare was disturbed and there were flecks of blood, most of them partly covered by snow. Ethan put a finger on the thickest spot of blood, and it smeared slightly under pressure. Almost frozen, but not quite.

"Indians," he said.

We felt a chill beyond that of the cold. Within the hour, no doubt much less than that, an Indian had taken a rabbit from that snare and killed it. He must have been inspecting his snares at the same time that the children were along the creek.

Webb was a hard man, but he had a child of his own, and he knew these children. "Injuns!" he said. "Injuns got them."

The tracks that might have told us more lay under the new fallen snow, and the storm was growing worse. It was only by chance that we had found the snare, for in a few minutes it would have been covered.

We had thought to find the children before they could freeze, perhaps huddled somewhere out of the wind waiting for us.

We were armed with pistols, but wary of freezing our hands, had carried no rifles.

Yet we could not abandon the search. The Indians might not have known they were there, and hearing the Indians, the children might have hidden themselves well. So we continued to search every clump of bushes, around the roots of blow-downs, under the hanging, snow-laden branches of the spruce, but we no longer expected to find them.

By the time the others came floundering toward us we had given up hope. Bunched together in the partial shelter of thick trees, stamping our feet and beating our hands against the cold, we listened to them, who had had no more luck than we.

Neely Stuart complained, putting the blame on Ethan, but the scout ignored him. From the look on his face I knew he was considering the Indians. Given knowledge of the country and the ways of redskins, a man might guess how far they had gone and where they might be camped.

Bad off as those youngsters might be, I almost wished my sister Lorna was with them instead of Mae. Lorna was pretty, too, prettier than Mae, but Lorna was like Cain in some ways, a cool-thinking girl. If anybody could have found a way out, Lorna could.

There was nothing to do but go back home. There was a chance they had found their way back, but nobody would have bet on it.

Ethan fell in beside me as we started back. He had faced directly away from that clump of trees, taken the wind at a certain angle on his face, and led off. It was the only guide in a storm like that, and although the wind might shift it wasn't likely to shift that much at this stage of the storm.

"Bendigo, are you game to take a chance? I've a notion where those Indians might be."

"Just the two of us?"

"We'd not make it out and back tonight. Are you with me?"

To my dying day I shall remember that blizzard. Ethan moved up to Cain, who had taken over breaking trail. "Hold across the wind," he advised. "Let it take you on the left eye and nose, like. You'll reach sight of the valley in a few minutes. Once over that low ridge, hold along the edge of the trees above Mrs. Macken's and you'll make it."

Cain stopped. He turned his broad back square to the wind and looked at Ethan. "What about you?"

"Bendigo an' me, we've an idea. If worst comes to worst we'll just dig a hole in the snow and sit it out. A man can wait out a storm if he doesn't exhaust himself first."

We faced into the storm and plodded away, leaning against the wind. Darkness had come upon us, and the wind blew a full gale, cutting at our exposed brows like knives. It seemed an age before we climbed a knoll and stumbled into a thick stand of aspen where we stopped to catch our breath.

"The day we fetched up to this place," Ethan explained, "I spotted the sign of eight to ten Indians with their travois, lodges, and goods. Not wanting to frighten the women-folks I said nothing. Maybe they were passing through, but that snare was reset, so I figure they're close by."

It was almost still inside the aspen grove. The slim trunks stood so close they formed a barrier against the wind.

"The best place for those Indians to wait out a storm is in the hollow right below this hill, so we're a-goin' down there."

Cold or not, I loosened the buttons on my coat and laid a hand to that old pistol of mine. Never in my born days had I drawn against any man, and I had no mind to unless the need was great.

"You keep that handy. An Indian respects strength but mighty little else."

We went down the hill through the deepening snow, smelling smoke on the wind, and sure enough, the lodges were there, three of them, covered with snow except around the smoke hole at the top where the warmth had melted the snow away.

We listened outside each lodge until we heard Mae speak and some arguing among the Indians. Ethan lifted the flap and went in, with me right behind him.

A small fire burned in the center of the tent, and the air was stifling hot and smoky after the cold outside. Right off I spotted Mae and the youngsters beside her. They seemed unhurt, only scared.

There were five buck Indians in there. One young brave was on his feet arguing, and he was mad as all get-out.

The others were older, and the one at whom the buck seemed to be pointing his words was oldest of all. Now that one might be old, but his eyes were clear, and it seemed to me I saw a gleam of malice in those eyes, like maybe he didn't like that young buck too much.

Talk broke off when we came in, and the young brave put a hand to his tomahawk. The next thing I knew he was looking into the business end of my six-shooter.

Now he was no more surprised than I, for I'd no thought of drawing that gun. It just fetched out when the need came, and young as that warrior was, he knew what that gun meant, and he let go of his tomahawk like it was red hot.

Ethan Sackett, he started talking to that old Indian in Shoshone.

After a minute he stopped talking, and the old man spoke. Ethan interpreted for me out of the side of his mouth. "The young buck wants to keep Mae and kill the young uns, but the old man doesn't like it. He says the Shoshone are friends to the white man.

"He's right about that, but there's more to this argument than a body can see at first glimpse. I think the old man wants to take that young buck down a peg. Gettin' too big for his britches."

My eyes had never left that young warrior. He was mad as a trapped catamount and ready to pitch in and go to fighting.

"Tell them we are friends, Ethan, and tell them to come when the snow leaves and trade with us. Tell them to bring their furs, hides, or whatever. And thank them for saving the young ones from the snow. Tell them when they come in the spring we will have presents for them."

Sackett, he talked for a while, but before the old man could reply that young buck busted in with a furious harangue, gesturing now and again toward the other lodges, like he was about to go for help.

"We'd best take the youngsters and light out," I suggested. "This shapes up to trouble."

Ethan never turned his head. "Mae, get up and come over here and bring the young uns with you."

When that young buck saw what was happening he started to yell, and I belted him in the stomach with my fist. When he doubled over I sledged him across the skull with my gun barrel.

Not one of the others so much as moved, but the old man said something I didn't catch. They didn't seem much upset by what had happened.

Ethan took out his tobacco sack and passed it to the old man, with a gesture implying it was to be shared with the others. Me, I took out my Shafter-made axe, the best there is, and handed it to the old man.

"Friend," I said. Then indicating the axe I said, "It is a medicine axe, made from iron from the skies."

"The youngsters first," Ethan said, "then you."

"I'm holding the gun. You go ahead of me."

We floundered through the snow, which was growing deeper by the moment, and made slow time until we got to the crest of the ridge. My heart was pumping heavily when we topped out, and far off, behind us, we heard shouts.

Ethan led the way, but not toward home. With the youngsters to see to we were in no shape to tackle a trip home through the night and the storm. So Ethan took us into a hollow downwind of the Indians. It was a place gouged out by the fall of two pines whose roots had torn up great masses of earth that clung to a frozen spider web of roots.

When Ethan waded into the hollow he was shoulder-deep, but he floundered around, tramping down the snow. When I saw what he was about, I helped. We tramped down an area five or six feet across, but with snow walls five feet high facing the triangle made by the roots, it was all of eight feet high.

Scooping out a hollow big enough for the kids in one snow wall, I packed the snow tight with my hands.

Ethan found some heavy, broken limbs with which he made a platform for our fire, then he dug under the fallen trees for broken twigs and bark. Soon we had a small fire going, using the mass of earth and roots for a reflector.

We broke off evergreen branches and made a roof across the corner of our hole, and with the falling snow to cover it we soon had a snug snowhouse.

We were much too close to the Shoshone camp, and it was a worrisome thing to be without rifles. We had six-shooters, and each of us carried a spare loaded cylinder to be slipped into place if we emptied our guns.

Ann fell asleep in my arms, and Mae put her head on my shoulder, snuggling closer, I thought, than need be. Ethan fixed a bough bed for Lenny Sampson, and he was off to sleep, a mighty tired little boy.

Ethan looked across the fire at me. "We got us a family, Bendigo. Likely the only one I'll ever have."

"You've got no kin?"

He added sticks to the fire. "I've kin-folk aplenty, although I don't recall seeing any of them for years. One was a mountain man like me, a Sackett from the Cumberland River country of Tennessee. Ran into him at a rendezvous on the Green.

"I don't lack for kin-folk. There's Sacketts all over Tennessee and Carolina, but I lacked somebody of my very own. When I was shy of fourteen my pa was killed by Comanches on the Santa Fe Trail. Since then I've fetched up and down the country from Missouri to the shores of the western sea, but I hunger for a place of my own and somebody to do for."

Cain's daughter Ann had gone right off to sleep like Lenny, but that Mae was making me nervous, acting like she was asleep but snuggling like she was about to crawl into my lap. If Ethan noticed he paid it no mind.

Folks thought Ethan had eyes for the Widow Macken, and it needed no thinking to guess why. She was a mighty pretty woman and some years shy of thirty. Taller than most, with dark hair and gray eyes, she had skin that was clear and smooth.

Little things never disturbed her very much, and she had a quick, easy smile that pleasured a man. Along with it she had an honest, straightforward, no-nonsense way of looking at things.

She was one of us, but she held to herself, going her own way with quiet assurance. She was the real leader among us.

Riding with Ethan one time, I had said as much. "Yes and no,"
he'd said. "Mrs. Macken is a thinking woman who knows her
mind, but you watch and listen, Bendigo. You'll see she starts
things. She opens the ball but nothing moves unless Cain says
so."

Now I hadn't noticed that before, but when he said it I knew at
once it was the truth. Cain was not a talking man, preferring to
work with his hands, and he was sure and cunning at his craft.
Perhaps because of that he was a thinking man, for working with
the hands helps a man to consider. Cain was never stirred by
passing waves of excitement, never took off on tangents. His
judgments were arrived at quickly enough, and he was wrong as
rarely as any man I knew. I had learned something about my own
brother, and from a stranger.

"A woman needs a man, Bendigo, even a woman like Ruth
Macken. No woman, however strong, should have to stand alone.
Believe me, she's a stronger woman because Cain is there and
she knows he's there."

As I sat there in the cold, my face roasting, my back half
frozen, trying to keep those youngsters warm and feeding sticks
into the fire, I thought about the men of our town.

John Sampson, who came from the same town as Ruth Macken,
had probably undergone the greatest change. As he gathered
respect for his abilities, he also added a dignity, or perhaps we
had only then begun to notice it.

As some men quailed beneath the awfulness of sky and plain,
he grew taller, and his eyes held on the far horizon.

Far as the eye could reach and day after day, there was nothing.
We traveled seven, eight, maybe on a good day as much as
twelve miles. A time or two we camped within sight of our last
night's camp, but to John Sampson it was more than a journey, it
was a rebirth.

I thought of the men with whom we shared the town and
wondered if the town would change them as much as the plains
had, for even then I had become aware that it is not streets and
buildings that make a town, but men and women. I began to be
glad we had John Sampson, Ruth Macken, and my brother Cain,
and to wonder if I had it in me to meet the demands the town
would make.

At last morning came, a dead gray sky above the white hills of
snow, the trees somber against the sky, and to the north, towering mountains, white, sublime, and still. We climbed from our

shelter, circled wide the valley where the Indians stayed, and at last came to the ridge above our town.

The wind had gone down in the hours before the dawn and the cabins lay white in the morning's still cold, slow smoke rising from the chimneys like beckoning fingers that promised warmth and security. We stood there a long moment looking upon it, lumps rising in our throats. It was all so new, and yet it was ours, the place we had built with our hands.

A door opened and closed, and I saw my brother walking toward the corral with a bucket for the morning milking. A horse whinnied, and Cain took a pitchfork and began forking hay to the stock. Something made him look up.

We saw him stop, stare, then drop his fork and start on a run for the house. Sound carried well in that still air, and we heard him plain. "Ma! They've come back, and they've got the children!"

Doors burst open, and folks ran out upon the snow, shading their eyes to see. And then they started to run, floundering in the deep snow, and we started down the hill, running, too. All but Ethan Sackett, who had no one to run to.

Cain scooped Ann into his arms, and Lenny ran to his father.

Neely ran to Mae. His eyes searched her face. "You all right?"

"Of course I'm all right. Mr. Sackett and Bendigo fetched me."

Neely turned on Ethan, mighty uncomfortable. He thrust out a hand, but he was almighty stiff about it. "Thanks, Sackett."

Ethan brushed off the thanks with a gesture. "When folks are making a fresh start they have to tolerate." He indicated me with a jerk of his head. "It was Bendigo more than me. If he hadn't come out with that pistol when he did we'd probably never have got out alive."

We started walking back through the snow and my eyes went from one to the other. They were talking and happy, victorious over the first trouble that had come our way.

Maybe this wasn't how a town was built, but it was a beginning.

THREE

Our town began with five log cabins and a dugout faced with logs. This was built by Ethan Sackett, and as you might expect, it was the warmest, snuggest place in town.

When snow fell we were in no shape to face the winter. We had the walls up and the roofs on, and we tacked canvas from our wagon tops over the windows until we could hang shutters. As the ground was frozen and we could not bank our cabins with earth, we banked them with snow, pitching it as high as possible against the walls to make a cushion against the wind.

As we worked we watched the ridge and the trees for Indians, for we were few, and by now they must have taken a measure of our strength.

Yet there was another thing that had begun to show itself in our town, and my brother Cain put it into words. "There is determination, there is the will to survive, the will to endure. We have that, and few as we are, and no matter what trials we must endure, when spring comes we will be here to greet it."

Neely Stuart scoffed, yet he himself listened, and I know he profited by Cain's words, for about Cain there was something indomitable, something immovable as a mountain. It had taken Ethan Sackett to open my eyes to my brother's worth, but once opened I could see how much we all depended upon him and somehow waited for his leadership. He had the ability to impart

22

strength to others, and even Neely stood a little straighter because of what my brother had said.

Most of our time was devoted to the never-ending task of finding, cutting, and hauling fuel. We were cutting brush on the fringes of the forest to deny hiding to Indians when Cain commented, "It is no wonder the Egyptians could build pyramids."

"What do you mean?" Croft asked.

"It was an easy land they had, with a warm sun, no fuel to find, and a river that each year brought them fresh soil and always carried water in aplenty. I doubt not it gave them time to think on other things."

"There must be time for thinking here," John Sampson said. "We must give our children more than meat."

"What is it you have in mind?"

"A school with desks and blackboards. On the hill yonder I saw some sheets of slate, and we can find chalk somewhere about."

"A school and a church," Cain agreed.

"You are building a town before you have finished a cabin," Neely protested, but he was listening, and he was interested. Lately he had talked less of California.

There was a longing in me when they spoke of school, and regret, for I was past the age for school and had little learning, precariously come by. Ours had been a Bible-reading folk, and I'd spent time mulling over what the Bible had taught me. Mostly I'd read the stories for the wonder of them and less for the Lord's word than was proper, yet the sound of the words was a rolling music to my ears, and I longed for a command of them so that I might speak and write with wisdom.

There was much history there, too, and it worried my mind that I did not know more about the lands of the Bible. Those ancient people spoke of things I knew, of flocks and shepherds and watches by night, and I wondered if those who reared up the mighty walls of Babylon had once begun as we now did, from a few simple walls, a stream, and a few cattle.

The longing was in me for books other than the Bible, which was the only book we had brought west. Back at home I had read Jonathan Edwards' *Freedom of the Will*, which had been left at our house by a traveler when I was a child. It was that same traveler who'd left us William Penn's *Some Fruits of Solitude*.

My father, who died when I was very young, had been a follower of the Reverend John Witherspoon, a Scottish minister whose philosophy of down-to-earth common sense appealed to him. Vaguely I remembered some supper-table discussion of this, and no doubt it had more to do with shaping Cain's thought than mine.

Often when our wagons were rolling westward I would sit by the fire and listen to the talk of men, and especially, in the days before he died, to Ruth Macken's husband, who was an educated man. He was a tolerant and thoughtful one as well.

He talked much of writers long dead and of the thoughts they had left to us, and I longed to know such men, men who had painted, composed music, or written books. Once when I had said as much, Macken commented, "Often they are fine men, enough to be admired, but often they are sadly, weakly human, too. Remember this, Bendigo, that it is the work a man does that matters. Many men who have made mistakes in their own lives have created grandly, beautifully. It is this by which we measure a man, by what he does in this life, by what he creates to leave behind."

Ruth Macken knew of my longing for knowledge, of my longing for a larger, brighter world somewhere beyond the distance. She was a woman to whom a boy might talk of things dreamed. There was understanding in her, and sympathy. Also, I thought, there was a longing in her for the same things. An Indian arrow had taken away her husband only a few days out upon the plains, and he was one who had none but kindly thoughts of Indians. A woman less strong might have turned back, but she had little money, nothing to return to, and a son to rear.

She listened when I told her of John Sampson's talk of a school. "Of course, we must have a school, but the building is less important than the teacher. It is the teacher who makes the school, no matter how magnificent the building.

"A school is wherever a man can learn, Mr. Shafter, do not forget that. A man can learn from these mountains and the trees, he can learn by listening, by seeing, and by hearing the talk of other men and thinking about what they say."

Most of us in those days were pleased to have a roof above us and a solid earthen floor, but not Mrs. Macken.

"Mr. Shafter," she said, when I was counting my work finished, "is there a way you can make planks for a floor?"

She was educating me in more ways than she knew, and from her I was beginning to learn the wiles of women and how they work upon a man's pride and vanity to get things done. Her phrasing was a shrewd thing, for it was a challenge to my show-off.

"Planks can be made," I admitted warily. "They can be split from logs, but I'd say flat stones might do as well."

"I would prefer the plank, Mr. Shafter, and 'as well' is never good enough. The plank, if it would not be troubling you too much."

Each day I worked for her she would stop at midafternoon and sit at the table to drink tea or coffee. We would eat small cakes and talk. She told me in confidence that Bud needed the rest, but it was the custom she liked, something left to her from another life. It was not long before I realized how shrewdly she guided me along the path of my wishing. It was from her that I learned much of the world beyond the limits of our wilderness. I learned from her that a man's world need be no smaller than the mind of the man who scans it. And I learned from her and from Cain the beauty of building, and a hatred of all who destroy, of all who are heedless of the work of others.

The village people called me "Ben" or "Bendigo," but to her I was always "Mr. Shafter," and when I spoke she listened as if every word were important.

Eighteen I was, and a man grown these three years, but I had worked my life on an Illinois farm, and only gone to school a few months at a time. I had learned to read, to write, and to cipher, and the books of which I have spoken I had read over and over again. Ours was a house where people stopped, and when my chores were over I listened to the talk of the travelers.

When Ruth Macken spoke of the floor I knew I was in for it, and there would be more hunting and exploring to be missed, yet she was not one to settle for anything but the best, so I set to work splitting planks from large logs, using wedges and a beetle, which was a heavy wooden sledge borrowed from Cain.

One day when the floor was half completed she went to her chest. Now Mrs. Macken's chest had been a much talked of thing while the wagons rolled west, for it was heavy, and there were some who believed it was filled with gold, one of them being Neely Stuart's wife.

A time or two when her wagon bogged down we'd had occasion to lift it down, and four good men were needed for the lifting, unless one of them was Cain. Nobody had seen the cover lifted, although Ethan Sackett surmised what it contained.

That day in my presence she opened the trunk and what lay within was better than gold, for it was lined with three layers of oiled-cloth and tightly packed with books and a store of paper for writing.

"There are fifty of these books, Mr. Shafter, that would give you an education if you read them and no others. Many who consider themselves educated have not read so many or so well."

She took several books from the chest. "Some of these books my husband brought because he thought they might teach him something of the land to which we were coming.

"The rest were chosen carefully because of weight and because he wished to bring those books that would prove the greatest value to Bud and to himself.

"He often said he might have chosen another list that would be equally valuable. However, I am going to let you read first the books about the western lands. They may prepare you and help you."

She handed me books I'd not seen or heard of before, and I'd no idea people had written about the lands to which we had come, or those similar. She handed me Josiah Gregg's *Commerce of the Prairies,* the *Journals* of Lewis and Clark, *A Tour of the Prairies* by Washington Irving, and one but lately printed, *Three Years Among the Comanches,* which was the personal story of Nelson Lee, a Texas Ranger. This had been published in 1859, so was very new.

The books filled me with excitement, and, tucking them under my coat, I took them home. When supper was over I settled beside the fire with the first of them. I chose Nelson Lee's book and was soon lost in its pages.

Some of the men he mentioned I'd heard talk of about the fire, men such as Jack Hays and Ben McCullogh, for their names were well known. There was much about riding and shooting, fights with Mexican bandits and Comanches, and finally his capture by the Indians.

None needed to tell me how much the Mackens had sacrificed to bring these books, for no item was taken without its displacing some other, possibly equally important. Clothing and food made up much of the load, although wiser travelers carried a small sheet-iron stove with a boiler, for it was often windy, and fuel was scarce along the way west. Dutch ovens, skillets, plowshares, axes, saws, and augers, all these were necessary.

My brother and I had brought two wagons and Ruth Macken did also. My brother needed his tools, and she brought goods to open a store.

It was not recommended to bring over 2500 pounds, although those with strong teams packed more than that, figuring by the time rough country was met they would have eaten their load to half its size, and such was the case.

The days at our town went swiftly by, but I did not neglect
going up the ridge to look over the country around, and I often
rode abroad with Ethan for hunting or to learn the country.

Our town was located in South Pass, the great, wide open pass
taken by all the wagons bound westward. To the north of us the
Wind River Mountains towered against the sky, and we longed to
explore them as Ethan had.

We saw no Indians, but were not relieved, for they would
return. The young Indian would find others like himself, and they
would come to steal horses or take scalps.

When I could find the time away from the widow's home I
helped Cain, for we had large plans between us. We were setting
up the smithy, and when it was done we planned to build a mill
for the grinding of flour. For this we needed logs cut, squared,
and left to season.

"Our mother's family was a family of builders," Cain told me.
"They built ships, steamboats, bridges, and houses. Part of her
family came down from Canada and were French once upon a
time. Ma could speak French," he added, "and was an educated
woman."

Little enough I knew of my mother and I treasured the times
when Cain spoke of her; nor did I know aught of my family before
pa, although Cain being older had heard more.

There was not much food among us. We ate sparingly and
looked upon the months to come with unspoken fear. As long as
the heavy snow lasted there was no fresh meat, and we had eaten
deep into our supplies, saved against the cold months. Our stock
had grown poorly due to lack of forage, and as we looked upon
them we worried. During this time only Ethan seemed to find
game, and that was little enough.

Usually I was the first to rise. After my eyes opened I would lie
within the comfortable warmth of my blankets, staring at the gray
ashes in the fireplace and wondering if any spark remained that I
could coax into flame.

Suddenly, I would move; throwing back the blankets, I would
rush across the room, shivering in the bitter cold, stir the coals,
pile on a few slivers of pitch pine and bits of shredded bark to any
hint of an ember, then blow the coals to a tiny blaze. Once the
flames began to crackle I would heap on wood and duck back
under the covers until the room had lost its chill.

We banked our fires against the morning, but pine burns with a
quick, hot blaze, leaving little behind. When we tried a back-log
it would as often as not slowly gather all the fire into itself, then

smolder and go out. There were a number of ways of nursing a
fire through the night, and sometimes they worked.

The first one up in the morning would crack the ice in the
water bucket, or if it was frozen to the bottom, which happened
often enough, place it close enough to the fire so it would melt.

Once there were three days of such bitter cold that nobody
ventured out but to water and feed the stock, rustle fuel for the
fires, or do the few odd chores that had to be done each day.

We had dug a halfway sort of shelter for the stock from the side
of a slope near the town and banked high the snow around it. We
had almost no feed for them, but we had cut a hole in the creek
ice so they could water. During the worst of the cold it had to be
reopened every time they went for a drink, which was twice each
day.

We had managed to cut a little hay in the meadow but used it
sparingly, fearful of the months to come.

On the fourth day of the bitter cold worry began to draw lines
upon the faces of the men. The women-folks made light of it to
save their men trial, but food was scarce, and the bitter cold
killed any chance of hunting, for the wild game would be holed
in, waiting out the weather.

Come daylight on the sixth day I could stand it no longer, so
taking my rifle I left the cabin while it was still dark. Ethan was
up, huddling over his small fire, nursing a cup of coffee to warm
his hands.

He glanced at me, then at the rifle. "You gone crazy? There'll
be no game out in this cold! It must be forty, maybe fifty below
zero!"

"I was thinking of those snares along the river. We might find a
rabbit or something."

"All right." He got up and put on his coat. "I don't believe it,
but I'll go along. There's danger in a man being out alone in this
weather."

He took his rifle down and checked the loads while I looked
around. Ethan had less to do with than any of us, but he was a
man who knew how to contrive. He had a double bunk against
one wall and a fireplace with a chimney that drew well. He had
rigged the chimney so the smoke rose through a clump of brush
that spread it out and thinned it so that it faded from sight almost
at once. It was a trick I'd not seen before, but I tucked it away in
my thoughts for future use. Ethan was full of things like that,
most of them so natural to him he'd never think of telling anyone
about them.

We stopped on the crest of the ridge to catch our breath and to look over the country, yet as far as eye could reach the white expanse of snow was unbroken.

We watched each other's faces as we moved along, looking for the white spots of frostbite. When we saw one appear we would warn of it, and he who had the spot could warm it away with his hands.

No wind blew . . . nothing moved. There was no sound but the crunch of snow under our homemade snowshoes. It was easy traveling because all the rocks and rough places were covered by snow.

Our walk was for nothing. The snares were empty. As we started back I said, "I've been reading a book."

"I read when I can find aught to read."

"This is about Comanches, writ by a man who was prisoner among them."

"Lies, most likely."

"It isn't. It's gospel. He was a man who rode with Jack Hays, Ben McCullogh, and them."

"Learn you anything?"

"Uh-huh. He tells how they'd stop at evening, maybe an hour shy of sundown, build them a fire and cook up, letting their horses graze the while. Then they would douse their fire and ride on several miles before camping for the night."

"That's common sense. You don't need a book to tell you that. I've been doing that since I was a boy."

"I never heard of it before."

We plodded on. "They were in a fierce fight at a place called Walker Creek. Killed Indians there."

Ethan looked around me. "You don't say. Who wrote that book, anyway?"

"A man named Lee, Nelson Lee."

Ethan stopped short. "Nelson Lee wrote a book? I didn't know he could write his name."

"You knew him? You knew Nelson Lee?"

"Well, I should smile. I was at Walker Creek. I was in that fight. I lost a friend there, name of Mott ——."

"He mentions him."

"He should've. Mott was a friend to him also." When we had closed the cold out and were stirring the fire in the dugout he said, "I'd admire to see that book of Nels Lee's. I surely would."

"I'll have to ask. It belongs to Mrs. Macken."

"Ah? Out of that box of hers, I'll bet. Macken told me it was full of books, but I scarcely believed it."

Of a night sometimes I'd sit with Cain, making nails against the summer's work. It was a thing we could do inside, and it took our minds from the hunger in us and the fear. Cain was a man who never stopped doing. His hands were forever busy, and so were his thoughts.

The end of a nail rod was heated and hammered to a point, then the rod was laid across the sharp edge of a wedge and a dent made around the rod at nail-length from the end. Then we'd put the rod into a nail-header, which was a wooden block with a hole through the center big enough for the nail-rod. We'd push the nail-rod through the hole as far as the dent, then snap it off. Afterward the end was hammered into a head, put into water to shrink the metal, then dropped from the header.

In a day's steady work a man could make several hundred to a thousand nails, if he had the rods. For most of our building we preferred careful fitting and wooden pins, which lasted longer and did not rust and rot the wood around them. In all our building, we built to last. It was Cain's way, and it was mine.

We made lists of the timbers we would need for framing and the planks for siding and roofing. Three times, during that cold spell, I went cruising timber to pick the proper trees for cutting.

At table of an evening, after the supper dishes were cleared, Cain, John Sampson, and I planned the mill and the smithy.

We selected logs not only for size but for ease of hauling, and while coming and going from the woods I tramped down the snow over the route we must follow so the hard-packed snow would freeze and make easier the task of skidding logs.

There was no Indian sign, and once I scouted as far as the hollow where the Indians had camped, but the place was deserted.

"When it begins to thaw," Cain suggested, "keep an eye out for any bit of iron. I can use anything you can find. There might be odds and ends cast over by movers."

Ethan was with us that night. "You might find something southwest of here. There was mining done there a few years ago."

"Mining?" Webb was alert. "What kind of mining?"

"Gold," Ethan said, "and by all accounts they found it."

"What happened?"

"Indians."

Ruth Macken came to visit a time or two, but on those occasions Cain talked little, watching the fire and smoking. He was normally a silent man, speaking rarely and to the point.

On the ninth day the cold spell broke, and on the tenth day Ethan Sackett killed a deer.

FOUR

Nobody talked of leaving now, for everybody was talking of gold.

Of gold and Ruth Macken's floor.

Even Cain went along to see it, sizing it up, testing it with his weight, for he was an almighty heavy man, square, thick, and powerful. He studied the joining of the planks and the way the corners were fitted, and when he straightened up he looked over at me and said, "I never saw it done better."

I was a proud man.

Stuart, Croft, and Webb were after Ethan to tell all he knew about the gold. It was little enough. It began with miners returning from the California gold fields. They had camped nearby, and one of them had seen something in the makeup of the country that reminded him of a place he had seen near Hangtown. He ran a few pans just for luck and found color.

They settled and began mining and stayed until the Indians drove them out.

The need for meat was serious so Ethan, Webb, and I were out most days or some part of the day. Ethan killed an elk while Webb and I each accounted for an antelope. We came across the tracks of a bear . . . a mighty big bear.

Evidently that bear hadn't fattened up enough before hibernation, so he had awakened and gone on the prowl for food.

It was on that trip that I first saw Webb shoot. He brought down a running antelope with as neat a neck shot as I ever saw, and that antelope was just picking up speed. It gave me pleasure to see it, for I admired good shooting, and such shooting might be the saving of us all.

Ethan was the best rifle shot among us, although he claimed that I was. Webb and my brother Cain were as good, or almost as good.

John Sampson had hunted along the creek bottoms back home, and as a boy had done some Indian fighting. As to Stuart and Croft, I did not know. Both had hunted, and we presumed they could account for themselves.

"That's five who can be counted on to hit what they shoot at," Cain said, when I'd told him about Webb.

"Six," Sampson said. "There's Ruth Macken."

We just looked at him, and he nodded. "Mrs. Macken is an excellent rifle shot. As good as any of us. She's been shooting since she was a child."

"She's a remarkable woman," Cain said.

"We lived in the same town, although I knew her only by sight. Her husband had been a major in the army, and she knows Indians and can talk their sign language as well as some of the Indian tongues. There were Sioux all around us in those days, but she had lived on several frontier posts."

When it could be managed I slipped away and climbed to the loft. The loft was the warmest place in the house, for the heat from the fireplace rose and kept the loft warm longer than anywhere else in the cabin.

About half the ceiling of our cabin was formed by planks resting on the roof beams to form this loft, and it was a pleasant place. Getting into bed, I lit my candle and soon was lost in the account of Nelson Lee's pursuit of Rublo, the outlaw.

For security as well as for warmth the candle had been placed in a tin can into which hundreds of holes had been punched. The light was not very good but it was the best to be had away from the fireplace.

After my eyes tired I lay awake planning to make a window for the Widow Macken from some bottles I'd found where the miners had worked. There were at least two dozen bottles and by cutting out a window hole not so tall as the bottles, then setting them into a groove in the log at the bottom and a deeper groove to take the necks at the top . . . or vice versa . . . she would have a window that could let in light, although she wouldn't be able to see out of it . . . or not very well.

Short of noon the following day when I was at Ruth Macken's explaining my window, Ethan appeared.

"Bendigo, I've got to see you."

When I walked off a little way with him he said, "There's horse tracks on the ridge. Shod horses."

We went down to Cain's house, and the men gathered. "If they were honest men," Ethan suggested, "they'd have come down to talk and have some coffee."

"How many were there?"

"Three, I'd say. They sat up there quite awhile, sizing us up." Ethan Sackett paused. "There are renegades around, raiding wagon trains and laying it on the Indians. It could be some of them."

"What do you advise?" Sampson asked.

"Get set for a fight. Cain, if this sounds right to you, I'd suggest you, Sampson, Stuart, and Croft get inside and stand by to back our stand. I'd like Webb outside with us."

"What's to be done?" Stuart said. "Maybe they aren't hunting trouble at all."

"I'll talk," Ethan said, "and we'd best not reveal our strength unless forced. If trouble starts, shoot them down. We have no choice." He paused. "It's my guess they are after our stock and whatever we have, but mostly they want the women . . . the girls."

My rifle was up at Ruth Macken's, so I walked back and laid it out for her. She listened, then nodded. "Tell them Bud and I will be ready. From here we have a good view of the approaches and a good field of fire."

When I looked surprised, she smiled at me. "Mr. Shafter, you must remember my husband was an army officer, and I lived much of my life on army posts. I know all the language."

We all got out of sight then, except Ethan, who put his horse between himself and the open and commenced fussing with his saddle. We were ready none too soon.

They came down off the ridge in a tight bunch, sixteen or seventeen by count, spreading out a little as they came but not as if expecting trouble. They would have a fair idea of our strength, judging by the number of cabins.

"A tough bunch!" Sampson commented, watching them through his glass. "Bendigo, Lutrell is among them!"

Lutrell had been with the wagon train and had followed my sister Lorna to the creek when she went for water. When I came

upon them he had grabbed my sister by the arm, and I straight-
away knocked him down.

My fist is a hard one, toughened by many a day's work with axe
or blacksmith's hammer, but he got up and came at me with a
thick club he had laid a hand to.

Clubs were not a new thing to me, and I went under his blow,
throwing my left arm over and under his right and grasping his
shirt front. Forcing him back to his right, I clobbered him good
with my right fist.

Anger comes to me seldom, but this man needed a lesson. I
gave him such a thrashing that two weeks later he had to be
helped from a wagon at Fort Laramie, and he stayed there,
refused permission to continue with us.

When they were fifty yards off, Ethan lifted a hand. "Hold up
there!" he ordered.

They drew up, but a big, hairy man in a dirty buckskin shirt
yelled back at us. "What's wrong? We're just aimin' to visit a
mite." He had kept moving, but slowly, as he spoke.

"We've nothing to talk about. Be off now."

Webb and I had moved up alongside Ethan when talking
started, although keeping a bit of distance between us. Suddenly
Webb swore and turned sharply around. From the corner of my
eye I saw what he'd guessed. While those in front held our
attention, others were closing in behind.

"Stand where you are!" Webb shouted. Then in a lower tone
he said to us, "Take those in front. I will handle this."

He walked quickly away from us, his gun muzzle down. Backing a step, I tried to keep an eye both ways in case Webb should
need help.

"John," I said, speaking just loud enough for Sampson to hear,
"the back window."

There was a scurry of movement from within the house, and
the renegades pulled up, seeing their trick was revealed to us.
Yet it was plain they were amused rather than otherwise, for they
outnumbered us three to one or more and fancied themselves
tough men.

"Go ahead," I heard Webb say, "if you feel lucky." And then
he pushed it hard. "God damn you!" he shouted. *"Try it!"*

With his rifle muzzle down I guess the man thought he could
take him. He, like all of us, had a lot to learn about Webb; the
trouble was that man had just run out of time.

He made his move, and Webb flipped a six-shooter from beneath his shirt with his *left* hand and fired.

It opened the ball.

From the back of the house Sampson's big Spencer .56 boomed, and Ethan fired with almost the same sound. Dropping to one knee I shot three times as fast as I could work the action on my rifle. A man at whom I fired tumbled from his saddle, and the hairy man at whom Ethan fired fell, one foot hanging in the stirrup. His horse ran away, dragging him over the frozen ground.

From the Macken house a bullet caught a man who was riding at me with a pistol, and he dropped his gun, grabbed the pommel with both hands and rode away, blood all over the front of his shirt.

As quickly as that, they were gone. Most of them.

Three men, their leader included, lay sprawled on the icy grass and the frozen snow.

Out back Webb's man lay dead, a bullet through the skull. Another lay on the ground, trying to crawl, one leg almost torn away by Sampson's second shot.

Cain came from the house and stood beside me, an odd expression in his eyes. "We could have warned them off," he said. "There needn't have been a fight."

"Better to get it over with, Cain. They would have come back, and next time we might not have been ready."

"Webb tricked that man. I think he wanted to kill him."

"Well," I replied, "we taught them a lesson."

"Do you be careful of him," Cain advised. "I think there's a hunger in him."

Ethan was speaking. "Take their guns and what ammunition they have, and we will bury them, although the ground is frozen." He turned to Cain. "Will you read over them?"

Webb indicated the man Sampson had shot. "Wait for him. He'll go with the others."

Fully conscious the outlaw stared bitterly at Webb. "Give me a gun," he said, "and I'll . . ."

His voice faded out as Sampson came from his house carrying a small kit of medicine and bandages.

The man was dead, stiffening in a pool of his own blood.

Others emerged, shocked and pale from the sudden violence. The women held the children within the cabins that they might not look upon death, yet fascinated and fearful, they strained to see.

"We should find out who they are," Mrs. Sampson suggested, "and write to their families."

Nobody wished to go into their pockets. We did not want to

know who they were, or if they left anyone behind, as some of
them must have. It was easier to be impersonal about the
anonymous.

Their rifles and ammunition we would need, for we had too
little of either, and each morning we looked upon the hills with
fear.

Black Lutrell was not among the dead. In the melee that
followed Webb's shot he had blurred among the others, and we
had not seen him plain.

We gathered guns and belts, catching up the horses that had
not run off. Fine, handsome animals they were, stolen no doubt
from folks killed.

We from our town stood together, and Cain read the service of
the dead. We buried them upon the small knoll, the first to die
there in our time, and when it was over we had drawn a little
closer together.

Once more we had met with fear and emerged a little stronger
than before, a little more tightly knit.

Yet we stood a little further apart, too, I guess, because some of
us had killed, and we were not used to killing, nor to violence.

Only Webb, I think, looked upon what he had done with
satisfaction, and I, who knew what was happening out there with
a kind of instinct, knew that what Webb had done had saved us
all.

His sudden action had destroyed their timing. They had planned
to begin it, and his move, for whatever cause, had caught them
short.

FIVE

When I finished reading Nelson Lee's book I started on Washington Irving, and followed that with *Commerce of the Prairies*. Sometimes I talked about what I read to Ruth Macken, and she shared ideas with me.

Her talk stirred all of us to restlessness, I guess. Neely Stuart did not like her talking to Mae, and said it gave her "notions," which no doubt it did.

When Neely spoke to Mrs. Macken about it, she merely smiled at him. "Mr. Stuart, I have no doubt that she has ideas, and she should have them. Nobody got anywhere in this world by simply being content."

"What about Bud?" I asked. "Why do you want a school but for him?"

"I want the school for the town, as well as for Bud. I want him to like it here, but I want him to help it grow. I want him to understand what is happening here, then go on to something bigger, better. Happiness for a man usually means doing something he wants to do very much, something that gives him a sense of achievement."

She turned to me. "What about you, Mr. Shafter? What do you want to do? What do you wish to become?"

It shamed me to say I had no idea. I loved the life, but the feeling rode with me that it was only something passing. Maybe

we all had that feeling about wherever we were. We were not like
the Europeans from whom we had sprung, we were not settled in
villages or classes where we would stay, generation after generation.
We were a people on the move, and whether that was good or ill,
only time would tell. Many of those who came west came to get
rich and get out, but some of us came to stay, and most of us had
the idea of enriching the country somehow, although many had
no notion of how to go about it.

What I wanted to do, I did not know. I had wanted to come
west, but now that I was west I was not sure. I wanted to help
Cain with his smithy and his sawmill, but even as I planned the
building of it I knew I'd no idea of staying on. The country was
too big, there was too much to see.

"And then what, Mr. Shafter? What happens when you have
seen most of it, and you are no longer a young man, and you take
stock of your life?"

She had a way of worrying a man, and I left her almighty
discontented with myself. She had asked me some dangerous
questions. Such questions were like a loose tooth or a nail in the
shoe; the mind kept worrying about them, unable to leave them
alone.

The books were opening the gates to a wider world, and in part
I read for the love of learning and discovering. There was little
time for it. To live was to struggle, and to keep our homes
supplied with food and fuel was an unending task, allowing little
time for considering things beyond the range of our daily lives.
What we did not possess we had to make for ourselves or learn to
do without, but the little I learned helped me to build a defense
against the change that time would surely bring, to teach me that
to live was to change, and that change was the one irrevocable
law. Nothing remained the same.

Ours was a land of movement. My people had come from
Wales, Ireland, and France at different times. My own parents
had come from Pennsylvania to Illinois and Wisconsin, and my
mother's grandparents had come from Maine and Virginia, but
the love of new lands was deep within us all.

It was no static world that waited upon decision, it was a world
where only a few positive virtues were required, and where the
rights and wrongs of things seemed sharply cut and clear.

Much as I loved reading I was wary of it, for I soon saw that
much that passed for thinking was simply a good memory, and
many an educated man was merely repeating what he had learned,
not what he had thought out for himself.

Of those with whom I lived only Ruth Macken had spent time among cultivated people. I envied her this, and longed to sit among people who were traveled and who had read and conversed.

Yet our town had begun as many of the first towns began, established by a nomadic people, and often when swinging an axe in the woods I wondered if in time man's brain might not become smaller, for as more knowledge was preserved in books or by other means, he might have to think less and contrive less.

We who lived upon the wild lands looked much at the sky, told time by the sun and our directions by the fall of shadows, the flow of streams, or the way the limbs grew upon the trees.

Ethan Sackett knew most about such things, and much of what I came to know was learned from him. His senses were finely attuned to the wilderness, and tracking a man or an animal was never simply a matter of following signs left on the earth or on brush, but of knowing the mind of the creature he was following. He often came with me into the woods when timber cruising, and we hunted together.

Felling timbers for the mill was more than simply dropping a tree, for once it lay upon the ground I would mark off regular intervals with the adze, then square the timbers into beams with a broadaxe. This was a short-handled axe with a bevel on one side and sharp enough to shave with.

We had no long stretches of continuous forest. The ridges were crested with timber, and there were extensive patches elsewhere scattered with meadows until one got up into the Wind River Range.

By the end of our first month I had felled and hewn ten great timbers besides hunting and doing daily chores. The timbers were placed upon sticks to hold them free of the ground to season rather than rot.

The days of cold and heavy snow had cut deep into our supplies, and without Ethan's hunting we would have seen hunger and grief. He butchered his meat and divided amongst us all.

We were sitting about the fire in Cain's place. "We've enough," Webb remarked, "if we take it easy. If it's an early spring, we can make out."

"We still got to think about waiting for a crop," Sampson commented.

"That's more'n those folks over east will do," Ethan said.

You never heard such a silence. Ethan had just come in, empty-handed, from a hunt. I wondered at it, for there was dried blood on the cantle of his saddle where he'd carried meat.

"What do you mean, Mr. Sackett?" Ruth Macken asked. "What folks over east?"

"Passel o' folks headed for Salt Lake. I never did see such a played out bunch. They're Mormon folk, come from the old countries to join up with Brigham."

"They're hungry?"

"Starvin', ma'am, an' sick."

"Let 'em eat their stock. I et horse a time or two," Webb said, "and it wasn't bad."

"They haven't any stock."

We just looked at him. No stock? That was impossible.

"They're afoot. Pushin' handcarts and the like. Many have died, but there may be thirty of them left. I guess they heard about those who came west that way years ago and decided to try it."

"Did you tell them about us?" Cain asked.

"Didn't figure I had the right. Settin' back like we are they could pass right by and never see us. I figured if we wanted to do anything we should all make the decision."

"Hell," Neely said, "there's nothing to decide. We've barely enough to last. They'd eat us out of house and home."

"I don't know, Neely," Croft objected, "I've been hungry a time or two."

"Whatever will they do?" Lorna exclaimed. "They'll all die!"

"None of our affair," Neely insisted. "Let Brigham take care of them."

"He'll do it," Ethan said, "and they sent a messenger through. If he makes it, and if help can get there in time."

"Bendigo." It was the first time Ruth Macken had ever called me by my first name. "Will you drive my wagon?"

"Yes, ma'am. I surely will."

"Now, see here!" Neely got suddenly to his feet but Mrs. Macken paid him no mind. She was going for her wraps.

Neely's face was flushed. "Mrs. Macken, you can't do this! You'll bring those people down on us like a flock of locusts."

She was buttoning her coat. Her eyes were large, the way they looked when her mind was made up. "You need do nothing. You asked me what I intended to sell at my trading post. I intended to sell food and clothing, and that's why we brought an extra wagon. I shall share with these people."

"You've got no right!" Mary Croft had never liked Ruth Macken because of her good looks and her independence. "You'll bring them down on us all!"

"Now, Mary . . .," Tom protested.

"It should be decided upon," Ethan said. "I move we vote."

"No help," Neely Stuart said firmly.

"Help," Croft said.

"No help!" Mary glared at Tom.

"I have already voted," Ruth said. "How about it, Bendigo?"

"He can't vote," Mary protested.

"I do a man's work. I'll cast a man's vote. We help them."

"No help," Webb said, after a minute.

"I can't turn my back on suffering," Sampson said. "I believe we should help."

Mrs. Sampson and Cain's wife voted for, as I knew they would, but all this time Cain Shafter had said nothing. He just looked up at me. "It's coming on to snow. You'll need runners on the wagon. You'll need two wagons and all the blankets and buffalo robes we can spare."

"You ain't voted," Neely protested.

Cain glanced at him. "Neely, I never gave it any thought. I was just setting here trying to figure out how best to do it."

Webb got up. "I don't believe in it, and I think we'll pay for it, but I'll drive that other wagon."

"You're a pack of fools!" Mary Croft said. "Let Brigham take care of them. He got them out here."

To get through the wind and snow to the stable I'd built for Ruth Macken was a problem. The ground had been almost bare of snow but the sky was gray and lowering. By sundown snow had started falling again with a few slow, drifting flakes, then it had come down faster and faster.

Cain, with Sampson and Webb to help, was fitting runners to the wagons. Stuart and Croft, with Neely still grumbling but doing his share nonetheless, worked on the second wagon. At the last minute Bud Macken claimed the right to come with me.

Ruth Macken said, "Bud, it will be brutally hard, unlike anything you have ever tried before, and if you go along you must do your part."

"I know it, ma."

Her big eyes were filled with worry, so as I gathered the lines I said, "He's pretty much of a man, ma'am. He'll stand up to it."

"I believe so. When he's your age I hope he is the man you are."

Her words stayed with me, and even with the cold and blowing snow I felt strangely warm. Ruth Macken had a way of saying the right words when they were needed.

We drove off, my wagon taking the lead, into the blowing snow. Within fifty yards we had lost sight of our town. Ahead of us was a cold drive that could bring death to the four of us.

Tom Croft was riding with Webb.

SIX

Ruth Macken's horses were good stock and in better shape than most because of the grass on that bench where she had chosen to settle, which was almost as good as in the meadow below. Her horses grazed in the meadow with the other stock, then grazed on her bench when the meadow grass thinned out.

We wanted horses because they were faster than oxen and more likely to find their way home if we became lost. None of us doubted the possibility.

Webb had a good, strong team, and he had worked them a good deal, hauling water from the falls. We had used our wagons for little else since arriving at the town site. Ruth Macken had water at her door, and I was thinking on a way to actually bring it into the house; the rest of us hauled water in barrels.

Actually, where we got the water wasn't a fall. It was too small to be called that, just a place where the creek spilled over a rock ledge high enough to set barrels under for filling.

We used to take a wagon loaded with four to six barrels and fill them to the brim. A good bit of water slopped over the side, turning that stretch of road into an icy pavement higher than the ground on either side by more than a foot.

It was a little more than a mile to the falls, which were near the main trail. The road home from the falls was along the trail except a few yards at the beginning.

44

When we had come down off the bench to make our start, Cain and Helen met us with several covered buckets. "Bendigo, this is soup," Helen said. "Now there isn't a lot here, so share it sparingly, but if you heat it when you get there it will give them warmth and strength for the ride."

It was cold. The wind was raw off the mountains, and the snow was thin and icy. We could feel the ruts under the wagons. Ethan had given us careful directions, and we held to a steady gait.

It was two hours short of daybreak before we actually got started, and we checked time by Webb's big silver watch. It was all of twelve miles to where the Mormon folk were camped, which meant three to four hours each way . . . if we were lucky.

Bud walked up and down the wagon behind me, beating his arms about him in the "teamster's warming" and stamping his feet to keep them from freezing. Both of us wore buffalo-hide coats and fur caps with ear laps. Mine had been given to me by Ruth Macken. It had been her husband's cap, but it fitted snug and fine. By the time we had been an hour on the road nothing was warm any more.

When we stopped for the third time to give the horses a breather, Webb walked up to join us. "I don't like it, Ben. We've got ruts to follow now, but if the snow keeps falling they'll be buried too deep by the time we start back."

"We'll make it," I said, trying to sound more confident than I felt. Much of the country we had to cross was a great, wide plain. To the south it stretched away for mile upon empty mile where the wind had a full sweep. If a man got off the trail he might never find it again.

"Check the time it takes us," I suggested, "and we'll watch the time as we start back."

The sky turned gray, and I could see the lead horses again. All around us the ground was white, an unbroken expanse of snow.

"Bendigo?" Bud said. "Can we walk for a while? I think my feet are freezing."

"Good idea." I pulled up and got down. Webb came forward again, and he nodded when I said we were going to walk.

His was a narrow, dark face but his eyes were cold and gray. With a stubble of beard showing where his handlebar mustache wasn't, he looked both cold and cruel. I thought then, as often before, that he was a better man to have with you than against you.

We knew nothing about him; only that he came from Missouri. He had a good outfit, but on the wagon train he made no friends, and his son made enemies quickly. Foss was large for his age with the instincts of a bully. Webb had none of that, so far as one could see. He minded his own affairs and worked hard, yet there was no friendliness in him.

He glanced at Bud. "How you makin' it, boy? My Foss was about to come. Backed out at the last minute."

"Maybe he was smarter than I was, Mr. Webb. I just didn't know when I was well off."

"You're game," Webb said. "I like that in a man."

We walked on. My face was stiff with cold, and ice gathered on the muffler near my mouth. I wished I had wolverine fur, which Ethan told me wouldn't collect ice.

We saw their smoke before we saw them. They were huddled together behind some canvas windbreaks they'd raised against the wind, their handcarts standing about.

Never in my born days did I see a more woebegone, miserable-looking lot of folks. Shivering with cold, they stood up to greet us; you never saw people more ill-equipped to face such weather. I didn't know whether to admire them for their faith and courage or to think them downright crazy.

They stared at us, hollow-eyed and unbelieving. Bud and I got down and carried the soup over to them while Webb turned the wagons and Tom Croft rustled firewood to heat up the soup.

"Do you come from Brigham?"

Turning my head, I looked at the tall, gaunt man in a flimsy cloth coat. He had an odd lilt to his voice that I took to be some kind of an English accent.

"No. We come from up the trail a piece. We haven't much ourselves, but our friend told us of you and we've come to help."

"The man who brought the meat? May the Lord bless him. May the Lord bless you all."

"We can't take your gear. Tell them to get what food you have and your clothes and guns. We'll take you to our town and you can return for your gear later."

He hesitated. "But it is all we have!"

"No, sir. You have your lives. You can always come back and get your goods."

Hungry and cold though they were, they were of no mind to leave their belongings, but there were twenty-nine of them, and we had but two wagons.

While they ate soup Webb and I rinsed the buckets and heated water for the horses to drink, covering them with blankets while we waited.

Their camp showed how little these people knew. None of them had reflectors for their fires, and they had brushed back the snow, exposing the frozen earth. The snow itself would have been a lot warmer, and reflectors built of sticks or earth would have thrown a lot of the heat back into their faces.

They were a thin, scrawny lot, wearied to death from walking in the cold. Two of them left bloody tracks on the snow where they stepped.

"Neely was right," Webb said, "they'll eat us out of house and home. Two or three days and we'll be out of grub ourselves, feeding this lot. It was a fool notion."

"Sorry you came?"

"No. I came because I wanted to."

"You're a good man, Webb."

He was startled. "Don't you never think it. I'm a pretty poor sort of man, and a mean one to boot." He was serious, I could see that.

Yet I was learning something about Webb. Hard, bitter, and irritable as he was, he was a man who rose to emergency. He might not agree with a thing you said or planned to do, but if it demanded strength and courage he would not be left out.

Nor was it a matter of pride, so far as I could see; it was simply that he was geared to trouble. There was no yield in him. He was a pusher, a man geared to last stands. He might have sneered at the patriots, derided the noble feelings, but he would have been at Valley Forge. He would have gone into the Alamo with old Ben Milam.

There was one newborn baby among the Mormons, and there were several youngsters too small for walking. One man had his foot bandaged and used trail-made crutches.

Their leader, Hammersmith, said he couldn't leave the carts. "Maybe we could tie them behind the wagons."

"Mister," I said impatiently, "if we get back home we'll be lucky. The wagons will be overloaded even if half of you folks walk. If you want to go with us, get in the wagon. Let Brigham worry about your goods."

My wagon led off again, and Webb was right. We would have trouble with the trail. No sooner were we out of the hollow than I pulled up and walked back to Webb. "How long did it take us to get here?"

"Better than four hours. Closer to five."

"And we were empty then, and there was only about half the snow." I studied it over. "You check your watch," I said, "and when we've put in four hours we'd better do some considering."

"Take us twice the time, I'm thinking. We won't be nowhere close in four hours."

We couldn't see the sun, but his watch was clear enough. It was noon now, and it would be long after dark before we got back.

The faint tracks of our coming still remained, and we followed them, but when another hour had gone by they had faded; once in a while in a sheltered place we would come upon some sign.

Bud and I got down to walk.

There was nothing to look at but snow. Mile after mile we plodded on. Most of the Mormon men were walking, and even a couple of the women. They had talked among themselves, had learned how far we had to go, and how heavy the going was. My hands and feet grew numb, and I had to stomp my feet and club my hands together to keep the blood circulating.

At the top of a small hill where we stopped to give the horses a breathing space, Webb walked back to me. He had taken over the lead to spare my horses. His face was a mask, and there was ice on his mustache.

He spoke in a low tone so nobody could hear. "We're off the trail, Ben."

"How long d'you think?"

"No idea."

It was like standing in a white cave, with snow falling around us and no way to see out.

"If those folks get the idea we're lost, they'll be scared."

"They mustn't know."

I was thinking back. We had not come far with the heavy pull for the horses and frequent stops. It had been desperately hard to keep to the trail, but I figured we were somewhere on the divide between Strawberry and Rock Creek. We might cross Strawberry without knowing it, but the chances were slight. Rock Creek was another proposition. Most of its banks were steep and if we didn't see them in time we might have a bit of trouble.

We figured to be heading north, but were we? The wind was, or had been, from the north. Now it was blowing against the right eye and ear. Had we altered course, or had the wind changed?

We walked out in front and kicked away the snow. Grass. Stiff, brown, frozen grass. We kicked around in a circle, but all we found was grass.

Which way to turn? We daren't stop hunting the trail because we might not find our way back. Nor could we risk another night in the open with these people. At least two of them were in bad shape.

"Let's go," I said.

"You chancin' it?"

"If I recall, the country west of the trail slopes off a bit, so if the teams did any drifting it would likely be downhill. Not that there's much difference."

So we started again, knowing we might be making the wrong move. We'd traversed several dips and hollows some time before and might have crossed a creek without being aware of it.

We took it slow. Bud spelled me on the lines, and he was a fair hand. Twice we stopped and scraped down to grass . . . the snow was almost a foot deep now.

"Are we lost, Bendigo?"

"I reckon."

"Ma will be worried."

When we stopped for a breather there was no sound but the occasional rattle of trace chains. Suddenly I made the decision that had been nagging at me for some time. "You handle the team, Bud. I'm going out front."

Walking up to Webb, I said, "Hold up for a while. I'm going to scout around."

"You'll get lost."

"I'll walk left two hundred paces. My tracks won't fill before I get back. Then I'll do the same thing on the other side."

The wind was stirring again, and the snow was falling heavily. A man could see thirty or forty feet ahead of his team, but no more.

I walked slowly, feeling the ground with my feet at each step. Swirling flakes were all about me, and my tracks filled faster than I had thought they would. By the time I got back the ones I'd made first were half-filled with blown or falling snow. There was no luck to the other side, either.

We drove on for half an hour, the horses making hard work of it in the deepening snow and with their increasing load, as more and more of the walkers played out and had to be taken aboard. Yet I felt sure the horses were climbing as well as pulling, and if they were climbing there was a good chance we were going right.

At our next halt both Webb and I walked out, one to either side. We feared now that we might drive right on by our turnoff and never see it. There was nothing west of us for more than a hundred miles.

If we had to stop for camp there was no fuel here and we'd have to burn the wagons for warmth.

"It's rocky," Webb said, "I think we're going right."

"I think so, too, but so much of this country is rocky and rough."

The wind was rising. One of the horses slipped to its knees. We got the horse up and started on, but I slipped and fell. I fell hard, and cold as I was it was no fun. When I got up and brushed myself off I called to Webb. "There was ice beneath that snow."

He and Croft came back. We kicked the snow away. It was ice, all right. Thick ice and the tracks of wagons.

"We're all right," I said, "we've found the water trail."

"The what?"

"Where water spilled, hauling from the falls."

Beneath the snow the roadbed was built up from many spillings and sloppings until it stood six to eight inches above ground level. Once we got the horses up on the road it was easy to know when one of them stepped off into the deeper snow.

We could see nothing. The wind was blowing a gale by now, whipping the wagon covers and blowing snow into our faces. Suddenly Bud yelled, "There's a light!"

The horses, sensing the barn was close, buckled down to pulling. I cracked the whip like a pistol shot above their heads and yelled.

Slowly the cabins took shape through the blowing snow, and nothing ever looked so good as to swing up to Cain's cabin and see them all come rushing out into the snow. It wasn't until we got into the cabin that Webb showed me his watch. We had been eleven hours coming back.

Cain, Sampson, Foss, and Stuart unharnessed the horses, rubbed them down, and fed them warmed up water and hay. They had put in a long, hard day in cold and snow.

Those tired, exhausted Mormons were brought inside and fed, then bedded down. We hadn't much, but we would share what we did have. The Widow Macken did most of it.

She had clothing and blankets to sell in the spring, and she outfitted several of those who were worse off and provided blankets for sleeping.

One of them, a lean, long boy of about my own age thrust out a hand to me. "Thank you, sir. You've been our saving."

"You thank Webb, Bud, and Croft," I told him. "They did as much as me."

I was beat. I was surely tired. When I'd eaten a bit of hot soup

I crawled into the loft and stretched out flat, falling asleep without even pulling off my boots. Later, Lorna did it for me.

When I fell asleep it was to the murmur of the voices down below, those people we'd saved, and I was glad, glad all through me that we'd done it. Yet there was an awful sinking in me, too, for they would eat, those folks, and we had nothing to spare. The winter months stretched long and frightening before us.

Ethan and I, we'd have to go out and hunt. We'd have to go far afield and risk trouble with Indians to find game.

If there was any.

SEVEN

Of the Mormons, who stayed with us five days, I came to know only one, the lean, tall young man whose name was Truman Trask.

On the fifth day the wagons came from Salt Lake, six big wagons with blankets, food, whatever was needed. Ethan saw them coming and rode out to meet them, who were fearful they would find only the frozen, starved bodies of their people.

They left us sugar, flour, and tea, although not nearly as much as we'd used in helping, and we saw them away on the morning of the seventh day, all of us standing out in the weather to watch them go. Within the hour, with the storm blown out, Ethan and I were on our snowshoes hunting game.

We went into the mountains, hoping to find some sheltered park where the game had holed up, but until night was almost on us we saw nary a track, and both of us were scared. We had hungry folks back home, folks wanting meat and trusting us to get it for them.

We found a sheltered place, built a lean-to and a reflector, chewed on some jerky, and ate some cold flour mixed with warm water. There we sat, talking of many things until the night was late for lonely hunters.

It was warmer next day and we found our way into a wide, deep canyon. The stream was frozen over, but there was melting on the south side of some pines. The air was bright and clear, and we began to see deer tracks, and of a sudden, the tracks of a bear.

Bears hibernate in winter, but unless they fatten up real good they're apt to come out when the weather warms up and try to find something to eat; then they'll go back and hole up again.

We found where he'd dug into the snow after roots and such. Given a chance bears will stick to a diet of bugs, grass, roots, and berries. They kill small animals occasionally, but with the exception of the grizzly they rarely kill for meat; even more rarely will they bother a man. This one was a grizzly. We knew that from the extra long claws on the forefeet.

We followed him up Twin Creek until he turned up a canyon along Deep Creek. "Let's look for something else," Ethan suggested, "this one's poorly. If he was fat he wouldn't be out." And then he added, "I never much liked to kill bears, anyhow."

Our way led along an easy slope into some trees beyond, then into a valley where there was a frozen marsh with trees trailing down to its edge. And there were four elk.

"How far do you make it?" I asked.

"Two hundred yards . . . maybe more. Over white snow, distance can be a tricky thing."

"Do we chance it?"

We were in the open. At any moment they might see us. The wind was blowing across, and their heads were down, scratching at something at the edge of the marsh.

So we walked toward them. Five yards . . . ten. We had our rifles poised for a quick shot if their heads came up. We advanced another ten yards before the big bull brought his head up with a jerk, looking at us.

With the first stirring of muscle we had frozen in place, and now we held perfectly still. The others looked up, and one skittish youngster walked off a few feet. That seemed to start them. If they began to walk, they would soon be running.

My shot was high. The bull dropped in his tracks, but I knew my shot was too high. Ethan fired and the second elk jumped, bounded three times then fell all of a piece. We went in fast and were within twenty yards when my bull came off the ground with a lunge, one antler hanging.

He came up running and I fired my rifle like a pistol from one hand. The bullet hit him behind the left shoulder and he ran on for thirty yards before he dropped. I levered a fresh cartridge into the chamber and went on to where he lay.

My first bullet had hit the base of the antler, stunning the bull.

My second was a heart shot and pure dee luck. I'd tried for the heart, of course, but with him running like that it was a chancy thing.

Cold as it was, we couldn't waste time but took our skinning knives and went to work. From time to time I looked over to where Ethan was skinning out his elk. We'd been uncommonly lucky and should be back to town by nightfall with fresh meat.

We were just finishing skinning when I happened to look up, and out of the corner of my eye I caught a flicker of movement in the canyon beyond where Ethan was working.

My meat was skinned out, and I'd been sacking it up in the fresh hide when I caught that move. My rifle was at hand, and I wiped my hands clean in the snow, watching that spot without looking directly at it. Of a sudden, a bird flew up.

My hand dropped to my rifle, and as I turned I saw a man rise up with a rifle aimed right at Ethan. I was down on one knee and there was no time for aiming. I fired from where my rifle was, the stock under my arm.

The man with the rifle reared up on his toes and fell full length from the brush.

Ethan looked up at the shot and looked right toward me, and in a flash I knew that somebody was probably sneaking up on me, too. So as I spun around, I fired.

I was fifty feet higher than Ethan, a good hundred yards from him, and an easy two hundred yards from the man who had appeared behind me. My bullet hit the dirt about six feet short of him, but he ducked back out of sight.

The sound of the shots faded, and all was still. Ethan had disappeared. Suddenly there was another shot and my bundle of meat jerked. Evidently somebody had mistaken the meat for me.

Lying still, my eyes searched for a target, but I could see nothing. Their attempt at surprise having failed, they had to make another try at it, but we were in a bad situation. Ethan was worse off than I was, for he was in the bottom near the marsh. There was good hiding down there but no way he could escape without crossing a hundred yards of white snow where he'd be as easy to see as a red shirt at a Quaker meeting.

My position wasn't bad. I was right at the tapering off point of the pines that came down off the ridge toward the swamp. There was some scattered brush, snow-covered rocks, and a few deadfalls. Our trouble was we had no idea how many we were facing.

The man I'd shot seemed to be dead. He lay sprawled on the slope back of Ethan. His hat had rolled down the slope a little, and he was lying all sprawled out. It gave me a turn to see him there because I wanted no dead men on my back trail.

It was cold. We hadn't waited more than a few minutes before I realized this could get sort of tiresome. My fingers on that rifle began to get stiff with cold, and I dearly wished to move.

We'd killed one, and there might only have been two. We might be close by their camp without knowing it, and if so we'd be surrounded in no time. It was time to move.

Picking a spot in the thicker stand of trees, I dug in my toes and took off with a lunge.

Nothing happened.

No shot, no movement that I could see. From my safer position I scanned the country around, watching trees, birds playing in the brush, and the like. After a minute I glanced over at the dead man.

His rifle was still gripped in his right hand, and I could see a lump on the back of his coat near the side that might be a pistol butt.

The others, if there had been others, were gone. Walking out, I took the rifle from his hand and stripped off his pistol belt and gun. The rifle was a new Henry .44, and they were a scarce thing. Cain and I, we had two of the first ones. Cain had worked in a plant in New Haven where they were made, only returning to Illinois when he started westward.

The pistol was an old cap-and-ball, much worn. His belt held thirty rounds of cartridges for the rifle.

Ethan came up to meet me, carrying his meat. I loaded up, and we led off into the trees, backtracking the man who shot at me. We found his horse tied to a tree with a blanket roll behind the saddle, two well-packed saddlebags, and a heavy coat. There were a couple of letters in the pocket addressed to *Win Pollard, Fort Bridger, Dakota Territory.*

"He was among them who attacked us at the town," Ethan said. "I recognize that horse. Had one like him, one time."

We loaded our meat on the horse and started back to our town. We stripped the saddle from the horse and hung it on a peg in the shed back of Cain's place. The folks were glad to see the fresh meat.

Webb went out next day and killed a deer. He rode by our kill, and there were fresh bear tracks, so the old bear had evidently found enough to keep him through until spring.

Webb told us about it when he got back. "Seen that body," he commented. "Didn't you say you found some letters?"

I showed them to him, and he glanced at the signature. "Well, you got you some trouble, boy."

"What's that mean?"

"Win Pollard. You killed him. I figured I knew that face. Win's got him a family. He's got some brothers and a mighty mean lot they are. When word gets to them, they'll come a-hunting."

"He bought trouble," Ethan said. "We were just cutting up meat when they came on us."

"It'll make them no mind," Webb said. "Those Pollards are vengeful boys."

For two weeks then we had a quiet time, with much hunting and some evenings of reading and talking. Taking the oxen so's to rest the horses, I went out and snaked a couple of big deadfalls out of the woods, then took a wagon up to the edge of the trees and loaded it with firewood.

Neely Stuart was out and killed an antelope. He said he saw some horse tracks over on Pine Creek, west of us. Four riders, he said.

When I came back to Cain's house for supper that day, Mae Stuart was there, helping Lorna get food on the table. She had her hair up and looked mighty pretty, swishing her skirts at me as she went by.

"We're going to have a dance, Ben! We're going to have a dance up at Mrs. Macken's!"

"It's true!" Lorna said. "Ruth Macken was down today talking to Cain and Helen about it. She said nobody had done anything but work since we arrived, and it was time we had a dance or a party."

"When?"

"Next week. Friday night. We're all going to make cake and cookies and whatever."

It would be like Ruth Macken to think of that, and it was true that it was time we had some fun. We had hunted, built cabins, improved them, cut wood, and we had our difficulties. Yet I felt guilty.

That dance was less important to me than getting another book from Ruth Macken. So much time seemed to be getting away from me, and in the east men of my years had gone to school eight to ten years and read besides.

Cain got out his accordion, and it turned out Ethan played a fiddle. Tom Croft did also, and Tom had his with him. Everybody was talking about the party except Webb and me. I was thinking of books when Webb came up to me.

"One of those men got away," he said. "We've got to do something about them, Ben."

"What can we do?"

"Go after them. If they can ambush, so can we."

"I never laid out to shoot any man," I said. "If they come for us, I'll fight."

"We've been lucky, mighty lucky. Suppose they come on us unexpected? Or when most of us are away?"

"What do you have it in mind to do?"

"There's been no snow since. We could backtrack them, make it so hot they'll pull out and leave."

It made no sense. There were too few of us to risk, and they'd already come against us twice and had come off hurting. They might have learned a lesson. We had trouble enough without borrowing it. Yet I had to admit we'd been lucky. If I hadn't caught that move out of the corner of my eye, Ethan and I would be dead, and if Webb hadn't been quick on the shoot that first day we might have lost that fight.

"We can talk to Ethan," I said, "and Cain."

"No," Cain said, when I mentioned it to him at supper. "We'll not borrow trouble. We'll just have to keep watch as best we can."

That night I walked up the hill to Ruth Macken's cabin. It was clear, and the stars were bright in the dark sky. I stood for a long time, just dreaming, wondering what the years would bring and filled with a nameless longing that I could not find a place for.

It was pleasant inside. Mrs. Macken had curtains at her windows and in front of her bunks, and she had a real candlestick. Two of them, in fact. I had heard Lorna and Helen talking of Mrs. Macken's "things," and longing was in their voices. I had learned long since that women set store by such fixings.

They were just up from supper, so while she did dishes I stood by, talking to her and Bud about the country, the way animals lived, and the plants. She dried her hands and went to the trunk again and took out another book. It was *Walden,* by Thoreau.

"He was a friend of Ralph Waldo Emerson," Mrs. Macken said, "and a thinking man. I believe you will enjoy the book, Mr. Shafter, and you will enjoy meeting Mr. Thoreau."

"He's here?" I was surprised.

"In the book." She smiled at me. "He'll tell you about himself. Sometimes I think if it were not for books I could not live, I'd be so lonely. But I can take a book out of that trunk, and it is just like talking to an old friend, and I imagine them as they were, bent over their desks or tables, trying to put what they thought into words.

"In that trunk I have some of the greatest minds in the world, ready to talk to me or teach me whenever I am prepared to listen."

"Is it enough?" I asked.

She turned her gray eyes on me and said quietly, "Yes, Mr. Shafter, it is enough. Some might find this hard to believe, but I never wanted but one man. We had a wonderful life together before he was killed, and now I have Bud to think of.

"No, my life has been fulfilled in many ways. I don't want to marry again, although I would not have missed my marriage for anything. He was a good man, a strong man. We had love, and we had respect for each other, and that's a lot."

The truth of the matter was that I'd never heard of Emerson, but I said nothing of that. It seemed likely that I'd hear more about him before long. In the meanwhile there was *Walden,* and I carried it with me when I went up the mountain in the morning.

The weather had moderated. It was mild enough to work without a coat. The snow had melted in exposed places, but we all knew that was temporary. It was a fine day for woodcutting, and I went to work early.

Everybody was talking about the party, but I could hardly wait until lunch time to open the new book. It was a quiet place up there on the ridge, but I was no such fool as to sit in the open reading. I'd found a hiding place behind three towering pines that stood before a hollow in the rock.

It was not a cave, just a hollow that permitted nobody to approach me except from in front where my position was masked by the trees. I sat there and read, then put the book aside to think of our town, and of me.

Christmas was only a few weeks away, and spring would follow after. When grass was green would our people remain? Would others come? We wanted others to come, and expected them, but we were a little jealous, too, for now the town was ours, our creation.

What of me? What of this person I was? What of the man I might become? Most of all I needed what all men need, a destination. I wanted to become something, for in the last analysis it is not what people think of a man but what he thinks of himself.

It was there, in Thoreau. "Public opinion is a weak tyrant

compared with our own private opinion. What a man thinks of himself, that is what determines, or rather indicates his fate."

What I was to do in the world, this I did not know; yet for all my years there had been within me a vague yearning to be something, to hold a responsible place in the world.

Putting the book away where it would not become damp, I returned to my work and worked hard until almost sundown. Then it was that I saw the wagon.

It was a large wagon, drawn by six fine, big horses, and there were two outriders, both with rifles. Taking up my rifle, I walked down the hill. Webb was outside, gathering an armful of firewood, and when he saw my gesture he went inside, emerging with his rifle.

By the time I was standing before Cain's house I knew that all our men were in place and waiting. The wagon was coming into what we called our street.

The first rider rode out ahead, a stocky, powerfully built man with cold gray-green eyes.

He held out his hand. "We come as friends," he said, "to repay the help you offered our brethren. I am Porter Rockwell."

We knew the name. Rockwell was said to be the leader of the Danites, Brigham's Destroying Angels. It was whispered that these were the men who eliminated those troublesome to the church, and back in Missouri his name had been legend. In Illinois, too, for that matter.

"It was good work," he told us, "and we are obliged. I am to speak to Mrs. Macken, in particular."

Cain came from his house, Ruth Macken and Helen following. The wagon pulled up as they emerged, and the driver and the others, for there had been three armed men hidden in the wagon, began to unload.

There was flour, sugar, coffee, salt, a barrel of pickles, and much else. There were bales of blankets, robes, and clothing to repay Mrs. Macken for those she had so freely given.

"We're beholden," Rockwell said. "We have found less of kindness and more of abuse, and had you not gone to the aid of our brethren they would surely have perished."

The other outrider was Truman Trask. He looked better than before. He was lean, hard, and in fine shape. He was also better dressed.

When they had unloaded a part of their cargo the rest was taken to Ruth Macken's. Truman and I went up the slope to help the unloading.

"The Prophet has told all his people to trade with you," Porter Rockwell said, "if they are nearby and have need."

Later, I stood beside Rockwell and watched the wagon begin its homeward journey. They had need to return at once, and no time was lost. Rockwell was watching Webb with narrow eyes. "That one. I seem to know him."

"He came west with our train, as we all did," I said. "He's a good man with a gun."

Rockwell turned and looked straight at me. "You will have need of him," he said bluntly, "when spring comes."

Porter Rockwell swung into the saddle. He had a magnificent horse, and was noted for the horses he owned and bred. He gathered the reins. "There will be more of our people over this road. Do you help them if there is need."

"Of course," Cain said.

Trask emerged from Stuart's house, and they rode off after the wagon. We watched them until they were out of sight.

"I never knew any Mormons before," I said.

Cain shrugged. "They are people," he said. Then he turned to me. "Have you given thought to Christmas, Bendigo? The younger children will be wanting toys."

"I hadn't done anything about it," I confessed.

"I know." There was a shade of wistfulness in his voice. "You've been reading Ruth Macken's books. I always wanted more of an education, and you can learn much. Read as many as you can."

He looked at me thoughtfully. "I am expecting great things of you, Bendigo."

I blushed. "Of me?" Then I said, "I will try, Cain. But I do not know what I wish to do."

"Give it thought. There is time." He hesitated a moment. "Ethan Sackett told me about the Indian you hit. He said you were very quick. He had never seen anyone so quick with a gun. It is a thing to value, but it wants care, Bendigo. When one acts quickly, sometimes one acts too quickly."

"I will remember that."

Neely and Tom had built a cabin together in order to build faster when snow began to fall, so now Tom Croft began to build his own. He was a good workman, and he worked swiftly and well. Twice he went to the forest with me and looked thoughtful when I told him how I cropped the trees.

"But there are plenty of them," he objected. "The mountains are covered with forest."

"They are now," I agreed, "but more people come west with

each season. Also, the mountains need their trees. Without them the water runs off, and there is no game."

Ethan Sackett rode up the hill to us. "They're gone," he said, "pulled out, lock, stock, and barrel."

"You found their camp?"

"It was east of here. Over on the Sweetwater, and there must have been thirty or forty, judging by the number of fires and what I could make of their sleeping places."

"They'll come back," Croft said.

"They've gone off on a big raid, I think," Ethan said.

Mae Stuart was at the house when I returned, making paper decorations for the dance, helping Lorna. Lenny Sampson was there, too.

Cain was sitting by the fire, making nails. He pushed a nail-rod and a header toward me, and I looked around for a steel wedge, trying not to look at Mae.

Mae was wishful of being looked at, and a pretty girl is hard to ignore. On the wagon train there had been so many folks it was easy to fight shy of any particular one, and Mae had seemed flighty and man-crazy. Now being man-crazy can be a bad thing unless you're the man she's crazy about.

Yet even as I thought that, a warning voice told me that Mae's swishing skirts were a trap. She could be mighty pretty and enticing, but supposing something came of it?

What Mae had in mind, I didn't know. Maybe she just wanted attention, and maybe she wanted a man, and maybe she was thinking of a wedding, but a wedding for me at eighteen would be no good thing.

A wife and family don't go along with dreams. They hamper a man's movements, they restrict the risks he can afford to take to get ahead, and even the most helpful of women is usually more expense than a very young man can bear.

No doubt Mae wasn't thinking of that. Seemed to me she was hearing the mating call and wasn't thinking of anything else. Well, I was. And besides, Mae was no girl for me. Yet no doubt she had her dreams, too. Trouble was, I don't think they had much to do with mine.

So I kept my eyes away from her and tried to close my ears to her laughter.

But it wasn't easy. Not by a long shot.

EIGHT

We lived with hope, but we lived also with fear. Without hope and faith we could not have come west, nor could we have established our town, but fear was ever-present, not only of renegades or Indians, but of man's age-old enemies, hunger, thirst, and cold.

Gathering fuel or hunting pleased me because they offered time for thinking, and now I thought of how close hunger and cold must ever be. Man's civilization is a flimsy thing, a thin barrier between man and his oldest enemy. Truly, man must be like the beaver, a building creature, only man must build cities as a beaver must build dams. There may be no reason in it whatever. Give a man a pile of sticks, and he will start to put something together, even as we had here.

A town means order, and order means law, and without them there can be no civilization, no peace, and no leisure. Surely, the first towns came when men learned to domesticate animals and plant crops, but the first culture and good living began when man learned to share the work and so provide leisure for music, for painting, for writing, and for study. As long as a man is scrabbling in the dust for food and fuel, looking over his shoulder for enemies, he cannot think of other things.

Yet I could see that the more involved a civilization became the more vulnerable it became, and any disaster, war, fire, flood, or earthquake can put man right back to the hunting and food-gathering level on which we now existed.

No one of us is ever safe. There is no security this side of the grave. A shipwreck or a hurricane can put man back to the brink of savagery, both in the means he uses to get his food and the lengths he will go to get it. The more ill-prepared people are to face trouble, the more likely they are to revert to savagery against each other.

Our town was an example of what could be. The leaders of our community were the hunter and the fighter. Ethan and I had done more than all the rest to bring meat to the people, and whenever we were gone they looked eagerly forward to our return. When spring came Cain and Ruth would be looked up to, but now it was us.

Cain worked quietly, doing his share to gather and cut fuel, but always looking forward to spring, to building his smithy and his mill. Cain was not a hunter but an artisan, a sharer of labor, a builder of civilization.

"When spring comes there will be more people," Cain said to me, "and we will need some law. If we are to be free to work we must have somebody to wear a badge."

"Can't we do without that?" I asked.

"No. Until man can order his own affairs, until he ceases to prey on his brothers, he will need someone to maintain order. A lawman," he added, "is not a restraint, but a freedom, a liberation. He restrains only those who would break the laws and provides freedom for the rest of us to work, to laugh, to sing, to play in peace."

I had not thought of it that way.

Twice, hunting beyond Limestone Mountain I came upon pony tracks. It was a distance to go for fuel, but I remembered bitter cold days and wanted to leave the closer fuel for days when we could not go so far afield.

There was an old travois trail leading up the mountain through the trees, and I had followed it for a short distance. One day on that trail Ethan Sackett rode up to me. He got down and helped me to throw wood into the small cart I was using to collect it.

"Game's staying far out. I haven't seen a track today."

"Might be a good time to ride to Bridger. Lay in a few supplies while the weather is mild."

"Take you a week, if all went well."

"Worth it," I said. "Are you going to fiddle for the party?"

"Tom is. I'll spell him, time to time." He gave me a sharp look. "Watch yourself, Bendigo. Mae Stuart is settin' her cap for you."

My ears grew hot. "Aw, no such thing! Anyway, I ain't about to marry."

"I'd caution against it. Not to say a word against Mae, but she's flighty and marriage won't make a spell of difference." And then he added, "Many a man who had no thought of marrying suddenly finds himself in a place when he's either got to marry or run."

My eyes ranged the edge of the woods. I leaned against the wagon watching the steam rise from the horses. It was cool, but pleasant, and time to be starting for home.

"Have you ever been to San Francisco, Ethan?"

"A time or two. You figuring to go there?"

"Maybe . . . I haven't decided yet. I want to make something of myself, and I don't want to live out my days here. Not that I don't like our town, but there's not many folks."

He grinned at me. "Not many girls, either."

I got red around the ears. "All right, there aren't. Girls are part of it, but a man needs room to swing an axe, and I want my axe to cut deep and true. Maybe I'm a damn' fool," I added.

"You're not. You've got good ideas." He looked over at me. "Ruth Macken thinks you'll make a great man, someday."

I flushed again, but I was pleased. "She said that?"

"Uh-huh . . . if you don't get your foot caught in some girl's trap before you get started."

He got up in the saddle. "We could trap some beaver, you and me. There isn't the money in it that there used to be when everybody wore a beaver hat, but a body can still get a price for prime fur."

"I'll need money, but I'll need education. Mrs. Macken says the big cities have libraries, some of them free for the use of anybody."

We started down the mountain. "I'll never be the smith Cain is, and I'm not cut out for farming. With learning I might find my way to something."

"This country needs cattle. No town can depend on hunting, and all the stock you folks have got won't last. There's cattle in Oregon, Bendigo."

"Do you reckon a man could drive a herd from there?"

"What a man wants to do he generally can do, if he wants to badly enough. Following some rain, a body just might make it." He glanced at me. "You figuring on that?"

"It's in my mind. If you'd come along to keep the boogers off."

He chuckled. "Seems to me you'd do pretty good at that yourself."

"Trouble is, it takes money to buy cattle, and we don't have it."

"You might find gold. The first gold was found here back in 1842."

"Gold is a chancy thing. Still, a body might find enough to buy a few head and make a start."

When we reached town he headed off for his dugout, and I stopped by Ruth Macken's to throw down some wood.

She came out with Bud, and whilst Bud was stacking wood I told her about my idea of buying cattle in Oregon.

She did not laugh as I half expected she would but asked me about the trail, and I told her what Ethan had said.

"Bendigo," she said, after a bit, "when you've gotten rid of your wood, come back by and have supper with us. We'll talk about it."

Well, now. I won't say the idea hadn't been in the back of my head. Helen was a fine cook, but she cooked plain. Ruth Macken fussed over her meals. Helen's was straight, honest food with no nonsense about it, but Ruth did a little extra to everything she fixed, and it was tasty, mighty tasty.

So while she cooked and fixed at supper, I sat astride a chair, my arms on the back, and told her my thinking. Most of it had just come to mind while I talked to Ethan, but once started it worried at my thoughts like a coyote over a fresh buffalo hide.

"Ethan would go along. We could scout for water and grass on the way out and plan each day's drive to end where there was water, even if the drives were short. We could hire a couple of men out there, bring back a small herd, and if it turned out well, go back for another."

When I was fifteen I'd helped drive three hundred head from Illinois to New York state, and I told her of that. We ate, talked, and then Ruth Macken said, "Bendigo, if you decide to go I will buy a share in your herd and take my money in cattle at the end."

Well, I just looked at her. There'd been no such thought in my mind. All I'd been doing was hunting a good meal and a chance to tell my idea to a good listener. I wanted to hear it take shape in my mind as I talked. Now, all of a sudden it was no longer just talk, the chance was staring me right in the face.

"It would be a long drive, Mrs. Macken. I'd be wrong not to warn you we might lose all we started with."

"We need cattle here, and I believe you can do it."

Cain was sitting by the fire when I came back down the hill, but the rest of them were all asleep. He was putting a long splice in a rope so I sat down, fed a stick or two in the fire, and explained my idea.

"You'd have to have an outfit, and grub for the trip," he said, "and money to buy cattle."

"Ethan would go with me."

Cain took a strand of rope and tucked it into place, working it tight and snug with his hands. "The idea is a good one, but you'd best give it some thought. I doubt if we could spare both of you."

Well, I should have thought of that. Ethan and me, both gone for months on end. It would be a danger to the town, and they'd have less meat.

"There's Webb," I said.

"Yes, there's Webb." His tone said a lot. Cain did not trust Webb in a time of violence. Webb was eager, far too eager. Such a man might bring trouble where there was none.

"Well, maybe next year," I agreed, reluctantly. Another year seemed far, far away, and I'd been building plans and thinking what to do with the money I'd make.

"You could go alone," Cain said. He turned the rope in his hands, studying the splice. It was so perfectly done as to scarcely increase the dimension of the rope. "The risk would be great, but you've good judgment."

Alone?

"If you go with Ethan you would learn, but you'd be dependent, too. He knows so much you'd be apt to let him lead. If you go alone you'll do it all yourself."

There was a lot in what he said, for when I went out with Ethan I always stood back a mite. Much as I knew, he knew more, and it was easier to let him have the responsibility. Suddenly the trip seemed a whole lot longer, yet more exciting, too.

One thing I realized. If I would make it back to our town by the following fall, I must have my herd and be ready to begin my drive with the first grass of spring, and that meant I must leave sometime after the new year, while winter was still upon the land.

Thinking about it, I lay awake long and slept late, a rare thing for me. When I awakened there was laughter in the house, and I could hear Mae down there with Lorna, and it came to me that today was party day, and everybody was fixing for it.

It shamed me to be getting up from bed with all those folks downstairs, and me the one who was always the first out of bed.

I'd got into my pants and was reaching for a shirt when Mae stuck her head over the edge of the floor.

That girl was a caution. She had climbed right up there with Lorna daring her. She was looking at me with eyes dancing with fun, but there was something else in them, too, something that made me wonder what she'd have done if we'd been in the house alone.

She was a bold one. She reached right over and put her hand on my arm. "Oooh! Look at all those muscles! I had no idea you were so strong!"

"Lorna!" I yelled, embarrassed. "Get this girl out of here!"

Lorna just laughed at me, and I grabbed for a shirt, and pulled it on. Maybe it was a good thing I was taking off down the Oregon Trail. She was pretty, too pretty to be running around loose, and I thought Ethan implied truly when he said marriage would not keep her from running.

"You get down from here," I said, "you've got no call to come up here like this. You're a big girl now."

"I didn't think you'd noticed," she said, laughing at me. "That nice Mr. Trask surely did. He wanted me to come to Salt Lake with him."

"Which wife were you to be? Second or third?"

"I'd be first, no matter when he married me!"

Well, I got into my shirt and climbed down to where my boots were, smelling all the good things cooking and baking, and watching the girls sewing clothes and chattering away about the party. I'd never seen such excitement in our town, and for the first time I began to feel excitement myself. For the first time also I began to realize that the event itself is not more important to women-folks than the chattering about it, before and after, and the fixing up and doing for it.

Cain was down at the shop, sharpening a saw. He paused, holding the file in his hand. "I'd have to leave right after Christmas," I said.

"I was thinking of that."

Much as I wished to go, in another way I didn't want to at all. The town would have one less rifle to defend it and one less to hunt for game to survive the winter. A late spring could mean disaster.

Yet we would need cattle; not only for my own gain, but for both milk and beef, and to build supplies against the winter that would follow.

It was too soon to worry but not too soon to plan. I would not leave for another month, and in the meantime I must go over the trail with Ethan.

And tonight was our first party, the first entertainment in our town.

NINE

Tom played the fiddle, and John Sampson played the fife, and we danced until the sun came up over the eastern hills. Cain played the accordion for a while, and I danced with Lorna and Mae, with Ruth Macken and Helen, and with Mary Croft and Neely Stuart's wife, who did not like me, I think.

It was a fine night, gay with laughter and singing. Few of us sang well but we all loved to sing, and the sound of our voices went out across the snow to the wintry hills beyond.

Yet we did not forget, in all our fun-making, that our lives were lived with danger, and every now and again one or the other of us would step out, walk away from the inner sounds to listen to the night.

Let it never be said that a man does not develop a sixth sense, a feeling for danger when there are no outward signs of it. Perhaps subconsciously he perceives things not registered on his conscious mind, but whatever the reason, I have myself been warned time and again of danger lurking, and so have many whom I know.

So listening was not only listening, it was sensing, registering the feel of the night.

The moon was clear and the eye carried far out across the snow, down the valley and along the towering cliffs, very white now in the moonlight. Nothing was seen.

Lorna came out and stood beside me. She was flushed and happy, her eyes bright with gaiety. "It's grand, isn't it, Ben? I'm awfully glad we came."

"You left friends behind."

"I hated to leave them, too, but I will make new friends. I've seen so much and learned so much that I'd not have learned at home. You have too, Ben. You've changed."

"Me?"

"Oh, yes! You're so much older, and wiser somehow. I think you've changed more than any of us. Even Cain has spoken of it."

A change in a man is never so evident to himself, but of course, I had experienced new things. The experiences of the long trek west, the Indian fights along that trail, the responsibilities, rustling food for the people of the town, working, watching, thinking. Even as a man shapes a timber for a house or a bridge, he is also shaping himself. He has in himself a material that can be shaped to anything he wishes it to be. The trouble is the shaping never ceases, and sometimes it has gone far along one line before a man realizes it.

"I can hardly wait for spring. I want to get out and walk upon the hills."

"You be careful. There's Indians, you know." I paused. "And I won't be here. I am going away after Christmas."

"Oh, no!"

So I told her our plans, and of my long ride to Oregon alone, and how it would need much of the year to make the homeward drive.

We had turned to start back inside, for the cold was reaching into us, but as I held the door open for Lorna I glanced back.

There was something on the trail, something that had not been there before.

Only a black dot, only a shadow of something, only something that would alter the shape of my own life, but I could not see that. I could see only that something was there that had not been before.

My pistol was in my waistband. To get my rifle might interrupt my people at their fun, so I told Lorna I would be right in, and then I closed the door and went to the edge of the bench to look again, and to look around also, to be sure it was not a trick, something to lure us out away from our buildings.

I tucked my right hand under my coat to keep the fingers warm for my gun and started down off the bench toward the trail.

The black spot did not move. With my hand on the butt of my gun for a quick, smooth draw, I went closer.

It was a horse, head hanging, standing over a man who had apparently fallen from the saddle.

Squatting, my right hand on my gun, I slid my left under his coat and felt for his heart. I seemed to feel a faint beat, but there was something else. His shirt was stiff with dried blood. He was not only in a fair way to freezing to death but wounded as well.

Lifting him into the saddle I steadied him with one hand and spoke to the horse, who moved off quickly, eager for the lights of our town.

The horse had not been ground-hitched but had preferred to stay with the man. It must be quite a man who could command such loyalty from a dumb brute.

I went right to John Sampson's house and carried the wounded man inside, stripped off his overcoat and covered him with a buffalo robe, all by firelight. Then I lit a candle and moved the hot water pot closer to the fire.

Looking down at the wounded man, I studied his face. He was no one I had ever seen. His was a narrow, aristocratic face, finely boned and handsome. He was, I guessed, about thirty-five, but might have been younger. His hair was the color of buckwheat honey, his mustache darker.

Lifting him carefully, I eased his arms out of his black broad-cloth coat, then removed the vest, which was dark with the stain of blood. The gold watch he carried was expensive, the most beautiful I'd seen. His gunbelt was of hand-tooled leather, and the pistol was oiled and in fine working condition. It was the pistol of a man who knew guns and used them.

I removed his tie and his collar. He was going to need help, more help than I could give him. Help of that kind in our town meant John Sampson, better at treating wounds or sickness than any of us.

The buffalo robe and the fire would warm the chill from his body, and in the meantime I would care for his horse and get John Sampson.

It had grown colder. I led the horse to the stable, stripped off its gear, rubbed it dry with a little hay, and put some more hay in the manger. Due to the smallness of the stable and the presence of our own stock, it was warm.

At the Macken house the music had stopped and everybody was eating, laughing, and talking. Ruth came toward me with a plate but I shook my head, and catching John's eye, motioned him to the door. Quietly, I told him of the wounded man, and putting down his plate he got his coat and followed me out. The youngsters did not notice, but Webb did, and so did Cain.

Leaving John to care for the stranger's wounds I went back to the stable. A thought had occurred to me: What was a man doing so far from anywhere without even a blanket roll?

The saddlebags had been heavy. Lighting a lantern, I opened them up. One contained several clean white handkerchiefs, rare in this country, and a sack containing several paper-wrapped cylinders. Each cylinder contained forty gold eagles. There were twelve of them.

There was a thin volume in some foreign tongue, a folded newspaper with a San Francisco dateline, some odds and ends, a few small coins, and some letters. I caught the name.

DRAKE MORRELL

PALACE HOTEL

SAN FRANCISCO

It was a name I had heard. Curiously, I opened the newspaper. Two months old, but not much worn. I doubted he had had it long.

There was a headline over a column on an inside page:

MORRELL TO HANG

Morrell had killed a man, and not the first one, and he had been sentenced to hang on August the twenty-ninth. It was now only a few weeks to Christmas.

Refolding the newspaper to leave no indication it had been opened, I returned everything to the saddlebags. I took his rifle from its scabbard and went back into the house.

Morrell had been stripped to the waist and the blood washed away.

"The bullet went through," Sampson said, "but he's lost a lot of blood and he's in bad shape." He glanced at the saddlebags. "Is there a razor in there?"

Before I realized it, I said, "No . . . no razor."

"There's something wrong here," Sampson said. "No bed on the horse, and this man shaved not later than yesterday. That means he must have camped somewhere within a day's ride."

Morrell stirred, the first movement I'd seen him make. He stirred and muttered something.

"I'll make some soup," John said, "and some coffee."

He indicated the table. "I found that, too."

It was a derringer, .44 caliber. A sleeve gun with a band to fasten it to the wrist. The draw from the sleeve was one of the fastest and was fancied by gambling men.

I hung my coat over a chair and when I turned back to the wounded man his eyes were open and he was looking at me.

"Better lie still. You've had a rough time of it."

"Is this the new town?"

"Well, it is a new town. I don't know whether it is *the* new town."

"You have women here?"

"Yes."

He seemed relieved, then tried to sit up. "I've got to get out of here."

"Lie down," Sampson said. "If you move you'll start that wound bleeding, and you haven't the blood to lose. If you start bleeding you may not last until morning."

That sounded pretty drastic, but Morrell did lie down. "Who found me? Where was I?"

"Quarter of a mile down the valley. I found you."

"I followed your wagon tracks. Look, you've got to leave right now. You have to backtrack me."

It was a cold night and I had had enough of traveling in the cold. I said so.

"There's two youngsters," he said, "they're in a cave about seven miles south of the Sweetwater, near Oregon Buttes."

Now I knew nothing of that area, but it seemed likely to be further than he said, close to twenty miles from here. There was a chance it might be a trap.

"What are they doing there?"

"We holed up there because there was fuel at hand, but when I realized I had no chance to make it without help, I told them to sit tight. After all, they were warm there, and I might pass out along the trail and leave them in the cold.

"I knew about you people and hoped to reach you while I could still travel. I must have passed out just after I saw your lights."

"How old are they?"

"The girl's twelve and the boy's a bit younger. Eight or nine, I'd say, and sick. He's got a bad cough and a fever. That's another reason I didn't want them in the cold."

There were a lot of questions unanswered, but Sampson was shaking his head to get me to stop talking. His story made a certain kind of sense, but I was wondering what a man sentenced to hang was doing out there, miles from nowhere, with two children obviously not his own.

"How do I find this place?"

He told me, and he was good, I'll give him that. He knew how to pick landmarks and how to give directions. In the west that was quite a skill, for many a man traveled a thousand miles on directions given in a few minutes over a drink or traced in the sand with a stick. From the directions he gave I knew this man had covered a lot of country and knew what to notice.

"I'll get my wife," Sampson said. "She'll be wondering what happened."

When he had gone, I looked down at Morrell. "I am going after those kids," I said, "and this had better not be a trap."

"Why should it be?"

"We buried some renegades on the hill," I said, "and they have friends."

"I am not one of them," he said ironically, "although I expect I am enough of a renegade. I travel alone. Or did until I ran into those youngsters."

"What name are you using?"

He gave me a cold, intent look. "That's a good question," he said. "Did you have anything in mind?"

"A man's name is his own affair," I said, "and out here a man's name is less than what he is. I looked in your saddlebags and saw a name there, but I'll call you anything you like as long as you play your cards above the table."

"Fair enough." For a moment he closed his eyes. It was wasting his strength to keep him talking, but there were things I wanted to know. "My name is Drake Morrell. It has always been a good name, and I'll use it."

He closed his eyes again, and I shouldered into my coat, not relishing the long ride in the cold. The last thing before I left I placed his saddlebags where his hand could rest on them.

The horse I saddled was the buckskin taken from the renegades. My own horse had been hard-used these past weeks and needed rest. The buckskin looked tough, a mustang, and a horse used to living out in all sorts of weather. He wanted to go no more than I did, but we started, a bait of grub and a roll of blankets behind the saddle.

We headed south into a night bright with stars, the wind icy cold on my face.

Ethan had pointed out the Oregon Buttes direction one time, and with what Morrell had told me, I felt sure I'd find the cave.

The day dawned cold and gray. There was no sound but the hard pound of the buckskin's hoofs on frozen snow or ground where the snow had blown away.

For the last few miles of my ride I had the Oregon Buttes to guide on, for they stood out well against the sky, towering above the country around. Closing in, I smelled smoke . . . at least, they still had a fire.

The tracks of Morrell's horse led me into the draw where the cave was, only it was not exactly a cave but a walled up dugout with a hollow log for a chimney. A girl was outside picking up sticks. She straightened up, watching me with wide, dark eyes.

She was not afraid. She simply stood, waiting, to see what I was and what I wanted. She was a child, but a rarely beautiful child.

"I am Bendigo Shafter," I said, "and Mr. Morrell sent me for you."

"Is he all right?" She was anxious. "I was afraid for him."

"He was all right when I left, although he'll be needing a lot of rest."

She opened the door with her free hand. "David is sick. Will you come in?"

Ducking my head, I followed her. It was warm inside. There were four bunks and a table, two benches, a wash basin, and a bucket.

On the lower bunk lay a child, shockingly thin, his eyes wide and feverish. His brow was hot under my hand, his breathing broken and unsteady.

There was a door across the room. "What's in there?" I asked.

"A stable. There's a little hay in there."

There was an outside door that opened among some boulders, and I led the buckskin in. He ducked his head and walked right to the manger, so I had a hunch that buckskin had been here before.

I added some wood to the fire, then got out my grub sack and a pan I'd brought along. I threw pemmican into the pan, added some snow, and when it heated up I made her eat some of it. The boy refused at first, then swallowed a little, making a half-hearted effort to eat.

We had to get out of here, but the boy would never survive a twenty-mile ride in the cold.

"Is he your brother?"

"Yes."

"Are you related to Drake Morrell?"

"Oh, no! Of course not. He knew my mother, and he helped us."

Knew? I hesitated to ask the question but she looked at me with those great, dark eyes, holding her hands tightly clasped in her lap and said, "My mother died last week. He . . . Mr. Morrell . . . buried her. He was taking us to St. Louis so we could catch the steamer for New Orleans."

"I see."

"Only there was a man waiting for him at Fort Bridger. He put a rifle on Mr. Morrell and said he was going to kill him, but Mr. Morrell shot him. Then somebody else shot Mr. Morrell and we had to ride away."

"We'll go to my town," I said. "There are women there, and some children. You'll like it there. We even had a party last night with dancing and singing."

"I can dance. And sing, too. And I can play the violin and banjo."

Bad as it was to remain here with the fuel running out and a risk of outlaws returning, for I was sure this had been one of their places from the way the buckskin acted, I simply dared not start with the boy in the shape he was in. Yet, if I could get some strength in him from the hot stew, he might be in better shape by daylight. It was a sure thing he would not recover here.

There wasn't fuel enough to last the night so I scouted along the riverbed. Here and there I found a broken limb from a tree, washed down from above, but in two trips I'd found everything within walking distance, and it wasn't much.

Several times I tried to feed the sick boy, but he refused it. I wished John Sampson was with me, or Helen or Mrs. Macken.

All I could do was keep them warm and hope for the best. After a while the girl fell asleep, and I was alone with the sick child, trying to keep the place warm. Finally there was nothing for it but to burn the stable door, so I brought the horse in with us where his body heat would help and broke down the manger and burned it and then the door. Somehow I kept the fire alive through the long, weary, very cold night.

Sometime about daybreak I fell asleep myself and was awakened by a hand on my shoulder.

"Mr. Shafter?"

I sat up, ashamed of myself for sleeping. "What is it, honey? What's wrong?"

"It's my brother, Mr. Shafter. He's gone, I think."

And so he was.

TEN

Drake Morrell tried to sit up when I walked into Sampson's house. "Did you find them?"

"The boy didn't make it."

"I was afraid of that. How did she take it?"

"Like a soldier . . . so far."

"Their mother was a fine girl, a very fine one." He looked up at me. "I knew her before. Long ago. She was ill. In very bad shape. So was the boy. I knew they had people in New Orleans, and if I could get them to St. Louis they could catch the steamboat."

He was silent for a while. He looked better but was far from well. He would be weak for a good long time.

"Where is she now?"

"At Ruth Macken's. She's a widow with one son, not much older than the girl. She had the most room, and she was the best person for a girl to be with at a time like this."

He had that book on the table beside him and when I left he began reading again.

Webb was in Cain's house when I entered. He looked at me. "Do you know who that man is? He's a riverboat gambler and gunfighter. He's killed a half dozen men."

"So?"

"Figured you'd like to know."

"He conducts himself as a gentleman should, and as long as he does I'll find no fault in him."

"We can always use a good man with a gun," Webb agreed.

Two nights later when I was invited to Ruth Macken's for supper, I saw again the girl I had brought back from the cold. Mrs. Macken had contrived a dress for her from an old one of her own. She greeted me with a curtsy and led me to the table. She seemed somehow older than her twelve years, a grave, beautiful girl with large dark eyes.

This was also the night I was finally returning *Walden*, which I had read twice, so Mrs. Macken went to her trunk for another. This time it was Plutarch's *Lives*, a book about ancient Greeks and Romans whose lives were somehow similar.

"More great men have read this book, Mr. Shafter, than any other unless it be the Bible. I think you will enjoy it."

We ate by candle and firelight, no casual meal as in the other cabins, but a formal dinner, carefully done and carefully served.

When we were alone for a moment Ruth Macken said, "She's very brave, but a strange child. She never mentions her brother, but at night I've heard her crying."

"I shouldn't wonder, losing her mother and brother so nearly together. Does she know anything of her relatives in New Orleans?"

"Only their names. She saw them only once, when she was very young, and she remembers they lived in a very grand house and did not approve of her father. He was an actor and played in London and Paris as well as New York."

"What happened to him?"

"She hasn't said, and I haven't asked." Ruth Macken smiled at me, amusement in her eyes. "You have an admirer, Mr. Shafter. You are her hero now. You came out in the storm and rescued her, just like in the stories."

I felt myself blushing. "I did nothing," I said.

She changed the subject. "What do you know about Drake Morrell?"

"He is a gambler. He was sentenced to be hung in San Francisco, but we don't know the circumstances. How he escaped I have no idea. I am sure he's a man of good family, and with some education. He is reading a book now, in some foreign language. I believe it is Latin.

"Webb knows something about him. He said he had been a riverboat gambler. He has supposedly killed several men, but so have we."

"Only a decent man would allow himself to be saddled with two youngsters while escaping from enemies. I think he will bear acquaintance, Mr. Shafter."

The days that passed were days of work, and for me, days of planning. I spent many hours with Ethan, going over the Oregon Trail in our talk, talking of water holes, where grass might be found, and such things. Our celebration of Thanksgiving was quiet, a brief sermon by John Sampson and then we sang hymns, the old ones like Rock of Ages and Come Ye That Love the Lord.

Drake Morrell recovered slowly, but before he did he hired Tom Croft and me to build him a cabin. We took our pay in gold, a twenty dollar gold piece to each of us. I hoarded mine against the Oregon trip.

He bought needful things from Ruth Macken, and I was present when he made his purchases. When she answered the door he said, "Madam, I understand you have blankets and clothing to sell?"

She led the way to her storeroom, and he selected blankets and the usual kitchen utensils. He was polite, yet there was something about him that froze off any questions.

"Is there a post?" he asked. "I mean, can a letter be mailed from here?"

"At present, no. We sent some mail by Porter Rockwell when he was here, but there has been no reply."

"Rockwell comes here?"

"He came to thank us. We helped some Mormons."

"You were fortunate," he commented dryly, "Porter's visits usually have less happy results."

He studied the matter. "Then you've no regular post?"

"Not yet. There's talk of a stage line when spring comes again. It has been running off and on for several years, but the Indians steal their horses."

"I'll be going west after Christmas," I said. "I am going to buy cattle and drive them back. I could take your letters then."

He looked at me thoughtfully. "You are enterprising. Yes, thank you. I shall write a few." He gathered his packages. "Do you have many visitors?"

"Almost none. When spring comes we hope that will change."

"I'm sure."

He bowed again and walked out into the air. "A handsome woman," he said, "and a lady."

"She lends me books."

"Books?"

"I am reading Plutarch," I said.

He glanced at me. "You are fortunate. He was a man of great understanding, a man of the world in its best sense. Yes, he is well worth reading. And Mrs. Macken? Does she read Plutarch?"

"Her husband did. I believe she has also."

"What happened to Mr. Macken?"

"Indians . . . on the way out. Over on the Platte. He'd been a major in the army and served in several frontier posts as well as in the east."

When we put down the bundles, I said, "I noticed you were reading."

"Yes, I have many books, but only the one with me." He smiled. "You will understand, Mr. Shafter, I had no time to pack."

"Well," I said, "he who reads and runs away lives to read another day."

He glanced at me again, but made no comment. Then after a moment he said, "When a man has put one bullet into you, and you have been trusted with the care of two children, you do not risk a second bullet. No doubt the gentleman and I shall meet again."

"That book . . . it was in another language."

"Latin . . . the *Satires,* of Juvenal."

Turning to the door, I hesitated. "Mr. Morrell," I said, "I like you. We would like you to stay as long as you wish, but there is one thing. I understand you have had several gun battles."

"Not of my choosing. Not," he added dryly, "in every case."

"We have a man here named Webb."

"I have seen him."

"He is a good man, but a difficult one. When there is trouble he is always ready for it, no matter what kind. We need men like that. But he is touchy . . . he has never hunted trouble, but is very quick when it comes."

"Why do you tell me this?"

"Because I do not want trouble between you and would not want it to come from a careless word."

"Thank you. I will remember what you have said." He turned away as I started out, then asked, "Are you the town marshal?"

"No, sir. We do not have one."

"You'd better. I mean before spring comes. This man Webb, perhaps?"

"He's too quick."

"Then you? You have handled this situation very correctly."

"I'll be gone," I said, "and I don't want the job."

"Sometimes the job selects the man," he said.

For several days then we saw very little of Drake Morrell. He spent most of his time indoors, occasionally walking down to Beaver Creek in the evening.

And then we had the chinook.

I awakened in the night. Something was different, strangely different. At first I could not realize what it was, and then I knew.

It was warm.

Lying there in my bed I could hear water dripping from the eaves. I went down the ladder to the window. Cain was sitting on the edge of the bed, listening. "What is it, Cain?"

"Sounds like rain, but it can't be. Not at this time of the year."

We opened the door and looked out. Water was dripping from the eaves, and where the night before there had been a solid field of snow there were now large patches of black where the snow was no longer. A warm wind touched our faces, and the snow was vanishing as if by magic.

"It's what Ethan told us about," Cain said, "it's a chinook."

By daylight there was little snow left, and the road to the falls was black with mud. The air felt wonderful, and I bathed my face and upper body in a tin washbasin outside the door.

For a few days we had fine weather and Cain and I turned to working on the tub mill we planned to build, marking out the ground and beginning the foundation. Croft had gone hunting with Neely Stuart, and all was quiet in the town.

We worked steadily, hauling rocks and building them into a wall, with smaller rocks for a chimney. Cain worked without effort, the largest boulder seeming nothing to him.

"You were with Morrell when he bought blankets?" he asked suddenly.

Straightening to get the kink out of my back I said, "He bought clothing as well. I think he means to stay."

Cain was silent. After a while he took his pipe from his pocket and lighted it. "We can use another man. He's an educated man, you say?"

"Yes."

"He will be a companion then to Mrs. Macken. I do not doubt she has wished for somebody with education."

Surprised, I glanced at him. "I hadn't thought of it that way. They had nothing to say to each other."

"Give them time. No doubt she misses educated talk. I heard her husband talk a few times, and he was a man of parts, very bright, and a fine speaker. Whatever he spoke had meaning." And then he added, "I never had a gift for words."

"What you say is to the point, and that's important."

He returned to work, but the conversation puzzled me. There had been a note of wistfulness, almost of uncertainty in his voice. He was always so calm, so sure. I think he made fewer false moves than any man I ever knew.

He had always seemed so complete a man that I never thought of him feeling any lack in himself, yet now I knew he did. The lack of education disturbed him, made him less sure. And there was something else there, too. Something that I could not, at the moment, put a finger to.

After a bit we left our work on the mill and went over to the places chosen and paced off the spots for a schoolhouse and a church. As we gathered tools at the day's end, Cain said to me, "We are invited to Ruth Macken's tonight. There's to be a performance."

"A what?"

"The little girl you brought to us. It seems she is an actress, as well. She is going to recite and sing."

"An actress? Her?"

"They begin very young, sometimes. At least it will be a change."

We walked to Cain's cabin and he put down the tools under the overhang of the shed. "I hope Mrs. Stuart will cause no trouble."

"What sort of trouble?"

"She doesn't believe in the child exhibiting herself, as she puts it, before a crowd of people. She was very outspoken."

"It will probably do the child good," I said. "She probably feels we have given her everything, and she has done nothing. As for Mrs. Stuart, if she doesn't wish to come, she needn't."

The weather remained warm, and after chores we all walked up the hill to Mrs. Macken's. Ethan, with Bud's help, had placed some planks on chunks of wood to make benches where we could sit.

Neely Stuart and his wife were there, looking very prim and proper. Tom and Mary Croft were trying to look the same but not managing it as well. I don't know what they expected or what I expected myself. Probably something like what you'd get at a church pageant or a social, or on visitor's day at school when the children would each stand up and say a "piece."

It was nothing like that.

She walked out very quickly and said, "I am Ninon Vauvert, of New Orleans and Boston, and now of your town."

She did not seem at all a child but was perfectly poised and composed. She sang "The Old Oaken Bucket," which was popular at the time, following it with a song from John Howard Payne's opera, *Clari* . . . "Home, Sweet Home."

She sang in a sweet, but a surprisingly strong, well-trained voice, and Morrell, seated beside me, whispered, "She is even better than her mother was . . . much better."

She seemed nothing like the slight, shivering child I had held before me on that freezing twenty-mile ride from the Oregon Buttes.

She danced a clog, something amusing I had seen a Negro do in St. Louis, and recited a poem by a journalist of Philadelphia, who had died a few years before. His name was E. A. Poe, and the poem was called *The Raven*. None of us had heard it before but Morrell, who had known Poe through a mutual friend, another writer named George Lippard.

Nobody quite knew what to do when it was over, although we all applauded. Suddenly I felt very awkward toward her. Cain took her hand in his and said, "Miss, that was the most beautiful singing I ever heard!"

Mae Stuart ran to her. "Ninon, will you teach me to dance like that?"

Neely turned sharply around. "Mae! Don't make a fool of yourself!"

When everybody had gone, Drake Morrell, Ruth Macken, Ninon, and I sat around just talking. Oddly, I had not known her name before.

She had been carried on the stage while still a baby, she played Cora's child in *Pizarro*, and the child of Damon in *Damon and Pythias*, and from that time on had worked most of the time, playing in New York, Philadelphia, Baltimore, Mobile, New Orleans, and San Francisco. After the closing of their show in San Francisco they had started for New York, and her mother had died in the mountains to the west of us, of pneumonia.

"You are welcome here as long as you wish to stay," Ruth Macken told her. "We would love to have you."

"She has family in New Orleans, Mrs. Macken," Morrell said, "but she has no wish to go to them, and I have no wish to see her go."

"Then don't go," I said bluntly, "we haven't much, but I'll do my share to see you have enough."

"I don't know. I don't know what I want to do."

"There's no hurry," Ruth Macken said, "it is best to think about it and make up your mind without being hurried."

We walked outside while Ninon got ready for bed. Standing under the stars, Morrell said, "Ninon comes of a very old and very good family, Mrs. Macken. The acting was on her father's side of the family, but they were more than simply strolling players. One of her ancestors wrote some excellent chamber music, another was organist for a king."

"Her family disapproved?"

"Very much so. They were aristocratic, very straitlaced, strong on tradition and all that." He glanced at Ruth Macken. "I know exactly what she went through and how Paul Vauvert must have seemed when she met him. He was a handsome chap, a really fine musician, and an accomplished actor.

"She had always loved to sing, to dance, to perform. What she lacked in talent she more than made up for in vivacity and personality. Ninon is like her. She is like them both, with a strong touch of her grandfather, also. Ninon is intelligent, more than the usual."

"I miss the theater," Mrs. Macken said. "We never lived where there were more than a few companies of traveling players, but we visited Boston, New York, and Washington."

"Ninon's mother played in *Lady of Lyons*, *The Duchess*, and *Our American Cousin*. She also played both Juliet and Rosalind. Ninon knows most of the roles. She has a fantastic memory."

We talked a little longer, of our town as well as of the eastern cities. Most of the time I listened, for there was much to learn, and I knew nothing of such places.

After Mrs. Macken went back inside Morrell and I walked off down the hill. "You're staying on?" I asked.

"I have been thinking of it. It is restful here."

"We need you. I mean, there has been trouble, and we are expecting more in the spring, and if I leave, our town will need every gun it can get."

"You'll go alone?"

"We can't spare anyone. Ethan Sackett knows the way, but he's our best hunter."

"You are better off alone." Morrell bit the end from a cigar. "Begin to depend on no one but yourself. The fewer people whom you trust, the fewer on whom you rely, the better for you. Especially when traveling.

"If you know it is entirely up to you, you will be more careful.

The greater the number of travelers, the greater the carelessness. Be wise, my friend, travel alone. You'll ride faster and farther."

"And when I bring the herd back?"

"Hire men as needed, get rid of them immediately if they cause you trouble, and don't trust any of them. Most of them will be trustworthy, I have no doubt, so you will have lost nothing. Others will try to steal from you or kill you, but you will be on guard."

We parted, and he walked on to his cabin, and I stood watching until he was within his door, thinking of what he had said. I did not entirely agree with him but his words stuck in my mind and would not leave me.

Softly, I opened the door. All within were asleep. Only the firelight played upon the simple, homely things about the room, and I felt a pang to know that soon I would be leaving all this, this place I was coming to love.

Adding fuel, I carefully banked the fire against the cold of the night and the morning's rising.

For a moment then I sat alone beside the fire, remembering the clear, lovely tones of Ninon's voice singing the words of "Home, Sweet Home." I had never heard the words before, but they were to ride with me for many a mile. I knew it then.

I tiptoed in my sock feet, carrying my boots, and climbed to my bed under the eaves.

Hands clasped behind my head, I lay awake long, watching the flicker of the firelight on the roof beams until sleep came.

Drake Morrell's telling of the love of Ninon's parents remained in my thoughts. It was a fine thing, that. To find a girl who loved you and to go on together. Had it been that way with Ruth Macken and her husband? And what of Cain and Helen?

What of Cain and Helen?

ELEVEN

It was Neely Stuart who found gold. He found it on Rock Creek about six or eight miles from our town, and he brought the news like the Indians were coming.

Cain and I were hoisting a timber into place on the mill when we heard a horse running like mad. We put that timber down quickly, and both of us grabbed our rifles and dropped down behind the low stone wall we had already put together.

We saw Sampson break and run for his house, and John was past the years for running. Webb ducked into the door of his cabin, pushing Foss aside, and emerged with a rifle in his hand.

It was Neely, running the legs off his horse, and nothing behind him that we could see.

"Gold!" he yelled. "I found gold!"

"It'll keep," Cain said. "Where did you find it?"

Neely thrust out his hand dramatically, and truth to tell, there was a nugget in his palm. It was about as big as a bean, but a nice piece. Webb came over, and then Croft.

It worried me, us bunching like that, so excited though I was, I pulled off a few yards to keep a lookout. The way they were talking I could have heard them fifty yards off, and Neely was so excited he was yelling.

On Rock Creek, he was saying. He had decided to go over and run a few pans now that the ice was gone, temporarily, and he had come up with a show of color right off. The first pan netted him four or five colors and then the nugget.

Webb led out his horse and saddled up, leaving Foss to do the chores. Tom Croft went along, and I couldn't hold off. If I could find a little gold I could buy cattle, a lot of cattle.

Yet to tell the truth I wasn't happy at the discovery of gold, for it would bring in folks who had no desire to stay. I was young, and I wanted to hunt for gold, but I didn't want it to happen to our town. When getting rich became the only incentive, folks didn't care much about a place and left as soon as the chance was gone.

There were signs of mining. I left them panning and walked my horse along the creek. The first gold had been found there about 1842, and several times since men had tried mining only to be driven off by Indians.

I paused to take samples from the creek bottom, for all of us had gold pans. Young though I was and accustomed to looking on the bright side, I remembered folks who had come back to my home country full of big stories but with no gold to show for it. Standing in cold mountain streams or struggling over mountain passes from one strike to another is a quick way to get old.

The only man I personally knew who came back from the gold fields rich was one who had opened a store out there.

There would be gold hunters coming when the news got out, but I intended to be selling them beef. Whatever game there was would escape to the high country with increased hunting, but if we had cattle to sell we could get along fine.

Our town site had been well chosen, for it lay back under the Beaver Rim, free from much of the wind that blew along the levels or along the slopes of the mountains. From a high place I looked back. I'd climbed so high so quickly my friends looked no more than ants. The air was fresh and cool, so much so it was like drinking water from a spring just to breathe it.

"A good place from which to look," I thought, but rode on toward the high, lonely places.

Yet the sun was leaning toward the west and I was an hour from my friends, nearly as much from our town. I was high on a shoulder of Limestone Mountain. I wanted to ride on, but had no blanket with me, and no food.

The shortest way home was along the rim of the mountain. Moreover, I might come upon an elk, and we were always in need of fresh meat. I turned southeast and skirted the edge of the trees, then started back.

As always I rode with caution. My senses were alive to what the wilderness could tell me; it never ceases to send out messages to those who will listen. Two hundred yards ahead of me a bird swooped in toward a bush, veered suddenly upward and away, and instantly, I swung my horse into the deeper shelter of the trees.

That bird had planned to land in the bush . . . what had changed its mind? Chasing an insect? Or fright at something hiding in the brush overlooking our town?

Had I been seen? I had no way of knowing. My left was sheltered by a thick growth of aspen, the right by a steep declivity on the mountain's face. Easing myself from the saddle, I spoke warningly to my horse. The buckskin was as alert to danger as any wild thing. My rifle was in my hand, and on this day I wore moccasins.

Nothing about my horse was obvious. The buckskin and his gear faded easily into the aspen trunks and leaves. If he remained still, he would be invisible at only a few paces.

Creeping forward and lowering myself to one knee, I examined the approaches to the place from which the bird had flown. The position was well chosen, if it was occupied.

For several minutes I studied the place, seeing no sign of movement. I moved forward, hesitated in a hollow from which at some time a boulder had rolled, and almost at once moved to three low-growing trees. There I waited.

A glance at the sun told me my time was short. Soon the man I sought would be leaving his position, and might even have left already.

Then I glimpsed a game trail, a narrow, low tunnel among the leaves of brush and trunks of aspen, not three feet high but almost that wide. I went into it, gained thirty yards or more, then worked my way along the slope.

I saw the place: a neat hollow where a split boulder offered a natural, easy view of our town. Around it were trees, some of them leaning above it, offering both shade and shelter.

Whoever had been there was gone. Yet the way the grass and leaves were pressed down indicated my quarry was human.

"Right cur'ous, ain't you?"

My muscles stiffened, then slowly relaxed. The voice came from behind me, and if I turned quickly I would surely be killed.

For a moment I lay still, and then I said, "Wouldn't you be curious?"

There was a dry chuckle. "I reckon. You're a purty good Injun for a younker."

Slowly, I turned around, keeping my grip on my rifle. The man who sat on the edge of the trees behind me was not disturbed. His rifle was centered on my chest, and there was no way he could miss, no way I could bring a gun to bear before a .56 caliber Spencer bullet had torn a hole in me big enough to put a fist through.

"I take it you've some reason for not coming down to the town," I suggested. Gently I released my grip on the rifle. My pistol was inside my buckskin hunting shirt and thrust behind my waistband. Did he know that? Had he noticed that my hunting shirt was not the pull over kind, but laced halfway up the front?

"You make it right. Man down there I'm fixin' to kill."

"Well," I said dryly, "if what they tell me about this country is true, you wait until spring and the Indians will do it for you."

He chuckled again. "Cool one, ain't you? Now mebbe I just better shoot you before you try somethin'."

The fact that he had slipped up on me was irritating, and I'll not deny I was itching to even the score. Besides, had he not said he intended to kill one of us?

"You shoot me, and everybody down there will know something is wrong. I am the only one out of the village, and you'd never get away with it. I've a friend down there who would track you down."

"In that bunch of pilgrims? Ain't one of you down there could find me on an alkali flat at high sun!"

"Ethan Sackett could."

He gave me a sharp look from those foxy old eyes. He was a narrow, high-shouldered man, rail-thin yet wiry, and he wore a dirty buckskin hunting shirt and leggings with a bedraggled coonskin cap.

"Ethan down there? That do count. It surely do count. I never reckoned on him."

"You know him?"

"I should reckon. We done trapped beaver on the Yellowstone together, an' fit Diggers on the Humboldt. So old Ethan is down there, is he?"

He took out a plug of tobacco and bit off a healthy thumb of it. "What you folks fixin' to do? Dig for gold?"

"We've started a town. We plan to stay, raise some cattle, plant crops, trade with the wagons."

"You ain't got long. Rich folks will be travelin' by the steam cars, or so I hear."

My pistol was under my shirt, my shirt bagged, my hand was close, yet the man I faced had no gamble in him. He would shoot.

"Who are you after? We've good folks down yonder, never made trouble for any man. All we're wishful to do is build a church, a school, and raise our families."

"Well now, ain't that nice?" He grinned at me, then spat a stream of tobacco juice near my feet. "I never cottoned much to towns or town-folk. Gimme a squaw an' a buffalo-hide teepee."

"Fine," I said, "why don't you go get it right now and leave us be? You've wasted time scouting folks who've done you no harm and aren't likely to. Unless you're one of that bunch of renegades from over east."

"Them?" He spat. "A pack o' murderin' blackguards, that's what they are." He chuckled. "You gave 'em what-for. I liked to smiled."

"Have you been here *that* long?"

"Here an' about." He gave me a foxy look from those sharp little eyes. "You taken on any comp'ny lately? I mean any new folks?"

"We're just a lot who turned off from a wagon train," I said carelessly, for now I thought I knew at whom he was pointing. "We didn't figure we could make it over the passes before winter."

"You think right. You was kee-rect. What I mean is somebody lately. A man and a couple of younkers, maybe?"

"We found a man alongside the trail some time back. He lived long enough to tell us where the children were. One of them died," I added, "the boy."

"A shame. I got nothing against the younkers. You say he lived long enough, but that don't say he ain't still livin', does it? And I reckon he is. Drake Morrell ain't the kind o' man to die that easy."

"Is it Morrell you're hunting?"

"You're darned tootin'. I'm fixin' to kill him."

"I've heard he's handy with a gun."

"He is. And might beat me if I face up to him, which I'm of no mind to do. He fights his way, I mine. And mine's Injun. No man in his right mind risks losin' his hair just to stand up to a man. I don't care if he knows who kills him just so he dies. An' he'll die."

It was nigh to sundown, and I was still a good way from home. My stomach was growling from hunger, and I was of no mind to sit here talking about shooting when what I needed was a meal.

"If you aren't going to shoot," I said, "I'm going home."

With that I moved to rise, and when I did I slid my gun into my fist. Now as I've said, I handle a pistol almighty fast. I can't claim credit for it, it just comes natural, but there it was and him looking into it, but I didn't shoot.

We just stood there, a Mexican standoff, each of us with the drop on the other. He had the most power in that .56, but I was sure I'd shoot as fast as he could.

"Well, now. Right foxy, ain't you?" He grinned at me, in no way disturbed, yet I watched him like a cat, my finger easy on the trigger, for this man would kill.

"I don't like to have anybody slipping up on me," I said, "I don't like it at all."

"You could have waited. You might git a shot at me off guard."

"You? That would be a mighty long wait. And I wouldn't shoot a man in the back."

"You're a fool. You should live Injun for a while. You'd see the thing is to win, no matter how."

"I wasn't aware that was an Indian idea," I said. "Most of them take pride in their victories and would rather count coups on a live, dangerous enemy than a dead one."

"Some o' them," he admitted grudgingly. "They ain't smart."

"I'm going to leave. I'm not anxious to kill you or be killed. I'd as soon leave you for Morrell." Keeping the drop on him, I stepped back toward the brush, but curiosity overcame me. "Why do you want to kill him? It takes a good man to risk his life to protect those youngsters as he did."

"Mebbe he just used them for shelter," he suggested. "Mebbe he figured I wouldn't kill him with them dependin' on him. An' he was right," he admitted, surprisingly, "I wouldn't. Not any child, let alone hers."

"You knew their mother?" Now I was surprised.

"Knew her? How'd the likes o' me know her? No, sir. I didn't know her but by sight, only that voice of hers. She sang like an angel. You know what that means to a man lonely for women-folks? I mean decent women-folks?

"I heard a feller say she couldn't sing for sour apples, but after he picked the teeth out of his face, he apologized.

"She was the on'y woman I'd heard sing in fifteen year, and she sang songs my ma used to sing. It was a sound from Heaven, believe me.

"It was a sorry thing when she died. If the thought'll pleasure you," he said, "I done put flowers on her grave after he buried her."

"But still, you want to kill him?"

"That's the switch of another tail. Yes, sir. I'll fetch him to Hell with my Spencer. He notched his gun for two of my brothers."

"Maybe they took in after him?"

"Surely they did, and that was their affair, but when he notched them he opened the war. I'll see him buried or left for buzzards."

"You'd better think about it, friend," I said. "I didn't know your brothers, but Drake Morrell is a good man, a damned good man, and that girl depends on him. Do you want her left to get along by herself in this country? In a couple of years she'll be a woman . . . what kind of woman?"

He glared at me, but I'd finished talking. I picked up my rifle and backed off into the brush, and he did the same. I went to my horse and rode back to town. It had started out to be a quiet day, but a man never knows.

Anyway, I had words for Drake Morrell, and I feared for him.

Ethan was gathering stove wood when I rode up to town, so I pulled in and told him the story. After I described the man, he chuckled without much humor.

"Stacy Follett . . . yeah, I know him. Morrell's treed himself an old he-coon, that's what he's done. An old he-coon."

TWELVE

By lantern light I fed my horse, rubbed him down with a handful of hay, and while doing so I thought of this place we were building, this island in the wilderness, and the dangers that lay about us. So it must have been with the first settlers building their first towns, surrounded by hatred of their strange ways.

For as no man stands alone, neither does a town, nor can a change be made in the terrain without ripples moving out from it. Our coming had caused the game to move back into the hills, had shortened its supply, and when spring came our plows would bite deep in the soil. It was not a rich soil, but it was the soil with which we must make do. With our hands, our strength, and the cunning learned from farmers of all times, we would enrich the soil, grow our crops, and our harvest would come, for better or worse.

Stacy Follett lurked in the mountains outside our town, a threat to one of us, indirectly to us all. Each man among us was necessary to us, and none could be lost without weakening the whole, and so exposing us to danger. Stacy Follett was not my enemy, yet I thought him so, for his rifle could remove part of our wall of strength against the Indians.

We did not wish trouble with the red man. He had his way and we ours, yet he fought for pleasure, for loot, and because he was faced by a nameless threat he could not grasp, yet feared.

He did not know his way of life was doomed, not by the guns of the white man, nor by his countless thousands, but by his goods.

The death of the red man's way came when the first white trader came among them to trade what the Indian could not himself make. From that day on his desire was aroused, and he must by trade or capture acquire those things he desired.

The needle, the steel knife blade, the gun and gunpowder, the whiskey, and the various ornaments. These were the seeds of his destruction, and what he warred against was the desire in his own heart. There were those who protested against using the white man's things, but their voices spoke into the hollow air, and no ear listened.

I could have lived the Indian way and loved it. I could feel his spirits move upon the air, hear them in the still forest and in the chuckling water of the mountain streams, but other voices were calling me, too, the voices of my own people and their ways.

For it was our way to go onward; to go forward and to try to shape our world into something that would make our lives easier, even if more complicated. Our struggle was for time. Our leisure was bought from hardship, and we needed leisure to think, to dream, to create.

Drake Morrell was in his cabin when I came to the door. He invited me in and listened while I told him of Follett.

"I have been expecting him," he said. "He is the best of a poor lot. They gambled with me, and were very clumsy about it, and when they lost they accused me of cheating. I invited a soldier who was waiting for the stage to step over and feel under the table, and as I knew he would, he found four hidden cards on their side.

"They had been trying to cheat, but so clumsily any fool could have seen what they were doing. I told them so, and what I thought of them, and they left.

"They waited for me outside, and when I came out I left by the rear door and came around the building. I saw them there, guns held upon the door, and I called them.

"Those Spencers are a terrible weapon, but heavy to handle swiftly. Only one got off a shot, and it went into the dirt. I killed them both, left and right like a brace of quail.

"If you expect me to be sorry, you will be mistaken. They tried to beat me at my own game, cards. When that failed they tried to shoot me down without warning.

"Stacy Follett is another thing. Without him they could not have lived as long as they had. He is a dangerous man."

"I think so."

"What is there to do? Be careful. I have always been that."

"You are a brave man, Morrell."

"A man does what he has to do. A brave man? What men call a hero, Shafter, is merely a man who is seen doing what a brave man does as a matter of course."

He turned away. "Let me get my pipe and we'll walk up the street. Have you finished Plutarch?"

"No."

"Take your time with him. He is worth it." He pulled the door shut behind him. "You are luckier than you know. I mean in the books you have to read. People who come west cannot bring much, so they try to bring the best, and from all I hear Major Macken chose wisely.

"I envy you, starting out like this. A mind, like a home, is furnished by its owner, so if one's life is cold and bare he can blame none but himself. You have a chance to select from some pretty elegant furnishings."

He changed the subject suddenly. "Shafter, you could do something for me."

Surprised, I just looked at him. He seemed so complete, so in need of nothing. "I speak of Ninon. If Stacy Follett should be luckier than I think he will be, take care of her.

"She's going to be a beautiful woman, Shafter, and a rarely talented one. She'll not be content here for long. She has too much inside her crying for expression. Whatever she comes to be, her life won't be lived quietly. She has too much passion and fire and ambition in her."

"But she's only a child."

He shrugged. "How long is a girl a child? She is a child, and then one morning you wake up and she's a woman and a dozen different people of whom you recognize none."

"Being here may be good for her. It may give her time to discover herself, to find out who she is."

"You're talking nonsense, Shafter, and you know it. Nobody is anybody until they make themselves somebody. But it won't take Ninon long. I know her and the stuff she came from."

We ate that night at Cain's house, and Ruth and Bud were there. We talked that night of many things, of books and boots and mysteries, of haunts and swords and far-off places where temples were and gods once walked with men.

Lenny Sampson came in with his pa and listened wide-eyed while Morrell told the story of Ulysses and the Cyclops, and the

one about Theseus and the Minotaur, and Aeneas and the found-
ing of Rome.

It was good talk, and the room was warm and pleasant, and
when it was over Ninon sang a couple of songs, and we drank
coffee. When the youngsters had gone off to bed Cain, Morrell,
Sampson, and I, we sat and talked of the town.

"You must have a town marshal," Morrell said. "You will have
violent men coming among the peaceful ones, and if there is no
law there will be trouble."

"How about you for the job?" Cain asked.

"No." Morrell spoke positively. "I am well known. I do not
want to bring my troubles on your town. I will stay, if you will
have me, but not as marshal."

"Bendigo is the one for the job," Sampson said. "He has
judgment, and he can use a gun if need be."

"I will not be here," I said.

"Webb?" Morrell asked.

"No," Cain said. "There is trouble in the man. I like him, but
he is dangerous."

We talked of that, and of a city government, and for the first
time we thought of elections and the drawing up of municipal
regulations.

There was also the matter of land. Nobody had claimed anything except for two mining claims by Webb and Stuart, over on
Rock Creek. Nobody, that is, but Ruth Macken.

She had staked out the bench on which her house stood, which
comprised several acres as well as a corner of meadow that lay
beyond some trees. That meadow was not one in which we had
run our stock, being more visible from her house than from the
town, yet there were at least fifty acres in it, and it was well
watered.

We began to think of garden plots, for there would be vegetables to be grown, and a place to sow wheat. Cain and John
Sampson and I had agreed to work together, but now I would be
gone. A subtle change had taken place in their relationship to me,
one that even I had scarcely noticed. Since I had been hunting
and providing so much of the meat for the settlement, they now
accepted me as an equal.

There was to be a town council, and we discussed among
ourselves whom we should choose for mayor. Sampson and I
suggested Cain, but he refused. John Sampson was the man, Cain
said, and we finally agreed when it came to a vote we would
nominate him . . . or Cain would.

For several days the work went forward. Cain and I built the stone wall of our mill halfway up as planned, then began the use of timbers. By the end of the week we had it ready for roofing.

Neely Stuart was working on his gold claim. Croft had been adding to his house, making it tighter against the cold. He had scouted a small field where he planned to plant vegetables and grain when spring came.

Neely was gone much of the time, and at first he had success. Each night he returned to talk of his gold, and then he began to speak of it less, but to walk with more of a swagger. He did manage to let us know he was doing well, and several times he made small purchases at Ruth Macken's and paid in gold.

Webb worked occasionally on his claim but helped more with the gathering of fuel, the hunting, and the scouting. We never hunted alone . . . each time a man went out, somebody went with him.

Several times Webb and I hunted, and I let him get the best of the shots. He was careful with a gun, a good shot and he wasted no ammunition. We talked little, but I felt that he liked me as much as he liked anyone. Several times he made comments about Foss . . . the boy was lazy, he said. He needed a good whipping from some boy half his size to teach him a thing or two. To all this I made no comment.

From Plutarch I moved on to Locke's *Essay on Human Understanding*. It had been a book much read by the founders of our country, and it was different from anything I had read until then.

Twice, groups of Mormons stopped by, and each time we gave them shelter and provided them with supplies, for which they paid. We saw nothing of Stacy Follett, and when I scouted his old observation post I found no sign of him there. No doubt once discovered he was wily enough to move away. Christmas was upon us then, and we forgot about him . . . at least most of us did.

It had been our custom ever since arriving to hold a service on Sunday. Usually, it was a simple, friendly affair with Cain or John Sampson reading from the Bible and Tom Croft leading us in hymn singing. We had a few fair to middling voices amongst us, and we liked the singing.

And then Moses Finnerly came to town.

He was a tall, thin man with haggard features and hollow eyes, sharp eyes that missed nothing at all. He had two men with him, a short, stocky man with a bland, open face and eyes that revealed nothing but seemed merry enough at first sight. The other was a big, heavy man with fat jowls and a coarse, rough way about him.

They came riding up the trail one Saturday forenoon and rode right to Cain's. They had them a tent, and they set it up right off, and then Moses Finnerly came to see Cain.

We had just reared a timber into place, one of the crossbeams of the mill, and we were catching our breath. Webb, wearing a pistol, had walked over to stand with us as the three riders came up the trail.

My rifle was handy, and as always I was wearing a six-gun. In that country nobody went unarmed from sunup to sundown . . . not if he planned to live out his years.

"How do you do, gentlemen? I am the Reverend Moses Finnerly. These gentlemen are accompanying me. May I present Brother Joseph Pappin? And Brother Ollie Trotter?"

"Howdy," Webb said. "I'm Webb. These are the Shafter brothers."

"Pleased," the Reverend Finnerly said, "pleased, indeed. We understood you had a settlement here and thought it behooved us to bring you God's word."

"We have God's word," Webb replied, "each house has a Bible. Of a Sunday we have readings."

"Ah? Of course, of course. But the Bible, sir, must be interpreted. The Lord's word must not be profaned, but given from the lips of one ordained to the task."

"Get down," Cain said, "get down, gentlemen. We have little enough here, but we will share with you."

"Little?" Ollie Trotter looked around. "I heard tell this was a gold camp."

Cain smiled. "I believe some mining did take place some years back. We've only just settled, and we're planning to farm and trade."

For a moment disappointment seemed to show in their faces, but who am I to judge? The hour was nearing noon, and it was the logical place to stop.

It was a natural thing for a man to notice. Their horses had come far, were not good stock, and they were traveling almighty light. If they'd been anything but men of God I would have guessed they left wherever they'd been in a hurry.

Webb watched them go, then spat. "I don't cotton to 'em, Ben," he said. "That Finnerly's got him a mean eye."

They joined us at table, and I didn't cotton to them either, or to the way their eyes followed Lorna about. Moses Finnerly sat back and looked up at her as she passed. "Have you been saved, young woman? Have you been offered the mercy of the Lord?"

Cain turned half around but before he could speak, I did. "She has never been lost, Reverend. She doesn't need saving."

He turned hard eyes toward mine. "The Lord will judge," he said.

"You are right, Reverend. He will judge us all."

He did not like that very much, nor did he like me, but the feeling was mutual, and I did not mind. I am a man who has respect for the ministers of the Lord, but it has been my short experience that some of them need their own best services. We Shafters have always leaned toward a gentle and forgiving Christ, but unless I missed my guess, Moses Finnerly had in him the spirit of a witch burner.

He asked the blessing, and a long-winded one it was, and personally I favored men of God who could say what they had to say briefly when I was hungry. Also there was more in his praying of what God forbade than what he forgave.

"The big house," Finnerly said, after a bit. "The one on the bench . . . whose is it?"

"The Widow Macken lives there," Helen said, "a fine woman."

"I doubt it not," Finnerly replied.

As though she had been called for, at that moment she knocked, and I saw a flicker of irritation cross Cain's face. At our call, she stepped in, Ninon beside her.

We got to our feet, all but Ollie Trotter. Cain introduced them, and I could fairly see their mouths water. Moses Finnerly said, "Widow Macken, we are travelers without a place to put our heads. You have a large house. Can you provide?"

She looked at him directly, a cool, measuring look, and then she smiled. "My cabin is not as large as it seems, and all too small for three of us."

"Three?"

"My son. I am afraid you must look elsewhere, Parson, but it has been a custom for those who come to our town to provide for themselves. We will share our food, although we have little; our homes are small."

"We need but little," Brother Joseph Pappin said, "a corner away from the wind."

She did not smile this time. "Please do not think me callous, but my home has no room for men, and you should understand that a woman, almost alone, could not offer you a place."

He did not like it, but he bowed. "Of course. I did not think. You spoke of a son . . ."

"He is quite young."

She sat down, and Helen brought her coffee, and conversation began again. Ruth Macken was no fool, and she had liked their unctuous manner no more than Webb and I. After a moment she turned to them. "Have you come far?"

"Too far, Mrs. Macken. Yet not too far if we can bring the word of God to you who reside here."

"You come from the west?"

Finnerly ignored the question and started to speak of God and his works, and I sat there sipping coffee and thinking about the Devil quoting Scripture to his own ends, which was unjust of me for I knew not the men, nor what lay behind them. They might be good men. Yet even as I told myself that I did not believe it.

"We will hold services tomorrow," the Reverend Finnerly said, "and would be pleased if you would attend."

"We shall be glad to hear you," Cain replied. "We have done our own preaching until now." He got to his feet. "The hour is late. If you wish to bed down here upon the floor, gentlemen, you are welcome. I am sorry we have so little to offer."

They exchanged a look. "Isn't there an empty house? Or one with fewer people? We are very tired and . . ."

"There's Drake Morrell's," I suggested, moved by I know not what deviltry.

Finnerly cringed as if stabbed. "Morrell? Is he *here*? You shelter such a man within this village?" Suddenly his voice rose. "Drake Morrell is a murderer. An evil, evil man!"

"He has lived quietly among us," John Sampson said. "We find no fault in the man."

"He is a gambler, a murderer, and a defiler of women!" Finnerly shouted.

"I have found him a gentleman," Ruth Macken replied, "and I believe him to be a man of honor."

Finnerly turned sharply and started to speak, but perhaps it was something in Cain's attitude or mine that decided him against it. He controlled himself, but his eyes were narrow and mean. "He will hang!" he said savagely. "There is no place for him and his kind."

Turning abruptly, he stalked from the room followed by Pappin and Trotter.

Ruth Macken spoke, as I started to close the door. "Leave it

open for just a minute, Mr. Shafter. I believe we need some fresh
air in here, after that."

"He should be ashamed of himself," Helen said. "I like Mr.
Morrell."

"To preach the word of Christ," Sampson said dryly, "a man
should have a little forgiveness in him. I have no doubt Mr.
Morrell has had his difficulties, but so have we."

"John," Cain said, "I have been thinking about the north forty.
Why don't we sow oats? I've seen some wild oats growing around,
and I think it would do well, and we'll have stock to feed."

Lorna, Ruth Macken, and Helen settled down to making paper
ornaments for a Christmas tree, and as Cain talked to John he
worked at making nails. Opening my book, I began to read, and
from time to time I would look up from Locke and listen to the
soft rumble of conversation in the room, the quiet crackling of the
flames, and the sound of working hands. It was an evening like
many another, one of those evenings I was to treasure in the long
years to come. Fortunately, I knew it then.

Reading what John Locke had to say on knowledge and judgment made me think again of Drake Morrell and our discussion
with the Reverend Finnerly.

It was like the sudden flight of the bird that warned me of Stacy
Follett's presence in the brush. I did not know for a certainty that
anything was there. On the evidence of the bird's sudden flight I
merely presumed it a possibility. With Drake Morrell we had
only his present conduct and his risking his life to aid two children by which to judge him, so I would accept him as the kind of
man he appeared to be while reserving judgment until there was
more evidence.

Looking up again from my book, I watched those in the room
with me and was lonely within myself, for there was in me a great
reaching outward, a desire to be and to become. I looked upon
Cain and John Sampson and thought of Ethan Sackett, each in his
own way a man, and a complete man, or so it seemed.

Ethan was the hunter and the mountain man, as much a part of
the mountains and the wilderness as any wolf, beaver, or deer.
My brother Cain, the master craftsman, turning the steel in his
hand, striking surely and honestly, and when the striking was
finished he would have created a tool. And John Sampson, a
kindly man, secure within himself, a God-fearing man who was
tolerant, forgiving, yet strong.

And I?

I had been given certain flesh and certain brains susceptible of shaping, and the shaping was mine to do. Of course, I would be influenced by heredity, by the world in which I lived, and by the contacts, abrasive or otherwise, but still and all, the shaping was in my hands.

What kind of man was I to be? What sort of thing must I do to become that man?

THIRTEEN

C hristmas Eve was clear and cold. There had been a light snow earlier in the day, covering some of the bare places left by the chinook or blown away by the winds.

The Reverend Moses Finnerly and his two friends had turned to, and with help from Neely Stuart had built a half-dugout cabin in the side of a knoll not far from the town.

Ethan, Webb, and I had put in a lot of time hunting, and had brought in meat for the Christmas tables. Ollie Trotter proved a good hunter, too, and brought in an elk and a deer. So there was meat in plenty for the holiday.

Working every moment we could spare, Cain, Sampson, and I had roofed the mill, added a big fireplace, and we would use it for meetings, socials, and such until spring came when the mill went into operation, and we could afford to build a school. The school would be the church, too, until we could build one.

Drake Morrell took part in everything. He worked with us on the mill, trimming logs of their branches, stacking brush, and gathering firewood so we who were good with tools could work longer.

Shortly after the Reverend Finnerly arrived, I mentioned him to Morrell. He gave me a kind of amused look. "I am not surprised that he doesn't like me, and he has reason."

"What happened?"

103

He shrugged. "You haven't seen it yet, Bendigo, but sometimes I take a drink too much, and when I do I am apt to be unpleasant. Oh, I don't mean violent! Nothing like that. But sarcastic sometimes, and inclined to prick balloons that are better left to float away.

"Moses Finnerly," he added, "is everything I don't like. He is to my thinking narrow, bigoted, and basically mean. He puts on a pious manner, preaches a kind of so-called Christianity with which I have never been in sympathy.

"He's a gospel shouter of the fire-and-brimstone school. Everybody is Hell-bound but him, and their only chance of being saved is by him."

Well, that was my opinion, too, but I didn't say so. I just asked, "What about Pappin and Trotter?"

"Ollie Trotter? He's a bad man. Finnerly got him away from a lynch mob so he stays with him. He's a dry-gulching murderer, a horse thief, and a troublemaker. He's good with a gun, but you'll wait a long time before he faces anybody with one.

"Since Finnerly saved his neck he claims to be a changed man, but I don't believe it. Not for one minute.

"Pappin is the smartest one of the lot. He passes the collection plate when they have meetings and always has his eye out for the main chance.

"The three of them have been run out of a half dozen camps. They start by preaching, end by trying to rule, and you can be sure they'll try it here, too.

"Finnerly doesn't like me because I started questioning him about religion."

"I didn't know you were a religious man."

"I'm not. At least I don't fit into the usual pattern. When I was a child I studied the Bible with a very fine man. He was a truly great scholar who read Hebrew and Greek or Latin better than I do English, and he enjoyed reading and discussing the Bible. We were much together, and I learned a lot . . . without really wanting to, at that age.

"Men like Finnerly irritate me, but when I am sober I am tolerant. I know it is better to ignore them as long as one can. Unhappily, when I have a drink there is a devil in me that makes me want to prick the balloon of their assumed righteousness."

"Well, he won't stay long. That's one thing."

"Don't you believe it. Finnerly will stay if he can. West of here he got into too much trouble. They'll stay if they can."

Later, talking to Cain and John Sampson, I repeated what Morrell had said.

Sampson said, "All that may very well be, but they shall have their chance. It is simple justice. And so far, although their views are not mine, they have conducted themselves well enough."

A week before Christmas, Drake Morrell disappeared. He had been gone for three days before we realized it, but when I mentioned it to Ruth Macken she said, "He stopped by on his way out and asked if Bud would take care of his cabin, so Bud has been sleeping over there and loving it."

On that clear, cold Christmas Eve, Drake Morrell returned, leading two pack horses. He had ridden all the way to Fort Bridger and its trading post, and only then did we discover that he had ordered, weeks before, presents for the lot of us from Salt Lake.

Cain had built a roaring fire in the mill, and we gathered there for the services, and without allowing Moses Finnerly any opportunity to take charge, John Sampson quietly took over. He had conducted prayer meetings back in the States, and on the wagon train west he had usually taken charge and conducted services naturally and easily.

He was a fine-looking man with white hair, and he spoke easily and with sincerity. We had come to find comfort in his words; he was truly a good man, and they were few enough, here or elsewhere.

Finnerly did not like it. Sitting behind him I could see him fidgeting, wishful to take over and conduct the meeting himself. We had talked among us, and we did not want a meeting of brimstone and fire and somebody calling down the anger of the Lord upon us for our sins. We wanted a meeting of thankfulness and gladness, for we were lucky to have survived so far.

We sang the old hymns and some songs that were only loved and were not religious, and Ninon sang "Home, Sweet Home" again for us. We went to our homes happy and awaiting Christmas morning.

As the others were bedding down, I walked to the stable to see how the animals were faring and to listen into the night. I saw nothing and heard nothing, yet there was an uneasiness upon me. We had met our difficulties and faced them down, and the price of our success had been vigilance. Walking out from the town, I climbed the hill to look around, and far off saw a glint of something that might have been fire.

I waited a moment, then looked again. The light was still there, and it must be a fire.

What would a fire be doing in such a place, on such a night? It was not a good place to camp, if my memory served me, but the fire might be further off than I believed.

After a moment, I walked back to our town. Already the light was out in Cain's house but I needed my rifle. I tiptoed to the door, opening it softly. There was a rush of warm air . . . the fire had been banked; only a few tendrils of flame wove a weird dance among the shadows on the wall.

"What is it, Bendigo?" Lorna sat up, whispering to me.

"There's a fire . . . it's far out, toward the plains."

"A campfire?"

"It's in no good place for a camp." I paused, thinking it over. "It might be a signal."

"Who'd be out there?"

I grinned at her in the half-light. "Sandy Claus. Maybe one of his reindeer broke a leg."

"Be serious." She got up and came to me in her nightgown. "Bendigo, can I go with you?"

"Who's going anywhere?"

"You are. I can tell."

"It's no place for a girl. We don't know what's down there . . . it might be a trap."

The thought had not occurred to me before, but now it did, a way to lure a few of us away into what might be just that. Yet it was near the trail, and it might be some woebegone traveler, and this was Christmas Eve.

I pulled off my boots; I wanted moccasins for this. A man makes less noise in them.

When I stood up, Lorna was half-dressed. "I'm coming, Bendigo. Now you wait."

Well, why not? I was a damned fool to take her but she was a good shot with a rifle, and I might need somebody to stand off and cover me. Still, I didn't like it.

She bundled up in a hurry and was ready to go before I was. We slipped out, but before I left I scratched out a little note for Cain and Helen, just in case.

It was still and cold. The stars hung low in the sky, and the snow sparkled with a million tiny flecks of diamond. We went to the barn for horses, and I almost heard them groan as I reached for a saddle.

Hurriedly, we saddled up, and again Lorna was ready almost as soon as I was. She had brought her rifle, and she led her horse out and got into the saddle. I was riding the buckskin we had taken from the renegades at the time of their raid.

Lorna was excited. "Bendigo? What do you think it is?"

"Might be a trap," I repeated, "and it might be somebody hurt and in trouble. We'll not ride right straight up to that fire. You come along easy, now."

We rode out of the town and into the scattered trees along the bench, then, holding to partial cover of trees and brush, we rode toward the fire. Several times I paused to study the area, but could see no movement . . . only the fire, whose size seemed to grow less as we rode nearer. Perhaps from lack of fuel.

The trees grew fewer, cover less. It was harder to keep out of sight, and still nothing stirred. And then we saw something we had not seen before . . . a black spot on the snow some fifty yards from the fire.

"It's a horse, Bendigo," Lorna said. "I am sure it's a horse."

"Then there's a rider close by. It's a cinch that horse didn't build the fire."

We walked our horses closer, circling wide. It was a horse, all right, and there was a man . . . or his body . . . lying near the fire.

It looked like whoever it was had set fire to a low-growing bush of some kind to get a fire started. It must have flared up about the time we saw it, and then as it died down he had fed sticks into it.

Sometimes dried leaves and broken twigs will pile up under a bush like that, and in an emergency a man might get something going when he had no strength to rustle materials to build a fire properly.

"Better warm your hands," I said, "but go easy. We don't want to shoot anybody lest we have to."

Shoving my own rifle down in its scabbard, I drew a pistol and walked my horse closer and closer.

The man lay still, unconscious or sleeping. I could see where he had crawled from his horse toward the creek, his trail plain enough in the sprinkling of snow. The fire was doing him little good now, as he was lying on the frozen ground. Most of the snow had been melted or blown from the spot where he lay, and he had evidently passed out trying to get to a deadfall for more fuel.

I got down from my horse and walked the last few yards.

It was an Indian, and he had a broken leg.

Keeping an eye on him, I fed some sticks into the fire, then called to Lorna.

My movements or the call brought him out of it. He pushed himself up to arm's length and turned to look at me, and I knew that face.

It was a face I'd not soon forget. It was the young warrior who had wanted to keep Mae Stuart and kill young Lenny Sampson.

He grabbed for his rifle and I kicked it out of his hands. "You better forget that," I said, "you're in bad shape."

There was blood on the front of his quilled hunting shirt, too, so he'd been shot.

And then I saw why.

Fastened to his belt was a scalp, a fresh scalp. And it was white man's hair.

FOURTEEN

He glared at me, his eyes ugly with hatred. I stood over him with my pistol in my hand, and he was almighty sure I was going to shoot him. As I looked down at him I thought what a lot of trouble I might save if I did.

Lorna said, "Bendigo, he's hurt. He's been shot."

"Yes," I said, "and he's carrying two fresh scalps, and they aren't Indian scalps.

"I'd better keep an eye on him, Lorna. You bring up my horse, will you?"

She looked at me, long and steadily, but I shook my head. "I'd never shoot a man when he was down," I said, "but he'd do it to me. Indians don't feel the same way about things as we do."

"They can change."

"I think so," I said. "Lorna, this is the same Indian who had Mae and Lenny."

She turned quickly and looked at him again. "You don't mean it!"

"Better get those horses. This cold isn't doing him any good."

When I bent over to take his knife and tomahawk he grabbed at me, and I hit him . . . I hit him hard. "You mind your manners, redskin. I'm just trying to save your hide . . . although I don't know why."

When Lorna came up with the horses I picked up that Indian

and got him aboard my horse. But first I tied his hands, because I didn't want to see him riding off with that buckskin and maybe grabbing Lorna's bridle, too.

It must have hurt when I flopped him into the saddle but he didn't make a sound, just glared at me. Taking up the reins I started off for home.

"You keep that rifle handy," I said to Lorna. "If he acts up . . . shoot him."

I didn't think she'd do it, although you can never tell about women, but I said it for the effect on the Indian. He might not know the words but he would get the idea.

I've no argument against the Indian. He was a mighty savage man and he fought the way he knew how. Only toward the end was he fighting for country; mostly he fought just to be fighting.

No Indian could get a wife or be counted a warrior until he had taken a scalp, and Indians were celebrated among themselves for their victories, just as were the knights at King Arthur's court.

We went on back to our town, and I woke Cain up. He listened to what I had to say while we got the Indian inside and stretched him out before the fire. Then Lorna went to awaken John Sampson. Between us we set the Indian's leg and put splints on it. "You'd better keep his hands tied," I advised. "He doesn't know what's going on. So far as he knows we're getting him well just to kill him."

"I wonder where he got those scalps?" Cain asked.

He glanced at his watch, then looked up. "Merry Christmas, everybody," he said, "it's nearly one o'clock."

We all answered him and then I looked down at the Indian. "And a Merry Christmas to you, too!"

He glared at me, then spat.

"Well," I said, "he's got nerve. Lorna, you'd better get some sleep. Morning isn't too far away."

John Sampson went back to his cabin to bed, and Cain sat down and lighted his pipe.

"There hasn't been any snow," he said, "and this Indian must have left a trail."

Well, we looked at each other, thinking of what might result. This Indian killed two white people, one of them a woman, by the looks of the hair, and they might have friends.

"You go to bed, Cain. I'll watch."

"All right." He got up. "I confess I'm tired. But do you keep watch out the window, too."

"You don't look much like Santa Claus," I said, to the Indian, "and if you bring us any gifts it won't be what we want."

There was some soup Helen had put by the night before, and I warmed it up, and when it was warm, took it and a spoon. "Come on," I said, "and I'll feed you."

He spat at me, and I just grinned at him. "What's the matter, brave warrior? Are you scared?"

He glared at me, then opened his mouth, and I fed him the bowl of soup, spoon by spoon because his hands were tied. When it was finished I said, "You'd better get some sleep, redskin."

Fixing myself a cup of coffee, I then went up the ladder to my bed and got the book I was reading. Only this time she had given me two at the same time, and I decided to take both of them down. The first was the *Essays* of Montaigne. The second was the *Travels* of William Bartram.

I wanted to read both of them so bad that I'd started one, then the other, and would read a piece of each. Bartram was a plant-hunter, a naturalist they called him, and he wrote a lot about the Cherokees and Creeks who lived in Tennessee, Carolina, and Georgia, where he wandered about.

Sitting down there with a cup of coffee beside me, and the two books, I read until almost daybreak. A couple of times I looked up to see that Indian watching me. I figure he'd never seen anybody read before, and even though he said nothing the curiosity was in his eyes.

It was a strange Christmas morning. We had stockings hung over the fireplace for everybody, but at the last minute before the others came down, Lorna appeared with another stocking to hang over the chimney.

The Indian had slept little, but he watched her hang it with straight black eyes that revealed little. Then Ann, who was ten, and Bobby, who was just four, came down from the loft and rushed at the stockings.

There were others for Cain, Helen, Lorna, and myself. Then Lorna took the other stocking down and laid it across the Indian's lap. He stared at it, then at her.

Leaning over with my knife I cut the rope that bound his wrists. They must have hurt, for I'd tied him tight for the sleeping hours, but he did not chafe them. He watched us like a cat, opening the things in our stockings.

There was a carved wooden doll, dressed in clothes Helen and Lorna had made for it, for Ann. There were a half dozen wooden soldiers for Bobby, and two carved wooden Indians. Cain and I, we both worked well at carving, and these were very lifelike. There was some rock candy and popcorn balls, and some odds and ends for the youngsters.

In my stocking there was a red knitted scarf from Lorna and a new, beautifully made hand-axe from Cain.

The Indian turned his sock over, then dug into it. The first thing was a chunk of rock candy. He had seen the children eating theirs, so he tasted it, then popped it into his mouth. There were popcorn balls for him, too, an old clasp knife that once belonged to Cain, and a silver button, a small sack of colored beads, a packet of needles—much in demand among Indians—and some more popcorn balls and rock candy. He examined every piece.

Helen was busy over dinner with Lorna helping. Cain had been outside feeding the stock when suddenly he came to the door for his rifle.

"Bendigo?"

When I looked up, he motioned me to join him. Seeing he held his rifle, I picked up mine. Webb was outside the door with Stuart, Croft, and Sampson. They were looking down the valley, and we could see a dark cluster of riders, out in the open and coming on steadily.

"Who do you think they are?" Webb wondered.

"I think they're trailing the Indian," I said.

"Indian? What Indian?" Webb demanded. He turned hard eyes on me. "I've seen no Indian."

"We've got one inside. He's wounded," I said.

He stepped to the door and opened it. The Indian was lying down again, his eyes closed. He looked pale and sick. His gifts were clustered close to him.

"If they want him, let them have him."

"No," I said.

He looked at me. "Bendigo," he said, "I think . . ."

"Webb," I said, "we found him wounded, Lorna and I. He had two scalps with him, but he was wounded, helpless, and this is Christmas Day."

"Two fresh scalps? I'll kill him myself."

"No, Webb. Let him be."

He glared at me. "Damn it, Ben. I like you, but I'll be double-damned if any murderin' redskin can come in here . . ."

"We brought him in, Webb. In his village we would be safe as long as we stayed in the village. Let's give him the same thing."

"You weren't very safe this winter! You an' Mae. I could kill him for that."

"That was a camp. I don't think it figures to be the same thing."

The riders came on, a dozen tough men. They pulled up. "Howdy, folks. We're trailin' an Indian. A damned murderin' Indian. He killed two of our folks, an' we got a bullet into him, and another into his horse."

"And we saw some boot tracks and moccasin tracks around where he fell, back yonder. Have you got him?"

"He's inside," Cain replied.

"Good!" One of them swung down. "Ed, shake out a noose. We'll stretch rope with him."

"No," Cain said.

They stared at him. A big, bearded man leaned toward him. "Did I hear you say no?"

"You did."

"You mean you're protectin' that thievin', murderin' scum?"

"I don't know what he did, and if he did it to me, I would probably feel as you do, but we found the Indian dying in the cold. We brought him in. It is Christmas Day, gentlemen, and here he stays."

They could not believe it, and I had not expected they would. Few white men, unless they had been long in the west, regarded the Indian as anything but a danger and an obstacle, something to be wiped out, as one would any kind of vermin.

Most of the military felt different about it, I knew. They had fought the Indian and respected him as a fighting man. The mountain men, who often lived among the Indians, had also come to accept and understand the Indian for the most part.

"Now, see here!" The speaker was a tight-faced man with high cheekbones and a handlebar mustache. "We come after that Injun an' we're goin' to have him. We can have him give to us, or we can take him."

"You gentlemen are a long way from home," I said, "and this is Christmas. You are welcome to share with us. As for giving up the Indian, we will not, and taking him would not be a simple thing. Some of us might die," I added, "but you'd go back with some bodies across your saddles.

"There need be no trouble," I said, "but this is our town, and any shooting that is done here will be done by us."

Webb stepped a pace off to my left. "And that goes for me," he said.

Somebody coughed, slightly behind them and to their left, and looking around they saw Ruth Macken, holding a rifle in her hands.

And then Drake Morrell stepped into view. His coat was back, and anybody could see his six-gun, and almost everybody knew Drake Morrell.

"This is my town, too, gentlemen," he said, "and I concur with my friends."

Their eyes went left and right. Ethan had stepped out of the barn and was standing there, his rifle in his hands.

"That redskin murdered our friends," the bearded man protested, "now you're standin' up for him. You ain't heard the last of this."

"I expect not," I replied, "but we will hope we have. We do not want trouble, gentlemen, but you must remember that taking scalps is the Indian's way of life and you are strangers in the country.

"We do not condone what he has done and we have ourselves had trouble with this same Indian." Webb shot me a quick hard look. "Nevertheless, we found him wounded and freezing and we brought him in. If you want him you will have to wait until he leaves here and follow him into his own country."

"You're crazy!" The bearded man stared from one to the other of us. "You're blind, stinkin' crazy!"

"Perhaps," I said, "but there you have it. Will you join us, gentlemen?"

"Like hell!" The man with the mustache turned his horse sharply around. "But you ain't heard the last of this! Not by a damned sight!"

They turned their mounts and rode off, and we watched them go. Ruth Macken stood until they were out of sight, then came down to us. "What was that about?"

We told her, and she stepped inside. The Indian was lying on his pallet near the fire. Lorna stood by with a pistol in her hand, and the Indian looked up at us.

Ruth, who spoke Sioux as good as any Indian, spoke to him. He merely glared at her, so she tried another tongue. Ethan came in behind her. "He's Shoshone, ma'am," he said, and then spoke to the Indian. He talked, using sign language, and explained what had happened.

The Shoshone listened, stared hard at me, then at the others, but made no sound.

Webb looked down at him. "Is he the one bothered Mae?"

"He didn't bother me." Mae had come in behind him. "He might have, but Ethan and Bendigo fetched me away."

"I don't blame 'em. Hangin's too good for him," Webb said bitterly.

"But you stood by us," Cain said.

Webb turned sharply. "Why not?" he said. "What the hell did you expect? This is our town."

And that was Webb. A hard, bitter man with none of us knew what behind him, but if there was fear in him we never saw it, and no matter how he might differ with us, which was often and upon many things, he was always there when trouble came, and never the last to show.

We stood there on that cold Christmas morning, watching the riders depart, and there was within me a deep satisfaction, for once again we had stood together, strong for what we believed, wrong-headed though it might have been.

Looking about me at Helen, at Ruth Macken and Lorna, and at Mrs. Sampson, who stood bravely in her door, a shotgun behind her which I had not seen until then, I felt that our women would have compared well with those wives of Bavaria of whom Montaigne tells.

When besieged and defeated by the Emperor Conrad III, the gentlewomen were permitted to depart, taking with them only what they could carry and valued most. Those same gentlewomen took upon their backs their husbands and their children, and the Emperor, who had pledged to kill all the men, let them depart out of respect for their courage.

Christmas was a warm, pleasant day, and we passed it quietly, in good talk, the singing of songs, and the eating of good food. Ruth Macken and Bud had us up for supper at her house, and a fine meal she had prepared with Ninon's help and Bud splitting wood for the fire.

We took the Indian along for we could not leave him, fearing what he might do when we were gone, and he lay on the floor and watched our doings, wondering at us, no doubt, as we should have wondered at some Indian customs and celebrations.

Drake Morrell was with us, quiet this day, and talking little, content to sit alone much of the time and simply watch. No doubt he was, as all of us were, recalling other Christmases in other times, perhaps in his own home, wherever that had been.

He spoke of the south, of Charleston, Atlanta, and of Boston, too. I thought he had lived much in the south, yet there was a bit of an accent at times, a strangeness of tone that caused me to wonder.

We in the west asked no questions of a man. He was taken by the name he gave you, if he chose to give one, and judged by his actions. A man's affairs were his own.

That day I treasured, for it was the last of one world and the beginning of another. I think, sometimes, that it was the last day of my youth, although I did not know it then.

I should see the New Year gone, but the morning after I should be riding out, a horse between my knees and a gun on my hip, to a faraway place in Oregon where I would buy cattle. I should be on my own then, carrying the gold that was saved by us all, carrying it to make our first venture toward stability and success.

Were they wise to trust me so? And why did they? What had I done to deserve it?

I searched my heart while I studied the horizon, and I knew I must do what must be done. I would be a man riding a man's way, and into a far country.

PART II

PART II

FIFTEEN

The night after Christmas was not restful. The Indian lay before our fireplace, and we had no reason to believe him other than an enemy. The scalps he still carried were proof enough that he could kill and had killed.

Nor had he reason to love me, who had struck him down in one of their own lodges, before the old men. He had lost face then, and his only way to redeem himself in his own eyes and possibly theirs was to kill me.

He was our enemy, and the small gifts we had given him he would accept without gratitude. The ethics of the white man are his own, and contrary to what he may believe, are not shared by others. Not in all cases, at least. Each people has it own standards, often similar, yet with notable differences.

Yet we could hope that seeing us among our own would cause him to think and to wonder. We would fight him if we were attacked, we would feed him if he was hungry, we would ask nothing of him but to share this land, so little of which was used.

This captive Indian hated me, but not because I was of a different race, simply because at one moment I had bested him, shamed him before those to whom he had boasted. I did not hate him; but there has never been any hate in me for any man. Those I disliked, I avoided.

What I wanted in the world I felt myself able to get. The

problem was simply the one of shaping this raw material that was me, shaping my strength and my thinking into the kind of man I could respect.

"What are we going to do about him?" Tom Croft asked. "How long are you going to keep that Injun?"

"We will take him back to his people," Cain said.

Ethan glanced at him, shrugged, and said, "Easier said than done, but we can surely try."

"We'd better," I said. "He's a danger here."

"A bullet would serve him better," Webb said shortly. "I don't know what you're thinkin' on. He'll rise some night and murder the lot of you."

Now that had been in my own thoughts. He was some better, although his leg had a long way to go. He had been strong physically, and we had fed him well and treated his wound. I know our attitude puzzled him. Maybe he figured we were fattening him for torture, or something. I couldn't see behind those black eyes whose beliefs, ideas, and impulses were so different from mine.

When a body has been taught from boyhood that any stranger is an enemy he isn't apt to throw that belief away because of a belly full of grub, a warm fire, and a few geegaws given him.

What scared me was me going away and leaving the family there with that Indian, and Cain the only man. He'd have to sleep, and someday, somehow that Indian would get loose.

"I brought him here," I said, "and I'll take him. There's villages to the north. I'll take him yonder, build a smoke, and leave him where they can pick him up."

"Kill him," Webb said, "he can tell them all about us, now."

"They know about us," Sampson replied. "They know our strength and our weakness. We know that one mistake, and all of us can die, and that is our strength."

"We should never have brought him here," Neely grumbled. "The Reverend is right. They are a murdering lot of savages, and no mention of them in the Bible."

"What has that to do with it?" John Sampson asked.

"If there's no mention of them," Neely said, "they are animals, not men."

"I don't recall any mention of the English, either," I said mildly.

He gave me a mean look, then changed the subject. "We got to think of a school," he said. "We've talked long enough, and now we've got a man who can teach in it."

Cain looked at him and crossed one leg over the other. "Who?" he asked.

"The Reverend. The subject came up, and we asked him if he would, and after some argument, he agreed. As long as he is going to be the preacher here . . ."

"Is he?" Cain asked.

"Who else? He's felt the call. John here, he reads well enough, but he's no preacher. Not rightly speaking. Moses Finnerly is."

Nobody said anything for a moment and then Cain asked, "Has Finnerly started his building?"

Neely looked startled. "No. That is, why should he build a school? They aren't his youngsters. We sort of figured your mill wouldn't be used until spring, and we could hold school there."

"It is nice of him to offer," I said, "you don't often find a man to volunteer to give freely of his time, like that."

Neely shifted his feet under the table. "Well," he said, uncomfortably, "we had sort of thought we might take up a collection. His time is valuable, and his teaching. We have nobody who can give the time or has the knowledge."

Ruth Macken was there, and Helen. The meeting had come about sort of by accident in Sampson's place, and folks had a way of dropping in when anything got started.

"I think there is a man," she said.

Neely looked up. "Who?" he demanded.

"Drake Morrell," she said simply.

Well, now. If you'd fired a shot in that room nobody would have been more startled. Everybody sort of sat up and stared, not only at each other but into ourselves, wondering what we thought about that.

Mrs. Croft broke in. "You can't be serious!"

"The man's a gambler and a gunfighter, a killing man who drinks!" Mrs. Stuart was angry. "I declare, Ruth Macken, you're gettin' worse all the time! You and your notions!"

"The man has an excellent classical education," she replied quietly. "I do not believe anyone present, including myself, can approach him on the basis of education."

"Let's be serious," Tom Croft said. "The man's no teacher. And he's a hunted man, who has been sentenced to hang."

"The Reverend," Neely said stiffly, "has kindly agreed to teach. He's a man who knows the Bible, and he's a good talker. He'd be preaching to us all on Sunday, anyhow, and he could teach the young uns on week days. I figure that'll work out fine. In fact," he added defiantly, "I told him he'd be the teacher."

"We have always discussed things among us," Sampson said. "It is the only way any decision can be made."

"In any event," Cain said gently, "I doubt if we have to decide this morning." He got to his feet. "I have work to do, and so have most of us."

The meeting broke up, leaving Neely Stuart arguing with Tom Croft as they went out, angry at Ruth Macken for her suggestion.

Ethan waited for me outside. "If you mean what you say about the Indian," he said, "I'll ride along."

"Thanks. I leave in a few days. He'd best be out of here before then."

We caught up our horses and saddled them, and then another horse for the redskin.

Cain was at the door when we came for him. "Be careful," he warned. "I am not sure I like this."

"We haven't much choice," I said.

"We'll get shut of him," Ethan said, "an' when we leave we won't waste around."

And we didn't.

We headed off up country with that Indian between us, Ethan riding ahead and me bringing up the rear, and watching him carefully. It was a far stretch, and the snow-clad mountains lay white and lovely about us, the dark pines trying to shake off their snow to show their proud heads above it.

Nameless lakes we skirted, and deep ravines where streams struggled against the ice that held them down, and we plunged our horses through drifts, occasionally finding a trail. When at last we smelled smoke we took it easy down through the pines, avoiding the bare poles of the aspen groves.

The lodges squatted on the valley floor a thousand feet below, smoke lifting from them.

We sat our saddles a moment, studying them out, for in time to come it might be good to know.

"This is your village?" I asked.

He grunted at me, and I took it for agreement. "We can't spare the horse," I said, "so you'll have to wait for them to come and get you, or crawl. I'd wait, myself."

He just looked at me.

I made the sign for friend to him, but he just glared at me, then spat.

"All right," I said. "Have it your own way."

"I kill!" he said. "I kill all!"

"You'd better get some big Indians to come along for the job," I said, "you couldn't kill a bug with a stick."

We helped him down to the snow, then fetched a few sticks and put together a hat full of fire. When the smoke started to rise, Ethan fired his rifle in the air, and we took off.

"He's a mean one," Ethan said miles later when we'd slowed down. "There's no give to him. Them Sheep-Eaters are usually good folks. I've known a passel of them, time to time."

"Keep an eye out for him when spring comes," I said, "he's made his war talk, and he'll likely try to come down upon us."

Ethan nodded. "Wished I was coming with you," he said, "you're riding a far piece, alone."

"Well, I got it to do."

"A ride like that," Ethan agreed, "that'll grow hair on your chest."

"So long as I don't lose what's on my head."

That night at Cain's place we held council. We had no idea what cattle would sell for in Oregon, but I had money to take along, a good bit of it for those days and times.

Cain and I, we had put by a little cash to use in California, but some of it had gone into extra supplies at Fort Laramie. Now we studied it out, the gamble and what might happen, and I took a hundred dollars of my money and two hundred of Cain's. That left him almighty little and me but fifty to carry for expenses.

Ruth Macken had two hundred dollars, Drake Morrell put in four hundred, John Sampson forty, Croft fifty, Neely Stuart a hundred in fresh gold.

"I could afford more," he said, "but seein' this here is a gamble, I reckon that'll have to do."

Webb came up at the last and counted out sixty dollars. "Don't leave me much," he said, "but if anybody can do it, Ben, you can. Take her along and do the best you can. No matter what happens you'll hear no complaints from me."

"Thanks, Webb. I'll do the best I can."

Listening to their talk, I stood tall and lean, wide-legged beside them, knowing their trust in me and how much each had trusted to me that he could not afford to lose. I carried their futures on my western ride . . . their futures and mine.

Drake walked outside the door with me to look upon the night. For a time we stood there and then he said, "It is a lot of money you carry, and there will be men in towns who are thieves, as well as dangers on the road."

"I shall be careful."

"Trust no one. Not even the ones who seem most to be trusted. That way you will be safe."

He paused and then said, "Life being what it is, and a man not knowing from one moment to the next, I want you to know that if anything happens to me, whatever profit there is from this venture shall go to Ninon."

"I will remember."

"She has wealthy relatives, but she would not go to them beholden. A little of her own will give her security."

Ruth Macken came out. "Mr. Morrell, we are to have a school here."

"Yes," he said.

"For a school there must be a teacher."

Even in the half-light I could see the quizzical glance he threw her. "Who better than you?" he suggested.

"Neely Stuart and the Crofts want the Reverend Moses Finnerly."

"Oh, my God!" He looked at her. "You're joking?"

"No."

"That bigoted fool?"

"He professes to be a man of God, and he is ready to accept."

"Well," he said cynically, "anything can happen. Why not you? You've a gift for it, I think."

"There are several boys. Foss Webb is big, and he will be hard to handle."

"Just call on me, Mrs. Macken, whenever you need me."

"Thank you, Mr. Morrell, I am calling on you now."

"Now? What for?"

"To teach. I want you to be the teacher. I believe there are others who do also."

He stared at her as if she had lost her mind, and then he said, "You are too kind, Mrs. Macken, but please consider: I am a gambler, I have been known to drink more than I should, and I have killed five men in gun battles. I do not think you understand what you are suggesting."

"I do understand. I have heard you were an honest gambler, but skillful. I do not think you would drink while a teacher, and we have ourselves had to use guns. In fact, I am quite sure I killed at least one man myself.

"I did not wish to do it, but we were protecting our homes."

"You honor me, Mrs. Macken." He turned to me. "Bendigo, how far has this gone?"

"It has divided the town," I said. "I am for you. You have

already heard Mrs. Macken. John Sampson is for you with reservations, and so is Webb. Cain has not said what he thinks."

"And the others?"

"Neely, his wife, and the Crofts all want Finnerly, so it stands four and four with no vote from Cain."

"Mr. Morrell, you are a gentleman. You have dignity and poise. You have an education, that is obvious. I do not believe what we could pay you would serve as any inducement, but I beg you to consider the quality of the gentleman who would accept the position if you decline."

"That's unfair."

"Bud is my consideration, Mr. Morrell. Bud and Ninon, since she is now in my care. There are other children here. I believe they should grow up with a love of learning, and a respect for it. Living here they will have no trouble understanding the harsher realities.

"I want my son to learn what he can, but most of all I wish him to be a citizen, to judge issues, to use logic in his thinking, to respect his country and its people."

"That is a great deal. I must think of this, Mrs. Macken. Never in my wildest thoughts have I . . ."

"Please do." She shivered. "It is growing cold. Bendigo, will you walk to my house? There is something I must give you."

Outside her door she whispered, "Bud is probably asleep. Will you wait?"

She went within and closed the door softly behind her. When she emerged she pressed something into my hand.

It was a derringer.

"You may need it. My husband always believed in having a little more in case of trouble." She paused. "There is a way of carrying it up your sleeve. Drake Morrell can show you how. He carries one of his there."

SIXTEEN

Darkness lay upon our town when I rode away to Oregon.
We had decided it was better so. No watcher would see me
leave, neither to follow me or to know our town held one rifle less.

Nor was anyone out to say goodbye, for we had talked of that,
too, and goodbyes were said earlier and inside. With Cain and me
it was quiet talk about various things and a strong handclasp eye
to eye, and he turned away to go on with his making of nails.

Helen had packed a bait of grub for me, and she and Lorna
stowed it in my saddlebags.

When that was done I walked up to the bench to have a few
words with Ruth Macken, Bud, and Ninon. Cain walked out to
feed the stock, and while he was forking hay to them he saddled
my horse and loaded my gear on the packhorse I was taking.

Ruth had coffee waiting and I sat down, looking around the
warm, familiar room, so little like the shell I had built for her. To
build a house is one thing, but to make it a home is quite another,
and Ruth Macken had a gift for homemaking.

Ninon brought me a piece of dried-apple pie, and we sat
talking of odds and ends. Suddenly Bud said, "Ollie Trotter was
asking when you were to leave."

"When?"

"Today. He asked a few days ago, too. He said if you were
going to make it you'd best be on your way."

126

I did not like his knowing, for I did not trust him, and he and his friends were one reason we had been secretive. Neely was irritated because I had not asked his advice on the western trip, nor mentioned the day when I would leave.

"I want to go with you," Ninon said suddenly. "I really do! I know people in Oregon, and I know people in San Francisco. I could help."

"If there is trouble it will be long before I get there, and a man had best have no one to think of but himself if trouble comes."

"When will you be back?"

"Not until frost comes again. It is a long ride, and a longer ride back, with cattle."

We talked of many things, and before we said goodbye, Ruth Macken went to her box and got out two books. "I do not know if there is room to carry these. You can take one or both, but I think you will want something to think about when traveling, so one of them is Blackstone."

"I've heard of it."

"Much of our law is founded upon it, and I think you will learn more from it than any book I have given you to read."

Ninon came to the door with me. "I shall miss you," she said, her eyes very large.

"By the time I come back you'll have forgotten all about me."

"Never!" She looked up at me. "I love you, Bendigo. Someday I shall marry you."

"You're too young to think of that," I said. "You aren't thirteen yet."

She lifted her chin at me. "Almost . . . anyway, that is only five years between us, and there were nine years between the Major and Mrs. Macken. Mr. Cain is seven years older than Helen Shafter. I know. I asked them."

"Well," I said lamely, not knowing what to say, "you'll change your mind a dozen times. Nevertheless, I'm honored." I grinned at her. "And I hope you don't change your mind."

She stood up quickly on her tiptoes and kissed me lightly on the lips, no more than the brush of a butterfly wing, but it startled me. "Hurry back, Bendigo. I shall be waiting for you!"

Walking down to the stable alone in the darkness I felt kind of odd, and told myself she was only a youngster with foolish ideas, but she had always seemed so much older, maybe because of her acting and traveling. So I went to my horse, stepped into the saddle, and rode out of the stable and down the road toward the trail to Fort Bridger.

After a while I heard the stable door close and knew Cain had been out to watch me go, and by now was at the door of his house, still watching. Turning in the saddle I lifted an arm, but if he responded I could not see for he would be only another shadow against the blackness of the house. Yet inside me I knew he was there, watching me away, as I would have watched him.

He had been more like a father to me than a brother, but there had ever been a closeness between us, stemming from I know not what understanding.

After a while I veered from the trail, choosing a spot where the snow had been smeared by the falling of some animal, and going down into a creek bottom. Then I rode swiftly for two miles. I did not wish to meet anyone or be seen.

Just before daybreak I made a hidden camp in a hollow of a dry creek bank, melted snow for coffee, fried a little bacon, and then slept for a couple of hours while my horses pawed at the thin grass under the snow.

When I saddled up again I looked back toward home, but saw nothing. Our town had been hidden among the hollow hills long since, and only the Wind River Range, rising above me, was the same. Glancing westward I picked out my landmark. Tabernacle Butte showed its low brow above the Divide, and after studying the country around and seeing nothing I rode along the creek, then up on the plain. Westward I rode, alternating from a walk to a shambling trot. That night I camped in a wind-sheltered cove at Tabernacle Butte.

Before dusk but after sundown I climbed to a high shoulder of the Butte to study my back trail, remaining until it was too dark to see.

After banking my small fire I crawled into my blankets and considered the situation. Travelers usually went by way of Fort Bridger, and risky as it might be I intended to stop there.

First, I was curious to see the place. Second, I wanted to gather information about the weather and trails that lay before me. And I needed to buy a few odds and ends of supplies.

Anyone following me and losing my trail would expect to overtake me there, and it would be a good chance to see if I had been followed.

The post had been established by Jim Bridger, a Virginian who came west to be a mountain man. He had come to know more than probably any other man about the western lands but it was said the Mormons had pushed him out, or bought him out, or something. Later the Mormons had abandoned the fort themselves, after building a twelve-foot stone wall around it.

The army had established a temporary post there, and the soldiers lived in tents. I envied them not at all.

Two days later I rode into Bridger, saw the white tents in even rows, and heard the lovely sound of a bugle, although I doubted if it sounded so lovely to those soldiers who had to hustle to formation.

I found myself a place to sleep, unsaddled my stock, and then went to the store and ordered a drink. I was never much of a drinking man, but drinking men talk together, and I had much to learn about the news of the country.

There'd been a fight with a Shoshone chief named Bear Hunter awhile back, and he was troublemaking around again. From what was said I decided the young warrior with the two scalps whom we'd taken in had probably ridden with Bear Hunter.

Traveling was dangerous, but some were doing it, and I listened to a discussion of the Fort Hall trail, and of the road west, and tried to make up my mind what it was best to do.

There were a dozen soldiers in the room and as many rough-looking civilians, but you never knew who they were. The one you took for an ignorant mountain man might turn out to be a son of European nobility . . . there seemed to be plenty of them around.

About two years before, Richard Burton, the writer and explorer, had traveled this country, and as usual, stories accumulated. He talked to everybody, including Eph Hanks and Porter Rockwell, gathering information about the country and the customs.

There was nothing to keep me at Fort Bridger. I finished my drink, gathered my few purchases, and eased out into the cold. And it was cold.

It was nearly midnight and men were stumbling to their sleeping quarters, wherever they might be, but I had no such plan. Saddling up again, I rode six miles west before turning up the bed of a thin little creek and camping in a hollow under a deadfall, where I put together a small fire and slept with my pistol in my hand.

Before daybreak I was riding west.

It was Indian country and some of Bear Hunter's braves might be about, but I saw none, and passed no one. It was coming on to dark when I saw a settlement of a half dozen huts crowded together, along with as many haystacks. There was only one person in sight, a man driving a half dozen cows. He was carrying a rifle, which he brought casually into view when he saw me.

Riding up, I asked him about bedding down for the night, and he looked me over carefully, asking if I was a Mormon. "No," I said, "I'm from a settlement back at South Pass."

He looked at me again, more carefully. "Heard of it. What might your name be?"

"Shafter," I said, "Bendigo Shafter. I'm riding out to Oregon."

"It's a fur piece," he commented. "You're one o' them what fed some o' the Saints, ain't you?"

"Awhile back," I agreed. "They were trapped by snow and we got word of it. Good folks."

" 'Light an' come in. I'll do for your stock."

"Obliged. Seems to me you've got work enough for yourself without me troubling you. I'll care for the horses. All I need is a place to roll my bed."

He watched me work over the buckskin. "Don't find many folks who care for their horses like that. This is a rough country on horses."

"And women," I said.

He looked at me. "You married?"

"No."

"I got two wives. You'll meet 'em inside. Mag, she was the fust one. She done picked out the second for me. I surely couldn't have done better. Maybe not as well, although I'm figured a good provider.

"Comp'ny, that's what it is. They're comp'ny for each other, and they share the work. Makes it a whole sight easier."

We walked on up to the house. I took off my fur cap, and we went inside.

There were two women there, and four youngsters. The women were maybe seven or eight years apart, age-wise, both of them attractive women, steady-looking, too. One look at that table and I saw that this man had him somebody who could put grub together. Maybe two somebodies.

"Mag . . . Bess . . . this here's Ben Shafter, from over to South Pass. He's one of them who did for Esther an' them."

"Welcome," Mag said. "You just take off your wraps an' set up. Your name has gone about among the Saints, Mr. Shafter, and you'll find friendliness amongst us."

"We were pleased to do what we could, ma'am," I said, embarrassed by her words.

"We haven't met friendliness in many places," Bess said quietly.
"It is something to be treasured."

Well, we sat up and ate, and I was a hungry man, and those
two women brought us food aplenty, and they made me a bed by
the fireside, rolling out my own blankets for me.

It worried me some, when it came to undressing, for there was
just one big room. They fetched a blanket for a curtain, but I
worried nonetheless. That gold in my belt made quite a swelling
under my shirt. Lucky it was that I am a narrow-waisted man,
with wide shoulders, but anyone peeking would surely see it. Not
that I expected peeking, but folks are curious, and many a good
man has found his sense of right twisted by the sight of gold, or
the appearance of it.

I trusted these folks, but I didn't want to lead them into
temptation, either.

Yet I slept well, and sounder than I'd wanted, and waked so
late that one of the women was up and stirring the fire when my
eyes opened. It shamed me, that's what it did. Not since I was a
youngster had any woman ever built fire when I was around.

These were poor folks, that was plain enough, but they had
enough to do with, and grub to put on the table. The house was
clean and neat, and those women washed their children and their
potatoes.

When I came to saddle up, the man walked out to me. "Mr.
Shafter," he said apologetically, "you done saved my sister, and
the folks with her. We ain't got much, but a passerby left a book
here . . . I seen the books you had and figured you might cotton
to this one. It's one o' them story books."

Glancing at it, I saw a novel I'd not seen before. It was *Rienzi,
the Last of the Tribunes*. It was written by a man with two names
and a bridge between them, Bulwer-Lytton.

"Thanks," I said, and he could have given me nothing I would
appreciate more.

As I rode away, and when I got clear of things and looked
around over the bunch-grass levels and saw no one, I looked it
over. I hadn't read a story book since I became a man. Once,
when I was a boy, we'd seen a few, and I'd read a few stories, but
this didn't seem to be for children. I knew what a tribune was
because I'd read Plutarch.

The ride was bleak and lonely, with wide flats here and there,
rocky ridges, and a few scattered cedars. When I came to where
the station should be, there were only a few blackened timbers

from a fire months old and three ugly-looking holes filled with slightly alkaline water that trickled off into a mud hole.

There was no welcome here for man or beast, so tired though I was, I moved on over a plain scattered with sage and greasewood. Patches of snow lay in every shadowed place. The sky was a dull gray overhead, the earth a dull gray beneath.

The miles unrolled without end, and just when I was about to give up and bed down on the open plain, the trail took a sudden dip into a shallow valley.

SEVENTEEN

The weather warmed, there were patches of black mud where snow had been, but snow remained in every shadowed corner, under the shelter of banks.

Far rolled the land wherever the eye turned, gray, desolate, the only vegetation a stunted sage, the only lure the blue haze that shadowed distant mountains. I saw no sign of Indians, only occasional jackrabbits that leaped up, bounded away, then stopped and sat up to look as if wondering what manner of creature was invading their lonely hills and plains.

Occasionally, on some far slope, a black-looking cedar cropped up . . . there was nothing else. I came upon a sign that told me it was 533 miles to Carson City, but I was not going that way. The country flattened out. The plain was a dead white. Dust arose and covered me with a thin film. It got into my eyes, ears, and nose. The sage and greasewood grew scarcer, there were ugly patches of white salt like sores on the face of the land, and in the distance, Granite Mountain, a rough and craggy hogback. It was rumored there were springs at the base of the mountain.

I made camp that night near a pool of sulphurous water surrounded by some straggly rushes. There were rocks nearby and a place that could be defended if need be. The horses turned up their noses at the water, but finally drank as nothing better could be offered.

Putting a fire together from some dead cedar and using dried sage for kindling, I got some coffee started with water from a spare canteen I carried on my packhorse, a result of advice from Ethan Sackett. The night was cold.

About a mile away there was a low, ragged ridge of blackish rock that thrust up from the desert. There were some scattered cedars on its slopes, and obviously some deep coves along its flanks, an ideal place for Indians to hide and watch travelers who might stop at the spring, if such it could be called.

There was nothing about the place I liked, yet others had camped there. I found the remnants of their fires.

EIGHTEEN

Only a few days since I had left our town, yet it seemed long since I had left, and I wondered what they were doing now, and was glad that Drake Morrell was there, and Webb as well. Neither was a trusting man, and each was ready to fight if need be. Too often when trouble arises there is too much time wasted in trying to temporize, and it becomes too late for action.

By morning it had begun to snow. The flakes fell few and large, drifting swiftly down, and then the fall thickened and the flakes grew smaller. The wind moaned in the cedars. I rode back along the line, studying my back trail and the country around as well as I could through the thickly falling snow. There was no time when a man was safe from Indians, and at such a time they might easily attack.

They had observed white men traveling in the cold and had seen them muffle their ears with ear laps, turn coat collars up to narrow their vision, and huddle deep into their coats, seeking nothing but warmth. Sometimes it is better to be a little cold and remain alive.

Snow was inches deep upon the trail when I made the ascent toward Butte Station. Thomas, a Mormon who operated the station, saw me coming and poured hot coffee.

Butte Station was about thirty feet long, built of country stone, and about fifteen feet wide. One end was partitioned off with a canvas wall. Behind it were bunks for four men covered with ragged blankets. Beneath the bunks were heaps of rubbish, saddles, harness and straps, dried-out boots, sacks of grain and potatoes.

The door was the backboard of a wagon, scarred by bullets. From the walls, on wooden pegs, hung several cartridge belts, an empty canteen, a pair of shotgun chaps, and a buckskin coat, as well as several overcoats and slickers. The floor was of tamped earth, but unswept.

Thomas, who kept up a running fire of conversation, told me he had three brothers in the English army, and that he was considering a move to California, come spring.

The fireplace was huge, piled high with wood, and blazing comfortably. There had been a good stack of cut wood just outside the door, a reassuring sight with the weather as cold as it was.

"Have to sleep on the floor," Thomas advised. "With buffalo robes and all, it won't be bad."

It's just for one night, I thought. Tomorrow night I'll be at Ruby Valley Station, and it's much better.

I finished my coffee and took up my rifle. "I'll look after the stock," I said to Thomas.

Stepping outside, I found it was bitter cold. My boots crunched on the snow as I walked over to the ramshackle stable and pole corral.

My stock was under the stable roof and sheltered from any wind. I stood there a few minutes, talking to my horses, and then I stuffed hay into the manger for them and turned back to the house.

From where I stood I could see bits of light through cracks in the shutters and a thin trail of smoke against the starlit sky.

NINETEEN

It was quiet when I rode up to Ruby Valley Station with towering, snow-covered peaks looming not far off. It was cold, but the sky was clear, and it looked like a good day a-coming.

I stripped the gear from my horses while Uncle Billy Rogers told me of the happenings along the western trail I'd be following tomorrow.

When I asked about cattle, he warmed up. "Fine! Fine stock, son. Mostly Durhams and Shorthorns . . . mixed breeds, but mixed from good stock. The forage has been good so they're overstocked on the range. If you want to buy cattle, this is the best time."

He took me over the trail that he had traveled and about which he had listened to much talk. "There's bad stretches, but no way as bad as the trails out of California. There's more dry country to the south."

I studied over it, worrying about what I was about to do. They'd sent me out to use my judgment, and the deal I made for cattle could mean life or death for our town . . . and for some of its people.

Money was a scarce thing amongst us, and if something went wrong we'd not be able to send out another man with more money. Nor could we hope to stay on where we were without cattle to feed us and to build a future. With daybreak I breakfasted and took to the trail. Diamond Springs was next, and this was dry, dry country I was crossing. I rode carefully around every bit of cover, carried my rifle ready in my hand at the passes, and was ready to play my cards the way they fell.

It was a hard day, a brutal day. The wind was cold off the snow-capped mountains, and the road had been chewed up by passing hoofs and had frozen that way.

Constant watching was wearing on the nerves, and this was a country where one had to be constantly aware. Twice I saw antelope in the distance, and several times coyotes and rabbits, both of which seemed to abound in the country. Coyotes had begun to learn about trails—that where travelers were there might be the bodies of stock that died along the way or scraps of food thrown aside, so they stalked the trails, alert for any tidbit.

When at last I rode over Chokup Pass and saw Diamond Springs Station on the bench, I was ready to stop.

TWENTY

When I'd stripped the gear from my horses, I tied them to the manger in the shed that acted the part of a stable. It wasn't very convincing.

I'm a man who believes in caring for his stock. Western horses, most of them half-broken mustangs from the wild free range, were used to roughing it. Winter and summer they had run loose, finding what shelter as they could, fighting mountain lions, wolves, and men who chased them, and finally coming under the saddle.

They were accustomed to rough living, but when a horse gave me what I required of him, which was a lot of travel over rough country, he deserved the best care I could arrange. That shed at Diamond Springs Station was nothing to write home about.

Usually, these western places had only a corral where the horses would stand, backs to the wind and storm or whatever, and they survived. The shed was an advantage but the wind was picking up to blow so I stayed on in the shed patching up a few holes to keep the wind out. I fixed most of the holes, but there's work a man can do that's helpful to his thinking, and working with the hands is one way.

It was time I decided what I intended to do with myself. Buying cattle was only a venture for the town, but when it was over I'd still have my problems. Traveling at this rate gives a man a chance to think, if he'll take it.

The study of law was one means to success, and I'd given it thought. Ranching? Well, ranching promised well, but I was not sure. Mining, from what I'd heard, seemed chancy.

Reading books was making me ask questions of myself. I was learning how other folks lived and had lived, and I could see that as Ruth Macken had said, it was a larger, wider world than I'd known.

Working around the stable kept me busy for most of an hour. Suddenly I realized that if I was to get any sleep I'd better go inside and to bed. I found myself reluctant to enter the station.

I kept thinking of the folks back in our town and knew I daren't make a mistake.

I was alone, carrying the fortunes of my community, and with a long ride ahead of me.

TWENTY-ONE

Daybreak found me in no good mood, and for no good reason, and that was unusual for me. Usually I awakened in fine shape, feeling good and ready for the day, but this time it was different. I woke up with a chip on my shoulder and sense enough to know it and to warn myself to be careful.

I had killed a man in a gun battle, but I was not proud of it or wanting it talked of. It had been a matter of life or death, not only for me, but for those people back yonder who trusted me.

It was wild, rough country through which I rode that day, but I made good time and I saw no Indians. The only game was an occasional rabbit or a far-off glimpse of antelope. There was white sage and rabbit bush, and in the coves of the mountains, bunch-grass.

I rode with care, but it was a lucky thing that it must be so, for I saw the country. How many times have I talked with people who have ridden the trails where I have ridden, yet had seen nothing? They passed over the land just to get over it, not to live with it and see it, feel it.

There was beauty out there, even in the heat-shimmering white desolate lands that lay in long valleys between the mountains. I learned where to look for water, and when. I knew the birds or insects who might live close to water and those who had no need of it. The kangaroo rat, whom I came to love, manufactures his

own water within his body and has no need of a drink, nor does
the powder-post beetle.

The desert and the wild country taught me not only to look,
but to see . . . and there is a difference. Many look but do not
see, for the land about them that seems so changeless is changing
even as they watch, a change unbelievably slow yet nevertheless
there. A rock falls, stirring a small slide; a root grows and spreads
and splits the rock; snow falls into the crack, freezes, expands,
and splits the rock still wider.

I learned that the wilderness never looks twice the same, and
one must look upon it at different hours to even know the land
close about. The shadows of night and morning bring out hidden
canyons and cliffs, places that are blurred under the hot sun. Yet
the thing I watched for was movement, for where there was
movement there was life, and it might be trouble.

When I rode up to the stage station it was already dark. I called
out with a long *halloo* to let them know I was coming. In Indian
country it was considered proper to announce yourself, otherwise
you might find yourself ducking lead.

The door opened, throwing a shaft of light across the hard-
packed clay of the yard. At the end of the light I could see the
bare bones of the poles that formed the corral.

The stage station was newly built of adobe after the old one had
been burned. It was a solid, comfortable building with a couple of
rooms. There was a board table, benches, and near the fireplace a
couple of chairs.

There were two men at the station. "Was three," the station
keeper commented, "but Joe, he rode off one day to hunt meat
. . . three weeks ago. We ain't seen hide nor hair since."

"Hunt for him?"

"Yeah . . . we found tracks. Lost 'em six or eight mile out. We
hunted two, three times for him but I reckon the Injuns come up
on him."

How many had died that way? How many had ridden off, never
to return?

"Did he have a family?"

"He never said. Worst of it was, he was ridin' my horse. A
blaze face sorrel with three white stockings . . . one of them
white clean to the shoulder. Long mane an' tail. I used to keep
'em combed like a baby's hair . . . best horse I ever did have.
Smart, too."

The food was good. The best I'd had since leaving Fort Bridger.
The station keepers talked all through dinner. I guess they

were glad to have outside company and neither of them drew a breath for long. When one wasn't talking the other one was.

After the dishes were cleared I moved to one side and opened my Blackstone, although not much in the mood for reading. I was thinking about Joe . . . one of the many who died somewhere out there.

They had looked, but there was small time for looking. Just to exist in this country took hard work and there was little time for idling, or for anything that had not to do with the business of living. And these men had to keep horses ready for the stages that came along, had to prepare food for the passengers, had to change horses and get in hay, and all the while stay alert for Indians.

TWENTY-TWO

I rode out before daylight, determined to get my bearings and some useful information.

"Cattle?" The blacksmith looked up from his work. "We've had a killing winter, man. You'll be lucky to find any for sale, but ride over yonder," he said, pointing with his tongs, "and talk to Ben Snipes. He knows ever' cow crittur in the Klickitat Valley by its first name. Tell him Ike Lancaster sent you."

When I rode up to the house a stocky man of some five feet eight inches, weighing about one seventy or a bit better, came to the door. He was wearing a white shirt and suspenders, his sleeves rolled up.

"I'm Bendigo Shafter, and I'm up from the South Pass country to buy cattle. Ike Lancaster said you could help me."

"Get down and come in." He turned to an Indian boy who had come up. "Charlie, put the gentleman's horses in the corral, will you?"

He turned toward the door. "We're just setting down to supper. Will you join us?"

After supper he pushed back in his chair and lit his pipe. "We've had a rough winter, so there's not much stock around. I've got a few head of steers."

"I want breeding stock."

"Figured you would." He drew on his pipe. "Fellow over on the creek has a few head . . . have you got cash money?"

144

"I have."

"Then you can buy. He needs money. I don't, and if I had the stock I wouldn't sell. This winter was bad but it's only one winter, and this is cattle country. This fellow I speak of, he's running scared.

"I'd say he had about sixty, seventy head that pulled through the winter. Young stuff, mostly, and at least one good bull. He wants to sell and get out."

"Why don't you buy his stock?"

Ben Snipes chuckled. "I'm short of cash money myself. I'm going to sell the steers for beef and borrow to buy cattle. That sixty head wouldn't be a patch on what I want, so make your own deal." He grinned at me. "I don't figure you plan to pay much, do you?"

"I'll pay what I have to. From what I hear all this stock is in bad shape, and I'll be taking a risk moving it out of here, but if I take it slow I think I can make it."

"All right." He took up a tablet and drew a map on it. "This man has a good place over there, but the winter scared him, and scared his wife worse. He'll sell cheap."

"How about horses? I'll need a few."

"Buy from the Indians, but be careful. They are shrewd traders and they'll skin you out of your eyeteeth if you aren't careful. They've got a lot of horses, good, tough stock, mountain bred and used to cold, and they make fine horses for working stock."

It was a good time to listen, for despite the killing winter they had been through, I sensed that Ben Snipes was a good cattleman, a man who knew what he was about, and a man to learn from.

Ben Snipes was right, of course. The man he told me of was in an itch to get out, but I had nothing to say about buying, not at first.

When I stopped by Tellegen's house he asked me to light and set, as was custom in the western lands, so I sat up to table with him, and we talked of the hard times, of the rough winter, and of the chance for good grass, come spring.

"I am going to buy some cattle," I told him frankly, "but I'm looking for somebody who wants to sell cheap. I've got cash money, but the folks I represent are poor and they have little enough to do with."

"I'll sell you mine for ten dollars a head," he said, putting down his cup.

I shook my head sadly. "More than I can afford. You see, all this stock up here is in poor shape after the winter they've been through, and it is not yet really spring. We'll have some more bad weather, and some of the stock around here won't last the time until grass grows.

"I'd have to take very slow drives. They can't stand much, and finding grass is going to be a hard thing to do. If I started out of here with a hundred head I doubt if I'd get to the river with sixty. That raises my price per head by a good deal."

They were good people, but neither of them was cut out for this country, or this life. She was eager to be out of it, and deep down, so was he. I knew they were going to sell those cattle, and sell them cheap, because it might be a couple of years before anybody came along again with gold to pay for cattle.

We had ridden around over his place. Snow still lay upon the land, his stacks of hay were about gone, his cattle were skin and bones . . . but they were Durhams, young stuff mostly, and had good conformation and their eyes looked clear, bright, and healthy.

Our count showed fifty-two head including one good bull and one young one coming on.

"This is good country," I said. "A man would ride far to find better country than the Klickitat. I am sorry I hit it just after a bad winter. I'd better ride back down to Oregon and buy there."

"I might cut my price," he said, at last.

When I made my deal it was for five dollars a head, and I hired an Indian boy he had working for him to help me. The boy was about fourteen, I'd guess, a Umatilla Indian from the eastern Oregon country.

My buying the cattle would have put him out of a job, but I needed the help. Tellegen told me he was a good, trustworthy boy. "Won't sleep on the ranch," he added. "Come night he takes to the hills."

That didn't disturb me, as we would have hills to take to wherever we were. He agreed to hire on, then began to look worried, and as we moved the cattle eastward at a slow walk, I got the idea something was on his mind.

We made only five miles that first day, but I had located a pretty fair patch of grazing where the snow had blown away, and I wanted to make it that far. We broke the ice for the cattle to drink, then turned them on the grass.

They were not trail broken by a long shot, but were far too tired to give me any trouble. Also, the grass I had found them, while poor enough, was sufficient to keep them busy.

When I started to cook, that boy started to fidget, and finally I

asked him straight out what was bothering him. It took awhile to
get the story from him but finally I did.

It was his grandfather. The old man was living in a cave about
three miles back, and the boy had gone each night to take him
food. He wanted food for him now.

"Bring him down to camp," I said. "We'll take him with us."

So I had two Indians and had made a better deal than I knew.

Uruwishi was old . . . I never could guess how old, and his
time for death was near. He had sung his song to the Great Spirit,
but there was strength in him still, and despite the fact that he
had prepared his way, he lingered on, as he told me, to see Short
Bull, his grandson, grow strong.

The Umatilla were a small tribe, but its warriors had been
brave, great trackers and hunters, he assured me, but Short Bull
still had much to learn.

Now I'd always had a feeling for Indian ways, although I'd had
little enough to do with them. Ruth Macken knew Indians and
their tongues, and she had often told me of their ways, as had
Ethan Sackett.

Now, seated beside the fire, I told the old man of my plans.
"The cattle are poor," I said, "the winter has been hard, and the
man who sold them to me did not expect to see them come even
this far.

"My people need the cattle to raise other cattle, and if they are
hungry, to eat. I must get them to Wyoming, and it is many
suns."

Uruwishi talked to his grandson and then Short Bull turned to
me. "My grandfather asks where you will cross the great river?"

I shrugged. I had been giving that a good deal of thought. Near
The Dalles might be the easiest place, but I had thought little of
that and planned to use a ferry if need be, no matter what the
expense.

Uruwishi spoke long and Short Bull explained. "You must cross
at Umatilla Landing, east of here," he said, speaking slowly.
"There is grass, and by the time your wo-haws get to the Landing
they will be stronger."

"Grass? Where?"

The old man drew in the dust. We were near Golden's place,
and east of us he drew several creeks flowing into the Columbia,
or creeks that we must cross if we went east along the north side.

"Rock Creek," Short Bull said, "beyond it Pine . . . Alder
here. There is grass." He looked up from the drawing. "There are

also men there who have cattle. They do not like strangers. They are bold men, and fierce."

"I'll be passing through," I said. "I hope they'll not mind."

They looked at me but they said nothing, although the old man was grim. Short Bull listened to him, then turned to me. There was a kind of wry amusement in his dark eyes. "Uruwishi says he is an old man. It is his time to die . . . but is it yours?"

"If the grass is good, we will drive that way," I told them, "and I do not think it is my time to die . . . or yours. Anyway," I told Uruwishi, "you cannot die now. You have hired on to ride to Wyoming with me."

He chuckled a little, then put out his pipe and went to his bed.

Short Bull was with the cattle, and I remained by the fire trying to think things out. No news from home worried me . . . there should have been a letter somewhere along the line.

I wanted to hear how our town was getting along, but I also wanted to hear from Ninon. Somehow she stayed in my thoughts even when I tried to forget her.

Also, I needed help with these cattle. They were tired and hungry. Once they got fed up they'd be a handful. And I needed horses, needed them the worst way.

We drove a slow five miles or a shade better on the second day, reached Rock Creek, and forded it before bedding down. There was good grass in the meadows not far from the creek, and the cattle were willing to stop.

Short Bull pointed toward the mountains to the north. "There is Horse Heaven," he said.

"There are horses there?"

"Many . . . and Indians."

"Your people?"

He shrugged. "My people are few, and not there. They are Yakima."

"Do you know them?"

"I do."

"Could you trade for horses? Or get them to come to me here?"

He shrugged. "Maybe so."

"Try," I said.

He spoke long to his grandfather and the old man talked a little, and then Short Bull rode away and I remained in camp with old Uruwishi.

The night was a long one. I lingered by the fire until it was dark, then rode out around my cattle. They were a small bunch and clustered pretty well together, so there was little riding to do. These cattle were used to people and not as scary as some cattle I'd known, so part of the time, to rest my horse, I walked.

After midnight the old man came out to me, although I'd not planned for it. He shook his head and waved me to camp, so I went on in, drank a cup of coffee and lay down, not figuring on sleep. Next thing I knew it was daylight and the old man was shaking me awake.

"Men come," he whispered.

Tugging on my boots, I got up and slung my gun to my hip.

There were three of them. For a moment they drew up and looked at my cattle, then came on up to camp. Uruwishi had disappeared.

I stood there waiting for them, me in my old run-down boots, my pants hanging over them, and a beat-up old hat on my head.

They came on up, looked at me, then looked sharply around.

"My name is Shelde." He spoke with an arrogance that told me he figured the name meant something. "Norman Shelde."

"Howdy," I replied. "I'm Bendigo Shafter."

"You're on my range."

"Passin' through," I said, "bound for Umatilla Landing."

"Like hell. Nobody passes through here. Your damned worn-out cows will infect my stock. You turn right around and drive them out of here."

"My stock are in poor shape because they had a bad winter over near Ben Snipes' place." I paused. "I don't figure on driving them a foot farther than need be, and my way lies straight on."

One of them started to speak up but Norman Shelde stopped him. "You a friend of Ben Snipes?"

"I know him."

"You buy them cattle from him?"

"Read the brand," I said. "You know whose brand that is."

"You talk mighty big for a man alone."

"I'm not alone," I said. "I've got a Colt and a Henry, and they've come a far piece with me."

One of the riders started to edge his horse to one side, and I said, "Mr. Shelde, you tell that man to keep his horse still, and if he can't, to get off him. I'd not like to think he was tryin' to flank me."

Shelde didn't know what to make of me. I was nowhere as scared as he figured I should be, and it worried him. He had to believe I had an ace up my sleeve somewhere, but all I had was a six-shooter that I'd learned how to use, and would use if they pushed me to it.

"Where you takin' them cattle?" Shelde demanded.

"South Pass," I said.

"Alone?"

"If need be."

The heavyset man who had been trying to edge over until I spoke to him spoke up. "How do we know you didn't steal them?"

"You can accuse me," I said, "but when you do you'd better not do it unless you have a gun in your hand."

One of them pointed to a white stick well beyond the fire. "If you're so much on the shoot," he said, "let's see you hit that."

"When I take my gun out," I replied, "I won't be shooting at no stick. I'm not a trouble-hunting man, but I never stepped away from any, either."

Shelde reined his horse around. "You heard me," he said roughly, "you're on my range. You got to get off."

"And you heard me," I said, "I'm driving right through." I pointed with my left hand. "I'm pulling out of here in about an hour, and I'm riding due east with my Henry across my saddle bows.

"You can stand clear and let us through or you can object. I figured I might have trouble with you folks so I brought along a shovel and a Bible."

They didn't like it, but neither did they feel inclined to call my hand. That heavyset one was fairly itching to try it, but he wasn't sure. They all carried rifles in their hands, and I had only a gun in a holster, and they knew nothing about me getting into action fast. That was something only two or three men did know.

They'd come out there to scare somebody, but when I didn't scare they were no longer so sure of themselves.

"We told you," Shelde said as he rode off, and I let him have the last word. I'd nothing to prove to anybody. Maybe I was young but I'd already learned a few things, and one of them was that if you throw your weight around somebody is going to call your hand . . . and he might be a whole sight tougher and meaner than you.

These past few months I'd seen a few tough men go to meet their maker unexpected. I'd seen Webb in action, and the man he'd killed hadn't expected to die.

The way I saw it, if you asked for it you were going to get it.

TWENTY-THREE

When they had gone old Uruwishi came out of the brush with his old Hawken rifle. I'd no idea where he'd been, but all the while the old coot had been lying back there with one of those men in his sights. It gave me a good feeling to know he was around.

He might have years behind him, but those hard old eyes could look down a rifle barrel as well as any young warrior whose first scalp was not dry.

We held our place, letting the cattle graze and waiting for Short Bull. He would find us, but I hated to move on leaving him to ride into trouble unaware of it.

Yet he was gone less time than expected, for he met four Yakimas on the south side of the mountain where they had gathered after a hunt. They had horses, and they were ready to trade. It had been a hard winter, and there was hunger in the lodges, so we talked, fed them, drank coffee, and they smoked. In the end I drove a close bargain. I was to get six horses for two steers and forty dollars. Many an Indian pony had been sold for ten dollars, but times were bad and these were to be especially good stock.

I sent Uruwishi along to pick them out and remained alone with the cattle.

Before they pulled out we shifted the cattle to a meadow

several miles further along, with two of the Yakimas to help. We
watered them, bedded them down, and then the Indians rode
away.

With my horses and rifle I pulled back atop a small knoll. The
cattle were fifty to sixty feet lower down and contented to be
resting and grazing. My lookout gave me a good view over the
country around so I could see anybody who might come up on
me.

Building a small fire, I put on a coffeepot and settled down with
a rock at my back and a view of the stock. Nothing was going to
come up behind me with those horses of mine feeding nearby
. . . they'd warn me in time. Nonetheless, from time to time I
took a careful look around.

One time I picked up a little dust, maybe a half mile off, but
whoever it was seemed content to look. I made no attempt to
conceal my fire. Anybody with half a mind could see that I had
good cover, and anybody coming up on me would be in view for a
good quarter of a mile or further.

Several times during the long evening I dozed a little, knowing
the rest would do me good, and when night came I tightened my
cinch, mounted up and rode down the slope, and began my
riding around the cattle.

They were a small bunch, so it was no problem, and I generally
stayed back a little. Whenever I closed in I sang to them.

After a while they got up, took their stretch and grazed a bit,
then lay down again. I drank coffee, added fuel to the fire to keep
it smoldering, then went back to the cattle. About daybreak when
the cattle were up I loaded up and moved out, trusting to the
Indians to follow, for there was little enough time for the long
drive ahead. With any kind of luck I hoped to buy more cattle as
we moved along, for much of what we had to go through was
cattle country.

Shelde and his outfit were probably the first in this area, and
his kind did not always last long. He'd come up against the wrong
outfit and he'd be planted somewhere along the slope to make the
grass grow better for latecomers.

I drifted the cattle slowly, letting them graze and water when
they were of a mind to, and when it was close by. They were
beginning to show the results of good grass. A couple of times I
saw riders. . . .

On the fourth day I was camped on Alder Creek when the
Indians came back, and they had six head of good, tough Indian
ponies.

We saw no more of Shelde or his friends during the drive to Umatilla Landing.

This was a new place, scarcely a town, yet as towns were in those days we might have called it such. A half dozen buildings had gone up in a few days and more were building. It was the point where the Umatilla flowed into the Columbia. Long ago, Uruwishi told us, there had been an Indian village at that point.

At the point where we crossed the river a man in a fur cap rode down to watch our herd bed down for the night. "You ain't buyin' cows, be you?"

"Maybe," I said. "Depend on what was offered and for how much."

"Wal," he said, curling a leg around the saddle horn, "I've got some young stuff up yonder, an' mighty little feed. I'm bein' crowded off my range."

"It looks to me like there is plenty of that," I commented. "Who's crowding?"

"Feller name of Shelde. He pushes an' he pushes hard. My old woman, she wants us to pull out, says they'll kill folks."

"I met him," I said, "and he did seem kind of ornery."

"Well, I need cash money. If you've got cash money for cattle, I'll sell. They taken most of my stock. When I spoke of it they said to come over and name what was mine, but they said I should bring a gun when I come because they didn't figure to shoot no unarmed man."

"You drive your stock down here," I said, "if you want a reasonable price."

"Well, if'n I keep 'em they'll be stole and I'll get nothin'. What would you say to six dollars a head like they stand? Fifteen for the bull?"

"All right," I said, "you bring them in."

There was a store and a saloon on the Washington side of the river. I bunched our stock on the meadow nearby and left the Indians to watch, then rode down to the store. I needed supplies, but most of those I'd get across the river and save carrying them over, but I had a small hunch riding me and bought a sack of fifty .44 cartridges that would fit either my six-gun or the Henry.

I stepped up to the bar and had a drink. The bartender was a baldheaded man with a black mustache and rolled up sleeves.

"You know the Shelde outfit?" I asked.

"I know them."

"Do you know the man who was just talking to me?"

"Pierson? Yes, I know him. He's an honest man and a hard worker, for all the good it will do him. There's no law around here, friend, except what a man carries in his holster. I think left to himself Pierson would back up and fight, but his old woman won't let him, and he's got two girls to think of. Shelde's already made trouble that way, and so has Bud Sallero, one of his riders."

"How many of them?"

"Five, six usually. Can be twenty or more. Most of them scatter out to find what they can find. Bud sticks close to Norman Shelde and his brother Frank."

I took my time with my drink, then had coffee. After a bit I stepped into my saddle and rode back to the camp. The cattle were resting easy, and the Indians had a fire going.

Short Bull was packing a rifle and he walked over to me. "Somebody watch," he said. "Two man."

"All right," I said. Then I explained that we might get more cattle.

He looked at me. "I don't think so," he said. "I think those men say no."

"Well, I need more cattle. This man Pierson has cattle to sell. Do you know where his place is?"

Short Bull explained, and I got up. "I'm going to ride up and complete my deal. If Pierson wants to sell, I'll just drive those cattle down myself."

I saddled up again, and I looked over at Short Bull and Uruwishi. "You take care of yourselves," I said, "and keep out of sight. If anybody bothers you or those cattle, you handle the situation, d'you hear? I'll back you from hell to breakfast."

When I'd stepped into the saddle I looked down at the two Indians. "If it is you or the cattle," I said, "let the cattle go and save yourselves, but if you can keep them, do it."

"We will keep the cattle," Uruwishi said, and I believed him.

Pierson Ranch wasn't much of a place. A log cabin built against the side of a hill, so probably it was half dugout, a pole corral, and a ramshackle barn. There were several horses in the corral, and a dozen head of cattle were grazing nearby.

I rode up around the barn and stepped down, tying my horses just out of sight behind the barn and among the trees. There was a trail leading into the hills through the trees.

Pierson and his family greeted me, and I was invited to sit down. Elsa Pierson was a buxom, heavyset woman with a wide, friendly smile, but there were lines of worry around her eyes now, and I noticed that she jumped at every sound.

She got out the coffeepot and she had cookies. The girls were young, almost women, and lovely enough in a healthy, friendly way.

"We want to get out," Elsa Pierson said quietly. "We do not want any more of this."

Obviously better educated than her husband, she had a quiet strength and certainty that I liked . . . it had carried over to the girls.

"I met Shelde," I said. "I had a bit of trouble with him."

"Be careful," Pierson warned, "that bunch is likely to take a shot at you. They're mean."

We drank coffee and talked. Pierson had sixty-odd head of cattle, and he would sell at six dollars a head. Most of them were within a half mile of the house. It was the best and closest water, and he had been saving the grass nearer the ranch, so now he'd brought them in close.

"The girls he'ped," he said, "but it ain't safe for them no more. That's a mean lot, and that Sallero is bad around women."

"We'll make our own gather," I said, "but you can help us, Pierson. I wouldn't want the women-folks involved." I looked over at Mrs. Pierson. "Can you get out of here, all right? I mean, how can you get away?"

"There's a man coming to the landing. He'll pick us up and take us on down to The Dalles. There's a man there who'll hire both me and the wife."

"All right. It's a deal then." I held out my hand. "I'm buying the cattle, everything wearing the P Bar . . . is that right?"

"Yes, sir. It surely is."

We shook hands on it and I ate a last cookie, picked up my hat, and turned toward the door.

"*Pierson!* Come out here!"

It was Norm Shelde's voice. I would have known it anywhere. Pierson started for the door and I stopped him.

"You'd be a damn' fool to go out there. Ask him what he wants."

"What you want?" Pierson yelled from the crack of the door.

"I hear you been talkin' to that damn' Yankee Shafter! Now you get this! You sell him one head of stock an' we'll kill you!"

My hand was on the door latch, and I opened it and stepped out. There are some things that make me mad, and one of them is a man who bullies other folks. Right now there was something coming up in me that I didn't like the feel of, but it was there. I stepped outside.

"I've bought every head of stock Pierson owned," I said. "What have you got to say to that?"

Well, you'd have thought I'd slapped him. He hadn't seen my horse and had no idea I was anywhere around. It might have made no difference, but I think it would have. Men of his stripe don't want witnesses or other men who'll stand up to them.

He had the same two men with him, the one I picked for his brother Frank, and the other this Bud Sallero.

"I don't like it," Shelde said. He was surprised but he was mad, also. "I don't like it at all. My suggestion to you is to get on your horse and ride out of here."

"All of which I intend to do," I said, "when I have bunched my stock so's I can drive it with me. Pierson and his family are coming along."

He didn't like me one little bit. He rolled his quid in his jaw and spat. "You're askin' trouble," he said, "an' I'll tell you once more . . . get *out!*"

Sallero had his rifle in his hands and so did Frank Shelde, but it wasn't a thing that mattered to me right then. My eyes were on Norm, and he was trying to decide how much of me was talk and how much was man.

All of a sudden his manner changed. He'd been trying to make up his mind, and I felt him change right in front of me. There had to be a reason and my guess was that somebody else had entered the picture . . . another man.

But where was he?

"Pierson," I said, "leave Norm Shelde for me. You can have Sallero."

Shelde's eyes flickered, and I knew where the other man was. Near the shed . . . must be the far end because there had been no sound from horses. If I'd put Shelde at twelve o'clock on a clock dial, that would put this other man at ten o'clock. If I were to step quickly back and left as I drew, he'd be likely to miss . . . of course, a man never knew. You have to play them the way they're dealt.

"Pierson?" Shelde sneered. "You got you nothing at all there. He wouldn't shoot."

He glanced quickly to his right, then said, "All right, boys, shoot him!"

My foot went back and left and I shot at Shelde, then turned, dropped to my knees and shot at the man by the corner of the barn.

At the same instant there were a half dozen other shots, then silence.

Bud Sallero was hanging to his saddle horn with both hands, his eyes round and staring. His rifle lay in the dust where it had fallen, and his face grew red from blood, then turned gray. There was a spreading stain of darkness on his shirt.

Frank Shelde was in the dust of the ranch yard, and Pierson had stepped out of the door, holding an old Sharps .50.

Sallero slowly let his hands slip off the horn, and he fell from the saddle into the dust.

The man at the corner of the barn was crawling. Pierson nodded at him. "He's gettin' away, Ben."

"Let him go. He won't travel far with what he's carrying. I know where I put it."

Norman Shelde was still in the saddle, and he was alive. Either I'd shot too quick, trying to get the other man, or his horse had stepped over, for my bullet had smashed his gun hand, cutting deep into the web of flesh that joins the thumb to the hand. The bullet had gone right up the forearm and smashed through the arm at the elbow.

We just stood there, I don't know how many seconds, and the shock was getting to me. I was shaking a little from reaction, and to cover it I started to talk.

"The odds weren't just like you figured, Shelde," I said, "so now you're finished. Unless you're pretty good with your left hand you'd better just ride out of here to some place where nobody knows you."

The blood was dripping from his hand and arm, and when he moved the hand it looked like the thumb was dangling. That his arm was smashed at the elbow anybody could see.

He just stared at me, then at it. He was numb, shocked into silence.

"I didn't want to kill anybody," Pierson said. "I'm a friendly man. I never figured to hurt anybody at all, but they come at me."

Elsa was out there. "You did just fine!" she said. "You did just what you had to do, and I'm right proud of you! You'd have done it before if I'd kept still, only I knew they'd never leave you to one man. It wasn't like them."

"I still want to leave here," Pierson said. "I want to go to The Dalles."

"Let's round up those cattle," I said, "it's a long ride to South Pass."

TWENTY-FOUR

I had picked up mail from home at the last station, but there had been no time to read it. Hurriedly, I had stuffed it into my saddlebags and had been busy on other things.

Now I was trailing southeast toward the Blue Mountains with one hundred and twenty-two head of mixed stuff, most of it young. The grazing was fairly good, and by scouting ahead and locating likely meadows I would have little trouble with my small herd.

I had picked up three more horses from Pierson, and he and his daughters had helped with the crossing and to get started on the trail away from the Landing.

At the end of the first day Pierson drew up and thrust out his hand. "Ain't likely I can ever thank you enough," he said simply. "I would have faced those men but ma couldn't see me leaving my two girls without a pa in this country, an' she was right. I'd likely have got one or two, but they'd surely have killed me."

"Maybe," I said. "You never know. Anyway, your family will do better at The Dalles, I'm thinking."

I lifted a hand to them and turned away. The heads of the cattle were bobbing, dust was lifting from the road, and deep-marked in the sod to left and right were the ruts of long-gone wagons, the pioneer wagons, the first to cut this road.

The Blue Mountains hung in the misty distance, shadowy,

changing, elusive, until a man could not say if they were mountains or only a mirage of mountains. We worked the cattle slowly
on, taking our time, letting them fatten for the long drives to
come, and saving our few horses.

Uruwishi, ancient as the ancient hills, rode like a young boy,
and the gleam in his eyes was good. Once, reined in beside the
road to let the cattle pass, I said to him, "I would like to have
seen you as a young man, Uruwishi. You must have been something then!"

"I was a warrior," he said simply. "I counted plenty coups, took
many scalps."

"What do you want for Short Bull?" I asked. "What do you see
for him?"

He stared after the young Indian and then said, "I would wish
he could ride the land as I did when I was young. Now he cannot,
for the land has changed. He must go the white man's way."

"You think it is the best way?"

He looked at me. "No," he said, "but it is here."

After a while I told him, "Both of you can stay at South Pass
with us. You're good men, and we need good men."

"In a white man's town?"

"It is a man's town," I said.

To tell the truth I'd never given much thought to that side of it
and thought there might be some argument from Webb and
Neely. Webb would grumble, but when he saw the Indians
would stand to their guns in time of trouble and do their share of
what had to be done, he would say no more. As for Neely, I was
used to him.

Of course, I had not opened the letters yet.

It wasn't until a few days later, camped under the pines at
Emigrant Springs, that I finally read them. There were three,
from Ruth Macken, from Lorna, and from Ninon.

I opened Mrs. Macken's letter first, for she was the one who
would tell me most about our town and the people in it, and I was
hungry to know. It seemed I had been away for such a long, long
time.

Dear Mr. Shafter:

*You will wish to know what has happened, or is about to
happen, but first let me say there is no sickness here. That
all is well I would hesitate to say. Since you left there has
been a great change, and not all of it for the better.*

Neely Stuart has done well with his mining. I believe he

exaggerates what he takes from his claim, but it is considerable. He has hired both Ollie Trotter and that Pappin man to work for him on his claim, and that gives him more time to stir trouble.

Moses Finnerly has taken to preaching. John was holding services in the school building so Neely built Finnerly a church of his own, which the Stuarts, the Crofts, and several new families attend. I gather he devotes most of his time to preaching against. Against Mormons, Indians, John Sampson, our school, Drake Morrell, and often veiled references to your brother or myself.

Ninon will tell you what she wishes in her letter, but she is discontented. Since you left she has been unhappy, continually wishing you were back, and fearing you will marry somebody while gone. She has been used to a more exciting life than we can offer here, and I know she yearns for the theater.

Moses Finnerly has several times stopped her and tried to get her to come to his church, to sing in his choir. He wants her to be a soloist. I am not sure his motives are what one would expect of a minister of the gospel, but our Ninon is not one to be misled. She is young, but much too wise in the way of the world to be fooled by anyone as clumsy as the Reverend.

Mr. Stuart has evidently been paying Pappin and Trotter very well, for both men spend more than any honest workman should. Mr. Webb still attends our church, and has taken a profound dislike to "that gospel shouter" and his cohorts.

We still do not have a marshal, although Mr. Trotter considers himself such. Mr. Stuart appointed him guard at the mine, and Trotter has taken to wearing a badge. Two weeks ago a stranger in town suddenly untied one of Mr. Webb's horses and started to ride away. Webb came to the door and shouted at him to come back and when he kept going, Mr. Webb shot him. I saw it, and it was a very good shot. It was with a Dragoon Colt and the man was at least one hundred yards off. The man fell, hit the dirt and started to rise, and Mr. Webb shot him again.

Ollie Trotter was in the saloon (oh, yes, we have one of those!), and he stepped to the door with a gun in his hand and demanded who had shot, and Mr. Webb turned on him and said he had, and what did he propose to do about it?

Mr. Trotter looked down the street at the horse thief, then at Mr. Webb, and went back inside the saloon.

The saloon was opened by a huge man who calls himself Dad Jenn. I suspect that part of the money came from Mr. Stuart from the way Jenn defers to him and to no one else. There are several toughs hanging about there much of the time.

My store is open, and I have done well. On the day it opened a dozen Mormons appeared and bought supplies. The freighting is done by a young Irishman named Filleen who has a livery stable. At last count we had sixty-two people in our town and four business establishments. Bud is working for Mr. Filleen and conducts the store for him when Mr. Filleen is out of town, freighting.

There was a little more, but that was the gist of it, and I wondered at how much had happened in the short time since I had been gone. The other letters I saved until later.

We moved on to Meacham's Blue Mountain Tavern, nooned there, where I mailed a brief reply to Mrs. Macken and a note to Cain. We drove on into the Blue Mountains with the Wallowas a purple haze off to the east. After crossing the divide we turned over into a mountain meadow and bedded down. The next day we drove to Brown Town and bedded down southeast of town. I needed more help—the old man wasn't going to stand up to this night work, and there was also the question of supplies. We'd managed to keep eating, all right, shooting an occasional deer, elk, or big horn, but we needed coffee.

Leaving the Indians with the stock I took a packhorse and rode over to Brown Town.

A few years before, maybe two or three, a man named Ben Brown had come back up the country to establish a home on a bench above the Umatilla River. Later he opened a store in his house as Ruth Macken had done in a like situation. A couple of other places had sprung up nearby.

"Howdy," Brown said as I came through the door. "Seen your cattle. Where you headed?"

"South Pass, and I need another hand. Close up your store and come along."

Brown chuckled. "Now that's an idea. Fact is, I'd like to. Always wanted to prowl around in them Wind Rivers. The mountains, I mean. Afraid I can't help you thataway."

He took the list of supplies I'd made out and glanced over it.

"Well, I can't come up with most of this stuff." He indicated my herd. "See you got a couple of Injuns along."

"Umatillas. The old man is Uruwishi. I hear he used to be a big man among them."

"He still is." Brown looked at me thoughtfully. "That Injun was a big warrior in his time and a great wanderer and hunter. How'd you get him to ride along with you?"

"His grandson is with me, too. He's sung his deathsong, and says this is his last ride."

"I'll believe that when I see it. That old coot can ride forever and outlast most of the young bucks in his tribe. Get him to telling stories, sometime. He knows 'em."

He filled my order while I stood there, smelling the good smells of freshly ground coffee, of canvas, new leather, dry goods, and the like. I ate a couple of crackers from the cracker barrel and cut myself a slice of cheese from the big cheese he had on the counter.

This man had a nice little business going for him and I did not blame him for not wanting to pull out. I'd said it just in idle talk, anyway, but looking around me made me think of my own future. By the time this ride was over I should have worked out some sort of a plan for myself. From what Ruth Macken had said our town was growing, and I wasn't altogether sure I'd like what I'd find.

"Got some paper? I'll take the time to write a letter."

Brown shoved a box across the table at me. "Help yourself. The ink's there. Only got a quill pen . . . make them ourselves. Hard to replace others, this far out."

So I sat down there on a stool by the counter and wrote out a letter to Cain. I told him a lot of things, but nothing about the shootings. That I hoped would be forgotten, and that the story would never get to them at South Pass.

We have one hundred and twenty-two head of young stuff, I told Cain, and they are coming on fine. By the look of things we will have several calves before we get to South Pass. The grass has been fair so far, and old Uruwishi says he knows the good meadows along the way.

We have had good weather, but clouds are building, and it looks like rain.

The way it looks now we will drive down Baker Valley, cross the Snake above the mouth of the Boise, go up Indian Creek to its head, across Camas Prairie, then across Wood

*River, and on across the Lava Beds near the sinks of Lost
River. We will cross the Snake again near Eagle Rock, then
take the Lander Cutoff through the mountains.*

*All of this planning may have to be thrown out the win-
dow if grass is not there or if conditions change the situation.*

Brown told me the country ahead was in good shape. "Union's
the next place you'll reach . . . it's an easy drive, and there's
good grass. Better drive on past before you bed 'em down,
though, so's you won't have trouble. They're good folks but they
take notions against people comin' along and eatin' up all their
grass."

We started them up in the morning when the dew was fresh on
the grass, and the trail we took was traveled, for it was the way of
the rolling wagons. This was the way they had come, those people
bound for Oregon, this was their trail. The ruts they cut in the
grass were there and the names they carved on the trees. The
graves they left at the trail side were there, too, to mark the ones
who did not finish the journey to the promised land.

Like them we had traveled on, stopping short of where we had
planned to go, and suddenly when we topped out on the rise
above the Grande Ronde, a wide bowl-like valley in the mountains,
I knew this was the land where we had intended to come, to such
a place as this. Yet we moved our cattle on, two calves to follow
now.

We rolled down to the town of Union, scarcely begun yet, and
bedded our cattle down beyond the fences that marked the land
of Conrad Miller, the first settler there.

He came out to greet us, and to try to trade for our calves, but
we would have none of it, for troublesome as they might be upon
the trail, they would be the beginning of something at our
destination.

At each place we stopped I asked for books. I was given some,
and I bought some, and I traded for others. "You're luckier than
you know," one trader said to me, "and you're getting better
books than you will five or ten years from now."

"Why do you say that?"

"Travel will be easier. People traveling west will not have to
consider each ounce of weight. Now they only bring the best, the
ones that can be read over and over with profit, so the books you
trade for are the good ones. Later the trash will come."

"I'd find something to learn in any of it," I said, "for even a man who writes trash has to think, to select, to try to write as well as he can."

"Maybe." The man was doubtful.

"I am an ignorant man," I said, and there was no modesty in me when I said it, for it was simply the truth. "The little I have learned only shows me how very much there is to learn."

"You won't read much tonight," he said, "even with four new books in your duffel. Unless I'm mistaken that storm has caught up with us."

Oh, he was right! Far righter than he knew, for the clouds moved on and hung low and the rain pelted down, and the cattle got up, their horns glistening in the lightning flashes, and we were busy to hold them. Thunder rumbled in the hills nearby, and the trees bent before the wind, leaves lashing under the whipping of rain and wind.

There was no rest that night, for we rode round and round. Old Uruwishi did his bit, and we held them there on the grass until the storm had gone. Then we returned to our beds, to find them soaked and wet, but we crawled in anyway and slept.

Short Bull turned me out a few hours later. "There's men coming," he said, "maybe they make trouble."

"Thanks," I said, and walked out to meet them.

They pulled up, a half dozen hard cases if ever I saw them. The first one was a big man with wide, sloping shoulders and a shock of blond, long uncut hair. He had small, cruel eyes, and I knew him for a tough, dangerous man.

"You drivin' this herd?" He spoke roughly.

Now the night before had been long. I was tired. I had slept all night in my clothes, I hadn't had a shave, a wash, or coffee, and I was feeling it. Normally I am, I think, a cautious man, but there was no caution in me now.

"I am."

"We've come to cut them," he said, "you've pulled in some local brands."

"What's your brand?"

"That makes no difference. I'll know it when I see it."

"There are one hundred and twenty-four head here," I said, "counting the two day-old calves. I started out of the Landing with one hundred and twenty-two head. There isn't a brand in there but mine."

"We'll just have a look."

"Like hell you will."

He turned his eyes on me like he hadn't seen me before, and he looked carefully.

"You're asking for trouble," he said.

"I'm ready for trouble, mister. I was born ready for trouble. I started from the Landing with this herd and we left three dead men on Washington grass, and a fourth who'll carry the mark of that shooting his life long.

"Now I am in no mood for trifling. If you want to cut this herd you're going to ride right over me to do it, so deal your hand and pick up your cards."

They did not like it. They had thought to find some farmer or small rancher whom they could frighten into stealing half his cattle. I knew what they were and what they intended, and this morning I didn't care. I was feeling mean and ornery as an old mossyhorn steer, and I'd called their hand.

Suddenly from back in the brush somebody jacked a shell into a Winchester, and they all heard the sound and knew what it meant. Somebody else was there, somebody they could not see but who could see them. It was no longer robbing some quiet farmer, some married man with responsibilities; it meant getting somebody killed for a few head of cattle.

"You walk a wide trail, stranger," the big blond man said, "one day I'll call your hand."

"Do it now," I said. "I'm here, you're here."

"I'll wait," he said. "I'll wait until there's nobody lyin' up in the brush, ready to stretch my hide."

"I don't give a damn what you do, start shooting or start riding."

He turned his horse. "All right," he said, and then asked, "who'd you shoot up north?"

"We nailed three of them out of four," I said, not bragging but hoping he'd accept the lesson and keep away. "And Norm Shelde won't be shooting with that hand any more."

"Shelde?" He looked thoughtful then. "I know a man who rode with him. Bud Sallero."

"You *knew* him," I said. "He cashed in his chips."

The blond man looked me over again. "Maybe I'll have to pay more attention," he said. "Sallero was tough."

"He wouldn't make a pimple on a tough man's neck," I replied shortly.

They rode off then, walking their horses to show how they didn't care. They'd simply pulled in their horns for the time being and were letting me know they'd come back.

I walked back to camp. I could see Short Bull with the cattle. Uruwishi was still in his blankets, unaware anything had happened.

Then who was that in the brush?

Suddenly there was a dry chuckle behind me. "Think you're kinda salty, don't you, kid?"

I knew that voice!

Turning sharply around I found myself staring at a man in dirty buckskins.

It was Stacy Follett.

He chuckled. "Growin' some bark, ain't you? You faced up to those renegades like you was three or four men."

"I was in no mood for trouble."

He chuckled. "I reckon." He looked toward the campfire. "You got you some coffee?"

We walked over to the fire, and he dug a cup out of his possibles. I filled it, then my own. "You've a long road behind you," I said. And then I looked at him over my cup. "Did you kill Drake Morrell?"

He chuckled again. "Decided agin it." He sipped his coffee. "You know somethin'? After he started that there schoolteachin' I figured I had him dead to rights. I laid out for him, waitin' until he was out of school, and when he come out the door, I shaped up with my old Betsy girl here"—he slapped his rifle—"right on his belly. I had him where he couldn't move. There was young-sters all around him, and he stood there lookin' at me and never turned a hair. He had sand, that Morrell."

"Had?"

"Has. He's still around. You want to know what happened? I nigh got myself kilt. Five or six of them youngsters, weren't but two of them upwards of twelve or thirteen, they outs with their six-shooters and had me covered.

"They told me he was their teacher and he was a mighty good one and if I shot him they'd fill my hide."

He chuckled again. "An' you know somethin'? They'd of done it, too."

"What happened?"

"Nothin'. I pulled down my flag. Pulled her down right quick. I never seen so many youngsters with six-shooters."

"That's wild country. Some of them ride to school. A boy in that country needs a gun."

"Well, they still got 'em. I backed off and told him I was pullin' out, he was too good a man to shoot.

"And here I am," he added.

TWENTY-FIVE

He squatted on his heels, sipping coffee. "Mighty good," he said, at last. "I was plumb out of coffee an' I set store by it.

"Meat's no problem as long as I got the old shooter here"—he put a hand on the Spencer—"but grub ain't grub without coffee."

"We can let you have some," I offered, "but why not ride along? I need an extra hand, and I'll pay you."

He made no reply, finally looking up at me. "What you plan to do with all them cows?"

"We're building a town, and the game will move back into the Wind Rivers. We'll need milk for the youngsters and beef for all of us. Besides, we've got to grow. We've got to make something of ourselves."

"I don't see that." He waved a hand. "Lots of country. Move into it, live with it. A body don't need no more. There's grub out there for the takin'."

"Except for coffee," I said.

He grinned at me. "There's ephedra tea, and there's bidable beans that a body can use. Still," he agreed, "it ain't coffee. That N'Orleans coffee now, with chicory . . . that there's coffee!"

He refilled his cup. "Been a passel o' folks through this here country, an' some of them ain't made it all the way."

"I've seen some graves."

"Ain't all been found. Nor buried." He paused a moment. "You

167

folks stack up purty good." He chuckled suddenly. "I liked them boys back yonder, the ones who pulled iron on me to save Morrell's hide.

"Sand . . . that's what they had. Those boys will do to ride the river with. Youngsters with the bark on 'em. I favor any boy what'll stand for his teacher, and they sure enough backed me down.

"You can reason with a man, mostly. You might skeer him some, but there wasn't no skeer in those youngsters."

He sipped more coffee. "Tell you something. There's a valley over yonder"—he waved a hand eastward toward the mountains— "where there's fifty, sixty head of cattle."

I put my cup down on a flat rock. "Cattle? Whose?"

"Your'n, if you want 'em. Mebbe ten, twelve year back a few wagons come through, drivin' fifteen, twenty head. They turned them into a box canyon where there was good grass and water and they put poles across the openin'.

"Injuns come down on 'em. There was quite a scrap, but Injuns wiped 'em out, drove off the wagon stock, but never found them cows."

"And they are still there?"

"Them and their get. I eat one, a time or two, an' grizzlies have taken one here or there, but the herd's grown, there's water aplenty, grass, but no way to get out."

"What do you want for them?"

"Ain't mine." He threw his coffee grounds into the fire. "I s'gest you leave the old bull and four, five head of young stuff. The old one's mean as all get-out anyways. You leave some for seed, like. You never can tell when a body might need beef. Meantime you drive out the rest and build your own herd."

"That's fine of you."

"Pshaw! Ain't nothin'." His hard old eyes twinkled at me. "Need to be cleared out. They's gettin' to be too many head for the grass, an' if they ain't skimmed off there'll be some dyin' this winter."

Fifty or sixty head . . . if we took forty our herd would be a third larger, and we'd all be better off.

We moved on with the break of day, with a mountain to climb, and cattle handle mountain passes better if you tackle them early. The morning was cool, a light wind stirring the grass.

Baker City was booming but we avoided the town, keeping our cattle moving steadily. The grass was good, and the work could now be shared by the four of us. No more was said about the box canyon with its cattle. I only knew they were somewhere ahead of us, and Stacy Follett had been vague about locations.

As the cattle gained in strength the drives became longer. From pushing them only a few miles each day we moved on to ten, twelve, and occasionally fifteen miles, depending on the country and what Uruwishi or Follett knew about grass.

The old Umatilla and the mountain man seemed to find much in common; sometimes they talked for hours in a mixture of sign language and several Indian tongues. And here, at last, camped on a small stream with the Snake River not far ahead, I found time to read the letter from Ninon.

Dearest Bendigo:

There has been a letter from my aunt in New Orleans, and she is sending someone or coming herself to fetch me away. I do not wish to go without seeing you, but you have been gone so long, and they say I must go when they come.

It is so far to New Orleans, and I am afraid you will never come to see me. I know you believe I am too young to know what I want, but I am old enough, and I love you very much. I hope you will come to New Orleans to see me. My aunt does not wish me to be an actress, so I may not stay with them, but I would tell that to no one but you.

Please hurry back before I must leave. I do so wish to see you.

Ninon.

Ninon would be leaving. Well, it would be better for her. She was not geared to our kind of life, nor was there much in prospect for her if she remained with us.

Still, the thought of her leaving disturbed me more than I wished to admit. She was a child, no more than that. The fact that girls often married at fifteen or sixteen had nothing to do with it. Even if she had been old enough I was in no shape to marry or to even consider it.

I'd seen too many men marry young and slave their lives out carrying the burden of wife and children. No matter how much a man loves his family, it kind of hamstrings him to have them too young . . . or so it seemed to me.

Several slow days of driving followed. The grass was only in patches, for the year had not been a good one, and when we found good grass, and it was usually Uruwishi or Follett who directed us to it, we scattered the cattle and let them graze. The Snake was not far ahead of us.

When the cattle grazed and there was yet light, I found occasional moments when I could read, and more often than not I read Blackstone. There was a growing hunger in me to be something, someone.

I knew it was not going to come to me by chance or by a sudden gift. Whatever I became I would have to become by my own efforts, and the worst of it was I did not know exactly where I was going or what I wished to be.

Of one thing I was sure. I was going to be something, and I was on my way. All I could do now was to finish the drive and learn all I could en route.

There's nothing like a long, slow drive to give a man chances for thinking. By the time the cattle reached grass they were always hungry enough to need little care, and old Uruwishi and Stacy Follett scouted the country, hunted our meat, kept their eyes and ears and pores open for trouble.

At night, with Short Bull riding herd, I put my book aside and listened to the talk between Stacy and old Uruwishi.

The Umatillas were kin to the Nez Perce and once had controlled a vast sweep of country from the Rocky Mountains to the Cascades, from the Yakima Basin to the Blue Mountains. Occasional hunting parties had crossed the Rockies, but that was rare until horses came among them.

Uruwishi thought he could remember when that was. Other Indians to the south had an occasional horse, stolen from still other Indians, who had themselves raided deep into Mexico to obtain them. Uruwishi had been a child when the first raiding party returned with three horses, but by the time he was old enough to hunt by himself with a bow, they had many horses.

They had lived upon salmon most of the time. Uruwishi remembered when Lewis and Clark had come down the Columbia, trading with them for some salmon, freshly caught. They were the first white men he had seen, although his father had been down to Astoria, long before, and his grandfather had once seen some men who were shipwrecked on the coast to the south.

The white man had not seemed important, for there were too few of them. Indians accepted them or killed them depending upon the mood of the moment or the white man's ability to defend himself. For a long time there were only a few rare men who drifted through the country.

For more than ten years after the Lewis and Clark group, Uruwishi had not seen even one white man.

The Chinooks were pushing in from the west, encroaching on their land. Other Indians were moving in also, and the Umatillas, never a large tribe, suddenly found their hunting lands growing less.

It was a story I had heard many times, and was to hear many times again, the story of one tribe pushing another, moving in, warring against them in long sporadic wars, and then taking over their hunting lands. Each time they were pushed they themselves pushed against other tribes, or moved to distant, less occupied areas.

Vast areas had been uninhabited, especially in the years before the horse came to give greater mobility. The Indians clung to lakes and rivers where water was in good supply. Yet there was much warring back and forth with nothing more in mind than the taking of scalps, counting coup, or stealing horses.

There were, I gathered, vast differences in the temperament of the various tribes, some very energetic, others lazy, and those living in the Great Basin country to the south and west of us had the least interesting cultures, due no doubt to the desperate struggle to even survive in a land of little water and less game.

Lorna's letter was the last one I opened. Its date was one month later than either of the others.

Dear Bendigo:
I am sad to tell you that Ninon is gone. A Charles Pairman and his wife (he is an attorney) came for her. She did not wish to go, nor did we want to see her go, but Cain agreed they were fine people, and she will have a better chance. Her aunt, we understand, is a very wealthy woman, very aristocratic, and has no children of her own.

It is just as well she is gone, for there has been trouble here. More gold has been found, although Cain says most of it is scarcely enough for the miner to live on. Nobody is getting rich, not even Neely Stuart. Cain believes Mr. Trotter and that other man are stealing from him, but he is (Neely is) afraid to accuse them. Moses Finnerly has demanded there be an election, and has offered to run for mayor. Quite a few of the new people are for him. He has offered Ollie Trotter as town marshal and Mr. Pappin for justice of the peace.

Some people want Cain as mayor, but he favors Mr. Sampson, and so do most of us. Something must be done,

*for there have been several robberies, and Mr. Aylmer, who
discovered some gold on his claim, was murdered.*

*There was an election at the stable one night without
anyone being consulted, and Jake Robinson was made town
marshal. He came out on the street with his badge, and some
of the toughs around Dad Jenn's saloon took his badge off,
pushed him around, and beat him up.*

*A man tried to break into Mrs. Macken's two nights ago
and she ordered him off; he laughed at her and kept lunging
at the door, so she shot through the door. The man cried,
swore, and warned her he'd be back.*

Putting the letter down, I stared off across the fire. We were
still a good two weeks away from our town, but I had a hunch I'd
better start back . . . that letter was three months old.

With sunup the old trapper led us back through winding canyons into a hollow in the hills. I'd seen such places before, but
this was of singular beauty, wide open to the sun with a stream
running through it and a meadow of fine grass. It ran back into
the mountains for upwards of three miles, with several hollows or
basins, too steeply walled for the cattle to escape. The canyon
narrowed down to the rail fence that guarded the entrance, a
fence often renewed by the look of it.

"My own cache," Follett said, "got my own ranch. I never seen
no tracks but wild game an' my own. She's a lost valley, and that's
what I call it."

We drove our own cattle into the valley and let them stay the
night, and when morning came we carefully cut out those we
were to leave behind and headed the rest toward the gate.

Some of the wild stock tried to cut back, but our cattle were
well broken to the trail and the Durham and Shorthorn stock was
more inclined to be placid, so the wild cattle drifted with the
herd.

"All right," I said to Follett, "I am leaving you in charge. Just
keep coming as you are, but when you get closer to our town
you'd better keep your eyes open . . . somebody might try to run
off the herd."

"What about you?" Stacy Follett stared at me, his old eyes
thoughtful. "You're ridin' into trouble, boy."

"I know it. But I have it to do."

"What you figurin' on?"

"I don't know. I'll just have to ride in and do what I can."

I shook hands all around, had a word for each of the Indians, and then I stepped into the saddle. I was taking two horses, a gray horse with a little dappling on the hips and a buckskin.

In the clear light of morning, I started and rode the sun from the sky, swapping my saddle to the second horse at midday and continuing on. Two hours of rest and I was off again, and when midnight was well gone I camped, staked out my horses, and rolled into my blankets. At daybreak I was up, ate a piece of jerky, drank coffee, and was in the saddle.

Four days later, with my watch showing it was past ten o'clock, I rode up the street of our town.

TWENTY-SIX

From a half mile off I could see the lights of what appeared to be a saloon. As I drew nearer I could see there were other lights in a half dozen buildings. No light showed from the bench where Ruth Macken's place stood nor from where Cain's house would be.

When I'd ridden several hundred yards further I saw the road that turned up to enter the street, and there was a sign there. I couldn't make it out, so I stepped my horse closer and struck a match.

FINNERLY

DAKOTA TERRITORY

I had gathered the reins and was turning away from the sign when a voice spoke from the darkness.

"Well, what did you make of it?" The voice was a strange one, the tone pleasant, somewhat speculative, I thought.

"I made it out to be a mistake," I said quietly. "I know who founded this town and when, and there was nobody named Finnerly present."

"That kind of talk could get a man into trouble," the speaker said. "I'd soft pedal it, if I were you."

"You're not me," I replied quietly. "This settlement was put together by a small party of people who wished for security, who

174

wished to build something honest, something worth having and keeping. There seem to have been some changes."

He was walking toward me and I could make him out now. He was a shorter man than I, blocky of build, older I'd guess. He carried a rifle.

"The people who first settled the town are outnumbered now. They are peaceful people with families and homes. Most of the newcomers are without families and they couldn't care less about peace.

"There has been gold found here, and these men have come in hoping to pick up what can be found. They are not those who care about anything permanent or stable."

"And you?"

"I am a bystander, sir. I'd not say an altogether innocent bystander. I have seen many towns born, and I have seen several of them die."

"Of what did they die?"

"Lack of attention, I think. Lack of love, lack of the will to take a stand, a willingness to let things be, to not be involved . . . a peace at any price policy, I think."

"And where did you stand?"

"I am a watcher, sir. I belong neither here nor there. You come at a most auspicious time, my friend. If you are planning to take part in the election, I'd say a most auspicious time."

"Who is running?"

"Why, the Reverend Moses Finnerly is running for mayor, I believe, opposed by a white-haired old gentleman known as Sampson. A Mr. Pappin is running for justice of peace, and he is opposed, of all things, by a woman."

"Ruth Macken?"

"Ah? You know the name then? Yes, it is Ruth Macken. The Widow Macken, I believe they call her. It is a new thing for a woman to run for office in this country, a revolutionary thing, one might say."

"She is an educated, intelligent woman, the widow of an army officer, who was a man of some distinction. She has poise and balance. I would say she would do very well."

He was quiet for a moment, and then he said, "Ollie Trotter is up for town marshal, and I thought at first no one would oppose him.

"You see," the stranger said, "there have been three previous marshals here. One of them was made a laughing stock, run out of town. A second was murdered . . . mysteriously, as the saying is, and the third was killed in a gun battle, which the witnesses say was a fair fight, by Mr. Candidate Trotter."

"But someone is running?"

"A man named Cain Shafter . . . one of that small group who wanted security. I admire Mr. Shafter's courage, but not his judgment. I hope he is very good with a gun."

"Possibly," I said, with irritation, "if there were fewer citizens who were innocent bystanders he might not need to be good with a gun."

"Undoubtedly . . . you are, of course, correct. But you see, young man, I am a traveler, an interested traveler but no more than that. My home is in the eastern part of the Territory, where I have but lately come from Denver City and before that from New York."

"I see." I stepped down from the saddle, keeping my horse between us. "You seem to have noticed quite a lot."

"I am interested in towns, and in politics. In the affairs of men, let us say. But I am a reader and an observer rather than a doer, and in this town I see a rather unfortunate spectacle, a town that never should have been, coming to an unpleasant end."

"Never should have been?"

"Certainly. Consider the position. You have only a very small stream . . . inadequate water supply. You have no major industry . . . oh, yes! The gold. But I have seen the gold, and have seen many gold areas. I do not think it is here in any quantity."

"The town was not built for gold. Nothing was known of it. The town was built as a refuge, some believed it a temporary refuge, some were building for the future."

"Misguided I said. I am sorry, young man, but the town has no future. As a place to live, perhaps. As a center for a small group of ranchers, perhaps. The soil is not rich enough for farming, and the wagon trains will not need supplies for long. The railroad will come, but not here."

"Where?"

"Further south. That's the best trail. In fact the route has been scouted, building will soon begin."

The man made sense, reluctant as I was to agree. We who built our town had come to love it because it was *ours*, the work of our hands.

"A mistake is really only a mistake if you persist in it," I said.

He stopped, looking at me. "Well, now. That's a rather profound remark. Do you think they will persist?"

I shrugged, and said nothing. I did not know, and besides, we had come to the first buildings. Two ramshackle shacks had been thrown up, undoubtedly since spring, for nobody would live through a winter in South Pass in such shacks.

There was a store that I did not remember, and across the street from it, the saloon. There were four windows and some batwing doors. The evening was cool but pleasant, and the other doors that could be closed against the weather were open. Some kind of a music box was going within, and I heard rough talk, then laughter.

In the light from the door I turned to look at my unknown companion.

His beard was neatly trimmed, he wore a new gray hat and a black broadcloth suit, his pants tucked into his boot tops.

He held out his hand. "Henry Stratton, sir, at your service. I own a bit of property over east of here, near Cheyenne. I have some small interest in the railroad, too."

"Bendigo Shafter. This is my home. I have been to Oregon after cattle."

"Oh, yes! I heard something of that. I might say you are looked for. Maybe hoped for is the term. I heard Bud Macken say none of this would have happened had you been here."

"I'll be going up to the house now."

"You won't come in for a drink? You might give the boys a chance to look you over."

"They will have their chance. Good night, sir."

There were no lights in Cain's house, and I hesitated to approach it at night. Nor was there a light at John Sampson's . . . the only one was a light at the Crofts' and one up at Macken's.

Turning my horse, I rode up the hill, leading my spare. As I turned into the yard I swung down, calling softly, "Hallo, the house!"

There was silence, and I walked nearer, then tapped lightly on the door. For a moment there was silence, and then Ruth's voice said, "Yes? Who is it?"

"It's me, Mrs. Macken. It's Bendigo."

I heard a bar lowered, then the door opened a crack. Ruth Macken was there, a pistol in her hand. "Ben? Oh, *Ben!* Please come in!"

"If I may I'll put my horses up first."

"Please. I'll put on some tea."

Stripping the gear from my horses, I turned them into the corral; then rifle, saddlebags, and slicker in hand, my blanket roll thrown over my shoulder, I went back to the house.

She was the same. The same lovely, composed face, the same dark hair . . . seemed to me there was a strand or two of gray I hadn't noticed, but they might always have been there.

"Come in, Ben. Let me look at you." She stood back and looked.

I knew well what she was seeing. I was two inches taller than six feet and weighed right at one hundred and ninety. I needed a haircut and a shave as well as a bath, and my hat was beat up and dirty.

Her eyes studied me, shadowed a little, I thought. "Ben, you've grown up. You're a man."

"I reckoned I always was, ma'am. I'm just a year or two older."

She poured tea into a cup, and put out a plate of cold meat and bread. "You've come at a bad time."

As we ate she laid it out for me. The town had grown . . . there were nearly two hundred people in it now, many of them men of the rougher sort, and some women, but there were some good people, too. Many of them.

Drake Morrell was still teaching, and the rough lot who had come in had left him strictly alone. John Sampson was still conducting his church, which now held more than sixty members. In fact, the town had functioned as if it were two towns except for the occasional sound of gunshots and the killings.

Ollie Trotter had killed a man, a stranger who had come into town. The stories of just what happened were various. The man had been armed.

"Webb?"

"He spends most of his time at the saloon. He speaks to the rest of us, no more than that, but his son runs with the rest of that trash. Foss has taken up with Trotter, follows him everywhere. Trotter calls him his 'deputy' and you can imagine how Foss feels about that. He simply struts. It would be funny if it wasn't so tragic."

"How about your trading post?"

"It's been doing very well. I bought some more stock . . . Mr. Trask freighted it in for me at first, then Mr. Filleen. We still get a lot of business from the Mormons, although fewer and fewer of them are coming around because of the situation in the town. They wish to avoid trouble, and that is becoming more difficult with every day."

"How is this man Filleen?"

"He's a good man, Ben. Born in the old country but brought over here as a child. He lived in the east . . . Boston, I believe, and in New York. We talked a few times. He's a law and order man, Ben, and he has friends around town."

"Election is tomorrow?"

"If it happens. Ben, I think they are planning to kill Cain."

"*What?*" My cup came down hard, spilling some tea. "Sorry. What do you mean?"

"Bud heard some talk at school, one of the boys was bragging. He'd been teasing Foss . . . Webb's boy . . . asking him how much of a deputy he'd be after Mr. Shafter was elec.̲d, and Foss got very angry and said he'd still be deputy because there was only going to be one candidate . . . nobody would be running against Ollie Trotter."

"Might be just talk."

"Ben, I'm worried. Every day for several weeks Ollie has had Foss out in the hills, teaching him how to shoot and how to draw fast. Bud watched them several times.

"Bud saw something that worried him. You know, Bud is a listener, and he often listened while you and Drake Morrell talked about gunfights and gunfighters. He said that several times Foss would walk right up to Ollie, speaking softly, a gun in his holster. Then when right up close he would suddenly draw another gun from under his coat."

Well, I just looked at her. Then I got up. "I think I'll go have a talk with Webb."

"Be careful, Ben. Webb has been running with that crowd."

I shrugged. "Mrs. Macken, you know as well as I do that no matter what anybody says, Webb's his own man. He's a maverick."

"He was. For months now he has been trailing with them, spending his time around Dad Jenn's and rarely more than speaking to any of us. He's grown even more surly, if you can imagine it."

I took up my cup and drank the rest of the tea. "Do you think they're putting Foss up to killing Cain?"

"It would be like them, Ben. They are men without conscience, thinking of their own ends. Foss is a foolish boy, making a hero of Ollie Trotter. They tell him what a big man he'll be, that they will make him an official deputy with a badge and everything . . . and Foss has always resented Cain because Cain seems so unmoved by things. If Foss does it they are blameless, whereas if they do it there'd be resentment and possibly enough reaction to lose the election for them."

The more I thought about it the more I thought it best to wait

until morning. Webb would be touchy if awakened in the middle
of the night, and Foss might be home.

I sat down again and listened to Ruth Macken tell about the
town, and I told her about the drive and who was bringing
the cattle up. I said nothing about the outlaw who had died near the
barn. The killing of a man was nothing of which to be proud. We
lived in a hard time, and if men took guns in their hands to force
others to their will, they had to expect to be killed. And they
always were . . . sooner or later.

That night I slept under the trees, listening to the trickle of the
water from Mrs. Macken's spring. I remembered when I had cut
the logs for her house, drunk at that spring, and how simple our
lives had been then.

We had only to think of shelter, of hunting game, keeping a
wary eye for Indians.

What of the Indians? What of that surly young brave whom I
had once laid out, then protected against those who would kill
him?

Day was breaking when I awakened, and tugging on boots and
slinging on my gunbelt, I saddled up and headed down to Cain's.
He had just come out with his milk pail when I rode up.

His broad face broke into a smile. "Bendigo! Well, of all
the . . . !" He started to turn toward the door, but I stopped him.

First, I told him about the herd. We'd had some additions
along the way, and we had one hundred and seventy head coming
up the country. I explained briefly about the Indians and Stacy
Follett. Lastly, I told him what Bud Macken heard, and what we
suspected. He listened gravely, nodding a bit.

"It's to be expected." He led the way on to the barn and
leaning his head against the side of the cow, he began to milk. I
listened to the changing sound of the milk in the bucket as it
filled, thinking about the day.

"Cain," I said quietly, "I want to run for office."

He looked up. "What office?"

"The one you're up for. Town marshal."

"Taking the monkey off my back, Bendigo? You needn't."

"It isn't that." Suddenly I knew I meant exactly what I was
saying. "I want to go into politics. This would be the best chance
for me. I'm good with a gun, and I think I know when not to use
it. I could be marshal here, maybe go on to something else. You
don't want it, I know. You never did. And before I left they were
asking me to take the job, even though I wasn't ready for it then."

"You are now?"

"Yes, Cain. I'm ready." He finished his milking. "Let's go see Helen and the girls."

Lorna came running. "Ben! Oh, Ben! I saw the horse and I just *knew!*" She was excited. "You're so *big*, Ben! You've taken on weight!"

"It isn't fat," I protested. "You don't get fat on the trails I've followed."

Suddenly there was a voice behind me. "Ben?"

Neely Stuart was standing there, and Neely had changed, too. His features were drawn and his eyes hollow as though he'd had no sleep. "Ben, you've got to help me."

"What is it, Neely?"

"Those two . . . Pappin and Trotter. They've taken my claim."

"Let's all go in and sit down. Helen's got breakfast on," Cain said. "I'm hungry even if you aren't."

"And I am," I said. "Come along, Neely. You can tell us about it."

When the greetings were over, we sat down. The warm, friendly room brought back memories with a rush, but the face I missed was Ninon's. It just wasn't there.

Would it ever be?

"They've been stealing from me," Neely said. "I've known it for some time, but well . . . well, I was afraid to brace them with it. I thought they'd kill me. Lately, I've got to figuring they intend to, anyway. I figured they were just waiting until Ollie was marshal or sheriff or whatever he's going to be, then they'd kill me, have their own inquest, and he'd go scot-free."

"So what happened?"

He hesitated. "Well, last night I closed the door. We've got a door on the mine. They put it up themselves, and they had the key. This time I switched locks when they weren't about, closed the mine, and hung a sign on it, 'Closed until further notice.' "

"A likely move," Cain said. "I think you were wise."

Neely shifted his feet under the table. "Yes, that's what I figured. Then this morning they came up to me. Pappin did, with Ollie right behind him. They handed me a bill-of-sale for the mine, and suggested I sign it.

"Pappin, he said, 'We've not been paid. We want you to give us the mine in payment. You just sign that there paper and there won't be any trouble. Ollie an' me, we don't want no trouble, do we, Ollie?' That's what he said.

"I told him I'd have to think about it. And he said I had until noon to do my thinking. Then I should bring the paper to them as

they'd be busy with the election. If I didn't bring it to them . . .
signed . . . they'd come after it."

"What do you want me to do?" I asked.

"I can't face them, Ben. You're good with a gun. Ethan said
you were the fastest he'd ever seen."

Cain looked at me, then nodded. "All right." He turned his
eyes to Neely. "Ben wants to run for marshal, in my place, Neely.
Would you vote for him?"

Neely glanced from Cain to me. "Yes, I would. I'd vote for
either of you."

Cain sat back in his chair. He was a heavy, powerful man that
might be considered fat by those who did not take a second look.
He was large-boned and heavy with muscle that showed not at
all. I watched him, wondering. Long as I'd known my brother I
had never been able to judge his strength. What he took hold of
moved . . . he was in his own way a phenomenon, but he was
not cut out to be marshal. He knew it, and I did.

He was a retiring man, a quiet man, with no wish for authority,
and no compulsion to command, yet I had seen him pick up a five
hundred pound barrel and set it on a wagon, and without seeming
effort. He had always been strong, born with it. Strong as I was
myself, I wasn't a patch on what he could do, and knew it. Yet he
was gentle and not the man to deal with what was down there in
town.

"Don't sign anything, Neely." I cut into the meat on my plate.
"I'll handle it.

"Cain? Would you step out of the marshal's race if I agreed to
run?"

"Yes," he said simply. "I didn't want it, but there was nobody
else. I'll tell them all that you're the man." He looked at me
thoughtfully. "You've come a long way these last months, Bendigo,
a long way. But you were always quick and sure. You're a man
who knows his mind."

"All right," I said, "I won't see our town going to hell in a hand
basket. I'll run, and I'll straighten it out. And don't you worry
about Trotter or Pappin."

Pappin . . . I thought about him. We knew very little about
him. He had seemed the brainy one, the shrewd one, but what
was he like in a tight spot? I had an idea I'd better think about
Pappin. Ollie Trotter would use a gun, and he fancied himself
that way.

Webb worried me. He was good, very good . . . but where did
he stand?

And there was his boy to think of, Foss, who we believed was to kill Cain.

Or me.

Well, he'd never do it with me. Suddenly I wished the cattle would get in. At this moment it would be a good thing to have Stacy Follett at my side.

A thought came to me. "Where's Ethan?"

Lorna had come in. "He's not around much, Bendigo. I think the only reason he stays around at all is waiting for you to come back. He told me he didn't favor leaving the town without you to look out for Ruth Macken."

"Is he up at the dugout?"

"I don't know. He's not a trouble-wishing man, and I think he lives up in the Wind Rivers most of the time. But he'll be around, once he knows you're back."

Helen came from the door.

"Bendigo? Ollie Trotter's coming up the hill. He's got two men with him."

TWENTY-SEVEN

Neither of the men was Pappin. Cain came up behind me, looking over my shoulder to see who it was. "Two of those roughs that lay about Dad Jenn's place," he commented. "The taller one is Nels Taylor, and the other is Vin Packman."

"All right," I said, "I'll handle it."

When I stepped outside to meet them I saw John Sampson's door was ajar, and it warmed my heart to think it was like it had been. Whenever the town was in danger, everyone stepped to the front. Cain would be there behind me, and Sampson yonder.

Trotter stopped abruptly when he saw me, frowning under the brim of his hat like he couldn't believe what he saw, but then they came on, the other two evidently asking him who I was.

It was a bright, sun-filled morning, and the valley was green and lovely. From where I stood I could see spots of color around Ruth Macken's house where her flowers grew. Slow smoke trailed from chimneys, and in the street in front of Dad Jenn's I could see two men standing, looking up the hill.

Trotter stopped. "Is Neely Stuart here?"

"Yes, he is, Trotter, but as his legal adviser I have told him to sign nothing, to leave the mine closed, and to institute an investigation as to the free gold that seems to be floating about. As gold is readily identifiable as to its mineral content, it seems possible someone has had access to gold that did not pass through Mr. Stuart's hands."

Now I was running a strong bluff, but since Trotter didn't know how much I knew, and a guilty man is very apt to suspect folks know more than they do, I figured I could make it stick.

"You ain't no lawyer!" Trotter said roughly. "You can't come that over me!"

"I have been studying law. As you should be aware, Mr. Trotter, I have been studying for some time now." He had seen me reading and had no idea just what kind of books they were, I believed he would buy that. I'd read Blackstone and a small book on the rules of evidence, and there was more than one practicing lawyer who hadn't read more than that. "How long does it take to become a lawyer?"

I knew he couldn't answer that one offhand, but what I wanted now was to confuse him, give him no excuse for gunplay, and to push the play back upon him and take the weight off Neely Stuart.

"Where's Neely? I want to talk to him!"

"Sorry. I have advised my client to say nothing." And then again I lied. "Naturally, the governor of the Territory will be sending an officer to investigate the matter."

Trotter did not like it and I was glad Pappin wasn't around. Pappin was shrewd and might not have bought my story so easily.

"He owes us money . . . wages. He's got to pay or we'll take the mine." Trotter put his hands on his hips. "This here ain't no affair of yours, Shafter, an' you'd better stay clear."

"It is my affair," I replied calmly, "and you will not take the mine. You have been paid. In fact, we plan to bring suit against you to have an accounting.

"In fact," I was lying again, "when Mr. Stuart wrote to me . . ."

"He *wrote* you?"

"Of course. And when he wrote I immediately began an investigation. A friend of mine has started inquiries as to your background, Mr. Trotter, that of Mr. Pappin, and of Moses Finnerly. We decided that if we had to go to court we wanted all the evidence in our hands."

Trotter didn't like it. Obviously, the possibility of an investigation into his own background was something he had not considered. To him it was a simple matter. He would bully Neely, a frightened man, into signing over his mine, and if he did not, they would trick him into a shootout and kill him.

Our town was far from anywhere, there was no law, and what

went on here would, they assumed, go unnoticed. My talk of courts, suits, and investigations confused and irritated Trotter. He was prepared for nothing of the kind, and he fell back upon bluster.

"This ain't the end of this. You just wait until after election. If you want this here to go to court, we'll just have our own trial, right here in town."

He turned and, trailed by the others, walked back down the street.

Turning to Cain, I said, "We've got to work fast. Get John and we'll take a walk."

"What kind of walk?" Bud Macken was coming down the hill toward us.

"We've got some electioneering to do. The three of us are going around, house to house, and talking to people about the election today. Some of them don't know me. I want to meet them."

Bud had stopped and was listening. Briefly, I explained what had happened so he could tell his mother. "Bud, you can do something for me. Ride up to Ethan's place and see if he's around. If he is, tell him I need him. If he isn't, leave a note for him."

Bud was off and John Sampson came from his house wearing his black suit, hat on his white hair. He was a fine-looking man.

With Cain we walked down the street to the Crofts. Tom and Mary came to the door. Quietly, I explained about Neely, and that I was now running for marshal in Cain's place, and that Cain was backing me.

"I don't know," Tom objected. "The Reverend's a good man. I'm not saying anything against you, John, but he's had experience. He's been top man in more than one town, and we need a strong hand."

"I wonder what towns they were?" Cain said. "And why he left them?"

"One thing or another," Tom said. "He wants to save souls. He's a preacher first and last."

"I believe you're right, Tom," I said. "It is a pity he has to take time from his preaching when John here could manage the town. The Reverend Finnerly is a real gospel-shouting preacher and that's what we need here . . . especially with some of the riffraff that have been coming in.

"He probably is not aware of what Mr. Trotter is doing. However, I believe he should be. If Ollie Trotter takes Neely's mine, he may realize how well you're doing with your farm and take that. The Reverend will have to be told, Tom, and if he is elected he must be told. And if he is elected, I would suggest you go to him at once."

Tom shifted his feet. The idea did not appeal to him, that much was obvious.

"You think about it, Tom. We've come a long way together, and we haven't always agreed, but we've made progress. I think before the coming winter is over half of this riffraff will have left the country, anyway. It is going to be a hard winter, and I suspect Ethan and I will be out hunting again."

We talked a few minutes more, then walked down the hill. A man named Robbins was next, a stiffnecked man who looked at us with some doubt. Obviously he liked John, but knew nothing of me but what he heard; but he listened. We did not appeal to his prejudices, but we did not oppose them, either. We simply stated our case.

"Bendigo Shafter was one of those who went to the Indians and got our children back," Cain said. "He hunted meat for us through that bad first winter, and he was a leader in the fight against the renegades."

"You the one went after cattle?" he demanded.

"Yes, I am. The herd should be in town within the next two or three days."

"That there's something, to drive cattle all the way from Oregon. And you taken gold money to buy them? You rode to Oregon with it?"

"Yes, I did."

"Takes some doin'. Most young fellers would have lost it or been tricked out of it. Well, I ain't sayin' how I'll vote, but you seem to be an upstandin' man."

There were a dozen men standing in front of the Filleen Livery Stable when we walked up, and they turned to look at us as we approached.

One of them, a square-built man with a rugged Irish face, thrust out his hand. "Howdy, Cain! John!" He turned to me, his eyes keen and measuring under tufted brows. "And you, I take it, are Bendigo Shafter? Word has come that you're runnin' for office."

"Well, well." The tone was cool, amused, somewhat taunting.

The crowd parted a little and there stood the big blond man who had tried to cut my herd back on the trail.

"You? Runnin' for office? What office?"

"Marshal." I grinned at him. "And I want your vote."

"You do, do you? Well, you got a nerve." He jerked his head at me. "I tried to cut his herd back on the Oregon Trail, but he stood me back in fine shape. Sure, Shafter, I'll vote for you for marshal. I think you'd make a damn' good one. You didn't crawl, you didn't stampede, and you were ready to back what you said."

He gave me a hard, taunting grin. "I may have to kill you some time, but I'll vote for you for marshal. You've got sand and you've got judgment."

He turned his back on me and walked away toward Dad Jenn's saloon.

"Well, gentlemen," Filleen said quietly, "there you have it." He held out his hand to me. "I'll go along with Colly Benson. There isn't a tougher hand around than him."

After a few more visits we walked back up the slope to Cain's place. It had gone off rather well. I'd never done any electioneering before, but I liked people, liked meeting them and listening to them, and I wanted to save our town.

What Henry Stratton had said rankled, but there was much truth in it. What trade we had would disappear when the railroad came in, far to the south of us. There would be a little trade with trappers, prospectors, and the like, but not enough for a town. The soil was sparse and the season short.

Why had we built a town at all? Because we needed it. We needed a refuge, and we needed a home and something to believe in. A town can be more than one thing to men. It can be a process of education as well as a place to live and make a living. But to build anything and to make it last calls for discipline, the inner discipline that a man provides for himself and the cooperative discipline that men give to each other.

Slackness, license, and ethical laxity meant death to any town, to any civilization, and it was here, in some of these latecomers. Cain was building, Filleen was also, and John Sampson . . . no doubt some of the others whom I did not know. Neely in his way, and Tom Croft in his, but Moses Finnerly, Pappin, and Trotter were leeches, contributing nothing, building nothing, but striving to fatten off the work of better men.

They were empty people, who believed they were the wise ones, who would ride on from town to town until finally they were suddenly old and worn with no place to go . . . if they lived so long. To such men death or prison was a kindness, for in the passing of time there came increased bitterness and usually a realization, too late, of the vanished years and the opportunities.

It was good to be back, even with the changes that had come. Lorna had changed, too. A lovely girl always, she was truly beautiful now in a quiet way, and I ached for her. I knew something and guessed more of the dreams she had, dreams that could never be in our town, for they were dreams of a wider, richer life somewhere in a settled community. Lorna wanted children, a husband, church on Sunday, the shade of trees, the beauty of flowers, singing at her work. She was one of the good ones who would rear strong sons who would walk their way in pride of home, of country, and of pleasure in their families.

"What do you think will happen down there, John?" Helen asked. "I mean when we go to vote."

"Nothing. They are too sure of themselves. They believe we are frightened."

Did John Sampson believe that? Or was he reassuring Helen and Lorna?

We talked idly of the old days on the trail, of the long westward marching, and what we had planned. Tom Croft was there, and he sat listening, the old dream returning to his eyes. "Maybe we should go on," he said, "the soil is thin here." He turned his eyes to me. "What did you see of the western lands, Ben?"

So I told them of the desert, of the parched and lonely miles, of the haunted nights and the Indians, but of the Grand Ronde also, and the green lands of Oregon. "It's a good country, Tom. A better country for you than this."

"What have we done here, then?" he asked.

"I've grown up," I said, "and I think all of us have, a little. Sometimes we have the dream but we are not ourselves ready for the dream. We have to grow to meet it.

"I don't know," I said, "and during the long nights riding west or the long days around the cattle I thought about it. At first I thought only of this town, of this place, and then little by little I began to wonder if this was not just a staging area for us, a place to live and grow in."

"Well," John Sampson said simply, "I've grown. I've changed. But I doubt if my life will ever be so simple again."

We sat there drinking coffee and watching the people come into the streets below. "I think we'll go down to town," I said. "Here comes Ruth Macken."

She was in her Sunday best, and so was Bud. John was dressed in his old black suit, and Cain emerged from behind an adjoining room wearing fresh overalls, polished boots, and a hat. I rarely saw him wear a hat, for he worked bareheaded, and he was usually working.

Tom got up and took his hat. "Mary will be back. She'll join us."

Neely got up. He had said little for the past hour, but he looked at us. "I wish Webb was here," he said. "He's the only one."

"And Ethan," I said.

"Aren't you going to count me?" It was Drake Morrell. "How are you, Bendigo? It's good to have you back."

He looked taut and worried. It took me a moment or so to see that was it, but it was there. He caught my look, then shrugged. "Things do not always go well, Ben. Sometimes things happen to a man . . . or he lets them happen."

"Well, come along."

The poll was at Filleen's Livery Stable. We walked along together, making quite a group.

On the porch in front of the saloon, raised three steps above the street, stood a man who could only be Dad Jenn. He was looking up the street at us. Moses Finnerly was on the steps, and beside him and a step lower was Pappin.

Several men idled about . . . too casually, I thought. "Be careful, Cain," I said. "They are ready for us."

"I'll let you call the turn, Ben," Morrell said. "I'm right with you."

"Helen," I said quietly, "you and the other women get back and to our right, so we can keep the fire away from you. Do you hear me?"

"Yes, Ben."

Ruth Macken spoke quietly. "I'll stand closer, Bendigo. I brought my pistol."

"Howdy, folks!" Finnerly was smiling. "Good to see you all together like this! First time in quite a while."

"We take our voting seriously, Mr. Finnerly," John said.

"Of course! Of course! Too bad about that. You got down the hill just too late. We've closed the boxes."

"You can open them again," John said quietly. "We intend to vote."

"Sorry about that." Trotter suddenly appeared, a shotgun in his hands. "We've closed the polls." He smiled at me. "I've been elected."

"Counted the ballots, Ollie?" I asked gently. "Even that?"

"Well, not exactly." He grinned. "But we'll count 'em."

"We'll all count them together," I said, "after we have voted."

The other toughs were moving in, grinning unpleasantly. They believed they had us.

"Boys," I said, "you all know Drake Morrell, here. Drake's with me in this."

Suddenly Webb appeared on the porch, emerging from the saloon. His face was flushed, and he had been drinking, but there was still that lean, dark face, the straight hard brows. And he wore a gun.

When he looked at me he was smiling; it was a sardonic smile, a strange smile.

"I told them, Ben," he said cryptically, "but they wouldn't listen."

"Drake," I said calmly, "when the shooting starts, kill Pappin. Get five bullets into him, Drake.

"Cain, you, John, Neely, and Tom, you cut loose into that bunch over there." With my left hand I indicated the toughs.

"What about me?" Trotter demanded. "Ain't I in this?"

I laughed at him. "Ollie, I wouldn't let anybody have you but me, I'm taking you and the Reverend there, I'm taking you myself."

And I drew my gun.

They were not expecting it. We were still talking, and then it was there, in my hand. Now there's nobody can draw so fast you don't see it. That sort of stuff is told in stories for children, but there are men who can draw very fast . . . and when you take them off guard it is easy. There's such a thing as reaction time; it takes an instant for a thing to register on the mind, then the hand has to move. I was still talking, and they hadn't thought I'd do it, not with the women present. And my gun was on the Reverend.

Now I didn't believe an old sinner such as I knew him to be would have all that trust in the Lord. And he didn't. I saw his face turn kind of gray.

Webb chuckled. "See what I mean? You ain't gonna steal a march on Ben." He looked over at me. "Where do I come in, Ben? Looks like you've taken the play."

"Take anyone you choose, Webb. I never doubted you'd be here when the going got rough. You know you always were."

"I was, wasn't I? All right, I'm here. What'll it be, boys?"

Dad Jenn had not moved nor spoken, but he did then. "Why, I guess we go on with the 'lection. Isn't that what you want, Mr. Shafter?"

"It is," I said.

"And move easy, boys," Dad Jenn said quietly, "that gent back there in the barn loft door might not know what you're fixin' to do."

It was Ethan Sackett. He was up there, and he had a rifle in his hand.

Dad thought I'd planned it that way. He looked over at me. "You never miss a trick, do you?"

But we almost did. So much had happened, it had all been so close to shooting, so near to death. Dad Jenn set the ballot box out on the porch and we dropped in our votes, still wary, edgy, but nevertheless quite sure it was all over.

Drake Morrell voted and then stepped back where he could look on, as Ethan was doing. I was there, my gun holstered again, not really expecting anything.

Suddenly someone spoke and I felt a cold shot of fear go up my spine. "Cain Shafter? Can I speak to you a moment?"

It was Foss Webb.

TWENTY-EIGHT

He wore boots with his pants tucked in, a vest, and a gun hanging low. His hair was long under his beat up old hat and the down on his face was soft. His eyes were staring, glassy. He was frightened but trying to look bold and confident.

He had seen nothing of what had happened. He had not even heard that I was running for marshal in Cain's place. Somewhere he had been hiding out, working up his nerve for what they had planned.

"Foss!" Pappin spoke sharply, but I do not believe Foss even heard him. He was intent on doing what he had been thinking of, and he wanted to do it boldly and right.

"Cain Shafter, I come to ki . . . !"

His hand came out of his vest with the hideout gun, and Cain's hand dropped to cover Foss's gun hand.

Even I, his brother, had not known Cain was that sudden. He was always so quiet, so deliberate, so easy sure in his ways. His hand dropped, covered Foss's, and squeezed.

"What is it, Foss?" he said gently. "What do you want, boy?"

Foss screamed. His face went white, and his weak mouth twisted, and Cain released his grip; the gun fell from the broken fingers.

Cain glanced over at Webb. "I am sorry, Webb," he said. "The boy was going to kill me."

193

Webb came down the steps and walked up to Foss. "Boy," he said, "what were you thinkin' of? Cain's our *friend*!"

Nobody else moved. Cain touched Foss's arm, and Foss winced away from him. "I'm sorry, Foss. I didn't intend to squeeze so hard. Maybe you scared me."

Webb put his arm over Foss's shoulders. "Come on, son. We'd better go look at that hand."

They went away then, and we saw the ballot box emptied and the votes counted. John Sampson won by fifteen votes, I won by eight, and Ruth Macken by one. Folks just weren't used to the idea of a woman holding office.

Colly Benson came out of the saloon with a beer in his hand. He looked over at me, grinning. "I don't think I'll try an' shoot you," he said, "somehow or other you'd come up holdin' aces!"

"Thanks, Colly. You had me worried."

He laughed. "Yeah. I'll bet."

When we walked back up the hill Bud Macken looked at me. "Who are you going to arrest first?" he asked.

"Nobody . . . I hope."

"But what they did to Mr. Stuart!" he protested. "They stole from him, robbed him!"

"We'd have to prove it, Bud, but I don't think we'll have to."

Lorna poured coffee, and we sat around the table. Ethan came up to the house and squatted on his heels against the wall.

"What's the next move?" Neely asked.

"We do what we should have done before," Sampson said. "We will draw up a list of ordinances, keep them few and simple, just enough to keep an orderly town.

"It will have to be pretty much on our own say-so because it's a long way to any other authority, but there's none of us wants anything but peace and quiet with a chance to work."

"Seen a couple of buffalo over east of here, Bendigo. Like to have you ride out with me," Ethan suggested.

"Let's see what Moses Finnerly and Trotter will do."

"What do you think?" Croft wanted to know.

"I think they'll pull out. They already have some of Neely's gold, and they may figure they'd better take it and run before that investigation I promised can get started."

"Or they may make a fight of it," Drake Morrell said. "Ollie Trotter liked being the power around here. He was careful where he stepped, but when he thought he could get away with it, he stepped hard."

"Drake, do you know Henry Stratton?" I asked.

"Yes, I do. Eastern man, cattle buyer, rancher, and what not. I believe he's invested in the Union Pacific, too."

"We had a talk last night. He says that towns grow according to their natural advantages, and that ours has none. It has only the gold and the trail, and the gold doesn't amount to much, and the trail will gradually peter out when the railroad goes through."

"He is right, of course," John Sampson said. "I have been thinking of it. In fact, Cain and I have talked about it. So far we have all done rather well, trading with the movers, and we've lived by hunting, and our planting has been successful only because we've had good seasons, but now is the time to think about the future."

"My mine will help," Neely said. "I think the reason they wanted to get me to sign it over was because they had found something special."

"That's possible," Morrell said, "but that's but one resource. We'll need more."

We talked it around, but when all was said and done it boiled down to running cattle on the range and perhaps getting a contract to cut ties for the railroad. They would need them, and we were close to the Wind Rivers and a good supply of timber. I think when everybody scattered out to their homes we'd decided to pull in our horns, spend as little as possible, and begin planning for a move.

When I walked outside with Ruth Macken I looked up the hill at her house. "I'd hate to see it empty," I said, "I really worked on that floor."

"Nothing is wasted," she said, "you learned a lot in doing it, and had the satisfaction of seeing your work completed and pleasing to others."

"Maybe that's all there is," I said.

It was quiet in the town. Just before sundown I took a walk down the street, and there were few people around. Filleen sat before his livery stable, whittling. Rumson, who was agent for the stage line, was sitting with him.

I went into the saloon. It was a simple room with a bar along one side and a half dozen tables. There was a barrel with a spigot, several rows of bottles on the back bar, and some tin cups and glasses. On one of the tables there was a deck of cards, scattered as if from recent play.

Dad Jenn was behind the bar. A man named Bob Harvey who had recently come over the plains with a dozen head of Holstein milk cows and a bull, was sitting at a table with a beer.

Dad's eyes were cool and measuring, very wise old eyes in the
face of a man not that old. I suspected he had worked the
end-of-tracks Hell Towns as the tracks moved west and there was
little he had not seen.

"I don't know you, Mr. Jenn, so take no offense at what I am to
say. Serve good whiskey and good beer, no knockout drops, no
house-operated games. The first man who gets robbed in here,
unless you can show it was done by an outsider, and the place
gets closed. Run it clean and you stay open . . . all right?"

"Fair enough," he said. "It's easier for me."

He leaned his heavy arms on the bar and looked out at the
street. "Heard stories about you," he said. "You've made a name
for yourself with that gun."

"It is a name I do not want," I replied. "For this town I want
only peace, good business, and a chance to become something.
Perhaps it won't make it . . . many western towns do not . . .
but let's give it a chance."

He nodded his heavy head.

"We're going to set up a meeting of the town council," I told
him, "and we will want you there."

"Me? I figured you folks knew what you was about and wouldn't
have use for me."

"We think we know what we're about, but you're one of the
town's businessmen. We would appreciate your ideas. From what
I understand, Mr. Jenn, you've had experience with towns before
this one."

He chuckled. "If you're pleased to call them that. Most of them
were towns only as long as the end of the tracks was there." He
straightened up. "I'll come to your meeting, Mr. Shafter, and
gladly."

I made the rounds, stopping to talk to people, shaking hands. I
needed to know them, judge their potential for trouble or for
support, and to learn from them as well.

My ideas, such as they were, had been shaped by experience,
by listening to more experienced men talk at home and around
the west-moving campfires, and by reading Blackstone, Plutarch,
and Locke.

What is it that shapes a man's life? Heredity? Environment? Or
is there some unknown element produced by certain times and
conditions that will shape a man to meet it?

I began to see that the westward movement, the pioneer
movement, had been a selective process, and that those who
came west were possessed of something distinctive, for better or

worse. More courage? Well . . . possibly. Some primitive throw-back to the times of migration?

Men had migrated for one reason or another from the beginning of time, but those migrations had been by nation, by tribe, or by group. They had been directed by a witch doctor, a chieftain, a king or a general, or perhaps a messiah. Such was not the case in America. These migrations were created by a multitude of individual decisions, of personal decisions. No one said, "We will move." No one said, "Tomorrow you are to go."

In thousands of homes the issues were debated, and then a family in Virginia or Pennsylvania, a man in Indiana or Ohio, a woman in Missouri decided to go west. Each on his own, of his own, financed by himself. Individually they moved to Independence, to Freeport, to any of the towns where wagon trains made up. There they met others like themselves, banded together, chose a leader, and moved out into the vast plains to travel a thousand miles or more toward a destination that shimmered in the silvery distance, beyond the sky, beyond the grass, beyond the horizon.

Why did some go and others stay? I did not know. Cain had a successful business. He was an artisan, skilled and aware, he could do well wherever he was . . . why did he choose to go? And Neely? Irritable, complaining, never sure he had done the right thing, but nevertheless having the will to shake off the ties and move out.

No movement in history was like it.

Many were to die, killed by Indians, dead of thirst, hunger, cold. The Indians killed them and killed them, and still they kept coming from some endless stream, pushing on westward, fighting dust storm and snowstorm, crossing swollen streams, casting off bit by bit what they had brought west, retaining only those things inherent within them, the love of home, of law, or of church, school, and their independence. Possibly the only motivating force, understood or not, was a love of freedom for its own sake.

They had given me the job of maintaining order. I had no wish for power, no wish to control, only to keep the peace.

There can be no living together without understanding, and understanding means compromise. Compromise is not a dirty word, it is the cornerstone of civilization, just as politics is the art of making civilization work. Men do not and cannot and hopefully will never think alike, hence each must yield a little in order to avoid war, to avoid bickering. Men and women meet together and adjust their differences; this is compromise. He who stands unyielding and immovable upon a principle is often a fool, and often bigoted, and usually left standing alone with his principle while other men adjust their differences and go on.

I saw nothing of Moses Finnerly, Pappin, or Trotter, yet I watched for them, and was cautious.

Colly Benson was in the saloon when I returned. I sat down and bought him a beer. "Staying around?" I asked.

He grinned at me, that tough, cynical grin. "Want me to leave?"

"Not at all. I want you to stay." When he seemed surprised, I said, "You're a fair man, Colly. We had trouble back on the trail, but you did not allow your feelings toward me to influence your judgment of me. A man like you is an asset to any town."

He looked uncomfortable, then laughed. "Shafter, if I stay around we might have trouble. I'm a hard man to get along with, and you and me, we both carry guns."

"But we have judgment, Colly. You showed it back there on the trail. Many a hothead would have got himself killed. That man back in the brush had a rifle right on you, and there isn't a better shot west of the Mississippi. You used considered judgment. You were not in the least afraid, you just weighed the chances and made your decision."

"I would have stolen some of your cattle."

"I know that, but if I'd left you in charge of them they'd have been safe. You're not a thief, Colly, not by nature or inclination."

"I've rustled a few head."

"So have a lot of western men until they realized it wasn't the right policy. Think it over, Colly. I may need a deputy. In any case, the town needs men who are willing to fight, but above all, who know when to fight."

After a while I went up the hill to Ruth Macken's place. She was watering her flowers. "Is everything all right?"

"Quiet," I said. "I was wondering what was left in that book box of yours. I'm fresh out of reading."

She led the way inside.

The books I selected were Alexis de Tocqueville's *Democracy in America*, and John Stuart Mill's *On Liberty*, the last one published not long before we started west. Then I also took *The Conquest of Granada*, by Washington Irving.

We drank coffee and talked. There was a knock on the door, and it was Henry Stratton. "May I come in? This seems to be the most likely place for conversation and a quiet evening." He turned to me. "Your sister told me she had seen you coming up the hill."

A few minutes later Drake Morrell appeared, and I sat quiet and listened. As I heard them talk of far-off cities that I had never seen, of people whom both knew or knew of, of plays and books, of music and actresses, of politics and politicians, I could not help but realize how very little I knew.

Stratton was carrying a bundle under his arm. "By the way, I shall be leaving tomorrow, but I thought you might like these. Some I brought with me, some of them have come to me since I arrived."

They were newspapers from Boston, New York, and Philadelphia. Even one from London.

My hand went out to them, touching their pages, as I thought of that wider world of which I knew so little.

And where, I wondered, was Ninon?

TWENTY-NINE

The cattle came in on the third day after the election, and we were all down in the streets at the first call that they were coming. I think it was the first time the newcomers gathered with those of us who had settled the town to celebrate something that brought good to us all.

At the very least it meant an assured supply of meat for the winter. At best it meant the beginning of several herds and of a new industry.

Bob Harvey, who had brought the Holsteins to the town, was there to watch. "I'm starting a distribution of milk," he said to me. "Would Cain's family be interested?"

"Sure. Have you talked to John Sampson? They'll want milk, too."

"How many head have you got?" Harvey asked.

"I'll have to check. We may have added some calves, but it will number close to one hundred and seventy head. We'll graze them higher up in the mountains in the summer to get the best of that grass."

"What about Indians?"

"We'll run that risk, and keep a sharp lookout. We will have to use that mountain grass while we can."

The herd came quietly, up the one street of our town, and we bunched the cattle on a rough flat below Ruth Macken's place and

behind the town. Only a few of them, ten or twelve head of those
Stacy Follett had led us to, were longhorns.

Everybody came down to look them over, and I introduced
everybody to the Indians as well. Follett grinned at Drake Morrell.
"I ain't huntin' you no more. Those youngsters convinced me I
had to be wrong."

"Glad they were there," Drake agreed. "We might have killed
each other."

The cattle were in good shape. During the last part of the drive
the grass had been good, and they had come along at a moderate
pace. Now they settled down nicely, seeming to realize the long
trek was ended.

For several days, all was quiet. The Indians took the cattle to
the high meadows. Stacy Follett and Ethan went off into the
Wind Rivers, setting traps for fur and hunting game.

On Sunday Finnerly showed up for meeting, but only a handful
attended. Neely and the Crofts were up the hill at John Sampson's
service, and oddly enough, Webb showed up.

Cain went to him at once. "Webb, I'm sorry about the boy."

Webb shrugged. "He had it comin'. Damn' fool, listening to
that crowd. Well, you cured him of wantin' to be a gunman. It'll
be months before his hand's any good, if it ever is."

"I guess I shut my hand too hard," Cain said. "I forget my
strength sometimes."

They stood and talked, then went into meeting together. I was
the last to enter, standing for a while and looking down the street
of our town. Either it or I was changing, for once again it seemed
familiar and was no longer a town that had become strange.

Three Oregon-bound wagon trains came through that week,
and we did a brisk business. I traded two head of strong steer for
three used-up oxen and a saddle with fifty .44 cartridges thrown
in.

Bob Harvey started sinking a well, and Cain picked up a
contract to supply ties to the railroad. The season was late, but
our town prospered, and we had put away food against the
coming cold. We had jerked venison, stored potatoes, carrots,
and onions, as well as canned berries from our gathering along
the creeks.

As town marshal I drew fifty dollars a month, but I augmented
my income from time to time by repairing wagons for passersby,
and trading. I swapped a bridle woven from rawhide for a colt,
newborn and too weak to stand the trek to Oregon.

Follett insisted I add the cattle he had located in the box

canyon to my herd. "See here," he argued, "you made the drive, without you there'd have been no cattle here. Them cattle are mine to give or leave. You take 'em. I live on wild meat, shot with my own rifle, and I don't take to cow meat, nohow."

So, with two oxen for which I'd traded, I now had fifty head of cattle, four horses, and a colt. Then I swapped a bearhide for a day-old calf.

On the third week after election nobody showed up for Finnerly's service. His sermons had grown increasingly filled with bigotry and hatred, and people preferred John's reading and our singing.

Several times I encountered Finnerly. He passed me by without speaking. Pappin spoke always; Ollie was surly, avoiding me.

With the first snow in the high country we brought the cattle down. Cain, John, Bud, and I had cut hay from several meadows and stacked it against the winter.

Alongside the hay stacks we built a pole corral, made into a wall against the wind on the north side, and a shed to shelter some of the stock.

When I went up the hill for supper I was thinking of the newspapers Stratton had given me. For the first time it would give me a chance to see what was taking place away from our town, and I began to wonder about what had been happening in the world far from our valley.

Those newspapers, of which I read every item, showed me how things were in other communities, in places where life was less simple than our town. A lot of lawing in those days was settled by the local justice of the peace and never went beyond him.

Back east business was picking up, and there was much talk of what the Union Pacific would do for the business of the country when it was complete, which would be soon.

I began to realize how little I knew of our country and what made it work. The more I'd read and observed the more I realized that the best intentions in the world will get a man just nowhere unless he knows how to get results and can enlist the cooperation of others. And cooperation means compromise.

Used to be that I'd get impatient that evils were allowed to be. I figured there ought to be some way of just shutting them off. The trouble was, there was no way short of dictatorship, and that meant worse evils. What was needed was to take one step at a time, not to be too drastic, and to bring about the changes with the least amount of friction. No changes could be forced upon people. They had to want it, to be ready for it. And public life

demanded folks who would do a little more than they were paid
to do.

Being marshal of a small town was not a full-time job, and most
marshals worked at something else, too. However, this was the
town where I lived, so I looked around. There was a mudhole
shaping up where the watering trough stood, and in front of Dad
Jenn's where the hitching rail got the most use there would be a
dust pit come summer. Without saying anything to anybody I
hitched up a team and hauled gravel from a pit a few miles south.
Between times I dumped gravel by the trough and the hitch rail,
filled the mudhole, and gravelled a good part of the street. It was
only two blocks long. With rain and snow it should pack down
solid during the winter months.

I asked no help, used my own team, did the work with my own
shovel, my own sweat.

Every night I studied the papers. Red Cloud's Sioux were
raiding in the eastern parts of the Territory. There was talk of
splitting us off from the rest of Dakota and forming a new territory,
called Wyoming. I mentioned it, and Cain smiled. "You've been
gone, boy. That's already done.

"Grant's been nominated for president against Seymour, they're
about to try Jeff Davis for treason. They tried to impeach President Johnson, but lacked the votes. There's been a lot going on."

Due to Indian troubles the stage did not run regularly, and
only a rare passenger stopped off in our town. News was scarce,
unreliable, and usually devoted to the sensational aspects.

We checked out the number of men able to defend the town
and warned each to keep a rifle close by. Follett and Ethan were
usually off in the hills. I took to riding up on the ridge as I had in
the first days, so we would have ample warning if the approach of
Indians was not first observed by Follett or Sackett.

We had snow from time to time but the grazing was still good,
and we held the cattle on the open plain a couple of miles from
town.

Handling the herd was simple. We held them on the grass,
moved them occasionally to a new area, and kept our eyes open
for Indians or cow thieves.

THIRTY

The town was quiet then, for three months. The snow fell deep upon the land, few people were traveling, and I took time to help Cain with tie-cutting. His mill was busy on the railroad contract, and I was felling timber back in the Wind Rivers.

A last wagon train came through . . . they had been thinning out before snow fell, and we all felt sure it was not only the winter. Many people would now be waiting for the steam cars to run.

That last wagon train was a worn-out lot, their hearts heavy with grief. The Sioux had hit them hard, driving off some stock, killing four of their men and one woman. The long stretch ahead was too much for them, and they stopped right there at our town, circled their wagons, and came up to see us.

Stacy Follett, Ethan, and I were sitting in Dad Jenn's when their wagon boss came in. We invited him to sit down.

"We're quittin'," he said. "We ain't damn' fools and with that desert and all ahead, and it being too late to cross the passes through the Sierras, we're just going to cash it in."

"There isn't much to do here," I said. "How are you fixed for grub?"

"We got aplenty, even with what was burned when the Injuns raided us, but me, I got a brother down Texas way. He wanted me to come work with him but I was hot for Californy. I reckon

204

I'll sell my outfit if'n I can find a buyer, and I'll keep my saddle horse and ride out for Texas."

"What about the others?"

"Four or five of them are pulling out come daylight for the south. It's cold, but they reckon they can make it down to where the railroad's coming through and be settin' there come spring.

"Two, three families figure to stick around here, if they can find a place. Miller Pine, that actor feller, he's in no shape to travel . . . got bad lungs. He'll stay on. You'll find him a right pleasant man . . . got a thousand stories to tell, all worth hearin'." He looked at me. "Marshal, there's good folks in that outfit, and some not so good, but one and all they'll need cash money. If you got enough to buy with, you can make you a deal, startin' with me."

"What do you have to sell?"

"Four head of oxen, in bad shape, six head of beef cattle, four of them heifers, comin' fresh in the spring. I got a wood-burnin' stove, some tools, kitchen fixin's, and an old printin' press."

"A what?"

"Printin' press. I ain't no printer, but I come on a feller in Laramie . . . there at the fort . . . who was. He had run out of eatin' money, and it looked like he was never goin' to start no newspaper in Californy. He swapped it to me for a side of bacon, ten pounds of beans, and a crow-bait mule so's he could ride out of there."

Mentally I took count of what I had and it wasn't much, then I took count of what they needed, and it was a whole lot, so I walked down to the wagon circle.

Certainly, they would be fools to try to go further. Once down off the pass they'd miss most of the snow, but they might come into it again in Nevada, and there was no way they could cross the Sierra Nevada until spring. They were in much the same shape as we were only they didn't have a Ruth Macken, nor a Cain Shafter, when it came to that.

Their stock was in bad shape. The beef and milk cattle were doing fine . . . they'd just walked along and the grass had been all right. The wagon teams, whether horses or oxen, were pretty dragged out and beat, and so were the people. Listening, I could hear they'd had a time of it. Indian fights, one wagon and a family lost swimming a river . . . several head of stock lost in a stampede of buffalo . . . a man killed there, another with a broken arm and leg.

"I am not one to take advantage," I told them, "but whatever I bought I'd have to buy cheap. Cash money is hard to come by."

"We done talked it over. The families that stay in your town will need all they have, but we who are to travel, we'll need grub for traveling and some cash money when we get there, if it's only a dollar or two."

We did some dickering, and I ended up with four head of oxen, two of the heifers, and a few odds and ends. Finally, when all else was completed and the only thing left was the printing press, he looked over at me. "I can't pack that on no horse, mister. You give me ten dollars and it's yours."

Well, why not? And to tell the truth I was fascinated by the press, although I'd never seen one worked and had no paper to use in such a machine. He pocketed the ten dollars. "A town like this needs a newspaper, anyway," he added. "Now you can go into the business."

A week later I hired a driver and put my oxen to work hauling logs for the sawmill. When spring came I'd start them hauling to the railroad. The printing press I stored in the corner of John Sampson's barn loft where it would be dry and out of the way, yet it stuck in my mind. A man might do a lot with a printing press.

The winter settled in, cold and still.

At the mill we had a square dance and a box supper. Each of the girls and women prepared a box with a supper inside, and these were auctioned off to raise money for new hymnals for the church. The buyer of a box got to eat with the girl who fixed it.

By that time nearly everybody knew the good cooks, and of course, the pretty girls were obvious. Lorna was both, and her box brought the highest price of the evening, the prize going to Miller Pine. It was a fine, fun time, and the music sounded out over the cold snow. I went outside, looking off into the distance where the dark line of the road led over the snow.

Where was Ninon? She would be nearly fifteen now . . . maybe older. I did not know when her birthday was. Girls married at that age in the south before the War, and perhaps they still did so.

Suddenly the door opened, letting out the sound of laughter and of someone singing. It was Pine . . . and he was singing "Home, Sweet Home," the song I'd first heard sung by Ninon.

Lorna came up to me. "A penny for your thoughts."

"I'm lonesome," I told her, honestly enough.

"I know. Bendigo, Miller knows her. Knows Ninon, I mean."

"Knows her? How?"

"He played New Orleans a few months ago, and Ninon was there with her family. One of his company remembered her as an actress and pointed her out. He said she was gorgeous, one of the most beautiful girls he had ever seen."

"She was that. She was lovely."

"Why don't you go see her? She was in love with you, you know."

"She was a child. I saved them out in the snow that night and she made something of it. By now she's forgotten me."

"I don't believe it."

"Anyway, how could I go? She comes of wealthy people. I am a town marshal making fifty dollars a month. I own a few head of cattle, and my whole wealth represents what her folks might spend in a week . . . maybe even in a day."

"Ben, you can be anything you want to be. Drake Morrell thinks so. So does Mrs. Macken."

We stood there together in the crisp, cold air, and after a bit I suggested, "You'd better go in, Lorna. It is cold."

"All right." She turned to go. "Ben? Take me for a ride tomorrow?"

"All right. You and Miller, if you want him."

"Ben, you're silly. I'm not getting a case on him."

"On who, then?"

"That's just it, Ben. There isn't anybody for me, either."

She was right, of course, and we had that in common. I waited, watching the stars twinkling in the cold night sky, listening to the sounds.

There were a few lights scattered over the town but everybody was here, at the mill, celebrating. It worried me, so I went down the hill to Cain's, opened the door, and went in. It was warm inside, and still. I filled a coffee cup, then got out my Winchester and my gunbelt.

At the party I had been carrying my six-shooter in my waistband, but now I transferred it to the holster. Putting on my buffalo coat, taking up the rifle and my gloves, I went outside and closed the door softly behind me.

They were dancing again, and I could hear the stomp of feet, the voice of the caller, and the whining of the fiddler and the fife. Slowly, I walked down toward the street, my boots crunching in the snow.

It *was* cold . . . must be all of thirty below, and not a night when Indians would be feared. No Indian wanted to fight in cold weather, and they did not do it when it could be avoided.

Slowly, I made the rounds, stopping at each store or house, just listening. When I reached the end of town, I stopped. Miller

Pine, who had been a chemist before he became an actor, had opened an assay office, and it was now the last building on the street. It was dark under the awning, and I stood there, rifle under my arm, rubbing my gloved hands together to warm them. From here I could see down the road a piece, but I had a good view up the street when I turned, and a view also of Ruth Macken's place on its bench.

Just as I was about to start back up the hill my eye caught a flicker of movement, and I stopped where I was, looking up the hill.

Somebody was up there . . . Ruth and Bud were at the mill. I'd seen them only a few minutes before, noticing that Bud was probably the best dancer of us all.

The movement had not been outside, but inside the house . . . somebody had passed a window.

Imagination? Maybe.

I'd have a look. Walking out from under the awning, I went up the hill. It was a five-minute walk . . . and it gave me time for thinking, for wondering.

Who could it be? Everybody was at the party . . . or almost everybody. Finnerly and his friends were not there, nor old Mrs. Wilson, one of the newcomers. There were a couple more.

At the door, I paused, slipping the glove from my right hand to take the action of the rifle. With my left hand I opened the door.

The stove was warm, its sides glowing red from the heat. There was no light in the room except that from a lamp with its wick turned low, and seated in Ruth's rocking chair by the stove was my brother Cain. His pipe was lit, and he had both elbows on his knees. He looked up when the door opened.

"I knew your step, Bendigo. Set down."

Standing my rifle close by against the wall, I pulled up a chair, then took off the heavy coat and my other glove. I put them down together on the bench. "Nice and warm," I said.

"I didn't want her . . . them . . . to come home to a cold house. Bud forgot to bank the fire and it had burned to nothing."

"Lucky you thought of it. I was down by the assay office . . . saw something move."

We sat there for a while, and I was uneasy. There was more to it than that. I remembered now that Cain had been gone for some time. He never did care for dancing, always kind of sat back and let Helen enjoy herself.

Suddenly, Cain said, "Bendigo, you've got to ride out of here.

Don't take a chance on being caught here, don't waste yourself in this place."

"It's our town," I said, surprised. "We built it."

"Bendigo, we built ourselves a place against the wind, but that was for us. Don't let it be for you. There's a larger world out there . . . I don't know what it's like, really. I guess I'll never know . . . but I wish I did, I wish I had.

"I got caught, Bendigo, I was caught in a trap I set for myself."

"A trap? *You?*"

"I planned to go to New York, Bendigo. You know how it is with tools and me. I could always do just about anything, make about anything. I had some inventions . . . just little things, but I had ideas. I wanted my own shop, in time, my own factory. I had big ideas, Bendigo, but I believe there was no reason why they should not have happened."

Well, I just sat there. I remembered now, when I was just a youngster, a city man who kept coming to town and wanting Cain to go with him, offering to put up the money for Cain's skill and his knowledge, but by that time Cain was walking out with Helen.

"I've been here before, Bendigo, when they were visiting . . . just to sit and smoke."

"Does Ruth Macken know?"

"I think so, but she'd never say anything, nor will I. You know, Bendigo, it is the easiest thing in the world to forget a man's responsibilities, chuck it all, and go following some red wagon . . . but it isn't a man's way.

"Helen is my wife, and we've grown along together. We understand each other, we mesh like gears . . . and I'd never find another woman like her. I could go chasing off, calling it love or whatever a body wished to call it, and I'd only prove myself a damned fool.

"The world isn't built around people who do what they want to do, Ben, what they want regardless of who gets hurt. It is built by people who do what they *should* do.

"You've been reading a lot . . . Plutarch, and the like. Well, the old Romans built what they had by being strong, inside as well as out, and they lost it when they began giving in, going the easy way. They lost everything, Ben, when they ceased to be *men,* and a man is one who does what he has to do when it has to be done, and does it with pride."

"Are you in love with Ruth Macken?"

"Don't ask that question, Ben. Don't even think it. I am in love with Helen.

"Maybe . . . just maybe . . . had Ruth and I met at another time, another place . . . well, who knows? Maybe she feels the same way, but I shall never find out because I don't want to. I married Helen, and we've had warm, friendly, wonderful times together. We've the children, and we understand each other. Any damn' fool kid can go tomcatting off after everything he sees . . . takes no particular knowledge, skill, or much of anything."

Cain got to his feet. "I grew up a long time ago, Ben. And I am glad I did. I miss the dream, but maybe if I'd followed the dream I'd never have found anyone like Helen.

"The thing you have to remember are the *years*. Not the hours, not the days or nights, but the *years*. When you want a woman you want one you can live down the years with. I have been dreaming, too, Ben, not of anything I have wanted to happen, not of anything I expected to happen, but just a kind of romantic thing that was there in my mind. But do you know something? I am glad you came up the hill tonight, we've had a good talk, and I don't think I'll be coming back here again. Let's go back to the party, Bendigo."

We walked back down the hill, and neither of us ever mentioned it again. Snow crunched under our feet as we walked, the breath showed before our mouths, and we heard the music as we went toward the mill.

Ruth looked up as we came in. She looked at Cain, and then at me, but she said nothing, nor did she move.

Slowly, I worked my way around, speaking to people, stopping to talk here and there. Webb was standing off by himself, and I stopped there beside him, not saying a word. After a while he said, "Nice evening, Ben. We need more like this."

"You helped make it possible, Webb. You did as much as any of them."

"It was Ruth Macken and Cain," he said, "and you."

"Webb, don't you ever forget. You were always there when the going was rough. You never sidestepped, you never welshed.

"You know something, Webb? I always knew you'd be there. I never even had to look."

"Thanks," he said, and a little later he went out, and just at the door, I stopped him. "Webb, Foss ought to be here. You tell him we'd like it if he'd come up and dance a couple."

Webb stood a little straighter. "Shafter, we don't need any . . ." He stopped then and stood watching the dancers. "He'd like to come. He was blue about it, Ben. He was afraid nobody'd speak, nobody would dance with him."

"Tell him to come on up. Hell, Webb! This is our town! He was one of the first of us!"

Maybe a half hour later, the door opened a crack and Foss stepped in. His hand was still bandaged up, but he had his hair slicked back.

Well, I caught Lorna's eye and moved my head a little, and she was over there. She danced with him, and Helen did, and then Ruth, and Mae Stuart.

Miller Pine, he led the singing of "Darling Nelly Gray," "Comin' Through the Rye," and "Annie Laurie," and then we broke up, stood around outside talking a mite, but it was cold for much of that, so we went home in the crisp, still air, the snow sparkling with a billion tiny stars.

One more time I walked around, making sure, from a distance, that Ruth and Bud got safely up the hill. They had a warm house waiting . . . with some smell of tobacco smoke in it.

Maybe that was just as important to comfort as a warm fire.

I don't know why it was, but that night when I went to sleep I was thinking of that printing press.

THIRTY-ONE

Miller Pine had brought with him a half dozen novels as well as a sheaf of plays, some of which he had performed, some in which he had hoped to appear. He let me have these to read, and I went through them quickly, fascinated and amused.

Anna Cora Mowatt's *Fashion; or Life in New York* was the first, followed by *The Black Crook*, by Barras. Then *The Octoroon*, by Dion Boucicault, and *Rip Van Winkle*, as played by Joseph Jefferson.

The days were bitter cold, there were frequent storms, and I found myself going again and again into the woods to haul fuel for the town. It was a task that needed all our efforts.

There was no travel. The stage ceased to run, the roads and trails were deep in snow, but there was constant fear of the spring. The Sioux were increasingly restless, we heard, and with spring there was certain to be trouble.

Several times I had gone to Sampson's loft to look at the printing press. Drake Morrell had worked as a printer's devil, or sort of errand boy and assistant to a printer, and explained much about it.

Occasionally I visited the Indians in their dugout near Ethan's, listening to their stories, talking of hunts and legends and stories of the past.

Often in the evening we would gather at Ruth's or Cain's,

talking politics, planning for the day when Wyoming would be a state, and of course there was much talk, and some joking about women's rights. Most of us were in favor of women voting, and in our own private elections they'd been doing it all along.

As marshal there was little to do. The bad ones had holed up for the winter, and ours was a peaceful people, too busy keeping ourselves warm and supplied with meat and fuel to create trouble.

When the storm broke, Ethan, Bud Macken, and I saddled up.

Ethan and I rode up to Ruth Macken's before daylight, but she was an early riser always and had coffee on and breakfast making. "Sit down, you two . . . and thanks for asking Bud. He's been wanting to go."

"We're going to scout back of Beaver Rim and maybe up the canyon. Maybe we can scare up a deer or an elk."

"By the way, Mr. Trask told me you could buy paper in Salt Lake . . . for your printing press."

That made it almost too easy. The trouble was, there was no way a man could make a living with a printing press in our town, even if he could sell some papers to the other settlements that were filling in along the creeks.

"There aren't enough people," I said, "but I've given it some thought."

"I am not sure, Ben. It isn't the deserted place it was. There have been some new miners moving in on Hermit Creek. They moved into those abandoned cabins over there and are getting ready for spring. There's some others on Willow Creek."

It was something to consider. Riding around over the country, I'd noticed a couple of small communities had sprung up, at least one of them abandoned shortly after the first snowfall.

"Ben," Bud interrupted, "there's a paper published over at Fort Bridger now. Called the *Sweetwater Mines*. Mr. Trask left a copy last time he was through."

The three of us started for the hills. It was a quiet, sunny morning. The snow was not deep on the level, and as always the folks in town were short of meat. The game had left the low country because of the people around, so we headed up the valley.

The Wind River Range was magnificent, covered with snow, only here and there a sheer face of rock showing black and bare against the whiteness. We saw rabbit tracks aplenty, but a man can starve to death eating rabbits . . . there just isn't enough nourishment in their meat . . . and we were hunting bigger game, hoping for an elk or two . . . if we were lucky a buffalo, although there were few of those around at any time.

We hadn't gone far when we saw two riders approaching. We pulled up and waited for them. It was Uruwishi and Short Bull.

"You hunt for meat?" Uruwishi asked.

"Yes, and you?"

"Also," Short Bull said.

"Ride with us," I suggested. "I would learn from the wisdom of Uruwishi."

We rode in silence for some distance, riding single file and weaving our way through the pines toward the higher country. Around us was the stillness of winter, with no sound but that of our own movements, the creak of leather, the occasional sound of metal, the hoof falls of the horses.

When we stopped again to let our horses rest, Uruwishi gestured toward the Big Horns, which lay off to the east. "Many days' journey to the north there is a place, a place to see. It is a stone wheel . . . a Medicine Wheel."

"A wheel?"

"Many days. It is high . . . a high, far place where a man can look all around. The Wheel is of stones."

"Standing up?" I was incredulous.

"On the ground. Many stones maybe so high"—he showed his hands two to three feet apart, moving them slightly as he spoke—"and many spokes."

"Who built it?"

He shrugged. "Who knows? The People Who Came Before It Was Light . . . maybe the Little People. They were there."

"Have you been there?"

"Once . . . when I was a papoose. My father prayed there, to the Great Spirit."

He turned his horse slightly. "I think it *is* a Medicine Wheel . . . I think it is *big* medicine. I think many moons, many lifetimes ago people came there to pray, to sit in thought upon the grass around the Wheel.

"On some of the ridges there are stone arrows that point the way."

"You say it was built long ago?"

"Long, long ago . . . it was built when the animals with long noses and long teeth were hunted. Men carved their bones then, and scratched upon them to count the moons, and to remember the planting times."

"Animals with long noses?"

"Bigger than buffalo . . . long hair. Noses they curled back when they charged. The people who lived before my people hunted them with spears, drove them into swamps, and stoned them for their meat."

"Do many Indians come to the Medicine Wheel? From many tribes?"

"They come."

"Why?"

"There is magic there. Nobody knows why . . . only that it is there. The Cheyenne know . . . they built their medicine lodges like the Wheel."

"Will you take me there, Uruwishi?"

The old Indian was silent. Then he said, "I am old, and it is a long way, yet I should like to see it again before I die. If the Great Spirit has not come for me when the snow is gone, I will ride with you."

"He is too old for that," grumbled Short Bull. "He will die there."

Uruwishi shrugged. "Then I shall die . . . who is it who lives forever? My days are finished . . . long ago I believed I was to die, and I sang my song of death, and then this white man came and he did not say, 'Sit by the fire, Old One.' He said, 'Come ride with me.' And I felt young again. What there is of my life is his, for he has given it to me. Where should I die? Seated by the fire? I who killed the great bear? Who hunted the buffalo and the wolf? Who drove the Blackfeet into their canyons? Am I to sit like an old squaw and wait for death? *I am a warrior! I am a chieftain!*

"When I swung my club, men fled! When I took up my bow the bears trembled!" He glanced sidewise at me, his old eyes twinkling. "These young ones! What do they know?"

"We will ride then, Old One. We will ride when the snow is gone!"

Higher we rode, skirting a canyon wall. Down below the water rushed, its banks edged with ice. We saw, suddenly, the tracks of elk . . . a half dozen or more. Uruwishi rode ahead, following the trail.

Snow tumbled from the heavily laden branches of the spruce. We rode single file again, trusting only the well-marked way. I was close behind Uruwishi. Suddenly we saw them. The elk were moving slowly across a clearing several hundred yards ahead and at least three hundred feet lower. It was a temptation to shoot, but the distance was hard to judge due to the snow and the lower level at which they moved.

Yet the wind was from them toward us, and they seemed to have no idea they were followed. We moved on, slowly, watching them into the timber on the far side. Minutes later, we were crossing the same snow.

Suddenly Uruwishi drew up, pointing at a limb where the snow had been brushed away. "Lion!" he said.

Evidently the lion had stretched on the limb, awaiting the elk, then the elk had passed too far away from him and now, judging by his tracks, he was stalking the elk.

Watching as we rode, we saw the lion's tracks stretching away before us, sometimes parallel to the elk trail, sometimes following right up the elk tracks.

On a slope where the snow had slid away toward the canyon's bottom, we saw the elk feeding. The cat was nowhere to be seen.

"Big one," Short Bull said.

Bud Macken rode up beside me. "Can I have a shot?"

"We don't want him, Bud. We want elk meat."

"You told me yourself it was good meat," Bud protested. "Stacy Follett said it was the best ever, and Ethan likes it."

"Maybe," I said, "but there isn't enough. We need a couple of elk . . . at least."

We edged along closer, the wind remaining the same. Still we saw nothing of the lion. It was unlikely he would attack a human, though when hungry they had been known to attack men, women, and often children. Our fear now was that the lion might frighten the elk before we were in position for a shot.

We had no animosity for the lion. He was hunting meat the same as we were, and usually predatory animals killed only the easy ones, the weak, the aged, and sometimes the young. The only thing was, we didn't want him to scare off the elk.

Ethan and I got down from our horses, and Short Bull did likewise. "Bud, you stick with Uruwishi. You'll get your chance."

"Aw, Ben! I figured . . ."

"Bud, we need meat. This hunt isn't for sport. All of us back there need meat if we're going to last the winter. After we get a couple of elk, you'll have your chance."

"Ben . . . ?" he protested.

"No," I said flatly. "You stick with the Old One. Listen to his wisdom. I've learned from him, and you can."

"All right," he said grudgingly, and took the reins we handed him. I knew how he felt, but we dare not risk missing a shot.

We had brought snowshoes, and now we put them on and moved out, taking our time. The elk had found a good place to feed and were unlikely to move unless frightened. Later, if unmolested, they would go to places where they could rest and wait out the day.

It was a slow business, and the air was cold. We moved with extreme care, working our way nearer and nearer. Short Bull was like a ghost. "We should have brought the Old One," he whispered once, "he can charm them to be still."

Finally I found the spot that I wanted. A clear field of fire, just over a hundred and fifty yards, and no branches in the way. There was a projecting limb that would serve as a rest, at just the right height.

"This is for me," I whispered. "I want the bull with the big rack of horns, and if I get a second shot, I'll take that one feeding by itself over there."

They agreed and moved on. A minute or two later, I saw Ethan stop. Short Bull was working closer and closer. I found a good spot for my feet and settled them in place, taking a sight on the big bull, relaxing and checking again.

Glancing over at Ethan, he lifted a hand to indicate his readiness. Short Bull had vanished, then suddenly he appeared, not more than seventy yards from the elk.

One elk had lifted her head . . . suddenly wary. I could see it in the poise of her head, the flicking of her ears. She was not just listening, not just testing the wind, she was suspicious.

I took my sight, trying for a neck shot, relaxed a bit, and eased out my breath tightening my finger ever so gently. The rifle leaped in my hands, and the bull took a magnificent leap forward. I knew I had scored a hit, and turning swiftly I caught the second one in a blur of action as it leaped, but I had thought of the swing, timed it in my mind, and the finger pressure was just right as I came on target.

The echoes of my shots were lost in the boom of Ethan's big .50 and the hard *spang* from that of Short Bull.

My big bull was down and threshing in the snow. The second one had vanished into the brush. Both Ethan and Short Bull had scored. There would be meat in our lodges tonight.

We went down through the snow to recover our meat. I glanced where the elk had stood at which I had fired my second shot. There was blood on the snow.

Red blood . . . it looked like a lung shot. Well, I'd been holding higher.

"I'm going after the other one, Ethan," I told him. "I scored on him."

Bud had ridden up, leading our horses. "He may run a long way. Do you have to go after him?"

"We need meat, Bud," I said, "but we want clean kills. I'll not have an animal suffering out there in the snow."

He knew, but he wanted to hear me say it. That's one way of learning, to have things repeated, but it settled the idea in his mind. He had asked me questions like that before, and in my time, I had asked them of Cain . . . and of Ethan, for that matter. Yet it was Uruwishi with whom I really wished to spend time.

I went off, moving at a swinging trot, following the trail. The elk had been a young one, but strong. I'd known them to run a mile or more with such a shot, but after seeing a few more drops of blood I was sure this one would not go so far.

In the excitement of the chase I had forgotten all else. I had forgotten my friends for the moment, and I had forgotten the lion.

The trail was downhill, winding through brush and scattered trees, with lots of young stuff springing up among the deadfalls and boulders. Suddenly, I thought I glimpsed the elk a couple of hundred yards away, and still struggling through the snow. It had gone down, gotten up, and plunged on, but now the deepening snow was slowing it down. I took my time, not wanting to fire again.

Back up the slope I could hear the voices of my comrades, but I was alone here.

To work up a sweat was no part of my plan. Pausing, I caught my breath, then moved on. The last thing I wanted was for the elk to go further down the slope. Taking it back to where the horses were would be a formidable task, but perhaps easier than bringing the horses down and moving them back in the deep snow.

I went up to within a dozen yards of the elk, but it lay sprawled on the snow. I was quite sure it was dead, yet I waited.

It was very still. Now, with more trees between us, I could no longer hear my friends, although had they called out no doubt it would have been clearly heard.

The Wind River Mountains towered above us, craggy, snow-covered, and lonely. As I looked I saw the wind catch a bridal veil of snow and draw it for an instant past some bare rocks, then pass on to leave them still bare.

The elk was dead. I put my rifle down on a deadfall after brushing its roots free of snow. Then I opened my sheepskin jacket and taking out my hunting knife, I dropped on one knee beside the elk to begin the skinning-out process.

Something scraped bark up and behind me, and I half-turned, a move that may have saved my life. Something struck me a tremendous blow on the shoulder and back, I felt a rush of hot, fetid breath, and jaws grabbed the upturned collar of my sheep-skin coat; in a panic I swung my knife back and around. It was razor-sharp, and I felt it strike home and jerked back and out on it.

Bent forward as I'd been, the heavy collar had stood straight out, my neck actually several inches away from it. His jaws had closed hard on that collar . . . I'd seen many deer killed by lion, and several horses, and that initial strike and bite usually did the job.

The lion's claws slashed at me, but I managed another slashing cut. We were in a frenzy of whirling cat, man, snow, and branches of the deadfall. No doubt they saved me on more than one occasion in those wild seconds. I thought nothing, felt nothing. It was a crazy struggle for life, and in that instant I was transformed into an animal at bay.

Turning sharply, I struck back with the knife again, barely hooked some flesh, and the lion fell free of me as I heaved myself up. Wounded, it sprang at me, and I had sense enough not to try to escape. To have tried to back away would have made me vulnerable, more so than I was, and I sprang at the cat, trying to get inside. I had my knife low down now, cutting edge up, and as we came together I drove my sheepskin covered forearm between his jaws, forcing it back so hard he could not bite, and then I ripped in and up with the knife, withdrew, stabbed again and again.

With my forearm filling its jaws the lion could not snap or tear. Again I stabbed with the knife. The powerful hind legs doubled, the wicked claws trying for my belly, then I stabbed again, and the lion dropped away from me.

Crouching, snarling, tail lashing in fury, the lion stared at me while I waited, swaying on my feet. Up on the slope I heard shouts, yells, and a crashing in the brush as my friends started down.

The lion made as if to leap, but the crashing in the brush made it hesitate, and I took a step back, toward my rifle. The cat snarled, and I knew it was no good trying for the rifle. Slowly, carefully, I shifted the bloody knife to my left hand and reached back for my pistol.

I drew it, not too fast, suddenly aware that my hand was bloody and wet. Lifting the gun slowly, I eased back the hammer, and the lion sprang at me. The hammer dropped and the heavy .44 slug caught the lion in the chest. Instantly I fired again, the power of the two hard-driven bullets doubling the lion up. It fell, and I stepped back, holding the gun ready, but it did not move. It was dead . . . quite dead.

Slowly I holstered my gun. Blood was on my hand, and all at once my friends were around me.

Ethan ran to me. "You all right?"

I just looked at him. "You tell me." Suddenly I backed up and sat down on the deadfall and began to shake all over.

Bud Macken was staring at me, awed. Short Bull went to the lion and turned it over with a grip on a leg. There were a half dozen stab marks; one, which we decided was my first one, had struck right through the lion's stomach, ripping a deep gash.

"We got to get you home," Bud said.

"Build a fire," I suggested, "melt some snow."

Ethan carefully took off my sheepskin jacket. It was ripped and torn, but without a doubt it had saved my life. The collar was bitten through and torn but the thickness had defeated the lion, as had my arm shoved back in his jaws too far for him to get the right leverage; and the thickness of the sleeve had protected me to a degree.

Yet the teeth had gone through the sleeve and bitten into my arm, not deeply, but enough to start the blood flowing, and there were lacerations on my legs as well, partly protected by the thick shotgun chaps I was wearing.

Ethan got a fire going and Short Bull and Bud put together a lean-to partly covered by the fresh elk hide. Then, with Ethan's help I bathed the wounds in hot water. I knew that the teeth and claws of a lion are usually poisonous from decayed meat, but nowhere had they penetrated very badly.

"They don't often jump a man," Ethan commented, "he must have seen the back of your coat, figured it was a part of the elk or that some other animal had jumped his elk."

When I was dressed again, the meat was cut out and hung up in a tree. We broiled some steaks over the fire, and settled down for the night.

Bud had gone back up the hill with Short Bull and brought down the horses. We'd planned to start back, but there was no chance of that now, and I was shaking . . . I wasn't as tough as I thought.

Ethan looked around at me as we sat by the fire. "Folks back east would never believe that," he said, "you whuppin' a catamount. You should write it up."

THIRTY-TWO

The shock of the attack hit me later, and long after the others were asleep I lay shivering in my blankets. Finally I rolled over, put more wood on the fire, and decided trying to sleep was no use.

The incident showed me on how short a string our lives were lived. There had been no way to prepare for such an attack. We had known the lion was about, but the idea that it would attack a man when others were close around had not occurred to us.

It was a big lion . . . not the biggest I ever saw, but it weighed about one hundred and seventy pounds, we figured. This wasn't the first lion I'd killed. I'd hunted them back east and killed a few, and I'd killed a half dozen, one time or another, since coming west. A lion stalking deer will try to get right up close before he makes his jump, often as close as four feet, and he likes to stalk a deer in thick brush, yet a big male, jumping downhill, would sometimes leap as much as twenty to twenty-five feet.

Thinking of all that as I lay there awake, I suddenly recalled what Ethan had said about me writing it up.

I'd read lots of writing, but had never thought of doing it myself. But I had thought of a newspaper, and that made me wonder if there weren't papers or journals or something back east that would publish something about the west, or about wild animals.

222

Maybe that was the answer. Maybe if I wrote some of what I knew I might get it published and then get a job on one of those eastern papers. It was a kind of wild idea, and I said nothing to anyone about it but started to think out what I'd say about lions, and the next thing I knew it was morning and the fire was burning, the coffee smell was in the air, and I was the last one to awaken. Even Bud was up before me.

Yet when I started to move, I groaned. They all looked around at me, but it wasn't the wounds. It was my back where that lion had hit me when he jumped . . . it was bruised, and badly. I didn't need to see it to know.

After a while I wrestled around and got myself up, tugged on my boots, and shrugged into what was left of a good sheepskin coat. I put on my chaps and eased up to the fire to partake of some fresh elk meat, biscuit, and coffee.

Ethan watched me putting the meat away and commented sarcastically that being jumped by a lion surely hadn't interfered with my appetite.

Drinking coffee, I studied on my idea of the night before. In the clear light of day I didn't shape up to have much chance, but I surely had access to the material. Between Ethan Sackett, Stacy Follett, and old Uruwishi I had men who knew as much about wilderness living, hunting, and wild animals as anybody alive.

We had meat enough, so we packed up and started down the canyon. Climbing out would have been a struggle, loaded like we were, so we decided we'd try going down canyon, knowing all the while that we might run into a big fall we couldn't go around and have to go all the way back. We lucked out, found a dim trail out of the canyon, and climbed out to a bench that followed along for miles.

The snow was patchy, and here and there the ground where the sunlight could reach was soggy from melting. Ethan was riding point and of a sudden he pulled in, looking up at a tree.

When the rest of us drew up and looked we saw the claw marks of a big bear . . . a bear stakes out his territory that way, standing up and reaching as high as he can before digging his claws into the bark. If a strange bear comes around and he can't reach that high, he keeps on traveling. Well, the bear that made these tracks was *big*.

Ethan looked at those claw marks and turned to us. "Either that bear was standing on top of a mighty big drift or I'm leaving the country!"

Of course, that was what had happened. Some bear, disturbed

in his hibernation or perhaps just restless and without a full stomach, must have come here when the snow was drifted deep. We all understood that, but Ethan always enjoyed telling about those claw marks. "Why," he'd say, "they must have been seventeen feet above the ground! I'm tellin' you, mister, I'll never go up that canyon again."

We hightailed it down the side of the canyon, riding through patchy forest, weaving among tumbled rocks and clumps of dense brush. We saw an elk ahead, and his head came up. "All right, Bud," I said, "there he is, and he's yours."

Bud took out his rifle, stepped down from the saddle and Injuned up a few yards closer. The wind was right, and he made it. I was waiting, afraid he would get buck fever, but he didn't. He squeezed off his shot.

The elk leaped, ran a few steps, and dropped.

We rode up, butchered him out, and while that was going on I went down to the stream to get a drink. The ice only fringed the banks; the center of the stream was running too fast to freeze. The water was so cold it made my teeth ache. I was just getting up when I saw something gleam down there on the sandy bottom, and I reached for it.

When I pulled my hand out of the water I looked at it, and what I held was gold.

It was a nugget, of rough gold, showing no sign of stream action at all, and it must have weighed an ounce or more.

Now it could be one of its kind, but it hadn't been under water long, and it hadn't traveled far, or some of that roughness would have been worn down by batting around among the rocks.

I stood up, dried my hands on my chaps a mite, then slipped that nugget into my pocket.

For a moment I stood there, listening to the talk on the bank about thirty yards off, then carefully I studied the layout.

That stream ran cold and fast where I stood, running over rocks polished smooth by the water, but upstream not more than fifty yards it cut through a ragged old ledge of crumbling rock.

There was a good chance that gold had come right from there, but I'd no idea of climbing back up there. In the first place my back was badly bruised, and every twist it got hurt something fierce, and second I didn't want anybody noticing or talking about what I'd done. I climbed back up the bank, then stopped and took in the layout.

The west is littered with lost mines, some good, some not, but those lost were usually lost because the finder was so excited he didn't find the right landmarks to guide him back. Everybody expects to come right back, but that's rarely possible due to one reason or another, so I took far-out landmarks, then closer ones, trying to find objects and estimate distances that would not be the same from any other direction.

We made it back to our town just after sundown, and sure enough, it turned into snow that night and by daylight the snow was eight inches deep on the level and drifted deep in every draw and canyon.

To make matters worse, one of those claw marks developed some infection with fever, and it was several days before I could get out and around.

One thing I did do. While lying in bed or sitting up I wrote a few pages on mountain lions. First, I noted down everything I knew about them, taking several days to recall it. I knew some people claimed a lion never killed except for meat, but that wasn't true. I'd seen a lion kill a doe and two fawns in just a minute or two, eat part of the meat, bury the rest under branches and such, and leave it. Occasionally a lion would come back to a kill, but only rarely would he eat from it again though he might move it to a fresh place so the meat would not spoil as fast.

When I had it all down I got out those newspapers I had and reread some of the stuff they'd published to see how others had done it, and then, trying not to be fancy for I didn't know a lot of words, I wrote everything I knew about mountain lions. I described a couple of hunts, including the lion who'd jumped me, only I wrote it like it was somebody else.

Stacy Follett dropped by Cain's one night, and I started him talking. He'd known of two men, one an Indian, one a white man who had been attacked and killed by mountain lions, and when he had gone I noted down what he had said.

Meanwhile I made notes on the location of the gold just as though it were material for an article on where we had killed the elk.

So far no gold had been found in quantity in the area, although Neely had taken out a good bit over the past two years, and Webb had also made a fair living from his claims.

Mail came through just before Christmas, and with the rest of it a bundle of newspapers, some of them dating from months back, but new to most of us. News came through by the occasional travelers, and it was rumored that by spring the telegraph wire was to come to our town.

Finally I put together my account of the mountain lion and

mailed it away. Without waiting for results I wrote an account of the cattle drive from Oregon to our town, including the stories of the gun battles, but writing it as though I wrote of somebody else. Then, suddenly filled with ambition, and having little else to do but rustle firewood and meat, I wrote an account of the rescue of Mae Stuart and the children from the Indians.

Most of what I had read would lead one to think that Indians were all of a kind, and even before I heard about the first story I received a letter from an editor doubting that the older Indians would sit quietly by while a white man knocked one of them out. Well, Indians had their personal animosities as much as any white men, and that young buck needed taking down a notch.

The long, cold days gave me time to think, and much of the work that needed to be done was the kind that was conducive to thinking. When a man is sawing wood his mind is free to wander, and mine did. So much was happening in the outside world of which I knew too little. The newspapers were telling me of it, and from a distance it seemed exciting, important, and filled with color. Yet even as I thought that, I knew that here on the frontier, what we were doing was even more important.

At night I would spend hours reading the papers that had been forwarded to me, papers from New York, Chicago, and Omaha, mostly. They had started an elevated railroad in New York, on Ninth Avenue, and the American-made pianos, Steinway and Chickering, had startled the world by winning first prizes at the Paris Exposition.

Nebraska had become a state. Jefferson Davis, who had been president of the Confederacy, had been released on bail put up by Horace Greeley, Cornelius Vanderbilt, and Gerrit Smith.

President Johnson had fired his Secretary of War, Stanton.

A man named Sholes had patented a typewriter and sold the rights to Eliphalet Remington . . . whoever he was.

They had even passed a law giving only an eight-hour day to government workers . . . it was getting so nobody wanted to work any more.

There was no letter from Ninon.

More and more I was thinking about that trip with old Uruwishi to the Medicine Wheel.

More travelers were coming along, despite the cold and the snow. Business had more than tripled over the past year, and although other settlements around had trouble, the bad ones avoided our town.

Colly Benson had built himself a dugout not far from Ethan and was snugged down for the winter. When I was out of town, he walked the streets and wore the star.

When he pinned it on, he gave me a hard-eyed smile. "What you tryin', Ben? You want to make an honest citizen of me?"

Tipping back in my chair, I grinned at him. "Not you, Colly. I'm just trying to keep the others honest."

"What's this talk about you going north come spring?"

"Ever hear of the Medicine Wheel, Colly?"

He nodded. "Yeah, I heard some talk. Never knew anybody who'd seen it. Just a ring of rocks, isn't it?"

"It is more than that, I believe. It's some sort of a religious symbol or shrine for some long ago Indians. I'd like to see it."

"Yeah." Colly knocked the ashes from his pipe and began scraping it with a knife point. "You know, when I was a youngster I lived down along the Carolina-Georgia border, and ma she went out one day and was washing clothes down by the river. When she came back she had a flat kind of dish, engraving around the edge. She'd found it stuck into the earth in the riverbank.

"We went down an' dug around some and we found ten, twelve pots, all the same kind. We washed them up and used them for years. It was better stuff than I ever saw among the fifteen or twenty Injun tribes I've had dealin's with. Which reminds me. There was a man back yonder in our village who'd been a ship's captain. He had him all kinds of stuff, spears, shields, pottery, baskets, everything like that. He'd picked it up in the South Seas or the like.

"Well, he had him one basket there that had a thin strip of oak for the rim. It was tied fast with some other strips, but it was a beautiful job. One day when I was talking to him a friend of ours, a Cherokee man, he came to see the Cap'n. He seen that basket and claimed it was Cherokee, but the Cap'n, he told him he'd gotten that basket in South America."

After he went away I sat for a long time thinking about the Indians. There were so many questions I wanted to ask, so many answers I needed, and I did not know where to find the answers. Worst of all, it was the old Indians like Uruwishi who had the answers, and so many times nobody asked them, and they'd never figure a white man to be interested. And of course, some of it was not to be told to any stranger.

Ethan came in that afternoon. "Seen some pony tracks, over east of here," he said. "They've been looking us over."

"Sioux?"

"Uh-huh. Ben, I don't want to worry the women-folks, but

come spring we're in for trouble. It's in the wind." He hesitated. "You know, the Sioux were pushing west when the white man interfered . . . they got themselves horses back there on the Wisconsin-Minnesota border country and they fanned out, their war parties raided south and west as well as north. They were headed toward conquering the whole country."

There was something in that. The horse had changed the Sioux from an earthbound people, hunting on foot and using only the dog for a beast of burden, to a mounted warrior, as fierce as any the old world ever knew. He was a knight without armor, fierce, indomitable . . . a conqueror.

West there were the Crow and the Blackfeet, both tribes of fighting men, the Blackfeet in particular. What would have happened when they collided no man would now know, but in America as in Africa a conquering tribe met the white man face to face. In Africa the Bantu, migrating slowly southward down the centuries, had met no enemy they could not subdue, and then they met the white man coming up from the south. What was left of the Hottentot and the Bushmen was caught in the meat-grinder between them.

1865 had been the bloody year on the plains, with the Sioux driving hard in attack after attack against soldiers, wagon trains, settlers. In 1866, just before Christmas, the Sioux destroyed the Fetterman command, wiped them out to a man. In 1867 there had been the Wagon-Box fight, led by a more skillful soldier who understood the Indian way of fighting, and they had defeated . . . or at least held off . . . the Sioux.

Some of this I said aloud. Ethan shrugged. "The Sioux and the Blackfeet have come together a time or two, and the Sioux and the Crow never did get along, far's I know.

"The Shoshone now, they're friendly. Most of that country we're going to pass through come spring will be their territory. Chief Washakie's no fool, and he's ready for peace. His tribe's not big enough, even with the Bannock's to help to keep off the Sioux, so he wants allies. He's doing just what they've been doing in Europe for years, he's getting allies where he can, and if he can't get us to help he can be sure we won't attack him whilst he's busy with the Sioux."

"I'm going east, Ethan."

The decision was suddenly made, right then. I suppose it had been in my mind for a while, but now it was out in the open where I could rope and tie the idea and inspect the brand.

He chuckled. "I figured you'd be doing that. You comin' back?"

"Of course."

"Drake's been hoping you would go. He's worried about Ninon, and he figures you're the man for her. She'll be sixteen or so now, and girls are gettin' married at that age all over the country."

"I do want to see her, but I've got nothing, Ethan. Her folks have money."

"I ain't worried about you. Neither is Henry Stratton."

"Stratton?"

"He told Drake Morrell he thought you were a coming man. He thinks you should go into politics."

It was a flattering thought, but I was not so sure. Who knew of me outside our little area? And what did I know of politics? Only enough to know there was an art to it far beyond what most men realized. Getting elected was one thing, but putting over a program after you were elected was another . . . much more difficult.

Once I'd put my decision into words I knew it was what I must do. Colly Benson was handling the town as well as I could, and it would give me a chance to see Ninon as well as to visit the publishers in the east. The more I thought of it, the more I knew it was what I must do.

"When I go," I decided suddenly, "I'll take Lorna with me."

THIRTY-THREE

It was a week after the lion jumped me before I was up to riding again, and I saddled up and headed out for the hills, leaving Colly Benson in charge at our town. Ethan was off somewhere, hunting.

The air was crisp and clear. I could hear the ringing of axes where several of the townsmen were cutting firewood. It was cold, but I was dressed for it.

Another Christmas was right close and the folks were decorating trees, rehearsing for the school play, and straightening up for the holidays.

Looking back I could see much activity along the streets. Several little settlements had grown up nearby, and there were stories of men washing out twenty-five to thirty dollars a day; nuggets had been found worth over a hundred dollars each.

Spring Gulch, Meadow Gulch, and Yankee Gulch were all being worked. There must have been several hundred people in the area now, but they were scattered, and our town was several miles from the nearest group.

The slope along which I turned was covered with timber, many small trees and a few scattered big ones. Here and there I could see the bare places where porcupines had climbed the trees to eat away the bark. Enough of that would kill the tree.

There was a wariness in me as I rode, for I well remembered

Ethan's warning about the Sioux. They were a warrior people, and anyone not of their tribe would be considered a potential enemy. Yet the forest and the mountains were always exciting to me, and I wove a precarious trail through the timber and the great boulders, passing a deserted beaver pond, noting a lion track. I walked my horse across a scarred flank of the mountain where a recent avalanche had torn a gash, fifty yards across.

What trail there may have been was gone, but my horse walked out, choosing his way with care, and we went on across and into the trees once more. Here there was an area of more rain or snow . . . all through the mountains there are scattered islands of climate where due to some formation of mountains or canyon, the rainfall is heavier, the growth thicker.

Soon I would reach the area of my gold discovery, so I pulled up under some trees to watch the trail behind. I did not believe I was followed, but it was good to be sure.

It was slow going, for there were many deadfalls from an old blow-down. The tree trunks lay gray and bare; most of them had lost their bark, and they lay about like the scattered bones of some gigantic monster. There was a place among the deadfalls where a small stream trickled down, fell over the end of a log, and into a small basin.

My horse drank, while I let my eyes drift across the steep slopes . . . no movement, nothing but a lone eagle, far above. Yet I had learned caution.

Nearby I could see where a white-tailed deer had been nibbling pine needles and browsing on some of the brush that appeared above the snow. After a few minutes I let my mustang pick its way down the steep game trail toward the bottom of the canyon.

Deliberately I had taken a wandering route as if merely hunting for game. I did not wish to ride right to the creek where I had found gold. I dismounted among some pines and boulders well up the slope, picketing my horse on a small patch of snow-covered grass.

Rifle in hand I went down the slope, following a route where the wind had blown away the snow. My boots slid in the loose rock, but at the bottom I went into the cedars growing from a red rock cliff. Crouching among them, I waited and watched both up and downstream.

Right below me was the crumbling ledge through which the stream had cut its way and where I believed the gold originated. After a few minutes I went down through the trees to the top of the ledge. Below me the stream was rimmed with ice, and there was a steep slide from the top of the ledge to the stream, some fifteen feet below. Carefully, I descended, using my hands on the rocks, as though going down to the stream for a drink. On the way down I gave all my attention to the rocks, but saw no gold, nor sign of it. At the stream, to complete the illusion for any who might follow my tracks, I crawled out on a rock and drank from the stream.

At the bottom were some fragments that might be gold. Reaching in, I managed to get two of the larger pieces. One, only slightly larger than a pinhead, was undoubtedly gold. The other was larger . . . perhaps twice as large.

I was close. I drank again, then turned slowly around and looked carefully along the slope of the mountain. Without a doubt I was on some small stream that flowed into the Popo Agie, an Indian name meaning "beginning of the waters."

I was alone.

I went along the ice at the stream's edge until I stood in the gateway of stone through which the stream passed. I crouched to study the rocks; it was ancient quartz, decomposing. I picked up a chunk in my fingers and could rub grains from it. I struck the chunk against the rock wall, and it fell apart.

No gold . . . at least none that I could see.

Where I now stood I could be seen only from upstream or down, and due to the twisting canyon the stream had cut, I was visible for no great distance from either direction. I studied the wall with care. Low, down right where the ice formed, was another streamer of quartz that disappeared under the ice.

Not wanting to leave any knife marks, I picked up a large chunk of rock and slammed it on the ice. In a few minutes I had broken down to the water. Running my hand into the water and through the gravel, I scooped it up.

There were three good-sized flakes in my hand along with some fragments of quartz and some sand.

I broke off several fragments from the quartz-vein where it lay under the water and examined them. They were seamed with gold.

I straightened up and dried my freezing hands on my shirt front, then held them under my coat and in my armpits to warm my fingers.

Gold . . . possibly just an outcropping, possibly much more.

It was winter, and there was no possibility of working a mine in such a place, nor of watching over it if it became known; yet I wanted the gold, or some of it. Worst of all, I should be returning soon if I intended to, and I had said nothing of the possibility of staying out. Nor had I any kind of tool beyond the hunting knife I habitually carried and the hatchet or tomahawk on my saddle.

A hunting knife was the most useful of articles, and I went nowhere without one, but the hatchet was useful also. As boys we had learned to throw them with the same skill with which some men throw knives. Often, when not wishing to use a gun, I had killed small game with a thrown tomahawk.

Returning to my horse I got my hatchet and went back to the stream. I enlarged the hole in the ice and began breaking off chunks of the quartz at the edge and beneath the water.

It was there, all right.

I'd heard much talk of gold mining, prospecting, and the like. From time to time I had tried my hand, with little to show for it. There was a prevailing notion that the deeper one followed a vein the richer it got, but I well remembered one old timer who claimed that a vein tended to peter out as it went deeper, that the richest ore was apt to be nearer the surface.

I had no idea which was true, but I guessed that if I'd found even these few colors downstream of this area, the deeper sands downstream must be loaded. When spring came I'd go down to bedrock on the nearest sandbar.

For more than an hour I worked steadily, trying to make no more noise than essential, prying away at cracks to break off chunks, and getting out the best stuff—jewelry rock, as the miners called it. Finally, when the shadows started to lengthen I carefully swept all the dust and debris into the hole in the ice and pushed a nearby chunk of driftwood over the hole. By morning it would be frozen solid once again.

My horse was more than willing to leave, so sacking up my stuff in an old blanket, I started back along the mountain. Several times I turned to look back. It was beginning to snow. With luck even my tracks would be covered before daylight.

It was a long, cold ride back, and midnight was near before I rode up to the blacksmith shop. I carried my sack inside, then went to put up my horse.

Cain came from the house. "Ruth is over," he said. "We were getting worried."

"Don't go in yet, Cain. We've some talking to do."

When the mustang was rubbed down and fed, I went back to the blacksmith shop. Reaching into the sack I took out a chunk of the ore. It was seamed with gold. I'd knocked away as much excess as I could, and the stuff looked great.

"Is there much of it?"

I shrugged. "Cain, I don't know. My guess would be that there is, but it might peter out in just a few feet. The gold that's been broken off over the years and washed downstream should be something, though, and there's probably several good bars right below. I'm no judge but my guess is that I've nearly a hundred dollars right here."

"We'll bust it up and melt it down," Cain said. "You've a good day's work, I'll say that."

We put the stuff in an old canvas sack where Cain usually carried odd bits of iron, and we hid it under some bits of planking, old rope, and odds and ends of harness.

Ruth and Bud were still up when we came back in. Drake was also there, and we sat down to an excellent meal. I was hungry and tired yet excited about my discovery. I'd never been one to place much emphasis on wealth. I wanted the respect of my fellow man and a chance to live my life, to think, to ride the high country.

"Are you going east, Bendigo?" Ruth asked.

"I am. I shall ride east and take the steam cars to Omaha, then to Chicago and New York."

"Not to New Orleans?"

I got a little red around the ears. "Maybe. But she's forgotten all about me. Besides, what use would she have for a wild country man like me?"

Ruth smiled. "You haven't looked into a mirror lately, Bendigo. You're a handsome man."

Well, I felt red and uncomfortable. I wasn't used to compliments and never knew what to say or how to react.

"By the way, Ben," Drake said, "there's a new magazine starting out on the coast. The *Overland Monthly*. A man named Bret Harte is editing it. Why don't you send him something? From what I've heard he is interested in everything western, and he might use something of yours."

"Thanks, I'll try him."

"We were just talking, Ben," Helen said. "Ruth thinks this will be the last year for wagon trains."

"There was a man stopped in at the post who had been working on the railroad, the Central Pacific. He says they are building east even faster than the Union Pacific is going west."

They talked quietly over their coffee and I sat with them,

thinking over the past time and all that had transpired. We had come here to a small, bare valley, and we had built our homes, and now for a time we had lived within them. We had raised our small crops, hunted and gathered in the forest and along the streams, and we had faced our trails.

What did it mean? What did we mean? Were we more than the beaver who builds for a while, harvests the country, and then retreats to easier, better places? Had we given anything to the land? To our country?

Listening to their voices I thought of them, of Cain, Helen, Ruth, of Webb and John Sampson and Drake Morrell . . . we all were passersby, in the last analysis, yet during this time we had lived our lives with courage, and each of us, I think, had grown.

We were a part of this now, a part of this land, of this forest, of these green hills now covered with snow. We had watered from its streams, reaped crops from its soil, and I, perhaps, had learned more than all of them, for I had the most to learn.

Here in this house, built of logs cut and trimmed by our own hands, I had talked to Plutarch, to Locke, to Hume and Blackstone; yet now I knew I must go on, and I did not know where.

Was it only Ninon that drew me to the east? Or was she the facade of something else . . . some vast yearning to be a part of that larger world as I was a small part of this?

"Ben?" Drake Morrell was speaking. "You are going east?"

"Yes. After Christmas I shall go. To New York first, I think."

"Don't be disappointed if your stuff doesn't sell. It rarely does, at first."

That made me smile. "I've been a trapper too long, Drake," I said, "a man has to set many traps to catch fur in one or two. I think it will be the same with writing."

There was a tap on the door, and then it opened. Ethan was there. He moved in, a man endlessly graceful, a man who moved like a blade of grass in the wind. I envied him.

He squatted on his heels against the wall, his rifle in one hand. "Ben, somebody picked up your trail today. Somebody tried to backtrack you."

For a moment I was very quiet, my mind sorting words for an answer. "*Tried* to?"

"He couldn't do it. It was snowing too much, and then somebody shot, and I guess it worried him."

"Somebody *shot?*"

Ethan was bland, innocent. "Yeah, I guess somebody figured that if that there person stopped follerin' now there'd be too much snow by the time he tried again. I wouldn't say anybody shot *at* anybody, but it was the sort of thing that makes a cautious man more cautious."

"Who was following the trail?" I asked.

"Offhand I'd say it was Moses . . . the Reverend."

They were all looking from Ethan to me. I should have known I could keep no secrets from him. I said as much.

He smiled. "Ben, you're my friend. What you've a mind to do is your affair, and I've no desire to horn in on it. Only thing is, I don't like nobody trackin' down a friend of mine . . . maybe gettin' in where he don't belong."

"Thanks," I said.

Ruth Macken changed the subject. "Bendigo, I got some books that I'd sent for. You might like to read them. A man named Timothy Dwight, writing about the New York–New England country."

"Thanks," I said; a part of my mind had moved after Moses Finnerly. Why was he tracking me? I often went to the mountains, so why this time?

"We need a larger building," Drake was saying. "We had only a half dozen students to begin. Now we've more than thirty. Even with Lorna helping, we'll need another room, and we should have another teacher."

"Maybe two more, Drake," I said quietly. "When I go east I am taking Lorna with me."

THIRTY-FOUR

"**N**o way you could have seen him," Ethan told me the next morning. "He didn't foller you, it was your trail. He tried backtrackin' you, and something about it struck me wrong, so I sort of headed him off."

"Did he have any idea who shot?"

Ethan chuckled. "Him? He's a pretty good Injun, but not that good. I just figured to kick up some snow, was all, and he took off."

"I've got to go back again," I said.

He shrugged. "Take a roundabout. Go through country where anybody who follers has got to come out in the open. Don't leave no other way for him, then set up high for a while and sort of look back."

"Good idea. Want to come with me?"

"Nope. Your affair . . . less you need he'p. You know, Ben, I sort of figure I've got all I need in this world. It ain't likely I'll marry, and if I do I can run a trap line. To me a showing of wealth would only cumber my life. It would load me up with watchin' after it, and I'd spend more time at that than roamin' the high country.

"I wouldn't trade all anybody could give me for one day on those mountain trails. I seen a big bear up there yesterday, Ben, the biggest I ever did see. A silver-tip grizzly, and he must've

237

weighed nearly a ton. He seen me, all right, an' he r'ared up on his hind legs and looked at me.

"I grounded the butt of my gun to show him I meant him no evil, an' we stood there, sniffin' the air and lookin' at each other for a while, and then he kind of lifted a paw . . . it was an accident, of course, but it looked almost like he waved at me, then he just turned his back an' walked off, an' I let him go.

"When he looked back again he was at the edge of the trees, an' I lifted a hand to him. He looked, then went on into the trees and out of the way. Ben, that bear was a big one. He's put in too many years in this country for me to fetch him now."

"I've found gold up there, Ethan."

"Figured as much. Well, if you go east after that actress gal you'll need it. Not that it would matter to her, but money shines with the old folks."

"I want to look around some. I've got to make up my mind about some things."

"I reckon." Ethan took out his pipe. "Ben, did you ever think about runnin' for office? I'm serious. I've heard a lot of talk. Wyoming will be a state. They'll need men with education. You've read a sight of books, and you're steady. I'd trust your judgment any time . . . you think about it."

Well, I had thought about it. Maybe that was a part of what our town meant, maybe it was a place for growing up, a place for teaching a man to think not only of himself but of a community, a training ground for learning to live together, to think for others, to plan for a future.

Yet I felt inadequate. There were so many questions of which I knew nothing, and that night I opened a fresh bundle of papers and began going through them. I must know why Johnson was dismissing Stanton, why they wanted to impeach Johnson, why men preferred Grant to Seymour.

Blackstone had greater appeal. I liked the even tone of his work, the effect he gave of considered judgment, the cool beauty of the principles he laid down. This was one of the books Jefferson had read, and Madison . . . all of them.

They had read Plutarch, too.

Two more trips I made to my mine, and each time I returned with gold. Cain melted it down in the forge, cast it into small ingots for me, flat and about as round as a silver dollar, but thicker.

On my last trip I rode out before daybreak. It was a clear, cold morning . . . freezing cold. On such a morning I would not have thought of going, but it would be the last time. Christmas was tomorrow, and after New Year's I would be going off to the east.

I rode swiftly up Beaver Creek, cut over toward the mountain, and climbed along an old game trail. It was a trail I knew very well, and when well up the mountain I turned sharply off and looked back.

Nothing.

It was too cold to wait long and I rode on, my horse eager to be off. On this occasion, I planned to bring back some gold I had dug and cached . . . a good load of it.

The air was very still, the sky gray and low. It was bad weather . . . a kind of weather made for sitting by the fire. I rode into the trees, down a long, snow-covered slope, into the trees again. Suddenly I pulled up.

Tracks . . . huge tracks. That big silver-tip was out and moving around. He probably knew we were in for a bad storm and wanted to have a full belly before it set in. Well, luck to him.

Cold . . . it was bitter, bitter cold, and it had grown colder since I started.

I had to get back. Tomorrow was Christmas Day.

Once, turning around a clump of snow-covered brush, I thought I caught a whisper of movement far behind me, but I looked and looked and saw nothing. My horse stamped irritably, eager to be moving, and we went on.

How I loved the vast stillness around me! No sound but the crunch of my horse's hoofs in the snow, the creak of stiff leather, an occasional crack of a branch in the cold.

Pulling up under some trees I stepped down from my horse into snow just short of knee-deep. My feet were cold, so I walked on, leading my horse. Then I mounted again, doubled back on my trail at a fast trot, and came suddenly into the open.

It caught them by surprise. There were three riders, and they were coming right down my trail.

When I rode out of the trees they pulled up sharply, and one of them made as if to turn. They were a good two hundred yards off and I considered. I had an idea who they were but no real reason to shoot . . . they had not attacked me. Not yet.

So I simply turned my horse and walked him back into the trees.

Three men . . . not one, but three. They were not simply following me, which one man could have done, they meant to kill me.

I turned up a dim game trail, only slightly tracked since the snow. I rode up, weaving a way in and out of the trees. I slid my horse down a steep bank, edged him between two boulders, slid down another bank through the trees and circled toward my cache.

Did they know of it? Had they located my mine? Or only the area? Unless they did know they would be foolish to kill me.

There was something in this I did not understand.

My horse wore caulked shoes so I turned him upstream on the ice and rode swiftly for several hundred yards, then up the bank and into the trees again. I disliked seeming to run from them, but I had killed men and this was known. The Reverend Finnerly still had friends and a few followers, and there was no liking between us. If I killed them or any one of them I would be in trouble, all my dreams suddenly gone down the drain. What I needed now was escape.

They were following but not too fast . . . why? Drawing up to let my horse catch his wind, I scowled: Why, if they wanted me dead, did they not close in and try to do the job?

They were obviously not in a hurry.

Why? The answer came to me suddenly . . . because they were not ready yet.

Why not?

Like a dash of cold snow down the back of the neck it came to me. Because there was somebody else involved, somebody not yet on the scene.

They were making no move to catch up. Despite the coming on of night they were willing to take their time. They were not even closing in to be sure I was within range.

In fact they acted just like . . . like men driving game or herding cattle.

That was what they were doing then, they were herding *me*, moving me closer and closer to some other enemy.

The worst of it was, I was in a canyon. There were places where I could climb out, but they were few, steep, and exposed.

At this point the canyon was about a half mile wide, the stream ran up the bottom, there were a few meadows, many trees, some steep, rocky cliffs, some slopes not quite as steep, some covered with trees, some only with snow.

What lay ahead? Enemies, certainly, but what enemies? Who?

There was also the night, the cold.

On my right the bank fell steeply away into the brush. Swiftly I turned my horse and slid down the bank into an avenue of trees. I would be herded no further. If it was fight they wanted, it would be now. I went into the trees on a run, turned right again down the canyon, and came up out of the trees to a level area to see the three riders pulling up . . . then, deliberately they turned their horses and started away.

Startled, I glanced behind me.

Indians. And they were coming toward me in an arc, walking their horses, closing in.

Starting forward, I found myself facing another group that was emerging slowly from the trees in the direction I was going. Shoving my rifle into its boot, I reached inside my coat and shucked my six-gun.

There was no chance to even think, there was only time now to do. My enemies had walked me right into a trap set for me and now they were pulling out. I slapped my heels to the mustang, and rode right into them.

They were not ready for it. They had expected me to try to talk, to ride to right or left, to try any way out. Instead I went right into them and I went shooting. My first shot knocked an Indian from his horse. The second tried to turn too fast, and his ordinarily surefooted pony slipped on the ice of the creek, and almost went down. I went into them, shooting.

It was almost dark. If I could just . . .

The Indians behind me hesitated to shoot for fear of hitting their friends, and shooting to right and left, I was through them. It was due far more to the caulks on my horse's shoes than to any skill or bravery on my part. The horse was sure on its feet, and in a moment I was into the trees.

I heard whoops and yells . . . there must be a dozen. How many were down? One man had gone down with his horse, but that was probably only momentary, and one I had wounded . . . I believed I had hit one other, but I'd been more intent on getting through them than killing anyone.

They were all around me. On my right the cliff went sheer . . . there was a chimney where a man *might* climb, no place a horse could go.

I dismounted quickly and stuffed the food from my saddlebag inside my shirt. There was also some ammunition, which I stuffed into my coat pockets.

"All right, boy," I whispered to my horse, "go home now!"

Rifle in hand, I went up the cliff, hung the sling over my shoulder and started to climb.

It was not easy. It was too dark to see properly despite the snow, and ice had dripped down from above onto the rocks. Slowly, carefully, I worked my way upward.

I heard the clatter of hoofs some distance off, a shout, then a shot, a yell . . .

I kept on climbing, and what seemed a long time later, I topped out on a narrow ledge. Along it I went, hurrying. Once I slipped and almost went over the edge, then pulling myself up, I saw a dark slit in the rock and peered into it. Some distance beyond I could see snow, and edged my way through.

Where they were now, I did not know, but Indians would not long be fooled. What had Finnerly done? Traded guns or whiskey probably and the promise of a scalp.

I crossed the clearing at a trot and climbed into a nest of boulders, desperately hoping for shelter. It was growing colder.

Then I worked my way back into the trees. In the darkness there, I stopped. Indians will rarely attack in the trees as the ambushing party has the advantage. Waiting there in the bitter cold, I thought of the long miles that separated me from home.

I climbed higher into the rocks and brush. There, on a shoulder of the mountain I found a small wind-hollowed cave. It was no such shelter as I wanted, only a ledge with some overhang above it, but as long as the wind did not get around to the east by south I was relatively safe.

There was broken rock so I built a small wall to protect a corner of the cave. From roots and brush I gathered together the materials for a fire. A pack rat had nested here, or some other creature. In the darkness I could not tell, and there was an old dead tree fallen half across the front of the cave.

Huddled there, shaking with the cold, I put together a small fire. It might attract some lead but at least I would not freeze, and the chances were I was so high and partially sheltered that they might not see me.

Far away to the south was our town, far away across the icy miles. They were there now, around their warm fires, sitting down to supper. Cain would be lighting his pipe, and perhaps Ruth and Bud would come down.

Tonight was Christmas Eve.

THIRTY-FIVE

The rock floor of the shallow cave was cold. The small fire I permitted myself kept me alive but little more. There was no room to stand in the cave, only to rise on my knees, yet I did so time and again, going through the motions of the teamster's warming to keep the blood moving.

There were no stars. Nor was there any sound. The chances were that the Indians had gone, yet I dared not risk it. From the brief glimpses I had of them they had seemed to be Shoshone, but the Shoshone were friendly to the white man, had even fought beside him.

All but one. And perhaps his friends. Had Finnerly heard that story? Of course. It was one of the most often told stories in our town, for it had been our first trial of strength against the wilderness.

Seated by the fire, adding fuel stick by stick, for there was little enough within reach, I contemplated my situation. Bitter as was the cold, it was in my favor. No Indian likes to fight in the cold, or even to move around, and the chances were they had planned for a quick kill and a return to their lodges. What worried me was that my horse would probably return to Cain's stable and they would send out a search party, ruining the planned Christmas.

As soon as daylight came I must try to get out of here. I must start back.

No shots came, no sound. Taking a chance, I built my fire a

little larger, and the waves of heat began hitting the back of the cave and reflecting from it.

Yet too much warmth was a danger. If I fell asleep my fire might go out, my enemies might come. Heavy-lidded and tired I huddled, shivering in the shallow cave.

Somehow the night passed. Right then I was wishing Santa Claus might come along for I'd relish a ride in a nice warm sleigh that could rise over the tangle of brush and rock that lay between me and home.

A faint grayness showed along the horizon. I warmed my hands again at the fire, warmed my mitts as well as I could without burning them, and slipped a hot rock into each coat pocket to warm my fingers.

It was bitter cold. I'd figure it twenty below zero or more, and I was a fair judge. After a man has lived in cold country he learns to tell by the crunch of snow, the cracking of branches, the very feel of the air.

For a time I crouched in my cave, studying the outside. Nothing stirred . . . certainly no wild animal or bird would be out on such a day, and the Indians were just as wise. Flattening against the rock wall, I worked my way out of the cave, momentarily expecting a shot.

When I crawled up through the rocks to the crest I looked all around. There were no tracks . . . nothing.

Far away to the south I could detect a thin trail of smoke from our town or one of the other settlements that had sprung up in the vicinity.

I started off at a brisk walk. Here, high on the mountain, the wind had swept much of the snow away, but ahead of me lay deep snow, not crusted enough to bear my weight.

For an hour I walked, then struck a dim trail that I believed I had traveled before . . . months ago. The snow had changed the appearances of things and I could not be sure, but south was my direction.

A bitter wind was blowing that intensified the cold, so I started down off the crest and into the comparative shelter of the canyon.

Several times I paused to stamp my feet, and soon I knew I must rest a little. Exhaustion is the greatest danger in the cold, for the body then has no reserves with which to fight its battle to survive.

At a turning of the canyon wall I came upon a huge tree that had tumbled from the bank above and lay at a steep angle, its top buried in the canyon snow. The roots still clung to the earth above, and the hollow beneath was sheltered by the snow that had packed itself among the branches and needles of the spruce.

Scattered about were the remains of dozens of other deadfalls. I had come several miles, but I would be a fool to push on and exhaust myself, so I went under the huge tree, and with the third match had a fire going. I then broke boughs from a living spruce nearby and laid them on the ground until I had a thick carpet.

Taking my time so as not to grow too warm, I did each thing with care. Soon I had put other branches over part of the face of the opening and had a snug place inside shaped like an Indian teepee, and almost as large as one.

There was no lack of fuel. Along any such woodland canyon there are always masses of dead timber, old trees that have fallen, other trees killed in blow-downs, and those that have died from insects, disease, or accidents.

I settled down to wait the storm out. I still had a little food, and there was a cup. In this I boiled water and made tea. Snug in my shelter, I enjoyed my fire, sipped hot tea, and considered how quickly a reasonably civilized man can become primitive. And how fortunate he is if he knows how primitive man survived.

It is a thing I must remember, that men must always remember, that civilization is a flimsy cloak, and just outside are hunger, thirst, and cold . . . waiting.

They are always there, and in the end, unless man remembers, they will always win.

Later, much later, I dozed, slept, awakened to add fuel to my fire, then dozed again. Toward evening I brewed another cup of tea, sipping it slowly. In my mind I thought my way over the route I must follow and considered whether I should try now, before the day was over.

This was a good shelter. I did want to be home for Christmas, but in such cold as I now faced it would be best to wait, conserve my strength, and be careful not to overextend myself. It was always my way to push on, to keep going, yet at this moment it was the wrong way.

Ethan, Cain, and the others knew me. My horse would probably get back safely and they would worry, yet they knew the country as well as or better than I . . . if I were wounded or hurt and down on the ground the cold would kill me before they could reach me, and if not, they knew I would be wise enough to hole up and wait it out.

I added more spruce boughs to the opening of the shelter, walling off the cold. Soon I grew warmer.

It was going to be a cold evening and a colder night, but now I was safe, I could last it out for days if necessary. I brought my guns closer to the fire . . . but not too close. I knew cold would stiffen the action, and I must be ready for anything.

All through the long night I thought, dozed, listened, and kept my fire going. How many men such as I must have huddled over fires in the bitter cold? Indians, and the men who came before the Indians, perhaps those who built the Medicine Wheel . . . The People Who Came Before . . . The People Who Had No Iron. Who were they? What were they? Why did they build their shrine in that place? Had it been a place of pilgrimage?

They must have known this canyon, must have walked the trails I had walked.

No doubt men who had huddled over just such fires as mine had pondered such questions. Ethan had told me the Hopi religion was one that merited study . . . he was not a read man, but one who thought clearly and to the point, and who had perhaps a greater grasp of Indian thinking than anyone I knew.

The trouble was that he was much like Indians I had known and did not pass on his ideas or discoveries to any chance passerby. The world from which I had sprung was a world excited by an urge to communicate, to tell, exhibit, relate. As soon as an idea came to one, or a discovery was made of whatever kind, it was our way to rush into print or to a platform. The Indian had no such compulsion. Of tales of war and hunting they had no end, and were expected to relate them with drama and excitement to the people of their village, but much knowledge was assumed to be known, whether it was or not.

Slowly the night dragged away, and with daybreak I decided to move. In all this snow there was no chance of my fire getting away, so I left it to burn out in case I had suddenly to return.

Turning south I went down to the vague trail and started walking steadily, calculating my time.

My mind was made up not to overdo it. Cold dulls the brain, yet I fastened there the thought that I must not try too hard, do too much. It was the exhausted who were killed by the cold, and even with the town close by, I must not risk trying too much distance. The air was cold, but not, I believed, as cold as the day before.

The trail was curving downward, and there was no wind. Several times I stopped when I saw small bits of moss or bark that had been sheltered from the snow beneath a rock or log. These bits I stuffed into my pocket where the heat of my body would dry out what moisture they contained. If I stopped to build a fire I wanted to be ready.

The creek below offered an easier path, but of that I was wary. The ice would be frozen thick, yet there are occasionally warm springs beneath the ice which, coming up from the creek bottom, cause the ice to be thin . . . a step through into the water beneath would be all a man would need in this cold. Before he could build a fire and dry himself he would be dead.

I could see the smoke from several of the settlements now, and the thought of a warm room and warm food pulled me onward.

Suddenly I caught a flicker of movement. My hand went inside my shirt to my pistol.

Three riders and a spare horse.

A hand lifted and waved . . . they had seen me. It was Ethan, Webb, and Stacy Follett.

"You all right?" Webb demanded.

"Well," I said, "I'm almighty cold, but most of all I'm figuring you boys ate all the Christmas dinner."

Stiffly, on the second attempt, I climbed into the saddle. "Anybody ride out of town a couple of days ago? Maybe three men?"

Webb turned sharply around in his saddle. "Three men? Well, three men rode out of town this morning, cold as it was. Looked like they were headed for the railroad."

"It was Moses Finnerly an' that bunch," Ethan said, "they took off."

PART III

THIRTY-SIX

The man who looked back at me from the mirror was a man I was only coming to know. The transformation had been gradual, but outwardly the result seemed to have been achieved.

My worn buckskins and shotgun chaps I had left in Cheyenne, and there I had bought a new suit of hand-me-downs.

"When you can," Stratton advised, "get rid of them. Nobody wears creased pants for they obviously came off the shelf. You've got the money, so go to my tailor . . . you have his name and address . . . buy several suits.

"Remember this: In New York you are known to no one so they must judge by appearances. If you look like a gentleman and conduct yourself as one they will accept you without question. The town is full of sharps of one kind or another, male and female, and they like the smell of money, so be careful.

"I have written to my attorney there, and he will call upon you. If you need advice, go to him. The Fifth Avenue is *the* hotel now. There are other good ones, of course, and you will find fewer western people there than at the Hoffman House or the St. Nicholas, but the Fifth Avenue is where you should stay.

"Don't expect much from your writing. They pay very little for such work, although it will open some doors for you, and it will give you identity. There are many writers in New York, but only a few are making a living. On the other hand, if you wish to read for the law, there is no better firm in the city."

"I haven't that intention," I replied. "I want to visit New York, and probably New Orleans. Then I shall return here."

"To Cheyenne? The town is growing, but so is Denver. You could do worse than to invest in either town."

And now I was in New York, looking into the mirror in my room in the Fifth Avenue Hotel. The man who looked back at me from the mirror was different, somehow, yet it was me. Six feet two inches, weight one hundred and ninety, tanned by sun and wind, wearing a carefully tailored dark suit, a white shirt and tie, Bendigo Shafter.

"You are a long way from the Beaver Rim, Bendigo," I told myself, "a long way."

Yet there was a reminder of the South Pass behind my belt. I had left much behind, but not my pistol. Straightening my tie again and taking up my coat and hat, I went out into the hall. I was walking toward my second ride on an elevator, an object of which the hotel management was exceedingly proud. It was said to be the first hotel elevator in the world. I had ridden up on it, but not down . . . what if it fell?

Two other men got on with me, accompanied by two girls who were giggling with excitement. I guessed it was their first ride, too.

When I reached the corridor, I glanced around. Lighted by gaslight, which I was also seeing for the first time, it shone with marble and polished wood, glittered with crystal.

A tall, fine-looking man with gray sideburns approached me. "Mr. Shafter? I am John Stryker. Mr. Stratton suggested I call upon you here, and when I saw you I knew at once you were the man I was looking for."

"Yes, sir. I was about to have dinner, sir. Would you join me?"

"On the contrary. You shall be my guest."

Over dinner we talked, and as we talked Stryker indicated various people who were dining or passing through the room. Some of the names I remembered from my careful reading of what newspapers had come my way.

"Stratton told me something of your . . . your adventures. He also mentioned your age, but you seem older."

"I am older," I replied. "On the frontier every boy wishes only to be a man. One is eager to be given responsibility and to be worthy of it. So if you do your job and act the part they accept you as you are. It is the willingness to accept responsibility, I think, that is the measure of a man."

"What about your town?" Stryker asked.

"Right now it is doing well. We've some cattle, and there's still business from the wagon trains, and then, of course, there's the mining. There's considerable gold there, but personally I doubt if the finds will prove to be extensive."

"I doubt if I would know gold if I saw it. Not in its native state."

I smiled at him. "I can show you some. Right now, in fact."

Reaching into my vest pocket I took out a nugget about as big as the end of my thumb. "There . . . that's raw gold, right from a stream bed."

His face flushed, and he stared at the nugget. "Really?" He picked it up and turned it slowly in his fingers. "Well, I'll be damned."

"Not unless you have too much of it," I told him, smiling, "and it isn't that easy to get."

A man had stopped near our table, and he was staring at the nugget. "Say there! May I see that?"

Stryker glanced up. "Yes, of course. How do you do, Mr. Greeley." He turned to me. "Bendigo Shafter . . . Horace Greeley."

This was the editor of the *Tribune*. Everybody along the Overland Trail knew of his famous ride with stage driver Hank Monk.

He was a man of about five feet ten inches, stout, with a partly bald head and white hair. He was dressed in a black suit, white vest, and a black tie that was slightly askew. He took up the nugget in his fingers, turning it to catch the light, and peering at it through his spectacles. "Yes, yes. Very nice. Very nice, indeed. Where did you get it, young man?"

"From a mining claim of mine in the new Territory of Wyoming. You know the country, sir. In South Pass."

"Yes, yes of course. Indeed I know the country. Not much of a pass, though, just a great big wide open prairie."

He sat down abruptly. "Shafter, you say? Yes, that's the name . . . Bendigo Shafter." He looked at me again. "I read a piece of yours. Something about a mountain lion."

"You read it, sir? But I . . ."

"I know . . . I know. I am interested in things western, and my friend showed it to me. Very interesting. Very interesting."

"You're a famous man out west, sir," I said, without smiling. "Everybody tells the story of your ride with Hank Monk."

"Monk? That stage driver? Was that his name? Oh, yes! Of course. Hank Monk. I should have known better than to ride with a man like that, and when I was in a hurry, too."

"But he got you there, Mr. Greeley."

Greeley chuckled. "Yes . . . yes, he did." He peered at me over his glasses. "Visiting in New York?"

"Yes, sir."

"He struck it rich in the mines, Mr. Greeley. He was just showing me what raw gold looks like."

"Hmm. Not much of it as pretty as that. Come and see me, young man. Come and see me. You write well, but what is more important, you think well . . . don't clutter up your work with a lot of nonsense."

He moved off, walking awkwardly.

"By the way," Stryker said, "are you interested in the theater? There's a new play opening . . . or I should say an old play in a new production."

"Yes, I am interested." I was thinking of something else. "I believe I shall be going to New Orleans soon."

"If there is any way in which I can be of service . . . ? Mr. Stratton was very emphatic, and if I fail to see anything or do anything you wish to do, I think he'll have my scalp."

"Don't worry. I've been seeing the town and learning about it, too." I looked down at my hands. Had they grown a little whiter already? Or was it my imagination? And had I grown softer? "Yes, I'd enjoy the play. What is it called?"

"*Fashion* . . . it was written twenty-five or thirty years ago . . . one of the first successes by an American, I think."

I was listening, but I was watching the people, wondering about them, enjoying the pageant they made. And then suddenly I was not enjoying it any longer.

My glass was in my fingers, and I almost dropped it, then placed it carefully upon the table. "Stryker," I said, "that group over there? Do you know them, by any chance?"

He glanced the way I was directing my attention. "The girl is Ninon Vauvert . . . she's from that play . . . the new one I was mentioning. The younger woman is in the play also, but the other fellow . . . I am sorry for her. She's in bad, bad company."

"Who is he?"

"His name is Jake McCaleb, or that, at least, is the name he uses here. He's been a riverboat gambler and several worse things. He's a dangerous man, Shafter, and I'd leave him alone."

"I know her."

"*You* know her? Ninon Vauvert? How could you? She's an actress . . . from New Orleans. She joined the show there and she's playing the part of the maid . . . it's a good part . . . in the play."

"Will you wait for me? I am going to speak to her."

"Be careful then. There've been a lot of stories told about the man, and they say his enemies don't last long. The police know all about him but have never been able to get enough for a case against him."

I'd been only half listening. Ninon was no longer a child. She was young, beautiful . . . but a woman.

I wended my way among the tables, and as I drew near, her eyes turned toward me. For a moment she sat perfectly still, her eyes widening. Then she came swiftly to her feet.

"Ben! Oh, Ben! Is it you?" Her fingers clutched both my sleeves.

"It has been a long time."

The other two were on their feet. McCaleb was speaking. "Do you know this man?"

"*Know* him? Of course, I know him! Ben, sit down, won't you? We've so much to talk about."

McCaleb's face was growing red. "Ninon, haven't you forgotten . . . ?"

She turned swiftly. "I have forgotten nothing. I told you I was not interested. Now I am telling you again." She looked down at the other man. "Come along, Charles. You will want to know Ben. He's . . ."

McCaleb came around the table. He moved swiftly and easily, and he seemed unhurried. He stepped in front of me. "You were not invited, my friend. Now I suggest you go . . . alone."

"Don't be silly," I said, smiling at him, and taking Ninon's elbow I guided her through the tables toward where Stryker waited.

When we were seated, I glanced back. McCaleb was settling his bill. Then he turned toward us, and I knew trouble when I saw it, but this was no barroom. It was one of the most elegant dining rooms in the city.

He was standing over us then. One of my boots slipped from under the table. "Look here, you . . ." His hand grasped my collar.

Hooking one toe behind his heel, I stood up suddenly, jerking the foot toward me. My standing up suddenly was all that was needed. He tried a quick step back as my toe jerked, and he fell, hitting the floor with a crash.

"Oh," I said, "you'd better watch it there. Here, let me help you." Before he could gather himself I leaned over as if to help him up, taking him by the shoulders to lift. My knee came up sharply and collided with his chin, knocking his head back as though it were on a hinge. Then I picked him up, made a show of brushing him off, and to the waiter and the captain who came over, I said, "I am afraid this gentleman is a little under the weather. I suspect you'd better call a cab for him."

Smiling, I pushed him gently into their hands and sat down.

He was groggy, shaken by his fall but knocked almost unconscious by the smash from my knee.

As he was taken slowly from the dining room I sat down. "Poor fellow!" I said, "I am afraid he has had one too many."

Ninon was looking at me, her eyes dancing. "Oh, how I wish I could have done that! That man has been bothering me for days, and everyone seems to be afraid of him. But how did you *do* it?"

"I was just trying to help him, you know. He seemed a bit unsteady, and well . . ."

The headwaiter came over to our table. "I am sorry if that man caused any trouble. You shan't be seeing him in here again."

"It was no trouble," I said. "He seemed upset about something."

Stryker was puzzled. "What did happen? When you got up he fell over, and then you helped him up, but I can't believe the fall hurt him as much as he seemed to be hurt."

"Don't let it worry you. He will be all right in the morning."

Stryker shook his head. "It will not be that simple. Jake McCaleb is a bad man, Shafter. He'll have some of his shoulder-strikers after you. They are a rough lot . . . some of that Bowery crowd. You've made a dangerous enemy."

"Ben"—Ninon put her hand on my arm—"how is everybody? Your brother? Mr. Sampson? Ruth? Lorna?"

"They are all well. In fact, Lorna is here with me. She wasn't feeling quite well this evening so she stayed in her room. But I thought you were in New Orleans?"

"I was . . . then I was offered this part . . . I am playing Millinette . . . my aunt wouldn't hear of it at first, but I was so eager to do it and she knew I'd not been contented. So finally she agreed and she came with me."

"She's here?"

"Well, it's only for a few weeks. You know, most plays don't run over a week, and two or three weeks is exceptional. When the play closes, I may do something else." Her eyes met mine. "I have been offered several parts."

"Mr. Shafter is something of a writer. Did you know that, Miss Vauvert?"

She was startled. "A writer? You, Ben? Somehow I never imagined you as a writer."

I shrugged, embarrassed. "I am not, really. Just some things about the Indians, the wild animals, and the life out there."

We talked, and she listened as I told her of my cattle drive from Oregon, carefully ignoring the gun trouble. It was nothing I cared to discuss, and I was hoping all that was in the past.

"You have a ranch, then?"

"Not yet, although I am running some cattle. Just before I left I bought sixty head from a man driving west who decided he'd had enough. I have a few mining claims, and I had been working one of them. I'm afraid, Ninon, that when the trail is no longer used our town will die."

"Oh, no!"

"We live in a changing time, and the railroads are going to affect all our lives. Anyway, our town did what it was supposed to do. It kept us through a bad winter, it gave us breathing time to take stock of what we really wished to do. I know I learned a lot there, from Ruth, from Cain, from Ethan, and from John Sampson. Yes, and from Webb."

"He always seemed so dark and morose. He would have made a wonderful Cassius."

"For his looks, yes. But if he had wanted to kill Caesar he would have done it alone, not with a crowd to share the blame. But he had depths of loyalty none of us realized."

Stryker got up. "I am going to leave you two alone. Remember, Shafter, if there's anything I can do, call on me."

"Thanks."

"And good night, Miss Vauvert."

For a moment we looked at each other, and I hadn't an idea what to say. I simply said the most obvious thing. "You're beautiful!"

She laughed at me, then she stopped laughing. "Ben, I've missed you! And strangely enough, I've missed your mountains. As long as I've been away I find my eyes lifting toward the hills and then looking around for Indians."

"They are there. That's one reason I cannot be away too long. Some think it will be another bloody year on the plains, as it was in '65."

"I hope not. Ben, what's going to become of them? Of the Indians, I mean?"

"Just what would happen to us in the same circumstances, and what has happened all the way across the world, I suppose. Some will go further and further back into the hills until they can go no further, some will fall by the way, but a good many will move out into this new world, and they will do well. The Indian is a Stone Age man, actually, but there is no question as to his basic intelligence. I've seen rifles Indians have repaired, and they were done as well as any gunsmith who had grown up in the trade."

"But will people accept him?"

"If he succeeds, they will. What is happening here has happened all across the world from the beginning of time. The migrations out of Central Asia into Europe displaced or absorbed other peoples. In Africa it was the same way. I was talking to a man the other day who believes the Bantu originally migrated out of Asia into Africa. Wherever two cultures collide, the one with the most efficient way of living will survive."

"Are you going back, Ben?"

"I have to. For a while, at least, but I will not stay. We've done all we can do there. I have some mining claims to sell, and I own some cattle. I may start a newspaper somewhere out there."

"Not here?"

I thought about that, and then decided. "No. I like it here, and I'll come back . . . often. But that's my country out there." I looked at her. "Ninon, you'll have to face it. I am at least half a mountain man. I like to ride the wild country."

Neither of us said much that was personal. We just sort of talked as people will, rambling on about those we knew, about the town, the snows, the mountains, and whatever came to mind.

"May I take you home?" I asked.

She laughed. "I am home, Bendigo. I live here at the hotel . . . with my aunt. You see, my play is in the Fifth Avenue Theater right behind the hotel. It is very close and convenient."

We got up and I took her to the elevator, and there I left her with a promise to meet the next day, and to meet her aunt.

When the elevator had gone up I walked across the hall and bought a copy of Mr. Greeley's *Tribune*.

Tomorrow I would call upon the editor who had my lion story.

Lorna was sitting up in bed reading when I knocked on her door. She put down her book and looked at me. "You've seen her? You've seen Ninon?"

"Now how in the world could you know that?"

She laughed. "I've had a guest, too. Her aunt." She put the marker in the book and closed it. "She's a very beautiful and very intelligent woman, Ben, but how she knew we were in town, I have no idea. But she did know, and she came calling."

THIRTY-SEVEN

We met at Delmonico's. It was, at the time, the most favored eating place in the city. If possible, Ninon was even more lovely than before, and her aunt, Mrs. Beaussaint, was a woman of forty or so, and very attractive.

When they approached the table where Lorna and I waited, I got to my feet. She looked right into my eyes, a searching glance that flickered with amusement.

"Well? Am I the ogre you expected?"

"You are Ninon's aunt. How could you be anything but beautiful?"

"Well said. You are very quick for a frontier savage," she said, smiling. "I was expecting someone in buckskins and carrying a scalping knife."

"I wear clothing suited to the activity in which I am engaged," I said, "and I don't think the buckskins would suit the situation."

"And the scalping knife?"

"That's another thing. However, I believe most of the scalping here is done with words . . . nothing so crude, or so clean, as a knife."

We sat together, talking quietly of many things, of the theater . . . I remembered now that I had read Ninon's play, *Fashion*, from a play script owned by Miller Pine . . . of books, travel, New York, New Orleans . . . I listened, talked, and let my eyes stray from time to time to the others in the room.

259

It was pleasant to sit here, relaxed and quiet, and the food was excellent, nothing like our rough fare on the frontier.

How far from here to the Beaver Rim! To the heights of the Wind Rivers or the canyon of the Popo Agie!

"Why did you come east, Mr. Shafter?"

I looked at her. "To see Ninon. It has been a long time."

"Nothing else?"

"Oh . . . there was a matter of some manuscripts I'd mailed east, but they would have replied sooner or later. As a matter of fact, I am glad I came. I have sold two articles . . . after I work them over a little.

"I spent an hour or two with the editor this morning, and he suggested how I might put them in shape. I'd spent too much time telling about it instead of telling it."

"What sort of thing do you write?"

"I can't claim to be a writer, but I'd seen there was interest in the west and in some of the wild life. I did a piece on mountain lions . . . pumas, panthers, whatever you wish to call them. I did another on a rescue from the Indians."

"Ninon has been telling me of your life out there. You must be very brave."

Was I? I had often wondered about that. I shrugged. "One does what one has to do."

"He rode miles and miles through the cold and snow to find me," Ninon said quietly. "If he had not come I would have died, just as my brother did."

"It was Drake," I said, "had it not been for his ride, and he was wounded and in very bad shape, I'd not have known where to go."

"Drake?" Emilie Beaussaint's eyebrows lifted. "Drake who?"

"Morrell . . . Drake Morrell. He knew Ninon's mother . . . your sister. After she died he started out to bring them to you, but he was badly wounded in a gun battle with some old enemies. When I found him he was passed out in the snow."

"Drake Morrell!" Emilie Beaussaint turned her eyes to Ninon. "You didn't tell me about him."

"Grandmother said I shouldn't. She said it would only make you feel bad."

"Did you know him?"

"Yes, I did. I knew him very well. He was an old friend of the family, and . . . well, I liked him."

"He's quite a man, and we've been glad he rode to our town. I suspect it has been a long time since you've seen him, but Drake

is a handsome man, a very wise one, too. From all I hear he has
been rather . . . well, rather sudden, on occasion."

She smiled. "You could say that. Drake gambled too much, you
know. We all liked him, but he would gamble. The worst of it
was, he was a very good gambler, and when one is successful
there is always a question of one's honesty."

"I know."

"What's he doing now? Is he still a gambler?"

"He's teaching school."

"*Drake Morrell?* Teaching school?"

"Yes, and very well, too." It was a good story, and I told it,
right down to the day his students gathered around him with
their pistols.

"They actually carry weapons into the schoolroom?"

"You have to remember, Mrs. Beaussaint, that our town is apt
to be attacked at any moment, and then some of the students ride
over from ranches or other settlements nearby.

"There's small chance of trouble, but when trouble does occur
it is rather decisive. One had better be prepared for it. There are
mountain lions . . . they don't often attack, but occasionally they
do.

"Or one might come between a she-bear and her cubs. In that
case she will always attack.

"It's customary for the boys to hang up their guns and gunbelts
along with their wraps, but at the time Follett came after Drake
they were about to ride home, and luckily they were armed."

"I can't imagine it."

"Of course not. It is very easy for people living in warm,
comfortable homes miles from the frontier to tell people on the
frontier how they should live, but quite another thing for the
settler to return home to find his wife and children murdered
. . . for no particular reason."

"What about you, Lorna?" Ninon asked. "Are you going back?"

"I don't know. I am still thinking about it, when I can find the
time. If I do stay here I would have to think of some way to make
a living, and that isn't easy. I am not an actress as you are, and
my brothers couldn't afford to let me live here and do nothing. I
think I shall go back, but not all the way. I may stop in Denver,
or some such place. Or even go on to California."

We finished our meal, and sat long over our coffee. I listened
to the easy sound of the voices and watched the people passing on
the street.

Suddenly, two men loomed alongside our table. One was Horace Greeley, the other a stranger. "May we join you, Mr. Shafter? My friend and I have been discussing the Indian situation and we thought a little on-the-spot information might be helpful."

"Of course." I stood up quickly, and presented them to the ladies.

"You mentioned the possibility of much fighting on the plains when spring comes. What can be done to avoid it?"

"Nothing."

"Nothing? Come, come, young man! Surely there must be something!"

"Possibly, but I am sure I do not have such an answer. What I have said is what I believe. Most white men do not understand the Indian, many do not think it important to try. They simply accept the Indian as an obstacle to settlement of the land, just as the buffalo is.

"The young Indian who would win honor among his people can do it only through hunting or war. He has no other avenue. The old Indians have fought their wars, they have counted coup, taken scalps, stolen enough horses to make them rich in their terms. They have status in the Indian community.

"But how is the young Indian to do this? If the old Indian wishes to make peace, the young wishes to make war. An Indian cannot get a wife until he has proven himself as a man, as a warrior, so he must fight. He must trade horses for his bride, so he must steal horses. She will want the things the white man has, and so will he, and the only means of getting them is by killing or by trading, and he has very little to trade these days. So he must kill.

"The white man's way is to work, but this has for long been considered beneath a man . . . to do manual labor is to demean himself. And we need not think this surprising for there are areas in Europe, and even some in this country, where men believe the same.

"The Indian sees the white man in his land. A wagon train to an Indian is like a Spanish galleon loaded with Aztec treasure to Sir Francis Drake. Many of the Indians who attack the wagon trains live nowhere near the route of travel, but they ride for miles to attack those 'treasure' trains.

"The problem is simply that we have two peoples face to face with different religious beliefs, different customs, different styles of living. War was a way of life for the Viking, and for several centuries it was the accepted route to success in Europe. With the Indian it still is.

"Reason, if you like, with the old Indians. They are wise men, and they will listen. Their minds are as quick, their brains as good as yours. But after you have reasoned and made peace with the old Indian, the young Indian who wishes to become a warrior still has his problem.

"Before there can be peace there must be a new code of values for the Indian, and such things take generations to develop."

"Hmm." Greeley rubbed his chin whiskers. "There you have it, my friend. I cannot say that I agree with this young man, but he has given us the most lucid explanation I've heard."

"We all wish there was an easy way to solve the problem," I commented, "but there is none. Everyone hopes for an immediate solution, but the only solutions to social problems come through time. We in America always believe we have only to pass a law and everything will be changed, but the truth is nothing is changed. There is only one more law upon the books to be ignored or broken. People only obey a law the majority have already decided to obey, and it must be a very large majority."

"You don't talk like such a young man," the other man commented. "I would imagine you've done some thinking on the subject."

"On the frontier there is no time for 'boyhood.' One is a child, and then one is a man. As for the Indian, we had better think about him for he is thinking about us. But I've been fortunate. I've had some good teachers. The wilderness first, my neighbors, and then of course, I've had Plutarch, Blackstone, Hume, Locke, and a few others to consider."

"You are going back?"

"Yes. I am marshal of our town, and if trouble comes we will need every fighting man available."

When they had gone Mrs. Beaussaint left us, and Lorna remained with Ninon and me. We talked long into the night, and when they went up to their rooms I stepped outside the hotel.

Fifth Avenue was quiet. The leaves in the trees on Madison Square rustled softly. A carriage went by, turning up Broadway, and I crossed the street and walked along by the park.

I strolled along a path under the trees, crossing toward the other side of the park.

Footsteps whispered in the grass. Somebody was following me, keeping pace a little to my left and behind me. Following me where? Soon I'd be out on the other side in the bright glow of the gaslights again, so what was to happen must happen soon.

They were clumsy at being quiet. Any child in our town could have done it better. My ears tuned themselves to the sound, and when they began to move closer I glanced carefully around.

The area of the park was about ten acres. On the east side I could see a handsome looking church on Madison Avenue. The Square had walks that led from side to side, and in the summer there were often band concerts. It was a fashionable area and a favorite promenade of the people who lived in the hotels or nearby homes.

Near the bandstand there were good lights, and I walked along toward them. As I neared the stand I saw why those following me had not closed in, for two other men, roughs by their look, stood waiting there. When they saw the direction I was taking they had evidently circled around.

I'd been mentally prepared for two . . . four was rather more than I wanted, and I'd no desire to get into a shooting scrape in a strange city where such things were frowned upon.

The two near the bandstand stepped out to block my way. "Hello, boys," I said cheerfully, "I've been expecting you."

"Take him," said another voice, and inadvertently, I glanced up.

It was Jake McCaleb, of course.

The shoes behind me suddenly scraped on the walk, but the two coming toward me from the front were closer.

Four of them there were, but it was still no fair chance for them, for I'd lived my life on a hard frontier working with pick, shovel, and axe, climbing mountains, riding horseback. These were undoubtedly tough men among their kind, but they'd lived too soft, drunk too much whiskey, lazed about, then beat up some citizen in the process of robbing him.

The two were coming in, and I did not wait. I closed in suddenly, and stepping off to the left to put the outside man out of position, I threw a high, hard right at the man on the left.

There's an old adage that to win a street fight one had best land the first punch. I did just that and landed it with the idea in mind that if it landed there would only be three to my one after it.

I threw the punch at his chin but actually toward a point four inches back of his chin. I was punching *through* . . . and he, bless him, was coming in fast.

My fist caught his chin like the butt end of an axe hitting a log, and he was cold before he hit the ground. I had thrown my weight with the right hand punch, but as the blow landed I rolled at the hips, throwing a left from where my fist was when the right landed. The second man coming in caught the left, and then a man leaped on my back. I had thrown myself far to the right with the follow through with the left hook, and he leaped across my back rather than on it.

Turning sharply, I was face to face with the fourth man while the third was climbing off the grass. My right hand brought the pistol out, and laid the barrel of it across the side of his head, then wheeled on the one who was getting up. I had the gun on him, but backed swiftly around to face McCaleb.

I had them both under the gun, and they stopped. I backed off just a little in case any of the others made a move to rise. One of them was on his knees, shaking his head.

"I am going to kill you," I said to the fourth man. He began to back up, pleading.

"Now listen, guvner," he pleaded, "this here's a mistake! I . . ."

"You!" I motioned to the man I'd hit with the left, who was getting up. "You two have just one chance of walking away from here."

"What? Now, see here! We . . . !"

I had moved a little closer. "You two," I said, "were hired to beat up a man, perhaps to kill him. Now you're going to earn your money."

They stared at me, but the gun offered little room for argument. "You're going to earn it," I said, "or when they sweep up in the morning they'll have your corpses to sweep away."

I pointed at McCaleb with the pistol. "Let's see how good you are . . . beat him up."

"What? Hey, now . . . !"

My thumb eared back the hammer, and the click was loud in the park. "You've got until I count three.

"One!" They hesitated. "Two!"

McCaleb turned to run, and they wasted no time. Leaping after him, they began swinging with a will. Both were strong men, if not in very good shape, but McCaleb was tough. He turned sharply around, and he was no coward. He plowed into them, swinging.

Had he attacked instead of trying to get away, he might have done it, but they'd landed several heavy ones before he got started.

It was a short, vicious, bloody fight, but in moments they had him staggering. He kicked, butted, and swung, and he had brass knuckles on his right hand . . . but so did they.

He went down suddenly, started to get up, and they both swung at his skull. He went down again, and they started to reach for him.

"That's enough! Now beat it!"

They hesitated, gasping for breath, then they turned and ran in a stumbling run toward the park entrance on Madison.

Suddenly a voice spoke behind me. "Ah, that was a lovely sight! A lovely sight, lad! Sure, 'n these four years I've been wishin' for such a chance! Beggin' all the saints for it!"

My gun was in my hand when I turned. The man standing there was a large Irish policeman, and he was smiling. "Put it away, lad. You'll no be needin' it.

"I want to shake you by the hand, I do. That spalpeen of a Jake . . . he's standin' in with some of them with political power in the town, and there's no touchin' him, but I've wished this many a time to put him behind bars where he belongs."

"They attacked me," I said. "I am afraid the gentleman and I had a few words over in the Fifth Avenue, where I am staying."

"I know that, lad. I heard of it. There's little happens about here that does not come to me, and I've had me eye on that Jake for a long time now. I was expectin' this . . . but not tonight.

"Oh, it was a lovely sight! Ah, man, you should be a boxer!"

"Thank you, officer. I think I'd better get inside. If you have no objections?"

"Oh, none at all! Go along with ye, an' carry the blessin's of Tom Mulrooney with ye!" He waved a hand. "Go along! Ye'll hear no more of this!"

When I reached the walk in front of the hotel I straightened my coat and put my hat back on my head. For a moment I stood on the steps, composing myself, then strolled inside, nodded to the clerk, and crossed to the elevator.

Suddenly, I felt very good. New York was quite a town, after all. Quite a town.

I could come to like it here.

THIRTY-EIGHT

Yet I found myself restless, and my mind returned again and again to the mountains and to my promise to Uruwishi. I thought I had detected in the old man's manner a wish to do just as I wished . . . to go to the Medicine Wheel. What it meant to him, if anything, I did not know, but he had been a great warrior. I knew he did not wish to waste away, to die slowly, seated by the fire.

On the night after my brief difficulty in Madison Square, I took Lorna to the theater. She wore a new gown she'd found in a shop on Broadway. At that time the fashionable shopping area was on Broadway between the St. Nicholas Hotel and Thirty-Fourth Street, and most of the great stores were located there. She found the gown she wanted in Stewart's, and as we were shown down the aisle to our seats I overheard many complimentary comments, as many from women as from men.

She was excited, and I was pleased for her. This was more her world than mine, for I longed for the feel of a good horse under me and the fresh chill of a wind from off the Big Horns. I wanted again the dark and lonely canyons where only echoes lived, the crash and roar of waters charging between the boulders, hurling themselves against a rocky wall . . . I wanted to skirt the deadfalls, gather the dead sticks from the ground, build a fire of cedar or pine, and smell the smoke.

267

I liked to sit in Delmonico's or the Fifth Avenue and watch the pretty women pass. I liked the swish of silks and the quiet tones of people talking . . . I liked to think they spoke of music, the arts, and the theater, and that they said witty things or ironic ones . . . but I knew that most of the conversation was dull and commonplace, of day-to-day things, a woman complaining because her corset was too tight, and a man wishing he could get outside for a smoke or a drink.

But I liked looking at them, though not so much as at my own country, so far, far away, and I whispered to Lorna, "I'm going back. I want to see the country again from up on the Beaver Rim . . . I want to ride the trails up the Wind Rivers and drink from the Popo Agie."

She nodded quickly. "I'm afraid I do too, Ben. Let's go home."

When the show had finished, we went backstage for Ninon. She was dressing quickly, and she looked around at me and laughed. "Ben, you look like a little lost boy tonight!"

"I am," I admitted, "I'm going back to the mountains."

"Tonight?"

"No . . . soon. Lorna wants to go, too."

"My show closes on Saturday, Ben. I think I will play Millinette for the last time, then."

"It is enough. You can come home with me."

She gasped, beautifully, teasing. "Lorna! Did you hear *that*? I think he's proposing." Suddenly she looked very prim, and she came right up to me and looked up at me, her eyes laughing. "Young man, are your intentions honorable?"

"Sort of . . . at least they are intentions."

There was one more thing to do, something I'd neglected. I called upon Stryker.

"There's a place called the Gold Exchange, I think?"

He looked at me curiously. "Yes, of course. You are interested in buying gold?"

"Selling," I said, "I want to sell gold."

He frowned a little. "But you see, they have no gold at the Gold Exchange. They are buying paper . . . speculating in gold prices."

"I want to sell gold," I replied quietly, "a considerable amount."

He sat back in his chair. "That can be arranged, of course. It might be interesting to see their reaction to some real gold. Do you have this gold? Or is it still to be mined?"

From my inside belt I took a bar of gold weighing about two kilos. "No, it is gold. Here . . . fresh, clean, unadulterated."

He was startled. "You are carrying that around with you? *On your person?*"

"Part of the time," I admitted. "At the going price I imagine that is worth about fifteen hundred dollars. I want to sell this one and eleven others just like it."

He sat back in his chair. He looked a little pale. "Shafter, I never knew anybody like you. You mean you have about twenty thousand dollars in pure gold? And you're carrying it with you?"

"Oh, I've been reasonably careful! Can you arrange a sale?"

"Of course, of course! A dozen bars of gold! Shafter, I never saw the like!" He sobered suddenly. "I suppose you can account for it? After all, that's a lot of gold."

"I have a little mine out there . . . I dug the gold myself; my brother and I melted it down in his blacksmith shop."

"A *little* mine? This would seem to be something quite substantial. How large a crew do you have at work?"

I shrugged, very casually. "I mined this myself. I hadn't much time, you know, just enough to get started before winter came on, and I made a few trips after the freeze up, but I'm no miner."

"But surely, you'll open it up in the spring? You could get a crew in there . . . no telling how much you might take out. It's worth millions!"

"Maybe. There's no question about the surface values. They are excellent, and I've no doubt I could get a good bit more out, but I'm no miner, as I've said, and I have some cattle now and am more interested in building up a cow ranch. I suppose I'll work at it from time to time, but I'm not that interested."

"Would you sell? I am not making an offer, understand, but well . . . this is *gold*, man. *Gold!*"

"I hadn't thought of selling. Of course . . . if the price was right . . . but how do you put a price on gold? I've only to mine what I want, buy what I want, and whenever I need money go back and dig out some more."

"But that's no way to do it. You need a crew . . . equipment. A mine as valuable as that should be a big venture. Why, there are men here in town who would jump at the chance."

"Maybe." I got up. "If you can find a buyer, I would appreciate it. For the gold, that is."

That twenty thousand, if I could get that much, represented freedom. A time to work, to plan, to decide just where I wanted to go and what to do. Whatever else I might do I knew that I would do some ranching. I had learned a little about cattle, and the market for beef was growing.

Good grazing land was to be had for the taking, and I believed some of the men now at our town would come with me.

But what of Ninon? Could she leave all this for the frontier? Many women had followed their men into the lonely lands, and from her brief experience with us she knew what it was like . . . but had I the right to ask her?

Well, why not? She could only say no . . . and I had almost asked her at dinner.

I shook hands with Stryker and left him hurrying back to his office. Twenty thousand dollars, the amount I hoped to realize from my gold venture, was a good-sized fortune in this day.

Lorna was waiting for me at the hotel. "Ben, we've a letter from Cain. There's been trouble."

"What is it?"

"Ollie Trotter shot Neely Stuart . . . wounded him very badly. It was some fight over Neely's mine. I think from what Cain says . . ."

I took the letter from her hand.

Dear Lorna and Ben:

Shortly after you left Finnerly, Pappin and Trotter returned to town. Nobody saw them until Neely went to his mine. They'd broken the lock off the door and were digging up some gold they had cached there before he sent them away.

He tried to stop them, and Trotter shot him. Colly heard the shot and went to see what had happened, and they rode off. Webb got a look at them as they left, so we have double identification.

Colly trailed them into the mountains but they got clean away. Neither Stacy nor Ethan was about, but Colly thinks they will come back.

The cattle are doing well. Business has fallen off some, but we've a half dozen wagon loads of ties to freight to the railroad.

Nubbin Taylor, his wife and youngsters were killed by Indians, their cabin burned, stock run off.

There was a little more, but what I had read was quite enough. If the Indians had attacked Taylor's place . . . he was only four miles east of town . . . anything might happen.

"Lorna," I said, "better get packed. We're going home."

She smiled. "Bendigo, I am packed. I knew you'd be wanting to leave."

THIRTY-NINE

She stood by the window, looking down into the street, and I looked at her and thought how different a world was this from our own little town at the foot of the Wind Rivers!

This sister of mine was tall, beautifully shaped, with clear, intelligent eyes, a wry, but pleasant sense of humor . . . what would her life be?

"There's one thing I must do," I said.

"Of course. You must see Ninon." She turned from the window. "Do that, Bendigo. I've some goodbyes to say, too."

"You?" I was surprised.

She laughed at me. "You've been very busy, Ben, and I can't blame you if you haven't noticed, but I have a friend, too. A very nice gentleman, in fact." She hesitated. "I wonder if you'd approve?"

"If you like him, I will like him," I replied simply. "Who is he?"

"His name is Fairchild . . . Jackson Fairchild. He's a doctor . . . a physician."

"I'd like to meet him."

"You shall. We are to have lunch together in a few minutes." She came over to me and put her hand on my arm. "Please like him. I do . . . very much."

"Well . . . if he's right for you. Remember, you're something very special to Cain and me."

"He's very special, too. He's from upstate New York, Bendigo, and he grew up on a farm, studied medicine, and he's been practicing in a small town in New Hampshire, but now he wants to go west."

"Where? I mean where in the west?"

"California, I think, but he's not quite sure. Only that he wants to be where things are happening, and he has an offer to go into practice in Colorado."

"Well, I'll talk to him. In the meanwhile . . ."

"I know. You're going to meet Ninon."

Their suite was on the floor above mine, and I went up the steps, then paused at a window looking out over the city. I knew so little of cities, even now, and so little of this one where there was so much to learn. In between times I had met people, Horace Greeley who might soon be a candidate for president, several writers, naturalists, and many would-be investors in land or mines. All were interested in the western lands, and all asked questions. What astonished me even more was that the answers came readily to my lips . . . at least, when their questions related to conditions or circumstances. On the Indian question I had no answers, no conclusions to offer.

I had fought Indians, hunted with them, talked with them, ridden miles with them, and many of them I liked. We could learn, each from the other, and I found the Indian very quick to adapt to conditions that favored him. But for most of our customs they had no use at all.

Yet the questions I had been asked had started me thinking, and when I returned to my own country I would try to learn. One never realizes how much and how little he knows until he starts talking.

Mrs. Beaussaint answered the door. "Ninon will be out in a minute, Mr. Shafter. You are going home, I hear?"

"Yes."

I spoke with some reservations, for although our town was still my home, I somehow did not believe it would be for long. All that had been said about its location was true, I expect, and with the railroad completed to the south, the new town would come into being near the right-of-way.

Ninon came in, coming quickly to me, both hands outstretched. "Ben! You're leaving?"

"I must. There's been trouble out there."

"It was always you, wasn't it, Ben? You were always the first to face whatever happened."

"I don't know. I did what was necessary."

"I know all about it. You went after Mae and the children when the Indians had them, and you went to help those Mormons in the snow, and you were out there in the street when the renegades attacked the town. It was you and Ethan Sackett who supplied most of the meat that first terrible winter. I heard all about it. And saw part of it."

"A man does what is necessary. And then I always had good men beside me. There was Cain, and Ethan and Webb . . . and of course, John Sampson."

"But it was *you*, Ben! You spoke for the town. You led the way."

"No, Ninon. It was Ruth Macken and Cain. They were always the ones."

She smiled. "In a way, it was. But it was you, Ben, more than anyone else."

"It was all of us. We were all changing, all growing up, all discovering what it takes to bring people together, to build something. I'm not sure we know anything even yet, but we'll do a better job wherever we go after this."

Mrs. Beaussaint had left us alone, and together we walked to the window. "Your show closes soon?"

"They've extended the time for another week. Then I am going back to New Orleans."

"You're not taking any of the offers you've had?"

She smiled at me. "None of those I've had so far, Ben. But you never can tell . . . if the right offer came along, well, I might listen."

"I was coming around to that. How about a run of the show contract? That's the only offer I could make. At this moment I don't even know where the show will be playing, and I am not sure of the town or the place . . . only the time."

"Would I be the leading lady?"

"Of course. And with top billing always."

"I'll take that offer, Ben. It's just the one I've been waiting for."

Well, I'd been getting to be quite a talker, but all of a sudden I wasn't so good any more, and I just stood there looking at her and she at me, but we didn't need to say much or do much; we both knew how we felt about it.

We stood there by the window holding hands and watching the traffic in the street below. "I've got a few cattle, and I'm going to buy more. I'll do some ranching, either in Wyoming or Oregon, and I'll write a little about the things I know best."

We talked . . . a lot of foolishness and some good sense, and then I told her about Lorna's friend.

"Ben! Let's go see him! Are they downstairs now?"

He stood up as we neared the table. He was tall, as tall as I was but probably twenty pounds lighter in weight, a mighty handsome man with a good, strong face and a firm grip to his hand. "Dr. Jackson Fairchild," he said. "Lorna has been telling me all about both of you."

We sat down and talked the hour away, and after a while I left the talking to them and remembered the rolling wagon wheels, the crisp brown grass of the plains, the river crossings, the bitter struggles, the times we had lost our horses and found them again, the Indian fights, and our town beside its small stream with the white cliff rising above it and the pines.

I was homesick for the smell of cedar smoke and the feel of a good horse. There was nothing here to remind me of the west except the six-shooter in my waistband. Even the girls seemed different. Ninon had grown from a child into a beautiful young woman whom I only slightly knew, after all, and Lorna was no longer a girl from our town but a young lady of fashion.

I listened to their laughter, listened to their talk of the west and of the town where we all would be together, yet I remembered the creak of a saddle and the seamed face of old Uruwishi. I remembered the cool wind from down the canyon of the Popo Agie, and the smell of powder smoke and the kick of a rifle butt against my shoulder. I remembered the day with Ethan when we were cutting our meat and the renegades had come upon us, and I remembered the smell of smoky, sweaty buckskins, and the far-off gleam of lights as we rode home.

Suddenly, I stood up. "I want to take a walk," I said. "I've some things to think about."

Outside the hour had grown late. We had talked long, and there were gray shadows already, for the sun was hidden behind a ceiling of dull cloud. I shrugged into my coat and walked off down the street, not too aware of where I was going.

The old smells were not here. These smells were of coal smoke and the city. Suddenly I found myself on the Bowery. Pawnbrokers' shops, third-class hotels, flophouses, low-class theaters and concert saloons. This had once been an area of farms, a place where lay the broad lands of the Brevoorts, the Dyckmans, the De Lanceys; and even old Peter Stuyvesant had a farm here.

It felt good, striding along the sidewalks, listening to the carriages in the slushy streets, watching the gaslights and the windows I passed.

Tomorrow I would be starting for home . . . tomorrow.

It could not be too soon.

FORTY

I sat in the car looking out over the vast white expanse. The snow-covered plains stretched away, losing themselves against a milky horizon.

It was cold . . . bitter cold out there. The stove at the end of the car glowed a sullen red, but its warmth extended only a few feet. Lorna sat near it with Dr. Fairchild and several others.

The train moved slowly, creeping along the icy rails. To be derailed at such a time and place would be about the worst thing that could happen, for we were now miles from anywhere and far out upon the plains. Fuel was scarce along the route and we must make do with what we had.

The conductor stopped by. "Aren't you a western man, Mr. Shafter?"

"Yes. I live up in the South Pass country."

"Then you know about this?" He waved a hand at the snow.

"I do."

"Folks are scared . . . there's some women-folks and young-sters in the next coach, newcomers. The men are tryin' to look brave enough, but they're as scared as the women."

"I don't blame them. If we got stuck out here . . . well, we'd have to tear up the tracks and burn the ties."

The conductor was shocked. "Oh, no! The railroad wouldn't allow it."

Well, I smiled at him. "Conductor, your railroad bosses are a long way off, and the cold is here, now. Believe me, if it came to that we'd burn the ties."

"What I was going to ask, Mr. Shafter, is whether you'd walk back and have a word with them. Encourage them a little."

"Of course." I got up, hitching my gun into position under my coat. Cheyenne was far away down the track, and there were miles upon miles of desolation ahead of us. Someday, no doubt, there would be farms or ranches along here, and towns. Now there was nothing.

A cold wind moaned about the creeping train; the piles of fuel looked pitifully small.

Balancing to the movement of the train, I walked back to the car behind. Stepping out of my car to the platform I felt the icy air . . . it must be ten below zero.

They looked up when I came into the car. Several women with scarves over their heads, a dozen children, and three men. At the back of the car a shabby rough-looking man with a handlebar mustache was sleeping. He seemed undisturbed by the cold.

"How are you?" I spoke to the nearest of the men. "Cold out there. Coming out to settle?"

"Yah. Ve go to Vyoming."

"To farm?"

"Ve look for goldt, I think. There iss goldt, I hear."

"If you're lucky." I had been. The $21,700 in several eastern banks spoke of that, yet I had known many who were not . . . and I'd not wasted my time looking. "Farming might be surer . . . or buffalo hunting. There's a big demand for buffalo hides."

"I cannot shoot. I haff never shot a gun."

Appalled, I just looked at him. He stared back at me, sensing my doubt. "Vhy shoot? I think the Indians are goodt folks if you are goodt to them. I do not vant to shoot them."

"Sometimes they are. I hope it is the good ones you meet. I've met both kinds. I think you should be prepared for the bad ones even while you hope to meet the good. You have a family."

He nodded confidently. "I do not worry. I haff a goodt family. Ve vork hardt, ve make it."

"The train will run slow through here because of the ice on the rails," I commented. "If the train stops, don't get out unless you are told to. People have been left out here . . . by accident."

They were listening to me, I could see. One quiet man said, "Thank you, sir. I am afraid we all have much to learn about the west. You say you have met Indians?"

"I have . . . often. The Sioux will be on the warpath when spring comes . . . they will wait for the grass to turn green so there will be food for their horses. There will be young men going out on their first scalp-hunting raid. I would suggest you locate somewhere close to a village or other people at least until you know the country."

"Are you a miner?"

"No. I run a few cattle, and I am considering a larger scale of operation. We've been building a town out there in the South Pass area, but I'd say our time is about up. We don't have enough to support a population."

"South Pass?" Another man looked up quickly. "Why, that's where the gold is! What d'you mean? Not enough to support a population?"

"A few claims have been located that are paying off. Most of the miners aren't making a living."

He did not believe me. "Tryin' to scare us off?" he said. "You can't do it, mister. We know all about it."

"I am glad you do and hope you find what you're looking for." I nodded toward the stove. "Make your fuel last. At this rate it will be hours before we can get more."

Turning, I started back. The man who thought I was trying to scare him off spoke up again. "You actually from out there?"

"I helped build the first houses," I said. "I was there from the beginning."

"I hear it's a wild place. Lots of women, shoot-ups, and outlaws. Why, they say there's a Mexican outlaw who's got 'em all scared to death. This Herrara . . ."

"Herrara did make some trouble around South Pass City," I said, "but they sent him packing."

He stared angrily. "They sent who? Why that town was scared to death of him! I read all about it!"

"Nobody scares a town where every man grew up with a gun. They let him swagger around a little until they lost patience, and then they ran him out of town just like his own people ran him out of Mexico."

"I don't believe that!"

For a moment I just looked at him. "My friend," I said after a moment, "what you have just said could get you killed where you are going. In this country if you call a man a liar you'd better reach for a gun when you do it. Nobody out here likes a loose tongue. You'd better learn while you can."

"Huh!" he said contemptuously. "If I have to use a gun, I will do it. I'm as good with a gun as any of them. They don't come any tougher out there than they do where I come from."

"Remember what I said about fuel. Stay close to the stove and burn it just enough to keep warm." I turned away and started back to my own car.

The nicely spoken man came after me. "Mind if I ask a few questions?" He gestured toward a pale, attractive young woman and a boy. "That's my family."

"All right."

"We have all heard of South Pass City. I'd like a turn at gold mining myself. Is it a good place?"

I shrugged, smiling. "My friend, most places are good places if your approach is right. There are fine people there, and there are some bad ones. South Pass City is only one of several small communities, and there is some mining along a half dozen of the creeks.

"Our own settlement is only a few miles from South Pass City, and we'd welcome you. However, I believe some of us will be leaving the area. Most of the good placer-mining claims have been staked, and the traffic along the Overland Trail will disappear when the railroad is in full operation, and I believe it is even now. I know the east and west lines have been joined, and by now they probably have scheduled trains . . . I haven't made inquiries beyond my own transportation.

"We'd welcome you, but you will have to think of making a living."

"You are in the cattle business?"

"In a small way. My brother and I operate a sawmill, also, but even that must be moved. We've been cutting ties for the railroad and timbers for some of the mines, although few have gotten so far along."

"Is it a violent place? Alec Williams here," he gestured toward the man who had spoken of Herrara, "has been telling us of the killings. He says the marshal there, somebody named Ben Shafter, is a killer."

"You won't need to worry about him nor about the community. There has been very little shooting."

Williams was listening. "A lot you know! That Shafter killed two men last year! Right in the middle of town!"

"Perhaps. His job is to keep the peace, but unfortunately there are always troublemakers. The two men who were killed were drifters, toughs, and not of the town at all. They came looking for trouble."

"Were you there?" Williams demanded belligerently. "What do you know about it?"

"Yes, I was there. I saw it."

Now I was eager to get away. The train was crawling now, and stooping to look out the windows, I saw the snow was falling again, thicker and faster. I heard the wind whine around the train.

"Save your fuel," I warned, "better stay close to the stove and to each other. This may develop into a bad storm."

Alec Williams was one of those who fed on sensation, and I'd known his kind before. Men were killed by officers of the law in eastern cities and villages, but nobody thought of building them up as killers or as gunfighters . . . they saved that for the west.

The train crept along. The stack of fuel grew lower. I walked back to the car where I had been riding and stood beside Lorna and Dr. Fairchild. "We're in trouble," I said quietly. "We're going to have a blizzard. The snow is falling and the wind is picking up."

Fairchild looked up. "But we're in the train. It will be safe here."

"These cars are not easy to heat, doctor," I said, "and there's very little fuel. If this keeps up we may get snowed in."

"Snowed in? You mean the train will stop?"

"We may even be covered with snow. It happens out here . . . this is a blizzard building up."

The plains that had stretched far away like a frozen sea had vanished. Now there was just the howling wind and a visibility of only inches beyond windows, which were swiftly frosting over.

I stopped the conductor. "We'd better get them all into one car, it will save fuel and keep them warmer."

"Good idea." He hurried away, his face taut with worry. I did not want to sit down. A restlessness was on me, and I was worried. I tried to remember what kind of country we were passing over . . . plains, yes, but had there been any stream beds? Any stands of cottonwood? Then I remembered that I had been asleep when we passed over much of this.

There was a station or a town. As the bunch from the other car trooped in, I asked the conductor about it. "No good," he said. "There's a station, but it's been closed, and the folks that were in the town picked up and left."

"How about buildings? Were there any?"

"Shacks . . . nothing but shacks and soddies. There was a store and saloon. Those folks were damn' fools. There was no chance for a town there. Nothing for it to draw on. Maybe if the country settles up there'd be enough business, but I doubt it. Somebody convinced them this would be the big metropolis of the plains.

"Why, I saw lots selling for a hundred dollars apiece right out there where there's nothing but prairie dogs and coyotes!"

"How far from here?"

"I dunno. Ten, fifteen miles. Hard to figure where we are when you can't see nothing."

"When we get there, stop."

"Mister, I daren't. Wheels would freeze to the tracks in no time. Anyway, there's nothing there. Nothing an' nobody."

I looked at him. "Conductor, when you get there . . . *stop*. There's fuel . . . or should be."

He went away and the train kept on. Some of the youngsters were whimpering. Lorna helped rock a baby to sleep, and the men went back to the other car to carry in what fuel remained. Nobody had much to say.

Williams came over to me. "It's mighty cold. Trains ever get stuck out here?"

"They could."

His face was gray. "It's my fault. I wanted to come out here. Pa said I was a fool, and Lil, she didn't want to leave. I just figured I'd do better. I wasn't making anything back there, just workin' sunup to sundown on the farm."

"It will be the same here," I told him quietly. "Wherever a man is, there is work to do. That's the best part of it."

"The *best* part?"

"The very best part. My friend, there is a Hell. It's when a man has a family to support, has his health, and is ready to work, and there is no work to do. When he stands with empty hands and sees his children going hungry, his wife without the things to do with. I hope you never have to try it."

The car trembled with the force of the wind. Blown bits of snow, each one a bit of ice, rattled against the windows. The windows were coated over with frost, and when the conductor next came through an icy blast blew in with him. He stamped the snow from his overshoes.

"Got to keep the doors open. They'll freeze shut. Anyway, with that stove goin' you'll need air, time to time."

"How far to that station?"

"You got me, mister. Ought to be soon."

There were five cars on the train. Three freight cars and two passenger cars and a sleeping car for the train crew. It was not really a caboose, just a freight car lined with tar paper with bunks and a stove.

He went on through, pulling the door shut behind him. After he had gone I looked at the snow that had fallen from his boots. The snow from his last trip was still there, unmelted.

The train whistle wailed into the night, a long, mournful cry. Lorna put the baby down on the seat and tucked the blanket around it.

The passengers were few. The nicely spoken man was Miller. "What about the town?" he asked. "Will there be people there?"

"No, I don't think so. It is one of those towns that had no reason for being." As I spoke I felt a twinge, thinking of our own town with sadness. "It has been abandoned. I've been thinking we might find some fuel."

The train was slowing, then it ground to a stop. The conductor put his head in the door. "Here's your town! But it's not empty. There's somebody got a light yonder."

With a rush we buttoned up and tightened collars and went down the icy steps to the platform. There were some stacks of firewood alongside the deserted station, and we rushed to it.

"We can tear down a building," Williams suggested. "It will make a good hot fire."

We started for the nearest one, and suddenly a man appeared with a lantern in one hand, a shotgun in the other.

"Here! What you doing?" he demanded angrily.

"Loading some fuel," the conductor replied. "We're about to freeze on that train."

Another man appeared, also with a shotgun. "You ain't loadin' nothin'!" he said roughly. "You uns are on a train. You're a-goin' somewhar. We uns are stuck here an' we got a long winter ahead of us. You jest git right back on that train an' git!"

"The wood by the depot belongs to the railroad," the conductor protested. "We're takin' that!"

"No, you ain't!" The shotguns came level. "We need that wood! Now you jest pull out o' here. You want to argy about it, you start in, but we aim to be shootin'."

"Forget it, conductor," I said quietly. "We've loaded some, and it will help. He's right, you know. These men and their families are stuck . . . they're here for the winter."

"We could take them on the train," the conductor suggested. "We could take them on to the next town."

"What? And leave all this here?" One of the men swept a gesture at the town. "Mister, we bought lots here! When the other folks pulled out, we done bought *their* lots! When spring comes this place'll be boomin'! We're gonna be rich! *Rich!*"

"Let's get back to the train before the wheels do freeze," I suggested. "We'll find something else!"

We scrambled aboard, the locomotive started, its wheels ground, then it reversed, started forward again, and slowly moved off into the blowing snow.

"Poor damn' fools!" the conductor said. "I hadn't the heart to tell them."

"Tell them what?" I asked.

"About their town. Folks left because they heard what's the truth. Come spring we're goin' to straighten the line through here and this town will be three, four miles from the track. His lots ain't worth nothin' . . . this here'll go back to prairie dogs, jackrabbits, and kiyutees!"

FORTY-ONE

Nonetheless, we had loaded what amounted to a cord of wood before we were stopped, and when the train rolled westward we went with a slightly greater margin of safety.

The conductor stopped by about an hour later. We had made coffee on the stove, and we poured a cup for him. He stood by, his clothes streaked with snow from crossing between the cars.

"Gettin' deeper out there. We're almighty afeared of the cut up ahead."

"Cut?" Fairchild asked. "You mean a cut through a hill?"

"Sort of. She's thirty feet deep and most of a half mile long."

"Have you got scoop shovels aboard?" I asked.

"I should reckon. Maybe a dozen. If we make it through the cut we can get on to the next settlement. There's folks there, and there's stores and grub . . . fuel, too."

Even as he spoke the train ground to a halt. The train reversed, then lunged ahead, then stopped.

I picked up my buffalo coat and with the conductor, went up through the cars. We climbed down the icy steps and jumped off into the snow. It was bitter cold even here where there was some shelter from the wind.

With the conductor breaking trail, we went up to the locomotive. The engineer was a burly Irishman. He leaned from the cab. "We're stopped, Walt. Big drift up there."

He got down from the cab and we walked forward, stumbling and pushing through the snow.

The drift had come down from the cut, slanting across the tracks. Where the locomotive had stopped it was at least eight feet deep and no telling how far it ran.

"We're about a third of the way through the cut, but I doubt if this drift runs far. If we could just get through here we might make it the rest of the way before daylight."

"Let's have those shovels," I said. "And if you've got any more lanterns, let's have a couple."

The wind swirled snow in my face, taking my breath. I hid my chin behind my collar and turned my face sidewise to the wind, walking back to the car where the shovels would be.

Taking a shovel, I walked back to the cow-catcher on the engine and began cutting out blocks of snow and tossing them aside. There was little room, but soon Fairchild joined me, and then Williams.

Williams was a talker, but he was also a good worker, and we worked steadily, shoveling the snow to one side. The slanting drift had filled in solidly on the far side of the engine, and we could dispose of the snow only where there was some shelter under the bank.

The work warmed us. We worked steadily, taking a moment now and again for a breather. Soon Miller came and took Fairchild's place while he returned for coffee, and two other men, their names unknown to me, came up and joined in.

The engine whistled, started forward, gained about fifty feet, and stopped again.

Snow swirled in our faces, frost formed from our breathing. My toes grew cold, and I stamped my feet on the ties to warm them, to restore circulation. We slugged away at the bank of snow, shoveling under it, then bringing it tumbling down about us.

We gained a few more feet, then a few more. When I returned to the warmth of the car and held my stiffened fingers to the blaze, I hated the thought of returning to the job, yet it must be done. I looked at the fuel box, then at Lorna. She was watching me, for our minds worked the same and she knew at once how little warmth remained to us. While we had worked the fuel had burned down to nothing.

Returning, I swung up to the warmth of the cab. "You know this country. Are there any creek bottoms near? Anywhere I could find some fuel?"

He shook his head. "Not that I recall. There's a crick up ahead, but she don't amount to much. No trees that I know of."

The fireman spoke up. "Yes, there's a few. Back about a hundred yards from the right-of-way the crick takes a turn, and I've seen treetops in there."

"You'll have to share with them back yonder," I said. "They're about out."

He gestured toward the tender. "We ain't doin' so well ourselves. Unless we have fuel we don't go nowheres, an' you don't neither."

An hour more we slugged away at the snowbank, and the locomotive gained a little more. We carried armfuls of wood from the tender back to the car and fed the hungry flames. The cold seemed to have grown more intense.

Suddenly, we broke through. The wall of snow before us caved in, and could see the rails ahead. Throwing our shovels into the freight car, we scrambled into our own passenger car to get warm while the train inched ahead.

A half mile long he had said, and we had come about a third of the distance when we stuck the first time. Now it must be almost half.

The train chugged-chugged ahead, occasionally spinning its wheels, then catching hold and going on, about as fast as a man could walk.

Fairchild looked at me. "Do you think that's it? Are we through?"

I shrugged. "There's no telling. There's maybe another drift ahead."

Wearily, I dropped into a seat beside Lorna. "Are you all right?" she whispered.

"Cold," I said, "and tired, but I've been cold and tired before this. Don't worry. We'll get through."

She glanced at Fairchild. "He's doing his share, isn't he?"

"He is that. He's a good man, honey."

She sat back, closing her eyes. She had lived with Cain and me too long, and she knew too well how we thought, and I expect she had worried about this, about how Fairchild would stand the gaff, and whether we would accept him. She knew we would accept him. She knew we would take him into the family, but she wanted more than that. She wanted him accepted for himself alone.

Still, the train was moving forward. How far had we come since we quit shoveling snow? A hundred yards? Two hundred?

Suddenly the train stopped. I sat still, my eyes closed, hating the thought of going out there again.

The door opened with a blast of freezing air. "Shafter? You got to see this to believe it." The conductor was standing at the door. "We're stopped, but it ain't snow this time, it's buffalo!"

"What?"

I struggled into my coat. I was tired, but so were the others, probably more tired than I. Fairchild was up. Williams, Miller, and the two of us followed the conductor back through the door. We got down and started forward, and suddenly I saw them.

We had entered the narrowest part of the cut, and the buffalo had taken shelter here from the storm. They were packed solid, wall to wall of the cut, and snow had drifted over and around them. As buffalo usually face into a storm, the heavy wool on their heads and shoulders was thick with snow. They stood stolidly, peering at us.

There was no way to judge their numbers, but a rough guess would say there were hundreds.

"They won't budge!" the brakeman said, standing near the cow-catcher. "They're alive, but they aren't about to move."

"If one of them got down on the tracks," the brakeman added, "it could derail the train."

Exasperated, we stood and stared at them. Heavy heads hanging, they stared back. They had found the best shelter anywhere around, and they were not going to budge simply because this puffing black monster wanted to crowd in where they had established themselves.

"We could shoot them," Williams suggested.

"And then what?" I asked. "Some of those right there weigh two thousand pounds or more. The smallest I can see will weigh eight or nine hundred. How are you going to move that weight after it's dead?"

"The shooting would scare 'em!" he insisted.

"Not buffalo," I replied. "Buffalo don't scare very easy. I've seen a buffalo hunter on a stand kill all afternoon from one position and the rest keep on feeding. They won't scare worth a damn. We're stuck."

"We could push into them. Maybe they'd move."

"You can try. You'll just get your tracks all bloody and slippery." Leaning closer to the conductor, I said, "There may be five hundred of them in there."

"What can we do then?"

"Try pushing ahead very carefully. You might start them. If you don't, our best bet is just to wait. When the storm eases, they'll move."

When a buffalo wants to go somewhere, he goes. If there isn't an opening, he makes one. Under some conditions buffalo can be stampeded, but in this cold, in such a situation, it was likely to prove impossible.

We walked back and climbed aboard the train. On the way my toe struck something in the snow, and when I kicked the snow away I saw that it was a broken railroad tie. With Alec Williams to help, we got it aboard. We had no axe, but we did have our Bowie knives and could cut loose pieces to add to the fire.

The train jerked, bumped a little, then eased forward, ever so slowly. A moment, and it stopped. Eased forward again and stopped again. Putting my head back against the plush seat, I let my muscles slowly relax. It was up to the engineer now . . . maybe he could do it.

Somehow I fell asleep, and when next my eyes opened the car was gray with morning light. Lorna's head was against my shoulder, and Fairchild was curled up on two seats and a sack laid between them, just across the aisle.

Williams was peering out the window, but looking out, all I could see was white. "Where are we?"

"Stuck," he said, "and the last of the fuel is ready to go in."

Easing away from Lorna, I got her head off my shoulder and on the cushion. Slowly, I got to my feet.

"Have we made any headway?"

"I dunno. I just woke up myself."

The others were fast asleep. I walked to the end of the car and opened the door. The cold air came in, and if anything it was colder. Suddenly a huge body brushed past the steps, almost at my feet . . . then another.

The buffalo were moving. The engineer whistled, and they started to gallop, then slowed down. I knew there was no steam to waste and that whistling would do little good. The engine threshed its wheels, then eased slowly forward.

We had cleared the last of the cut, and were on the downgrade when we sighted a square heap of snow that had to be a pile of ties. The train stopped, and we all got down, brushing the snow from the ties and loading most of them onto the tender. Several we carried back to our car.

"There's a town ahead where we can get some grub. Maybe some hot coffee. We'll stop."

Back at the stove I brushed the snow from my gloves and put them down on the seat. Lorna was awake, and so was Dr. Fairchild.

Alec Williams stopped by, grinning. "Well, we're on our way. How do you live out here, anyway?"

"Like anywhere . . . we do one thing at a time. It's a good

country for men, but as somebody said it's hell on horses and
women."

He chuckled. "Maybe . . . only my wife's been tryin' to talk
me into comin' west for a year."

He started away, then came back. "Say . . . didn't they call
you Shafter?"

"That's right, Williams. I'm Ben Shafter."

"Well, I'll be damned. I'll be forever damned." He shook his
head. "Wait'll I tell them back home I been workin' side by side
with Ben Shafter!"

Lorna had moved over to sit beside Fairchild, so I leaned back
and closed my eyes. In a few hours we'd be in Cheyenne, and
there would be a stop there long enough to do a little business.
The train whistled and the sound lost itself over the vast, snow-
covered wastes. It was no longer snowing, and the wind had gone
down. The last whisper of the wind stirred the snow like an
empty ghost, whirled it, and lacking energy to persist, dropped
it. Under the snow there was grass lying still, waiting for the
warmth of a spring sun, and where the snow now was there would
be buffalo walking, and when the buffalo were gone there would
be cattle, and then there would be wheat or corn or rye or flax.

The Indians would kill some of the newcomers. Cold, starvation,
drought, and storm would kill others, but there would be no end
for they would still come. Men like Williams and Miller, men like
Cain and Webb, men like Neely and Drake and Sackett . . . they
would still come. There was no end to them.

The Indian, like the buffalo, would pass from the face of the
land or become one with those who came, for they were all
caught up with change, the inevitable change that comes to men
and towns and nations. Men move across the face of the world
like tides upon the sea, and when they have gone, others will
come; and the weak would pass and the strong would live, for that
was the way it was, and the way it would be.

For a little while men might change that, but in the last
analysis men would not decide. It would be the wind, the rain,
the tortured earth, and the looming mountains, it would be
drought and hunger, it would be cold and desolation. For it is
these elements that decide, and no man can build a wall strong
enough to keep them out forever.

Lorna touched my shoulder. "Ben? We're coming into town."

FORTY-TWO

One who returns to a place sees it with new eyes. Although the place may not have changed, the viewer inevitably has. For the first time things invisible before become suddenly visible.

Our valley remained the same, as did the pines and the white cliff that backed our town. The trees along the hill had thinned out more than I realized, cut by indiscriminate woodchoppers hunting fuel or timbers for the mines.

Ruth Macken's home and trading post had settled against the hill as if it had been there always, and this I knew she had planned. The makeup of the building itself and the way it fit into the hill were perfect. She understood, as had the ancient Greeks, how the architecture must belong to the setting.

The trees there were still lovely, the silver in the sunlight on the stream, the snow melting under the morning sun. Someone was cutting wood there. I saw the flash of the axe blade, and a moment later heard the sound of the axe, with always that interval between testifying to the difference between the speeds of light and sound. I think there is no more lovely sound than the ring of an axe on a frosty morning.

Lower down and further back, our own place. Or I should say, Cain's place. The mill was ours. I had helped to build it and was a partner, and yet I had always thought of it as Cain's. He was the master here, and rightfully so. Yet the small cluster of original cabins sat well against the hill, and those built later were further down the small valley, closer to the road, the unpainted buildings weathered now and a little shabby.

We rode up into the street, and the first person we saw was Colly Benson.

"Howdy, Ben. We missed you."

We gripped hands. His was hard and strong. "Everything's quiet, Ben. Just like you'd want it."

"Thanks, Colly."

"There's been a few people driftin' in," he said, "and a few leavin'. I think more are leavin', Ben. More of the latecomers are just stoppin' by."

"See anything of Finnerly or Trotter?"

"Well . . . no. Only somebody took a shot at Neely awhile back, and a couple of days ago somebody tried to break into his mine. He'd rebuilt the door, set heavy timbers into the rock wall, and they made too much noise. But they got away before we could get to them."

We rode on up the slope, Lorna, Dr. Fairchild, and I. We could hear the ring of Cain's hammer from the blacksmith shop and the whine of the saw in the mill.

John Sampson came to the mill door and looked down the hill. We rode up to him, and a smile creased his weathered face. Time, which had used our town unkindly in some respects, had only laid a blessing upon John. His hair was as thick and white as ever, his eyes as clear and kindly, his face a little nobler. He made me think of Hawthorne's story about "The Great Stone Face," and the man who came to resemble the face on the mountainside. Age, confidence, and growing knowledge and usefulness had worked a miracle with John . . . or perhaps it had always been there, and we saw it only now. Yet I believe it began on the way across the plains, when for the first time men and women came to him for advice.

"We're home, John. And Lorna's brought a friend with her, Dr. Fairchild."

"How do you do, sir? Are you a medical doctor? Our town can use one." He turned his eyes to Lorna. "Lorna . . . you're a woman now, a beautiful woman."

She blushed and laughed to cover it. "I'm just a country girl, home from the city."

Cain came out, then Helen, and the others. On the slope Ruth Macken was shading her eyes at us.

"I've some coffee," Helen said, "and I've baked a cake."

"She's baked one every weekend since you left," Cain said, "expecting you home."

"Webb's coming up the hill, Bendigo," Helen said. "I'm afraid he's very lonely now."

"Now? What's happened?"

"Foss is gone. His hand got better and he pulled out, rode east. Said he wanted to ride north with the Texas cattle. He left right after you did."

Webb was gaunt, somber. He held out his hand. "Hello, Ben. Seems like old times."

"It does. I've missed you, Webb. You know there was a time back east when I had a little difficulty with some men. I found myself looking around because when we had trouble you were always there."

"If I'd of known, I'd have been."

"Come in, Mr. Webb. We're going to set for coffee and cake."

"Well . . ."

"Come on." I started to put a hand on his shoulder, then stopped. Webb was not a man you touched. Always, there was that aloofness in him.

We sat around inside and talked of things we knew, yet I felt myself a stranger here and looked across at Lorna. She looked wistful, and inquiring. I knew it was upon her, too, that strangeness of returning, for the secret is what Shakespeare said, that no traveler returns. He is always a little changed, a little different, and wistful and longing for what has been lost.

There was the smell of the wood fire, the warmth of the room, and familiar faces. This was home. I suspected, somehow, that it was more of a home than any other place I would ever know.

"What about Ninon?" Helen asked.

I looked up at her, smiling a little, and embarrassed. "She's coming out. We will meet in Denver."

"Good! She's a lovely girl, Bendigo. I'm happy for you."

Slowly the pieces were falling into place; the picture that was my town began to assemble itself once more. I looked down at my boots and listened to their voices, talking, laughing, bantering a little, these people who had not gone away.

"The tie contract is filled, Ben. I've been cutting timbers for some mines. We've been asked to move the mill down to Rock Springs."

"Rock Springs?"

"There's a town down there. Looks like it will grow."

I shifted uneasily in my chair, a chair Cain had made with his hands. I looked at the puncheon floor we had hewn from logs and fitted ourselves, yet I was not thinking only of the floor or of the chair, nor was I thinking of the cabins and the mill. I was thinking of these people around me, who fitted as solidly into our picture. Here in this place I had become a man, and here John Sampson had found his stature and his place, Drake Morrell, Dad Jenn . . . all of them had somehow staked their claims.

Ruth Macken came down from the hill, holding out both hands to me. "Bendigo! Why, you're handsome!"

I blushed, and she laughed at me. We sat together and talked and drank coffee. I mentioned Croft.

"They haven't told you? He's gone."

I felt a queer emptiness within me. "Tom? *Gone?*"

"He had a falling out with Neely, and of course his wife had never really liked us. He sold his place, and they pulled out, headed for some place in Nevada . . . Eureka, I think it is."

Foss Webb, who had always been an outsider in a sense, but one of us still, was gone. And now Croft. Uneasily, I emptied my cup . . . was this the beginning?

Rock Springs was not for me. I knew the place . . . the spring had been discovered in 1861 or about then by a pony express rider who was dodging Indians. Later, it was a stage stop, and some folks named Blair built in the neighborhood. In our country it never took much to start a town, and according to the last reports they'd found coal down there, and the railroad was interested in it as a source of fuel.

Other towns were building along the tracks, and there was much talk of them around the fire that first evening. Others were leaving town, and I decided to buy whatever stock they did not want to take along.

When we'd had supper I walked back up the hill with Ruth. Bud had been keeping store and he came out to meet me. He was nearly as tall as I was . . . maybe I hadn't noticed before.

"We're not replacing our stock, Bendigo," Ruth said. "Trade has slowed down, and we are doing much less business. I think when the stock is gone I will close up the store and move to California."

"I've known it would happen, but I hate to see it," I said slowly. "I love the place."

"So do we, and we always shall."

We talked of Ninon, of New York, of the hotels, the cafes, and the theater. "I miss it," she said at last. "And I want Bud to have a chance to go on to school. Drake has done well by him, and he's started the same books you read, but they'll have better schools out there, and I've done well with the store."

Ethan was squatting by the fire when I came in. He looked up. "Heard you was back. Stacy'll be around later."

"Have you seen Uruwishi, Ethan?"

"Seen him? I reckon. He's waitin' for you, Ben. He talks of the long ride you're takin' with him, far up into the Big Horns. That's about the only thing he talks about except for the old days, and I expect if you hadn't told him that, he'd have died this past winter. He's livin' for that ride."

"We'll take it."

"Want some comp'ny? Me an' Stacy would like to ride along. You'll need somebody to keep the boogers off your back."

"I'd be honored."

"Mebbe you would. Ben, give it some thought. Come spring the Sioux will be out. They'll be huntin' hair, an' we'd be likely candidates for somebody's coup stick."

"Scared?"

"Uh-huh, but scared never kep' me back so far. I'll be ridin' along." He looked up suddenly. "It'll seem like old times, Ben, like old times."

"All right . . . if they don't need us here."

The night was crisp and still. The Wind Rivers held their icy ridges against the cold night sky, the stars were bright, and underfoot the remnants of the snow crunched and the frozen ridges of mud crumbled.

There were more lights than I remembered, more houses, and they seemed scattered. In the distance the black streak of the road wound away down the valley. It was on that road I had found Drake Morrell, and down that road I had gone to find Ninon.

A wolf howled, somewhere back up on the Beaver Rim, and I listened to the wild, lonely howl. Something within me stood still, hearing the weird and lovely sound, a sound that found strange echoes in my own being.

If we left here would we ever find its like again? Not that this was the best of places. The growing season was too short, the winds blew too strong . . . there were many better places, and yet this had been, for a brief period, ours.

Would we ever again work together as we had here? Would we look to the mountains where there was no corruption? We had built with our hands and our hearts. We had tried to build homes, although in each of us there must have been the feeling that this was not forever.

It is this seed we carry with us, we Americans, the feeling that this is not the end. It would be better, perhaps, if we built our homes deeply into the land, built to last, built homes not for ourselves alone but for our grandchildren and great-grandchildren. Yet far away and long ago, we *moved*.

We moved . . . we left all behind. With our courage or our foolishness or whatever it was, we moved. And there remains with us the feeling that we can move again, that there is always a better place somewhere out beyond the rim of the world.

We are a people of the frontier, born to it, bred to it, looking always toward it. And when the frontiers of our own land are gone, when we have drawn them all into an ordered world, then we must seek other frontiers, the frontiers of the mind beyond which men have not gone, the frontiers that lie out beyond the stars, the frontiers that lie within our own selves, that hold us back from what we would do, what we would achieve.

I had yet to find my own place in the world. I was not so fortunate as my brother Cain, who turned the iron in his hands and it became steel, a steel that yet carried with it the tenderness, the knowingness that a craftsman needs to bring beauty from the cold material. I think we must beware not to stray too far from the hands of the craftsmen, the hands that weave, the hands that sew, the hands that weld and mold, for I think whatever man makes must carry pride in its making or we have lost much, too much.

The pride of a man who can stand back and look at what he has done, as I once had looked upon a floor, and say, "Yes, it is good, it is well done."

Turning from my way, I walked to the lodge of Uruwishi and spoke at the doorway, then entered. They were there, Uruwishi smoking by the fire, and Short Bull.

"The Old One waits for you, my friend."

Uruwishi looked up and gestured to a place beside him on the buffalo robe.

For a time he smoked in silence, and I sat beside him, watching the flames fingering the dry sticks that had once been trees, trees whose decaying roots and ashes would feed the earth where other trees would grow, other lions, other men.

"Short Bull warned me you might not come," Uruwishi said, "but I told him we would ride together toward the place where the winds gather."

"We will ride."

"I am old . . . old. My bones have felt many winters, and each winter they feel them more. It must be soon, my son."

"After two suns," I said, "this morning there was a little green showing where there was no snow."

"It is good. When you were gone our hearts lay in the shadow. Now you are back, and we are young again. After two suns, then. We shall be ready."

FORTY-THREE

L orna and I went up the hill to Ruth Macken's in the morning, walking with Drake Morrell. Drake looked thinner, I thought, and taller somehow. His clothes were neat, brushed carefully, and he was freshly shaved. Yet so it had ever been with Drake.

"How is the school, Drake?"

"The best. I've some fine students, Ben, although I am afraid I have used your name in vain more than once. They admire you, so I've not let them forget you've never ceased from learning."

"I guess that's why I like it, Drake. A man who is in love with learning is a man who is never without a bride, for there is always more."

"I hear you're riding again?"

"Yes, I'm going north with Uruwishi. I promised him, and then . . . well, I've a wish to see the Medicine Wheel. We always speak of this as a new land, Drake, a young land. But sometimes when I am on the mountain, or up there under the trees, I feel something very ancient. It is an old, old land, Drake, and I think men walked these trails far, far earlier than is now believed. I think Uruwishi knows it, too. I think he wants me to feel something, to know something while there is time.

"You've probably felt it yourself, but places have an atmosphere, a feeling about them. Sometimes in the mountains I feel as if the mountains wished to share something with me.

"This was Indian land before the white man came, and now we share it with them as the Picts came to share Great Britain with the Celts, Angles, Saxons, and Danes. The Indians we know were not the first, for others walked the land before them, and still others before *them*.

"We hold the land only for a time, and when our time has run out others will come to live in our place.

"Buffalo roam the plains by the million, but as long as they are there no land can be farmed, no fences built, no crops planted. There can be no homes, schools, churches, or hospitals, for the buffalo demand too much and stop at no fence.

"My heart is with them, perhaps because I feel that I am one with the buffalo and the Indian, and perhaps my time to pass along will be their time. I do not know.

"Old Indians will tell you hairy elephants lived here. Their forefathers hunted them. They are gone. There were bears larger than the grizzly and cats with teeth like curving tusks. I once saw an Indian wearing such teeth, passed along from who knows what ancestor? Or found, possibly, in some cut bank or cave? All of these are gone, but we only weep for those we see passing, we blame ourselves for what was inevitable.

"Only one thing we know, that all things change. If we leave here in a few years nothing will remain. Our roofs will fall in, timbers will rot, cellars fill with dust, the grass will reclaim the land. We've scarred it, but the scars are trifles, and the earth has been scarred by the fiery hand of God. But always the grass returns, and the trees, and in a few years men will come and look about and they will see nothing, or maybe a few relics that will cause them to wonder."

"Then why build at all?"

"The joy is in the building, I guess. And of course, some things last . . . for a while. That is why I want to see the Wheel. It has lasted . . . a thousand years? Two thousand? Ten thousand?

"Only the word can last longer. Uruwishi has songs, I think, that are older than that, and they were written on no paper, on no wall of stone, they were written only in the minds of men we call savages, and repeated, over and over."

Ruth came to the door, her dark hair blowing a little in the wind. "I have coffee on. It will seem like old times."

Ethan was there, squatting against the wall. He already nursed a cup in his hands. He nodded briefly. "She's got a gingerbread stashed away, boys. Don't let her fool you."

He sipped his coffee. "Stacy come in last night. The Sioux are making medicine."

"Well, we expected that, and if they want our hair they'll have to fight for it."

"They will." Ethan put his cup down on the floor. "That ain't all. There's a Shoshone brave who's broke with his people. He's picked him up a bunch of wild Shoshones and some other bronco Indians, and they are on a warpath of their own."

"A Shoshone?"

"Uh-huh. His name is Little Buffalo, and they say he's got his own blood feud with a white man."

"The same one?"

"I figure so. Stacy heard tell a mighty lot about him. He's a big man now. He led a raid on a railroad work party two years ago, and wiped them out. He ambushed an army patrol, and only two men got away. He raided the stage station at Three Crossings and drove off a dozen head of horses."

"But you saved his life, Ben! You brought him in when he was dying in the cold!"

"He don't see it thataway, ma'am. He says his medicine was too strong for Ben, that Ben intended to kill him, but his medicine was just too strong."

"How many has he got with him?"

"Eighteen to twenty . . . I guess more or less, depending on the time and place. You know how Injuns are. They come and go. But he's made a name for himself, and them he's tied to are a bunch of wild, trouble-hunting bucks."

The subject changed and we talked of newcomers, of the changing times, and after a moment I eased out of the conversation, and sitting back a little, let the words wash by my ears, not thinking of what was said, but just soaking in the good feeling of it, and of this place.

"I got the books you sent," Ruth said suddenly, "and the papers. It seemed like old times . . . in some ways."

"In some ways?" I asked.

"I don't know, but somehow a lot of the things they bother about seem so unimportant out here. It seems to me that the more money one has the more one worries about little unimportant things."

"Them Indians," Ethan commented, "mightn't be the only trouble that's shapin' up.

"Ollie Trotter. I picked up his sign a few days ago. I'd killed a deer and went down to skin it out and come on some tracks.

Seemed like an odd place, down in a canyon thataway, so after I taken my meat, I scouted around."

He drank a swallow of coffee and put the cup down. "Found a cut bank behind a sandbar in the creek. Been three, four men camped there."

"*Four?*"

"Maybe another one, too. Yep, anyway four men. The way it shaped up, the remains of fires, and the like of that, I figure they'd met there several times. There was some wood cut several weeks ago, some only a few days back. The tracks showed up to be both old and new."

"The same horses?"

"Uh-huh, and like I say, a couple of extries. I couldn't make 'em out, but I know four men camped there and I think five."

Finnerly, Trotter, Pappin, and who? Who else? That needed some thinking about, for there were a lot of strangers in our town and in the settlements close by.

"Maybe we should stake out Neely's place. If they did leave something else, they'll come back for it again."

"Somethin' else," Ethan commented. "That outfit ain't one to live out in the country. Trotter could do it, fair to middlin', although he's no woodsman when it comes to that, but not Finnerly. I think they've got themselves a place. Maybe over to South Pass City, maybe one of the other settlements around."

Yet, if they were living elsewhere, what could be done? They had stalked me and tried to kill me. I knew what Colly Benson thought of that. Find them, call them out, shoot them. He had even offered to help. For that matter Drake Morrell felt much the same way. I knew that if I dropped a word to Stacy he would hunt them down and shoot them like so many varmints. Stacy Follett was nothing if not a realist. You had an enemy, you killed him before he killed you.

Yet I was not one to borrow trouble, and it was likely they had other things in mind, although knowing them I doubted if they would leave the country without one more try for the gold . . . which must be there.

Ruth had set up her trading post with a long counter and a wall of shelves. There was a potbellied stove, several chairs, and benches. The room was pleasantly warm when I went in from the living quarters and began studying the shelves for what I might want on our ride north.

Long ago I'd discovered half the things a man might think of taking are never used. We had to go prepared for snow, for we were headed to high country, and the season was early. I bought some new socks and a pair of boots more suitable for hiking than those I usually wore and found a fine pair of elk-hide moccasins that would fit. These Ruth had in trade from some Indian, Shoshone, by the look of them.

I browsed around alone, picking out the various items I would need, then trimming the list from those I thought I'd need to those I knew I'd need. Yet, was it only that? Or was I savoring these last moments in a place I had helped build and in which I had spent so many happy hours? Ruth Macken was important to me.

Not in any romantic sense, and not simply for the books she had loaned me or the casual way she had guided me in many of the social graces. Ruth Macken may never have given a thought to instructing me, but she had set a standard of womanhood against which every woman I later was to know would be unconsciously measured. She was quietly beautiful, moving with an easy grace and confidence. She was tolerant, understanding, and intelligent, a good listener ready with apt comment; she understood my shyness and my eagerness to learn and overlooked my occasional clumsiness.

She had style, but for that matter, so did Drake Morrell. He had a dash, a flair, that made every boy in his school wish to be like him and every girl to be worthy of his attention.

The children who studied with him were of the country, of the backwoods, perhaps, but no one who knew them in the years that followed would have believed it. He gave them pride of bearing and appearance as well as a love for knowledge . . . I shall not say "scholarship," for that is often a different thing.

Soon I would be leaving this place, but as I idled there in the empty trading post, listening to the murmur of voices from the next room, I knew how fortunate I'd been to have known these people. To know Ruth Macken, John Sampson, Drake Morrell, and Cain.

Yes, and Webb.

He had prospered less than the rest of us, yet he had worked hard. Whatever else might be said of him, he possessed a quality of loyalty to comrade and principle given to very few. Whenever in the future my own stand would be put to the test, I knew I would think of Webb. Often I wondered if he knew fear; I know he had no doubt when the chips were down. He revealed nothing of himself, but I knew wherever I went in the future I would be conscious of Webb at my shoulder and would be stronger for it.

Several boxes of shells, a new ground sheet small enough to handle easily, a couple of wool shirts.

Ruth came in. "Are you finding what you want?"

"Yes."

"Be careful, Bendigo. An Indian woman was in, she is here often and is very friendly, and she warned me the Blackfeet would be riding the war trail in the spring."

"I know. Some other tribes as well, I expect, but we won't be long."

"I wish I could go with you. How many white men have seen the Wheel?"

"Not more than a dozen and probably only half that many. Ed Rose spent time in the Big Horn Basin as early as 1807, and there's a rumor the Spanish sent an expedition as far north as the Yellowstone many years ago. Whether they were east or west of the Big Horns, I don't know. The land didn't have many names then, and a man has to guess where they actually were. But there are old diggings all over the country.

"We only have written history to go by, and there was so much that went unwritten . . . most of it, probably. So far as we know it was well over a hundred years after De Soto saw the Mississippi until it was seen by another white man."

I stopped, my hands resting on the canteen I'd been checking. We would have small use for such a thing, for there was water everywhere . . . still, I was a cautious man.

"I want to go there, Mrs. Macken. I want to visit the Medicine Wheel . . . not just to see it. I've had it described and know about what it is and what it looks like, but what I want is to *be* there, to stand there . . . not for a minute or two, but to see the sun rise, the sunset, and the moon over it.

"I am tantalized by this country . . . there's so much we don't know. On the wagon train there was a man who lived in Ohio who told us about a great mound there, built by men. Maybe it was built by those we call Indians and maybe by somebody who came before them. I've heard of such mounds far to the south in Mississippi, and now I hear of this Wheel."

"Do you think there is a connection?"

"Probably not. But I believe that if I was there, if I was alone on that spot, I might grasp something intuitively that evades me now."

"You're a mystic, Bendigo."

"No . . . just an interested man. I never liked the term mystic as applied to someone or a way of thought. It covers something very profound and an awful lot of nonsense passes as profound thought.

"It is just that I have an idea that people who live long in a place leave an imprint upon it. Perhaps if I am there, where they were, I may catch some of their thinking. And maybe all of this is just an excuse to go wandering again.

"I like the wild, far country. There's a lot of Ethan in me, and Stacy, too. Do you think they were really hunting furs out here? Don't you believe it. They were seeing new country.

"Think what it means to top out on a ridge and look over a vast land beyond, which perhaps no other white man has seen? Or even an Indian? There were areas where they rarely, if ever, went. Much of Tennessee was hunted over only occasionally."

We walked back into the other room. "Trouble is," Ethan was saying, "an Indian an' a white man just don't think alike, so there's got to be misunderstanding. It's what Ben here calls 'the Christian-Jewish ethic.' We're all brought up according to it until we figure that's human nature, and it ain't no such thing. The Indian, he has his own way of thinking, and it's nothing like that at all. Each of us gets mighty upset that the other doesn't react the way we figure he ought to. Trouble is, there's no common standard."

FORTY-FOUR

Lean upon the hillside the old cow stood, watching as we passed, tall were the pines among the barren rocks, white the streamers of snow reaching ghostly fingers from their protecting shadows. I saw a deceptive spring being born upon the mountains, deceptive because the time was early and the danger of snow lingered.

We rode a narrow trail along the mountain's lumpy face, weaving among the trees, our horses walking with feet alert for shifting rock or snow, each step delicate, poised for a leap.

Five men we were, reining in upon a bare shoulder to catch a glimpse of the Big Horn Basin, far away. Meadows showed green at this distance and the forest was laced with a silver of mountain streams. We studied all we could see, our eyes searching for any hint of movement, any suggestion of enemies awaiting us there.

"I saw a smoke when the sun went down," Stacy commented, "a thin smoke, afar off. Injuns," Stacy spoke around his pipe, "movin' out to get a start on the grass. There'll be a stirring in the lodges now, and the braves will be painting themselves for war."

"We'll not be hunting trouble," I said, "only the Medicine Wheel."

"When you tell them that," Stacy said, "be looking down the barrel of your Henry."

There was dampness in the air, a dampness from earth turned

black from the melting snow and from a trickle of snow water running off. We ducked our heads under low pine boughs, skirted mossy boulders, and sometimes turned deep into the forest where no sound was.

Saddles creaked when the horses climbed, and when we stopped to let them catch their wind their breath showed at their nostrils. Today the icy peaks showed three dimensional in the deep blue of the sky.

Uruwishi sat beside me when our horses rested. "My heart is young again, as when I rode the war trail."

"Do the Sioux ride this far to the west?"

"A Sioux rides where he will. They are a bold people."

"Red Cloud is their chief."

"Huh!" Uruwishi was silent, then he said, "His words are spoken. The young men's eyes follow others now. Have you heard of Gall? He is fierce in battle. I think the young men will follow him . . . or Crazy Horse."

"Have you no wish to return to your own land?"

"My land is where the wind blows. Should I claim a land I cannot keep? Once my people roamed from the Yakima River to the Blue Mountains, from the Cascades to the Rockies. We were one with the Nez Perce and the Klickitat. Our war parties raided the Blackfeet and the Gros Ventres."

"You knew of the Medicine Wheel?"

"We have always known. Sometimes our wise men went there to dream . . . as I did."

We talked no more then, for voices carry in the canyons. Once we saw an elk move away, slowly as if aware we hunted no meat, and again there was an old brown bear, thin from a winter's sleep, who stood up on his hind legs and studied us.

"It's a long way to ride just to see a ring of rocks," Stacy said, skeptically. "Maybe there's a treasure buried there."

"They had no treasure other than treasures of the mind. If you
there looking for gold or silver you're wasting your time, for
ple who built it knew nothing of metals. They were
rine, or maybe a calendar to measure the equinoxes.
reason to measure time, for ceremonies and the
I think we'd all be better off if we had no
we might never get old, for we wouldn't

tacy said, dryly. "A time comes

"Ben, you know as well as I that if you hadn't come along the old boy would have been dead by now. You took him along, you asked his advice, and suddenly he had a reason for living, he was riding the trail again."

"It goes to show you. People don't wear out, they give up. And as far as trails go, there's always an open trail for the mind if you keep the doors open and give it a chance."

Uruwishi turned suddenly and lifted a hand. Ethan moved toward him.

I rode closer to Short Bull. "What is it?"

"Shoshone."

"How many?"

He shook his head, his eyes busy. We had stopped under a stand of aspen, the leaves dappling our bodies with the pale sunlight that fell through the slight overcast that held the sky. We were bunched there because it offered what we hoped was concealment, and because the view was good.

On our left was the high, bare range of the Wind Rivers above timberline. On our right was another bald mountain and to the right front still another bare ridge. Below and northwest of us, not too far away, a dozen small lakes were clustered . . . one was of fair size . . . amid parklike meadows and forest. Through an opening between the two bald mountains on our right we could see the beginnings of the basin.

Miles away across the basin thunderheads clustered over the Big Horns, and I saw a couple of distant rainstorms walking the hills. I remembered something Ruth Macken had said long ago when we first settled our town, that I was a man who loved to look upon distance, and it was true. There is no majesty like the grand sweep of miles upon miles of mountains and peaks with only the sky above and the silent canyons and timberline slopes below.

Uruwishi spoke, talking to Short Bull. "Five," he said, then to us, "Five men riding, since the first sun."

Five braves . . . not too far ahead of us and no way off the mountain here. It was a steep slide among rocks and deadfall into the canyon hundreds of feet below, and the mountain rear up, openfaced and without concealment, on our left.

Stacy turned around to look at me. "Shafter, if'n it was r turn off down Crooked Crick . . . she's a mite ahead . .
shut of the mountains. Git down off this mountain."

"Stace," Ethan spoke quietly, "if we skirt Moccas

know a way to cross the fork of the Little Wind River an' we can hold west of Bear Peak an' down into Sage Creek Basin."

"All right, Stacy?" I asked.

He shrugged. "Never tried that way. All right with me."

Neither of the Indians knew the way, so with Ethan to guide we started once more.

We were in high country, ten thousand feet or so above sea level. There was some good timber here and there, a lot of aspen, wild flowers already in bloom; and just above it the green played out suddenly against the slide rock. Most of the peaks were still covered with snow, and we saw several shadowed canyons where the snow remained, still eight to twelve feet of it. But there was runoff from all the drifts.

Here and there were vast slopes, gray with the dead trunks of fallen trees lying among other dead trees still standing in place. All had been killed with mighty winds that flattened whole slopes, laying the trees down like mown wheat.

Ethan led off, and within a few hundred yards suddenly turned from the trail we had followed, and the one taken by the Shoshone, into a notch where the dull gray of huge boulders, polished smooth by wind and ice, poked their ancient brows above the green of the new grass.

We skirted the boulders and went up through the notch. Ethan advanced slowly at the last until only his eyes looked through the notch. After a minute he motioned us on, and we all followed him down into Sage Creek Basin. There among some aspens and willows, we made camp on Sage Creek. "Over yonder," Ethan said, pointing northeast, "there's a cave. Never looked into it much, but she's there. Maybe three, four miles from here."

Soon we had a small fire going and coffee on. Moving out from camp, I found a nesting place among some fallen trees that offered a good view around and settled down to watch. There's always a lot to see in such places, but it never pays to get to watching one animal too closely . . . a man might lose his hair.

Yet I saw nothing. Nor did Short Bull, who took my place, nothing but a camp robber jay who hopped about from limb to twig to rock, watching for something he might steal.

We moved out before daybreak, riding down by the trail Ethan had suggested, then striking out across the basin toward Wind River.

Light was just showing when we topped out on the last ridge and started down into the valley of the Wind. Off to our right and far off we could see a lake. "Ethan," Stacy said, "ain't that Bull Lake?"

"Uh-huh. The Lake That Roars, so the Indians call it. The Shoshone say that some hunters once chased a white buffalo, a medicine buffalo, out on the ice, trying to kill him for his robe. The bull went through the ice and drowned, and the Shoshone say the wind sometimes gets under the ice, lifts it, and makes a groaning, roaring sound, but they claim it's the buffalo's anger that lifts the ice and makes the sound."

We lost some time working ourselves out of a tangle of deadfalls, boulders, and brush at the foot of the mountains, so it was coming up to sundown before we watered our horses in the Wind River. We pushed on while it was still light and camped close to Crowheart Butte.

"Big Injun fight here," Stacy commented. "Cheyennes, Gros Ventres, and Arapahos fightin' Shoshone. Story is the Shoshone chief ate the Crow chief's heart."

"When was that?" I asked.

"Twelve years ago, the way I figure. Washakie did sure enough have himself a fight here."

"Did he eat the heart?" I wanted to know.

"I wasn't there. They done such things. Figured it gave them all the bravery of their enemy."

"We'll sleep tonight in the Owl Creeks," Ethan said, "if we've still got our hair. This here is techy country."

"The mountains to the north? Aren't those the Absarokes?"

"Prime country!" Stacy commented. "I wintered there one time. John Colter come in there long before, him and two of his compadres. Mighty purty . . . rough country, too. Ain't no purtier country nowhere than the Absarokes."

We rode through the sagebrush bottoms, our eyes searching the country. Twice we picked up sign, all of it old, of unshod ponies. Several times we saw buffalo, but they were few and scattered. There had always been buffalo here, but not in the great herds of those further east. Yet toward night we saw one herd, afar off, that looked to be several hundred . . . maybe a thousand head.

The mountains hung low on the northern horizon, then seemed suddenly to loom large. The Owl Creeks were not high as mountains went, but there were some impressive spires here and there. Actually, although some referred to where we rode as the basin, the Big Horn Basin as such was north of the Owl Creeks, and where we rode was the Wind River Valley, or a part of it.

We were heading toward a pass Ethan knew, but suddenly he slowed up. "Stace? What d'you think?"

"Don't like it, Ethan. I surely don't. I never cared much for no pass, nohow. A pass is too easy."

"That's a purty deep canyon, the South Fork is, but I still don't hold no briefs for the pass."

Uruwishi spoke. "West from the pass, in the mountains nearer Owl Creek, there is a way. It is a lonely way, but it is there."

"I'll cast my vote for it," I said. "I trust the Old One. He didn't live this long without having a lot of savvy."

Uruwishi rode into the lead again and headed toward the mountains. There were a couple of creeks coming down from the slope that I could pick up afar off. Ethan was at my elbow. "That pass comes down about, well, maybe a mite east of the east fork of Bargee Creek. Looks like he's ridin' right for it."

"If they are up there, could they see us?" I believed they might, for the air was clear and the distance not that great.

"Sure. An Indian would see you. They've eyes that have been searchin' country like this since they were babies. A mite of dust you or I wouldn't see, they'll pick up right quick."

Suddenly, we dipped down into a wide hollow that was scattered with sagebrush and cedar. Riding straight ahead, Uruwishi headed into the thickest stand of cedar just like he'd done it a thousand times. A sandy ridge lay ahead of us, and we should turn right to skirt it; instead, he turned abruptly left.

This was behind the ridge and the cedar where our direction change could not be seen. "Sagwup Draw," Short Bull muttered, half to himself, half in explanation.

Now we rode more swiftly, our direction due west and away from the pass. The ridge grew higher, rockier, covered with scattered fragments of sandstone. Ethan pointed ahead and to our left. "That there's Red Basin, I think. I've heard about this country from Ed Rose an' Colter. I don't know where the Old One ever heard of it."

Suddenly, Uruwishi drew up to let the horses have a moment. He was scanning the ridge on our right, looking up toward the two highest points, two long ovals of rock. When he started again he rode right up the ridge on an angle across the face toward the narrow gap between the high points. If a trail existed we could not see it, but Uruwishi led on, holding to a good pace.

We made no dust, for the trail was among rocks, and when he turned again it was at right angles and a steep scramble into the gap. He was through the opening like a ghost, and we followed, through the rock-walled space in a matter of minutes and down the slope toward the valley on the other side.

The pass we had intended to cross was three miles east now, out of sight among the trees and shoulders of rock. Uruwishi led us, trusting to some ancient memory of a tale told by a campfire.

We found no tracks but those of deer and bighorn sheep. Off to our left now and less than a mile away, glimpsed occasionally through the trees, was Owl Creek Canyon. When we dipped toward the creek we were headed toward a crossing on the floor of the valley.

Stacy Follett pulled up. "Ethan, would you look at that now."

Behind us, to the east and south, several miles away, a thin finger of smoke pointed to the sky.

"I never did like passes," Ethan said.

FORTY-FIVE

It is my great gift to live with awareness. I do not know to what I owe this gift, nor do I seek an answer. I am content that it be so. Few of us ever live in the present, we are forever anticipating what is to come or remembering what has gone, and this I do also. Yet it is my good fortune to feel, to see, to hear, to be aware.

As much as I have read it has not turned me into one who lives only with the intellect, for most of life is not a life of the mind, nor is that the only good life. As I rode now I was aware, as we all were, of that finger of smoke behind us.

It was a signal, as we well knew, that we had not appeared where we were expected. It meant that they would be seeking out our trail, and of course, they would find it. Knowing Indians a little, I knew they would find it soon.

Yet that was the smallest part of my awareness, for my heart beat with the steady throbbing of hoofs beneath us. I was aware of the smell of trampled sage, and crushed cedar, the taste of dust, the glare of the sun, and the coolness of a wind from down a canyon.

The splendid arch of the blue sky above, the distant purple haze of mountains, the majestic strength in the face of old Uruwishi, the proud way Short Bull carried himself, the way my foot felt in a stirrup, the way a gun butt felt in my hand. Each, in its way, was a thing of beauty.

To live is not only to exist. It is not to wait for supper of an evening or for bedtime or for a drink at a saloon. It is all of these things and every marvelous moment that comes between. To live is to feel, and the senses have more to teach than the mind. More, at least, for the immediate moment. It is better, sometimes, to simply *feel*, to simply *be*.

We crossed the North Fork of Owl Creek and headed out across the flat toward Wagonhound Bench and rode toward an ancient shrine, a place of long ago. I suspect each of us rode toward a different shrine, the same only in name. For the destination men name is only the destination of surface: For each there is another, a different destination.

I rode toward a turning point in my life. I do not know why I knew this, and yet I did know it. Why had the Medicine Wheel such an attraction for me? Was it some ancient atavistic memory? Had some incarnation of me from a far distant time known this place? Or was there some recollection, deep hidden in my very blood and fiber, that called me to this place rather than to some other such place in some other land?

Turning in the saddle, I glanced back. The smoke was gone, the Shoshone were riding.

A Shoshone was riding, for I had no doubt it was my old enemy seeking me out. The Shoshone were a great tribe, and they lived, for the greater part, at peace with the white man. They were fine horsemen and great warriors, a fine people. It was my misfortune to have one of them for an enemy.

Short of sundown we stopped near a creek and among cottonwoods. While Ethan put together some food and made coffee, Stacy kept watch from a high point near the camp, and Short Bull, using his bow to avoid sound, hunted for fresh meat.

After I had eaten I took a cup of coffee with me and took Follett's place on watch. When the others had eaten we packed up the few items we had taken out and moved on for several miles, making a dry, fireless camp. Now if they had seen our fire they could go to it and find nothing.

Mine was the last watch of the night. Ethan awakened me about two in the morning, judging by the Big Dipper, and I moved out from the camp, the better to listen.

The night was starlit with only a few wisps of very high cloud, and all was very still. For a few minutes my ears sorted the sounds of the night, which were few. Once the special sounds of a place are known, the ears are quick to discern any other, and each place does have sounds particular to it alone.

In this case there was a broken limb high in a cottonwood that had dead leaves. They whispered and scratched when slightly stirred by wind. The wind over the sage flats had a particular sound also, and I listened.

I had always loved these last hours before the dawn when the stars are unbelievably bright and the night is very still. I enjoyed what many men did not, rising long before daybreak to get the feel of the night and the land.

Ghosts of the old ones walked this land; ghosts of warriors long vanished, and the blood from ancient battles had sunk into the soil along with crumbled leaves, decaying roots, and the drift sand blown by the wind.

The hours went by swiftly. I heard the dead leaves stir, caught the faint scent of sage, and saw the light fade the darkness from the eastern sky and our campfire grow brighter as some early riser prepared a fire for our coffee. My eyes searched the dawn-light distance and found no smoke.

We drank our coffee and ate fresh venison killed by Short Bull, and then we straddled our horses and led off to the north.

"Yonder's Black Butte"—Stacy pointed southeast—"and north of it lies Spanish Point, and there's a trail crosses the Big Horns yonder to the head of Soldier Crick. It's a fair way . . . there's game an' water."

How many times had I heard that? So it was that men learned of the western lands, even as the Indians such as Uruwishi learned of a country where he had never ridden. Such things were filed away, remembered in times of need, passed on to others. There were few maps, no guidebooks, but there was information passed in saloons, over campfires, or by men exchanging comments on the trail somewhere.

When I closed my eyes I could hear the voices of long ago, when I was a boy, the dry, drawling voices speaking unconscious poetry, singing the magical names of the far-off mountains and canyons. Ten Sleep, Meeteetse, Sun-dance, and Dry Fork Ridge, Wagon-Box and the Little Big Horn, which headed not far from Medicine Mountain. And now I heard them speak of Lodge Grass and Bucking Mule Creeks, Powder River and Bobcat Draw, and I'd ridden through Six-Shooter Gap and in the Sweet Alice Hills.

That was music, the music of a land whose only music yet was the chant of Indian voices, the wind in the pines, and the flutter of cottonwood or aspen along with the sound of snow water trickling and the bugle of an elk or the call of a wolf. Yet it was music of a very special kind.

We avoided the easy way through Granite Pass and rode on to the Dry Fork of Horse Pass. Skirting a canyon that dropped off a thousand feet or more, we topped out on the mesa and crossed to Cottonwood Creek and followed it to the head of Hidden Tepee and on northwest to Little Baldy Pass. We could see Bald Mountain ahead, and we were nearing the Wheel, which lay on Medicine Mountain, a sort of shoulder of Bald.

We traveled a far piece, and we camped here and yonder, always with a watchful eye for the Shoshone who rode our trail. By now they'd be hungering for our scalps, although a scalp was secondary to counting coup, and some Indians set no store by scalps, as Stacy would say, or Ethan.

We were nine thousand feet up now, and it was cold and clear. We stopped often to rest our horses although they were mountain bred and accustomed to the wild, rough land. We found much snow here, and only at midday did it edge with dampness from melting. Icy winds made us duck our heads.

We were strung out along the ridge, five men and four packhorses, riding barren, rocky country with the ridge falling away into a stand of spruce. Timberline through this country edges up to ten thousand feet, and we rode over bare rock or rock covered with snow and ice, yet only a few yards away was the edge of the timber, a low-growing spruce, and some wild flowers already showing through the snow.

Ethan pulled up and waited until we had bunched around him. The wind was cold and raw and getting rapidly colder. "We're not going to make it tonight, so why don't we go down off the rim into the trees and lay up?"

"Good thinkin'," Stacy agreed. "What d'you say, Ben?"

Bald Mountain bulked ahead, and Medicine Mountain was a spur . . . it could not be more than five or six miles further, but the weather was growing worse. "Lead the way, Ethan," I told him. "We'll hole up."

An hour later we were in a sheltered place among the boulders and fallen logs. Long ago some other seekers for shelter had chosen this place, using a corner of boulders and some fallen timbers. A sort of half corral had been made at the head of a canyon. The logs were very old, and there were evidences of ancient fires here as well as some more recent.

We grazed our horses on the wild flowers that grew in profusion nearby, and while Stacy put together a meal, watching the horses meanwhile, Ethan and I lifted dead logs into place to build a better corral and barricade for ourselves.

"No tracks," Ethan said when we gathered around the fire to eat. "Nobody's been up here since last fall, by the look of things."

"Do you think we lost the Shoshone?" I asked.

"No," Ethan said.

"They'll be some wrought up," Stacy commented. "This is Crow country, and north and east of here you'll find Sioux aplenty. Them Shoshone are feelin' mighty skittish about now."

"They ain't alone," Ethan commented dryly. "My scalp's been itchin'."

The night was bitter cold. There was no wind, not at first, but the branches creaked stiffly in the freezing air. We slept feet to the fire, and from time to time one of us arose to add fuel.

Of wood there was no shortage. The tumbled old gray bodies of the trees lay broken by the snows of many seasons, and there were broken branches for the fires of an army. Streams were born here, and when we broke the ice the water was clear, cold, and sweet. Those small streams seemed to flow from some ancient and hidden wells here at the crest of the world.

The tons of snow that lay all winter upon these high ridges melted into secret hiding under the slide rock; and now all summer it would be running in streams down the mountain to a thirsty bottomland. Here began the Little Big Horn, which ran down through the forest and out into the shallow valleys of Montana.

It was bitter cold when Short Bull awakened me. He squatted close while I tugged on my boots and shouldered into my heavy coat.

He looked at me, nursing his cup in his hands. "It is not a good night," he said, "I do not like it."

"Hear anything?"

"Nothing." He filled my cup with coffee and handed it to me. "We must get off the mountain."

"You think it will storm?"

"We must leave. The Old One is weak. It has been a ride."

"A long ride." I sipped my coffee, chewing on a strip of jerky. "He is a great man, the Old One."

"There is death on the wind. I do not like it."

A branch creaked in the cold, a faint wind stirred frozen particles of snow. I looked through the spruce at the icy dome of Bald Mountain.

"Short Bull? If the Old One goes, will you stay with us?"

He was silent for a long time. "I go back to my people. There are few left. I am needed."

I added sticks to the fire, listening to the night. "He is a great man," I repeated. "He has a home always among us."

Wind guttered the fire. The wind was rising, and it would be cold upon the mountain.

"We will start early. In an hour we should be there, two hours at most. An hour or so there and we can be off the mountain by midday."

Rummaging about I found a couple of spruce knots and added them to the fire. I finished my coffee and edged the pot a little closer to the coals.

Standing up then, I took my Henry and turned abruptly into the night, moving away from the fire. The stars were less clear than they had been. A sort of haze, scarcely to be seen, lay between us. I moved out, melded my body with the dark body of a spruce, and listened.

The wind was rising, the sound was a faint moaning in the thickness of the spruce. The skeleton arms of a dead one drooped a shaggy web of dead-brown needles, and the wind there made a different sound. I shifted my hands on the Henry, then tucked my right hand under my armpit, then my left.

The skin of my face was stiff from the cold. After a few minutes I went back to the fire and added fuel. All were asleep.

Prowling about among the spruce, I paused to listen. The mountainside below where we camped fell steeply away into a thicker stand of trees, and above where we were it thinned rapidly. Along a low ridge near us the trees were low, barbered by the wind until they resembled a trimmed hedge such as I had seen in the east.

For a moment, standing under one of the half-dead trees, I thought of going back and awakening them now, just to get a start. Or was it that? Was I not feeling what Short Bull felt? That there was death on the wind?

I shook myself, warmed my right hand again, and looked carefully around. The whiteness of the snow patches added to the light, and there were bare, black stretches and the trees. Above us loomed the bulk of Bald Mountain, stark and cold in the freezing air.

Nothing moved . . . nothing? My eyes shifted warily. No animal would be out, and what moved must move with the wind.

It was not a night for an Indian attack, and yet . . . the Shoshone had a hatred for me, and he believed his medicine was strong.

Like a shadow I ghosted from the spruce to another, and then another, beginning a circle of our camp. A horse stamped restlessly, and they came suddenly from the night in a soundless rush.

FORTY-SIX

They came up from the ground, ghostly and pale against the background of snow, trees, and rock, scarcely more than a mist of movement.

I fired my rifle from the hip, by instinct more than intent, and my shot seemed to strike and turn one of the attackers. My next shot knocked the legs from under another, but then they were too close, and I swung my clubbed rifle into the belly of the nearest.

He plunged face downward into the snow, but another closed in, cold steel winking in the starlight. Gripping my rifle by the barrel and the action in my two hands, I swung down and sidewise at the knife wrist, then brought the rifle to eye level and drove the butt against his skull. It struck with a solid *thunk*, and he fell beside me into the snow.

The Indian I had struck in the midriff was getting up, and I started to retreat when a sound from behind turned me, and I felt the brush of cold steel along my ribs as the turn saved me. Toppling back into the snow, I fell down the slope on the steep hill, and my attacker lit atop me. Lifting my legs high I turned a complete somersault, throwing him over me and down the slope beyond.

My rifle had been lost in the snow, but coming up I reached for my pistol. Something jerked at my sleeve, and a gun blossomed with fire. Crouching, I shot . . . too low. The bullet struck him in the groin, and he gave a queer, froglike leap, and as he landed his legs crumpled under him.

Pistol in hand I scrambled up the slope toward our camp by the fire, keeping low. I could hear the heavy thud of a buffalo gun and the hammer of a six-shooter and realized I had fallen out of the fight.

Pausing a moment to get my bearings, I felt the cold wind at my shirt collar, ripped open in the downhill tumble, and the wetness of melting snow against my cheek. My hand gripped my gun, and I wished I dared handle it without a glove.

A gun is an extension of the hand, but with a glove it becomes awkward and less easy to the feel. I hesitated, trying to judge my next move, for I dared not walk into an attacked camp where anything that moved would be sure to attract a bullet. They had no choice, with enemies all about.

Suddenly the shooting ceased. The heavy concussion of Follett's buffalo gun first, then the others.

Killed? Or the attack broken off?

I stood still in the snow, perhaps thirty yards from our fire, but downslope and out of sight. Against the snow, as long as I did not move, I resembled a broken-off tree, of which there were a number. If I moved I might attract a shot.

Yet the night was still. My rifle . . . I would need that rifle.

Where had it fallen? I struck one man, then another, then was jumped from the side and fell . . . over there, to my left. It must be in the snow, which was close to a foot deep, and our struggling might have kicked snow over it.

My fingers were cold. A quiet lay across the face of the mountain. Above me the icy rocks of Bald Mountain were hard and black, brutal and bold against the sky. Moving my hands carefully against the darkness of my body, I shifted hands and now tucked my right hand under my arm.

Carefully, moving only my eyes, I surveyed the slope as far to the right and left as possible. The slope was snow-covered except in places sheltered by boulders, fallen trees, or clefts in the rock. It was a maze of deadfalls and the larger rock slabs that lay at the foot of the frost-created slide rock.

Sidestepping to my left, I waited, but nothing happened. I stepped over again, then crouched behind a deadfall, scanning the snow for any gleam of metal that might be my rifle. It had been still more to the left, for I remembered my shoulders had struck only snow when I toppled back.

Where was the Indian who had pitched over my head? Down there in the trees, awaiting a shot? Or had they gone?

Their attack had been sudden, but complete surprise had failed, for my first shot must have warned the camp. Yet there had been two shots immediately upon the sound of my own, so someone by the fire must have seen them almost as soon as I had. It was growing paler around Bald Mountain; I could even see a little blue now.

Cold! It was bitter, bitter cold! The Shoshone must hate me very much or have amazing confidence in his medicine to attack on such a night.

The attackers must be gone. The Indian was ever a careful warrior, for brave as they were their people could not afford to lose warriors or their tribe would grow weak and small, unable to hunt or defend itself. It was their way to attack swiftly, and often if the advantage was lost to pull away and wait for another time. Yet crouching there in the snow, I waited while the sky brightened slowly and the shadows lost their war with the sun.

Atop Bald Mountain there was now a crescent of gold. I stood up and looked carefully around.

Walking to my left, scanning the snow with care, I found the place where my shoulders had struck, and just beyond it my rifle, fallen neatly into the snow with only a dusting of snow over it. Taking it up, I brushed off the snow, then tested the action, putting the ejected shell into my pocket.

From our camp I thought I heard a murmur of voices, and I shifted the rifle to my left hand, pulling the glove from my right hand and tucking it into my armpit to warm my chilled fingers.

The woods were still, and I looked up the slope toward camp. It should be safe to go in now, so I took one last look around. My eyes swept past the snow-laden spruce trees, over the fallen timber, and stopped.

He was standing there, not fifty feet off, and he was bringing the rifle to his shoulder as my eyes caught him. I had dropped my hand to button my coat, and as my eyes fastened upon him my hand was no more than an inch or two from my gun. I drew and fired in the same instant.

His gun stabbed flame, but I felt no shock and I fired again. He took a step back, slipped on the snow, and started to straighten up. I held my fire, waiting.

He started to lift a foot to get better footing, and then his legs folded under him and he went down. I waited while one might have counted four, then walked toward him, prepared to shoot at any movement. There was none.

He was lying on his side, but as I came near, in a futile attempt to get up, he slipped again and rolled over on his back.

Reaching down, I took the rifle from him and tossed it aside. He stared at me, his eyes alive with fury. From his actions or lack of them I decided my bullet must have touched his spinal cord, for he seemed to have lost the power to use his legs and at least one hand.

My bullet had gone through his body, my second shot a little lower, but well in the target area.

I knew he was dying and I spoke carefully, knowing he understood a little English. "I am sorry," I said, "I was never your enemy."

His eyes were black and hard, but at my words he seemed puzzled, and his lips fumbled for words that would not come. "It is a big country," I said, "big enough for all of us. I wanted to be your friend."

I thought he heard me, but I did not know. I squatted there beside him, reluctant to leave him alone. A cold wind rustled the spruces, a little snow blew from one, and a flake settled on his eyeball. The eye did not move or blink, and I knew the Shoshone was dead.

Slowly, I got to my feet, thumbed a couple of cartridges into my gun, and holstered it.

It was not until I started to button my coat that I noticed the holes. There were two of them through the left side of the coat about elbow high, and they were close together. Undoubtedly as I stood, my coat unfastened and my right hand under my left armpit and then dropping toward the holster, my coat must have hung loose, and he had shot where he believed my heart to be. Oddly enough, I remembered but one shot.

When I had scrambled up the slope for a few yards, I called out. "Ethan? Stacy?"

There was a moment of silence, then Ethan's voice called out, "Ben? Is that you? Come on in!"

Short Bull was down. He was badly hit, I could see that. Uruwishi was tending him, soaking some dried herbs he carried with him to pack on the wound. Ethan had a bullet scratch along his jaw, and Stacy had a bloody bandage on his left arm.

"We was in a good spot," Stacy was saying, "an' Ben here gave us warnin'."

"Somebody shot from camp," I said, "somebody fired almost as soon as I did."

Stacy pointed with his pipe stem at Uruwishi. "It was him. He was on one knee a-shootin' when I come awake."

"They'd rolled in snow," I said, "and some of them wore fur . . . wolf skins, maybe. They were so white I could scarcely make them out."

"You get any?" Stacy asked.

"One for sure," I said, after a minute, "and maybe three, but probably not. I know I scratched a couple or came close enough to worry them."

"I nailed one," Stacy said. "He run right at me. I had nothin' to do but squeeze 'er off."

"How bad is Short Bull?"

Ethan shrugged. "The Old One is some kind of a medicine man and he's fixin' him up. In this here cold he's apt not to get infection, an' he's a tough youngster."

We built up the fire and shaped around to eat. I drank some coffee and felt a little better. We had seen no dead Indians . . . except for me, that is, and the Shoshone down the slope.

They carried off their dead when they could, but of course we might not have killed any. It is easy to believe you are doing better shooting than you are.

We cut poles for a travois for Short Bull, and when we rigged it we mounted up. Even at the slow pace we must now take we would be at the Medicine Wheel by noon.

"Ain't human!" Stacy growled. "After all you done for him!"

"What is human, Stacy?" I asked mildly. "What we call human is what we believe to be right and sane, for in our world we have been brought up to believe certain things. We are apt to believe those things are human nature . . . whatever that is.

"Look at it from his standpoint. He took prisoners, and from the beginning of time as far as he is concerned the captor has the right to dispose of his prisoners, to kill them or enslave them.

"Our ancestors in Europe or Africa were doing the same thing for centuries. While he is arguing his case with the old men we come in, take his prisoners, then knock him out with a six-shooter in front of the very old men he is belittling.

"We disgraced him, dishonored him, and he must have revenge. We find him wounded. We bring him in, care for him, return him to his people.

"This to him was a triumph, for he believed his medicine was too strong for us or we would have killed him as he intended to kill me.

"To him our gifts were a cheap way to bribe him because we were afraid, and what we call gratitude had no place in his scheme of things. Nobody ever taught him to do unto others as you would have them do unto you."

We were riding out on a western spur of Medicine Mountain overlooking a vast sweep of the Big Horn Basin. The sun was warm, the sky clear, and before us was the Wheel.

It was almost round and seemed to be made of chunks of white limestone. At least seventy-five feet across and better than two hundred and fifty feet around. The stones were two to three feet above the thin grass of the ridge. In the center was a cairn of rocks perhaps a dozen feet across with an opening in one side, and from it radiated twenty-eight spokes, although there were scattered rocks that might once have been another spoke. Some of the rocks had been disarranged by frost or whatever.

It was high, barren, and the spur itself was cracked deeply in places, some of the cracks being all of four feet wide and a hundred feet deep.

We all drew up and sat our horses in silence. The wind touched our faces and stirred the hair hanging by Uruwishi's cheek.

We were white men, and we did not think with his thoughts, our blood did not run as his, nor did our memories stir with ancient secrets. These things were deep within him, deep in the flesh and bone of him, and yet as we sat with him I liked to think that we felt a little as he did.

Uruwishi did not stand alone upon this place. He stood with the spirits of all who had gone before.

"Many times!" he spoke suddenly. "Many times this place was shaped! Many times the wind, the snow, the ice . . . they have changed this place, they have made the stones move, but each time the stones have come back to their seats.

"There are places where a man can stand and be one with the Great Spirit, and this is such a place.

"This is a place to dream, a place to smoke, and a place to die!

"I am here! I, Uruwishi, have come!"

Slowly, weakly, the old man's arms lifted to the sky. In a quavering voice he sang once more his death song, and then he said, "I go now to join my fathers, I go where age cannot come, where flowers do not wither, where fish leap like silver in the streams. I go where the buffalo go, where the warriors, my brothers, have gone before me!

"Do not think that I mourn! I have come to this place with *men*! I have shed the skin of the old chief and ridden again with the young braves!

"I am here! I have come to this place! I am Uruwishi!"

Slowly, his arms lowered, and he bent far forward. We ran to him, all of us, and eased his body to the ground. His tired hand gripped my arm. His eyes held mine. "You said 'come ride with me,' and I came. You saw not an old man, tired and weak. You saw beneath my skin, which the years have wrinkled and withered, you saw the young warrior that lives in my heart! You saw Uruwishi!"

He died there, under the blue sky, near to the place where the men who had no iron had built their shrine, but he did not die alone or unmourned.

FORTY-SEVEN

We left him upon the mountain under the wide sky, but we did not leave him as he had fallen, although he might have wished it to be.

We did not know how the Umatilla would have buried him, and Short Bull was unconscious and unable to tell us. The day had not many hours to go, and our way was hard. The Bull lay upon his travois, and we must take him to a place beside a stream where his wound could be treated and where he could rest, this young Indian who was our friend.

So we buried Uruwishi as a Plains Indian might be buried, and if all was not perfect, at least it was done with respectful hands.

We cut four poles in the forest below the rim, and we stood them up in the ground and set them solidly there; then we built a platform of boughs and on it we placed the body of Uruwishi, his rifle beside him, with his ammunition belt and his medicine bag, and we covered him with his blanket and weighted the edges with stones.

He had brought his best clothes, knowing his time was near, and it was not until we stripped him to dress him in his best that we found the bullet wound, low down on his left side. He had bled much, but he had stopped the wound with moss and said nothing.

We could have let him lie where he fell, as men who die in

325

battle are sometimes left, but our respect was too great, so we lifted him up, covered him over, and then Stacy, who had lived among Indians, sang a song of the dead warriors.

When he had done we rode away, but once, before I went over the rim of the mountain and out of sight, I looked back.

The frame was stark against the sky, and I thought I saw the old man's hair blow in the wind, and I turned away, feeling I had left behind another father, one I had known a brief time only where the streams ran cold and clear and the stars stood bright in the sky.

Tonight he would ride the Milky Way, which the Cree call the Chief's Road, and I would go back to our town and after a while back to Ninon and the life that lay before me.